AS THEY ARE

A TURKISH TRILOGY - 2

PHYLLIS M SKOY

Black Rose Writing | Texas

ISBN: 978-1-68433-964-8
PUBLISHED BY BLACK ROSE WRITING
www.blackrosewriting.com

Printed in the United States of America
Suggested Retail Price (SRP) $21.95

As They Are is printed in Chaparral Pro

*As a planet-friendly publisher, Black Rose Writing does its best to eliminate unnecessary waste to reduce paper usage and energy costs, while never compromising the reading experience. As a result, the final word count vs. page count may not meet common expectations.

To Arthur
For his loving support.
He is the rock in my life and the love of my life.

ACKNOWLEDGEMENTS

Many thanks to my dear friend, acclaimed poet, Hilda Raz. It was her idea to have a prequel, and I listened.

Many thanks to my writing coach, Lynn Miller, for her sharp eyes and ears. I thank her for her constant belief in my writing over these many years.

Thanks to Damian McNicholl for his meticulous and sometimes savage critique. This book would not have been as good without you.

Thanks to my wonderful friend, Joan Schweighardt, for introducing me both to Damian and to Black Rose Writing.

Many thanks to Reagan Rothe and Black Rose Writing.

I want to express my gratitude to the Lynn C. Miller and Hilda Raz writing retreats and the contributions of my colleagues there: Lynda Miller, Cynthia Sylvester, Sarah Kotchian, Tina Carlson, Katherine Saluja and Stella Reed.

A lifetime of thanks to Kaicho Nakamura of World Seido Karate for all his years of support and lasting friendship. Without his mentorship, I would not have had the courage to publish.

Thanks to my right hand, Carolyn Flynn, for her belief in my writing and her valiant search for a publisher.

Thanks to all my patient readers, who saw many forms of this novel, especially Asher Rosenberg, Sara Zarem, and Ayşegül Hürdür.

A very special thanks to my Turkish friends who have allowed me into their lives.

My heart goes out to all the Turkish men and women who have suffered through wars and coups, as well as the minority populations who suffered through World Wars I & II and the establishment of the Republic of Turkey.

AS THEY ARE

PART I

Fusun Gives Birth to Fatma
Atatürk Gives Birth to the Republic of Turkey

CHAPTER 1

January 9, 1916: Fatma's anne (mother) expels her from her womb just as the Allies are expelled from the Gallipoli Peninsula.

Of course, Fatma knows nothing of these historical events, or the fact that Mustafa Kemal, Atatürk as he will later be called, is single-handedly responsible for this Allied retreat. He commands his men to die rather than allow themselves to be pushed back. And since he rides out in front, they follow.

Fatma is here because Fusun, her *anne*, fifteen and a virgin, has been raped by a couple of drunk Greek soldiers in an alleyway in Salonika. After this horrific event, Fusun's father, Ali, flees with his family to Constantinople, since Salonika is no longer safe for Turks.

Just eight months earlier in their tiny one-room home in Constantinople, Fusun's mother, Nur, confronts her. "Shouldn't it be your time of month now?"

The house is one large open space with dirt floors. The Greek family who had once lived there constructed it from materials they gathered from the scraps the Jews before them left in their haste. One small area behind a flimsy handmade tin partition is where Nur and Ali sleep. Another smaller area is cordoned off with blankets hanging from ropes housing a hole-in-the-floor toilet covered with a slab of porcelain. Holes have been drilled through by which urine and feces pass into the crudely dug sewer below. A small coal cooking stove sits in a corner next to a sink fashioned from a large pot with a faucet Ali has rigged to it. This sometimes brings water into the house from a common well and sometimes doesn't. Fusun sleeps on the floor on a carpet with pillows in the same room where they cook and eat.

"Yes, *Anne*," Fusun answers Nur cautiously, "it is my time of month."

"But I don't see any proof of this?" Nur is a tiny woman with a sharp tongue. Her dark eyes run up and down Fusun's pudgy body. Her daughter takes after her father, rather unfortunately, Nur thinks. When she looks at Fusun, Nur is dismayed to see Ali's beefy peasant face. Ali and Fusun must both watch their weight. What looks good on a man doesn't necessarily look good on a woman.

"It didn't come, *Anne.*" Fusun's eyes follow her mother's until Fusun drops her gaze to her feet in their heavy woolen socks.

"And what day was it supposed to come?"

"Friday. That's why I didn't want to go to the *hamam*. I was afraid it would start in the baths."

"That's already four days and now we can be afraid that it doesn't start at all. Such shame. Your father—."

"Please don't tell him yet. Maybe it will come. I pray that it comes." Fusun looks for a place to escape but there is none. She is forbidden to leave the house alone. In any event, she's been far too afraid to do so since that dreadful morning. The memory of it silences both of them.

****

Early that morning in Salonika, Nur sent Fusun to the market to buy whatever she could find for dinner. Supplies were so limited that Nur put together whatever was available, not what she would have chosen. She did say to Fusun, as she was walking out the door, "Make sure to see if there is any eggplant. I can do anything with that. Ah, what a treat that would be."

"Yes, *Anne,*" Fusun agreed, although it had been almost a month since she had seen any.

It was a hot and damp day, but as a good Turkish girl she was wearing long, blousy blue and red flower print pants, a white blouse, and a long, blue cotton jacket. Even though she was not yet married, she wore a deep blue headscarf to cover her black, curly hair. On her feet, she wore simple brown leather sandals with short, white ankle socks. Her face and her hands were the only skin visible. She carried a small purse inside her jacket pocket with the few coins Nur had given her to spend. And she had a burlap sack in which to carry her grocery items.

The marketplace was fairly empty. A few foreign soldiers slouched next to a *çay* kiosk. They stared at her. One said something in their language and all three laughed. Fusun kept her eyes lowered as she walked past them. She noticed that more men looked at her differently now. She felt their eyes on her in a way that made her uncomfortable, nervous.

As Fusun predicted, there were no eggplants to be found. There were some wrinkled peppers, some cheese, a bit of flour, beans, and rice for *pilav*. It would have to do. Ah, there was some parsley, probably past its time, but perhaps Nur would bake some pastry, if there were still some walnuts in the cupboard. Nur would complain no matter what Fusun purchased. Sometimes Fusun wished that Nur would go to the market with her so that she could see for herself how little there was available.

Fusun wondered if the soldiers made Nur anxious and if she sent Fusun instead because she thought they would not bother her. Nur did not handle wartime deprivation or occupation well. She yelled at Fusun ferociously, as if Fusun herself was responsible for the lack of supplies. Fusun could not remember the last time any of them had laughed.

It took her less than thirty minutes to bargain for the few things she could find. The old woman behind the peppers, both the peppers and the woman having seen better days, drove the hardest bargain. Since the peppers were the only other vegetable to be seen other than the wilted parsley, the woman behaved as if she owned a gold mine.

"Just a few," Fusun told the woman whose nails were long and cracked, thick with dirt. She wore a grease-splattered tan sweater over a shirt and a long, blue skirt. And though she wore a scarf on her head, it wasn't tied in Turkish style and Fusun thought she might be Serbian or Greek. Who knew anymore? She could have been Russian, for that matter.

The woman's Turkish was crude, supporting Fusun's assumptions. She stuck out one soiled hand and said, "Gimme."

Fusun reached into her purse and pulled out a coin. She placed it in the woman's hand without touching her.

"More, more," the woman said.

"No more," Fusun retorted.

The woman placed the peppers back onto the tray. "No more, no pepper," she looked into Fusun's eyes.

Fusun reached into the purse and removed one more coin. "*Tamam*, okay," she said. She placed it alongside the other coin in the woman's hand.

"More, more," the woman begged. "I have to eat, please."

"No more."

The old woman took two of the four peppers back off the tray and waved them in front of Fusun. Now it was Fusun's turn to say, "No, two more."

Fusun had to take back the now filthy coins and start to walk away before the woman called her back. The woman offered her three peppers at first and again, Fusun turned her back.

The woman cursed under her breath and called out to her. She held up four peppers, one a rather scrawny one, but this time Fusun did not object. This woman could have been her great grandmother and she probably was hungry. Everyone in this country was hungry.

The peppers were her last stop. She thought to sit and rest for a few minutes before heading back. This was the only time she would have any peace from Nur all day. But some Greek soldiers had gathered, smoking, and drinking what might have been beer, and Fusun thought she'd best get home as quickly as possible. She left the market and rounded the corner on the muddy, deserted dirt road back home. She had a sense of something she could not name, and she quickened her pace.

It was several minutes before she heard footsteps. Too frightened to look behind, she began to run. They came upon her quickly. She never would have guessed them to be so close. Rough hands jerked her legs up from behind, and she fell face forward into dried mud and small stones. She tried to kick her legs free, but her feet were being held too tightly. Fusun screamed. She could hear the ripping of her clothing and the guttural uttering of Greek words. These were words she'd heard before, but now they sounded like no more than animal grunts.

Fusun's pants and jacket were torn from her body with such force that she could no longer breathe, let alone scream. She could feel the dirt and stones scraping against her naked skin. Thick hands forced her face further into the mud, cutting off her air even further. She choked and sucked in dirt, breathing it into her nostrils. She was sure she was going to die.

A large weight climbed on top of her. She felt his zipper scrape her flesh. It cut her skin, but she wasn't able to utter a sound. Then there was a searing pain. This is it, she thought. I am going to die. She cried for her mother, *Anne*,

Anne, Anne. The thrusting and the searing pain stopped. The weight lifted and another took its place. This one was worse than the one before. He seemed to be grinding her entire body into the stones concealed in the mud and dirt. The pain was so severe that she could feel her world turning black. Mercifully, Fusun lost consciousness.

When Fusun awakened, her attackers were gone. They had left her naked in a pool of blood, lying face down in the road. Fusun struggled to sit up. Her torn clothing lay scattered nearby. She reached for her jacket to cover herself and saw that the pocket was torn. The bag of groceries and her small purse were nowhere to be seen. Fusun burst into tears. Nur would beat her for losing the food and coins. And surely, she would blame her for the torn clothing.

Fusun had no immediate thoughts of her own condition or what had just happened to her. Bracing her bruised hands against the dirt and rock, she managed to push herself to a standing position. Blood oozed from her insides and ran down her legs. She touched her face and could feel torn skin. She ran her fingers through her hair; they came out wet and sticky with blood. Her eyes closed and her head began to spin. She was compelled to sit down again.

After some moments, Fusun forced herself upright. She hesitated long enough to allow the dizziness to pass. Slowly she gathered the rest of her garments and covered herself as best she could. One of her sandals was ripped apart and would not stay on her foot. Her socks had disappeared. She carried the sandals in her hand and limped along the dirt road in bare feet. Her mind was empty; her feelings were dead. Later she would not be able to remember how she walked home.

Nur must have been watching for her from the window because before Fusun could reach the door, Nur came running out to her with a blanket. "Fusun, Fusun, what happened?"

Fusun could not speak.

"Your clothes are torn. Your face is bleeding." Nur wrapped the blanket around her and helped her into the house. "Please, Fusun, please say something."

But once she was sure she was finally out of danger, Fusun's body began to shake so violently that Nur could no longer contain her. Fusun fell to the floor in the blanket, rocking and shaking and crying until she finally went completely still. Nur bent over her and pried Fusun's hands from her bruised and battered face.

"My God, Allah, what has happened to you?"

Fusun shut her eyes, so that her mother could not look into them. She tried to say something, but the words would not form in her mind.

"Fusun, please, speak to me, say something, please."

When her mother let go of her hands, Fusun grabbed the blanket and tightened it around her body, covering her face as well.

Nur knelt down on the floor next to Fusun, wrapping her arms around the girl and the blanket. "Please talk to me, my daughter. Please tell me what has happened to you." But Fusun could not make herself utter one word. She opened her mouth to try but nothing came out. Nur settled down on the floor next to Fusun and laid Fusun's head against her breast, rocking her back and forth until Fusun drifted into sleep.

Fusun startled awake. She had lost all track of time. Nur had gotten up from the floor and placed a pillow under Fusun's head. Fusun sat up abruptly, looked around the room and called to Nur who was in the kitchen trying to find something she could use to prepare a dinner.

"*Anne, Anne*, how did I get here? What has happened to me?"

Nur came into the room and stared at Fusun. "I was hoping you'd be able to tell me what happened."

Fusun sat still for several minutes. She raised herself from the floor, tucking the blanket around her body, leaning against a table for support. She sat on a small stool and rubbed her head with one hand.

"What happened?" Nur insisted. "Someone attacked you. Did they steal the money and the groceries?" This was something that did occur frequently, as food supplies were so scarce, and families were starving. Along with these thefts, beatings were not uncommon.

The word "attack" shocked her: the weight of bodies, the scraping of zippers, buttons, stones. She ran her tongue over the dust and grit lining her teeth. She swallowed.

"I need to use the toilet and wash," Fusun said. "Then I will tell you."

"You did lose the money and the food?"

"Yes. I am very sorry."

"Ach, we still have rice and beans. It will have to do. No use in crying about it now."

Tears gathered in Fusun's eyes. She wrapped the blanket tightly around her body and half walked, half stumbled to the small toilet. She pushed aside the curtain that closed off the room and let the blanket fall to the floor. She removed her bloodied and torn clothing. There was no mirror to examine herself, but she ran her fingertips over the cuts and bruises on her face and body. She squatted over the toilet and saw that there was blood in her urine.

The men had done to her what Nur had cautioned her could happen if she wasn't careful. But she had been careful. She had not even looked at them in the market, but kept her eyes lowered as her mother had instructed. Maybe Nur wouldn't have to know what the men had done. Perhaps she could hide it from her. Nur had seemed more concerned with the loss of the food and money. Yes, they could have just beaten her, stolen her change purse and those crinkled peppers.

But now Nur pulled the curtain aside and entered with a large basin of water she'd heated. Nur set the basin on the floor so suddenly that some of it spilled on her feet. "My God, you are cut and bruised all over your body! Just look at your clothes!" Nur glanced down at the porcelain squat toilet that Fusun had not yet washed. Clots of blood glistened in the drain. "Oh, no. No, no. It can't be. What have they done to you?" Nur looked at her daughter and knew. "Ach, we are ruined."

Fusun quickly recovered the blanket from the floor where she'd dropped it and held it in front of her. "*Anne*, I never spoke to them. I never looked at them, I promise you."

Nur shook her head back and forth in despair and horror. "There was more than one?"

Fusun burst into tears of shame and anger. "It wasn't my fault. They followed me from the market. I didn't know they were following me. If I had known, I would never have left the market. I would have waited there until they were gone." But Fusun remembered her feelings of vulnerability, her sense of fear. Was it possible that she had been careless? Was all of this really her fault?

Nur gathered the clothing from the floor. "Wash yourself and do a good job of it. I will do what I can with your clothing." Nur disappeared to the other side of the curtain, taking the mangled cloth with her.

Fusun took the rag her mother had left in the water basin and began to wash. But the more she washed and rinsed the rag, the dirtier she seemed to be. Soap and water would never make her clean again, no matter how hot the water or how hard and long she scrubbed.

When Ali finally returned from the restaurant where he'd been working late that evening, Fusun could hear her *anne* and *baba* talking in the kitchen. When their voices rose, she could make out what they were saying. Salonika was now too dangerous. They would have to leave. Constantinople might be a better, safer place for the women. If only Ali would be able to find some work there. He would have to try.

"*Inşallah*, if God is willing," Fusun heard her father say, and her mother repeat.

"*Inşallah*."

No one mentioned the possibility that Fusun might become pregnant. They packed their few belongings to make the long trek, with many others, along the route to Constantinople.

****

Fusun's thoughts rush back to what is happening now, in Constantinople, in the present. She breaks the long silence between her and Nur. "Please don't tell *Baba* anything yet."

"Don't tell me what?" Ali steps out from behind the partition that serves as his bedroom. He is dressed and ready to go to the fish restaurant where he holds the title of assistant chef, a title in name only. He hopes to become a chef one day, but he's happy to have found any work at all in these times. He cleans fish, chops vegetables, makes salads and sauces, waits tables, sweeps the floor, and even washes dishes. He and the chef/owner are the only two employees, other than the chef's wife who does everything and has no title at all. Sometimes Ali disappears to the restaurant all day and most of the night. Now he looks at both his wife and his daughter with suspicion. "What is it that you don't want to tell me?"

Fusun looks back down at her feet. "She's late," Nur tells Ali.

"Late for what?" He stares at his wife until understanding spreads grudgingly across his face. "Oh, my God. Where is God? Where is Allah now?" He looks upward and shakes his fist. He demands a response, but of course, there is none.

"Maybe it will come yet." Nur sounds a bit like Fusun.

Ali storms out of the house, banging the door so violently that it springs open again. Nur and Fusun listen to him putting on his shoes outside and then hear his footsteps, clomping louder than usual, down the rickety steps and onto the walkway. Nur goes to the door and shuts it. "Such shame," she shakes her head, "such terrible, terrible shame."

When another week passes and her bleeding still doesn't begin, Nur makes an appointment with the doctor. Fusun is terrified. "I don't want him to examine me. I won't go."

"But what if you have some disease from those men?" Nur pleads.

"I don't want him looking at me," Fusun insists. "No!"

Ali has stopped speaking to Fusun directly. "Ask her how she will marry now?" Ali addresses Nur, as if Fusun is not right there in the room with them.

"I don't ever want to marry anyone! Don't worry. I hate men. I hate what they did to me. They held me down. It wasn't my fault."

"Please tell her to spare me the details. She must have done something. She must have looked them in the eyes."

"I never even saw them!" Fusun protests. "They attacked me from behind."

Ali shouts back at her and covers his ears. "Please, no more! Tell her not to speak of this to me. It's indecent."

Fusun bursts into tears. Why is he blaming me, she thinks, it's so unfair. I wish I'd never been born or that I'd been born a boy.

Ali leaves for the restaurant and doesn't come home for several days. Finally, Nur goes to the restaurant to coax him back. He doesn't say a word to either of them until the middle of the night when he's alone in the tiny bedroom with Nur. Ali tells her that he's stayed away to decide Fusun's fate.

"But we don't even know that she's pregnant yet," Nur tries to reason. "And she is refusing to let the doctor examine her."

"I can't look at her now. It is too hard to bear. I am afraid I will hurt her or kill her. I am afraid for her, afraid for myself. I love her and at the same time, I cannot see her right now. My heart is confused. I will take her to my parents. She's either pregnant or she's not. We can't afford the doctor and she's scared to death to go anyway. There will be a midwife there and if she's not pregnant, maybe my parents can find someone willing to marry her."

For four days and three nights, Ali and Fusun travel by bus together. They eat the food Ali has packed from the restaurant, mostly bread, cheese, and olives. Fusun doesn't utter a word. Although Ali has never hit her, she is afraid he might if she says the wrong thing. He has been clenching and unclenching his fists. She has never seen her father so angry.

Ali sleeps, sighs deeply and barks orders at her when they have to change buses. "Hurry it up. Move your feet. Why do you move so slowly?" Fusun is afraid to breathe too loudly. She tries not to cough or sneeze.

And so, this is the way Fusun is whisked off to her grandparents. It's a better place, Ali believes, for her stomach to inflate, and far enough away from the gossip of their Constantinople neighbors. The truth is that Ali doesn't really care about the neighbors. He doesn't even know them. He just can't bear to look at Fusun. Infidels have defiled her. Terribly violent and frighteningly erotic images flash through his mind. Anger is the only emotion he trusts himself to feel. This is anger at the world, but unfortunately, it is directly aimed at Fusun.

Since Ali does not want to risk that Fusun will talk to strangers, not that she ever would, he seats her by the window in each bus. He promptly goes to sleep, and she stares outside, in part to avoid thinking about having to go to the toilet. Fusun must wait for the bus to make a stop either because they've reached a destination or at the insistence of some other passenger who is braver than she.

Every now and then, there are checkpoints. Ali has to explain to soldiers from various countries, including his own, where they are from, and where and why they are traveling. Papers have to be produced at each of these checkpoints. Sometimes luggage is inspected, and everyone must leave the bus. This is a much longer trip than it would be under less difficult circumstances. The Great War is still in progress, and the situation in this part of the world remains extremely unsettled.

Fusun also sometimes drops off into sleep. One time she is jerked awake as the bus comes to a stop. It is midmorning, and the bus is refueling in a small city or village. Fusun wants to ask her *baba* its name, but she is afraid of making him angry. Instead, she gazes out the window, watching the farmers working in the fields, their children playing close by. The bus accelerates and hills and trees and fields go by. Eventually the bus comes to another small city.

Fusun sees that they are stopping in Kırıkkale, so a sign indicates. They are now in Central Anatolia. Ali is snoring, and even though Fusun would like to go to the bathroom, just in case the bus doesn't stop for a long time, she doesn't want to wake him. She watches the street from her window. It is after the noon call to prayer, and people are out and about. Even though Kırıkkale is not a small village, people are dressed more conservatively than they are in Constantinople. Women are veiled and fully covered. Fusun is not veiled, as she is not married, but she does wear a headscarf.

Fusun observes three women walking along the road. They seem to be coming from the market. They are all carrying large, heavy woven sacks in a variety of patterns and bright colors. Fusun's eyes fasten on the young woman in the middle. Her enlarged stomach is prominent, even under all the garments she is wearing. Clearly, she is in the late stage of her pregnancy. Fusun watches her awkward gait and wonders what it feels like to carry a baby. She closes her eyes and tries to imagine something that large pushing its way from her body and she gasps with terror. Unknowingly, she kicks Ali.

"What is wrong with you?" Ali asks.

"I'm sorry, *Baba*. I didn't mean to wake you."

Ali shrugs and stands up to stretch. "Do you need to use the bathroom while we're stopped?"

"Yes, *Baba*, thank you." Fusun makes her way up the aisle to the doorway with Ali just behind. He doesn't let her out of his sight unless she is using the toilet. The public bathrooms are next to the marketplace where Fusun thought the three women might have been shopping. Now she sees them standing in line at the public restroom. Fusun also recognizes several passengers from the bus. Some are purchasing paper bags filled with roasted hazelnuts from a food stall on the other side of the entrance to the market.

Ali motions to the stall. "I'm going to buy some nuts. They have the best hazelnuts here. Go straight to the bus when you are finished."

"Yes, *Baba*," Fusun speaks quietly. At least he isn't barking at her, and she will have several precious moments to herself. Fusun loves her father dearly, but her predicament, if she in truth has one, is causing him to behave erratically. Fusun suspects that her *anne* did not tell her father that she was raped until her *anne* knew there was a possibility that she might be pregnant. Since her father has known, he treats her differently, as if she has acquired a noxious odor that makes him ill.

Fusun lines up behind the three women from the marketplace. The pregnant one is in the front, but she turns to talk to the other two and is now facing Fusun directly. Although Fusun has been taught not to stare at people, she is unable to pry her eyes from this woman's stomach, and it seems to grow even larger as she stands there. Fusun knows that the baby is supposed to come out between the woman's legs. The size of something of this magnitude makes this appear impossible. She will be ripped apart. The woman catches Fusun's gaze and smiles. She turns and whispers something into the ear of the oldest of the three women. The woman clutches her veil in over her mouth to laugh. Fusun looks away, ashamed to have been caught staring.

A little girl Fusun recognizes from the bus vacates one of the three toilets, and the pregnant woman goes inside. Fusun wants to see what the woman's stomach looks like uncovered and at the same time knows that if she could, she would find it horrifying. Allah, Fusun prays silently, please don't let me be pregnant. Should she even be praying for such a thing? She has no idea. Perhaps it is another sin.

When it is finally her turn to enter one of the toilets, Fusun sees that her father has returned and is waiting for her near the bus. She steps inside the filthy latrine, covering her nose to avoid the awful smell. Flies buzz around her head and her bare buttocks as she squats and attempts to relieve herself. This is the worst part of travel, she thinks. Public toilets are always filthy, especially the ones at the hospital in Constantinople, where she had been once with her mother.

After Fusun washes her hands at the outdoor spigot, she notices that people who have boarded the bus are now getting off again and forming a line outside. Several men in tattered military gear, clothing so ragged that Fusun cannot tell if they are Turkish, Turkish Nationalists, or from some other army, step up into the empty bus. The driver is outside yelling at passengers to get out their papers.

But these men seem to have no interest in documented papers. They pull out bags and bundles, shaking out the belongings onto the dirty floor of the bus. One of the men stands on the bottom stair of the bus, aiming a rifle at the bus driver and his passengers. Even though this man is wearing a German jacket, his pants have some other language on the pockets. Fusun is not sure. And then it occurs to her that these men are not soldiers at all but robbers who have stolen their clothes from the dead, perhaps even from the living.

The men empty all the bags and then refill some of them with the items they've selected. They shake all the garments to see if coins are hidden or sewn inside. When they are satisfied that they have gotten all they can, they disembark. The men with the bags run off. The fellow with the rifle stays behind a moment longer. With an accent Fusun cannot make out he says, "If you try to come after us, we will shoot you dead." He backs away, hoisting his rifle over his shoulder and running off after his companions. Clamor accompanies the passengers back onto the bus, as they desperately search the remaining items for their personal belongings. Fusun shouts to her father through the crowd so that he will know she is okay, and he can go ahead and get into the bus to retrieve anything that might be left of their things. When Fusun finally is able to board, she is relieved to see that her small bag of belongings, shoved under the seat, has not been touched. But her father's sack of food is gone, and now all they have to eat are hazelnuts.

Baba speaks in a soft tone that Fusun recognizes for the first time on the trip, "Good thing I went to buy them." In their haste, the robbers have not checked the passenger's bodies and Ali shoved the bag into his jacket pocket after buying them. "They didn't get the money I hid on me either. We'll be okay."

Fusun is relieved, but she can see that the bus driver is shaken. He hurries the passengers into their seats so that they can quickly leave this place. He mutters under his breath, "They rob us in broad daylight. They have no fear. We are lucky to be left alive."

A young woman sitting up front near the driver interprets that he is talking to her. "They have some fear," she says, "or they would have raped us. They were Serbian," she adds, as if that explains everything.

Fusun overhears her and slumps down into her seat. If Ali has heard, he makes no comment. This trip is a recurring nightmare. How fortunate that she remembered to fill her flask at the water spigot. She hopes the water is clean and won't make her sick.

When they finally get off the third bus in their trip to Goreme, Fusun and Ali are tired, dirty, and hungry, but Ali doesn't take any time to stop anywhere. He pushes Fusun along the pebbled dirt road to the cave dwellings. Although it is not a terribly long walk from the bus to the caves, to Fusun it feels like a lifetime. She feels gravity pulling at her every step, and she must resist it in order to move forward. When they arrive at the entrance to his parents' home, Ali takes off his shoes and motions to Fusun, "Wait for me here."

Ali tells Fusun to wait outside because he hasn't told his parents that he's coming. Azime and Baler have only one son, just as their son, Ali, has only one daughter. Ali is confident that his parents will not turn him down. They are good and loving people, and he never thinks for one moment that they will turn Fusun away. They don't have a telephone, and it would have taken too long to send a letter and wait for a reply. And who can know in these crazy times if a letter would have reached them, or if a return letter would have made it back? Ali fears his rage too much. What if he were to lose his temper and hurt Fusun? He pushes aside the heavy carpeting that serves as a door and disappears inside.

Fusun sees some teenage boys climbing along the edge of the cliffs. They stare at her and make some comments she cannot hear. She keeps her eyes lowered to the ground. She is covered with dust from the long days of travel and the final walk to the caves. She sits on a rock and sets the cloth bag down that she has been carrying since she left Constantinople. The bag contains two changes of clothing, her hairbrush and comb.

"Hey, you girl, you girl," one of the boys calls out to her. "Who are you?" Fusun covers her face with her hands. When she doesn't respond, they lose interest and continue to climb and shout on the edges of the rock cliffs. Fusun does not look up even once.

Azime and Baler are religious people, but when they hear what Ali has to say, they are shocked by their son's attitude towards his daughter. Baler understands a bit more than Azime why Ali is so angry, but he also finds his son hard, callous.

"We don't want anything to do with this baby, *Baba*. We have to give it away," Ali tells him.

"Fusun didn't ask for this," Baler says slowly. "And how can you say that we should give away our own great grandchild? How does Nur feel about this? Have you said anything to Fusun?"

The cave is damp, and Ali is no longer used to living like this. He edges closer to the lingering warmth of the small coal stove in the main room. "I don't have to talk to Nur about anything, *Baba*. Nur will do as I say and so will Fusun. And we aren't even sure yet that she's pregnant. If she is, take the baby to the mosque or an orphanage and just leave it there. No one has to know." Ali reluctantly pulls some lira from his pocket. "I don't have much, but this will help to pay for a midwife and some food." He hands the money to Baler.

"I don't like to take money from you," Baler says, "but things are so difficult now with the war." Baler is as reluctant to accept the lira as Ali is to give them to him. He quickly hands the money to Azime. "Put it away for the midwife," he says. "We can decide about the baby later, if indeed there is one. I don't think you can make such a big decision by yourself, son. Your mother and I have always talked about these things together. We didn't raise you to be so heartless."

Ali does not argue with his father. And he does not say to Baler that he has never witnessed his parents making any decisions together. He knows nothing about how their decisions were made. When Ali was growing up, it had always seemed to him that Baler ruled the household, but perhaps his mother had more to say when she and Baler were alone. In any event, Ali knows he will soon be on his way back to the bus. For the time being, his problem is resolved.

It must be another hour before Ali emerges from the cave dwelling. He holds the makeshift carpet door open for Fusun and says roughly, "Take off your shoes and get inside now. I will see you later."

Fusun removes her dust-covered shoes, gets up and picks up her bag. After she steps inside, she peeks out the door. Ali is walking in the direction of the bus. He doesn't look back. She stares after him for a few moments before she lets the carpet slide back into place.

"Ah, Fusun," Azime hugs her as she enters, "make yourself at home. Baler is making you a place to rest, and I will get you some çay. The water for washing is this way." She lifts another hanging carpet door and points to a large clay pot inside a separate room. There is a dish of olive oil soap on the ground next to the water. A rudimentary squat toilet with a drain sits in one corner. "This water is for washing and for pouring over the toilet after use. The drinking water is where we cook. We get it from the well and collect it from the rain. It's been so long since you've visited, I don't know if you remember these things. We're so glad to have you."

"Thank you, *Babaanne*."

On the few trips that Ali and Nur have made over the years to visit them, his parents have doted on Fusun. When she was little, Azime would feed her little balls of *pilav* that she would roll in her hands. Azime would coat them in cinnamon and honey. Fusun could not get enough of them. She would beg her grandmother to make more. Now she is afraid they would just make her nauseous. Her mother has told her how sick she was when she was pregnant with Fusun, and even though Fusun has felt no ill effects yet, she is afraid to vomit so soon in her grandparents' home. Fusun is filled with worry. She has no idea whatsoever what to expect.

Baler enters the eating area and opens his arms to Fusun. "Fusun, my little charm. Welcome to our home. Now it is also your home. Come, let me show you where you will rest and sleep."

Fusun lifts her bag and follows Baler through the winding tunnel that is a hallway. He enters a room with a low ceiling but is roomy enough. Baler asks, "Will you be comfortable here?" There is a single bed next to one wall and a small wooden armoire across from it. The bed is piled with carpets and pillows. The floor is covered in a worn but thick handmade woolen carpet consisting of what were once deep vegetable dyes of red and blue. There is a small weaving of the prophet's name in Arabic and a blue glass eye to ward off evil. In one corner there is a chair and a table.

"Oh, it's beautiful!" Fusun has never had a room of her own.

"Do you really like it?" Baler asks shyly. "I made all of this furniture. In fact, I made all of the furniture in our home. I did it over several years when we first came here."

Fusun smiles for the first time since she's arrived. It seems that her bad fortune has led her to something much better. But quickly the smile fades. "*Baba* is very angry with me. I'm afraid he doesn't love me anymore."

"Of course he does." Baler takes Fusun's bag from her hand and sets it next to the armoire. "You will see in time, my child; the heart endures when the eye does not see."

"If I am pregnant and I have my baby here, can I stay and live with you? I don't think I ever want to go back."

"You may change your mind about that, dear little one, but of course, you are welcome to live with us as long as you like."

Fusun bows her head slightly in gratitude. "Thank you, dear *Büyükbaba*, my dear grandfather, I will try to never bring any trouble to you."

And Fusun is as good as her word. She is a quiet, shy child. She barely leaves the cave to go outside once her belly grows large, other than to take in a breath of fresh air. She does much more than Azime asks of her, learning her grandmother's routines and anticipating and completing tasks before Azime can ask. Up until the afternoon of January 8, 1916, when her contractions begin, Fusun is the daughter Azime has always wanted and never been able to have.

CHAPTER 2

Something strange happens to Fusun's mind during her labor. It snaps apart, breaking into hundreds, thousands, millions of tiny, jagged fragments. It is as if some force has plugged a live electric wire into her vagina, sending high voltage shocks into her body and up into her brain, shattering into splinters of broken glass.

Fatma does not want to come out into the world, and the pains come as fast as they go. Fatma shows Fusun no mercy, kicking and pushing while Fusun screams.

The midwife is almost as wide as she is tall. She comes from a nearby village and Azime cannot imagine how she is so fat in such lean times. She tells Azime that her name is Gülen. The name means a smiling person, but her blank expression belies this misnomer. She seems to be lacking in any humor, or more relevant now, any compassion. She yells at Fusun to push the baby out, but Fusun hardly acknowledges her instruction. Instead, she waves her arms wildly in the air, screaming, "No, get off me! Please, no more! Stop, please!"

Gülen ignores her cries. "Push, Fusun!" she calls to her, trying to make herself heard above Fusun's screams. Azime tries to help the midwife understand. "She's reliving the rape, I think, poor child. She's delirious. Allah, have mercy!"

"She was raped?" the midwife yells. "This is bad luck. I must go."

"No, please. There is no one else to be found." Tears pour down Azime's face. "Please have pity on her. There is no one here to help us. You must stay!"

The midwife says some words under her breath. Then she implores Fusun to push again. Fusun's voice becomes weaker and weaker as the

18

midwife's becomes louder and louder. These events continue on into the night and then into the morning. Baler waits outside his home, not able to bear Fusun's howls and wails.

Like the battle that has been raging on for ten months with no end in sight, Fatma is as unwilling to evacuate Fusun's despoiled body as the Allies are to evacuate the Gallipoli Peninsula, but both relinquish their tenacious holds on the infamous 9th of January. The midwife takes the baby, cuts the cord, and swaddles the wet baby girl.

The fight to release Fatma overwhelms Fusun. She is faint and feverish.

Azime tells the midwife, "Feel her. She is hot and soaking wet. Is she going to die?"

"Not as long as I'm here," Gülen retorts. "Get me more clean cloths, some water and some vinegar. Then clean off this baby and wrap her up again."

The midwife soaks several cloths in a mixture of water and vinegar. She places one on Fusun's forehead and one under each arm. "That will bring down the fever," she tells Azime.

Azime has cleaned the baby and tries to hand her to Fusun, but now that she is finally physically free of her, Fusun wants nothing to do with her. She wants nothing to do with anybody. She mutters through parched lips, "Her name is Fatma, daughter of the prophet." Azime is shocked by what seems to be a vengeful naming. But then she reconsiders. If the child has no father, she might as well be the daughter of the prophet.

Fusun refuses to suckle the infant and the midwife must call for a wet nurse. Fusun only leaves her bed to use the bathroom. Sometimes she does not even do that and so the sheets are soiled. Most of her food sits untouched. She sips a bit of water but lets her çay grow cold in the glass. She loses weight and for the first time in her life, she is thin. Her face is no longer puffy or swollen. She is pretty, against the odds.

The wet nurse, Fazilet, is brought from Gülen's village. She is young and patient and has just lost her baby. Although she doesn't know it yet, Fazilet's husband has already lost his life in battle. Fazilet's breasts are painfully filled with milk that she is only too willing to give to Fatma. Since Fusun makes no efforts to be Fatma's mother, or even to be in the world, Fazilet takes over the infant's care with Azime's close supervision.

It is a good six months before Fusun returns to life. When she does, it is as if for her it is just the day after Fatma's birth. She walks into the small room where Fatma and Fazilet have been staying and lifts the child from Fazilet's arms. "I'll take her from now on," she says. "Thank you."

Fatma makes no protest and curls up to her blood mother as if these are the only arms she's known. When a whole day passes without a single complaint from Fatma, Fazilet rolls up the small bundle of possessions she brought from her village, says her good-byes to Baler and Azime and slips away. Fatma seems none the wiser.

But this Fusun, Azime and Baler sadly note, is not the same Fusun they once knew. She is moody and withdrawn. Some days she stays in bed for half the day, and it is up to Azime to soothe the bereaved Fatma. Azime thinks about going after Fazilet, but Baler reassures her that all will one day be better with Fusun, as it was when she first reclaimed the child from Fazilet. "If we bring Fazilet back, it will be too confusing for both Fusun and Fatma," Baler tells her. "Let's give Fusun a chance." Azime hopes that he is right for many reasons, one of them being that she feels too old to raise a child.

As time passes, though, Azime sees that Baler is right. Fusun slowly takes over with Fatma and Azime does less. Fusun teaches Fatma what she knows, and Baler fills in a good bit that she doesn't. Azime is not educated, but she shares all the stories she knows with the little girl. By the time Fatma is ready for school, she is actually better equipped than most of the children her age in the village. With three parents as opposed to two, along with her native intelligence and joy in learning, Fatma will one day excel far beyond what Fusun could ever have imagined.

CHAPTER 3

1922 August 26 – September 9 Kemal's forces defeat the Greeks and capture Smyrna. Smyrna is burned to the ground. On November 1, 1922, Mustafa Kemal announces the abolition of the Sultanate. Fatma is six years old, almost seven.

"Are you sure you have everything you need?" Azime asks Fusun one more time, as if she hasn't asked her a dozen times already this morning.

Fusun is standing by the doorway and has tied together a blanket with clothing and food for her journey to Constantinople. Fatma, who has been watching her *anne* from a dark corner, runs to hug her. "Can't I go with you, *Anne*?" She asks for the fourth or fifth time.

"Not this time, little one. It's too dangerous for little girls. The fighting is still going on." Fusun pries Fatma from her and picks up her small bundle of possessions.

"Isn't it dangerous for you, too, *Anne*?"

"Don't be silly, child," Azime pulls Fatma to her. "She's all grown up and can take care of herself. And her father will be with her. Your *Babaanne* is not feeling well and so she must go to her. She'll be coming back soon."

"I hope so," Fusun mutters under her breath. She is wearing several layers of clothing. This is both to keep warm and to avoid having too much to carry. Fusun suspects that it isn't so much that Nur wants her daughter to come home to care for her as that Ali cannot manage without help. Fusun remembers well all the hours he spent in the restaurant, leaving her alone with her cranky *anne*. It's hard for her to imagine what Nur's mother must have been like. Azime is so kind and gentle. Even so, Fusun is reluctant to leave Fatma alone with her for very long.

Azime and Baler have aged in the time Fusun and Fatma have been with them. Baler is arthritic and has a retinal disease that has left him almost completely blind. The scarcity of good food and other supplies due to the wars going on all around them have taken their toll on everyone, the elderly most especially.

Fusun has not been back to Constantinople. Ali has made several trips to bring money and supplies to his parents, but he has not asked her to come home until now. Fusun has been working infrequently in the nearby town, painting plates and pots for the pottery family in Avanos when she is needed. Along with Ali's contributions, they've just been able to survive. Baler can no longer work, and Azime cooks and cleans for the potter's family on a part-time basis. Almost the entire community is living on rice and beans, along with the garrisons of soldiers fighting both the foreign occupiers as well as each other. The clash of Kemal's small but growing army and the sultan's remaining forces, composed mostly of criminals escaping their sentences by agreeing to fight, has created a civil war, and a nasty one at that.

Ali has gone on ahead and will meet Fusun at the bus. She could not travel safely alone, and she would not go at all except for her father's insistence that her mother is dying. Fusun has a hard time evoking much feeling for Nur, her last memory being Nur's undisguised disgust at Fusun's defilement. Unlike Ali, Nur didn't blame Fusun, but the disgust was there. Fusun had felt untouchable. If there were good times, Fusun cannot recall any.

"You know," Fusun says softly to Azime, "I don't think of her as my mother anymore. All those tears I cried for nothing. You are more of a mother to me. You've been the one to give us a home. I don't believe she even thinks of me."

"Don't be so hard on her, please." Azime says. "She's the wife of my son and you are her child. Of course, she wishes to see you."

Fusun shakes her head. "First they throw me out and now they want me to leave my own child to come back to be their servant. That's the only reason he's come for me." She wards off Fatma with her free hand. Fatma has wriggled away from her great grandmother's grasp, not quite believing she is to be left behind.

"You be a good girl," Fusun tells her. "Don't you make any trouble for anyone. You be sure to study your lessons and help *Babaanne* when she asks."

22

Fatma tries to grab onto her mother's skirt, but Fusun pushes her hand away. "No more than a few weeks. I promise." Fusun slips out the door.

Fatma bursts into tears. She has never been without Fusun, even when Fusun was at her most depressed. Fusun was at least there physically when she couldn't be there emotionally.

"I don't want to sleep all by myself," Fatma cries.

"It's okay, sweet pea, I'll come and sleep with you." Azime reassures her.

Fatma gives a few shorter sobs and then stops crying. She has learned that crying is of little use. She has never seen her mother or her great grandmother resort to tears. In her most depressed states, Fusun is merely silent.

"Thank you," Fatma tells Azime. "If you sleep with me, I'll be okay." And Fatma truly is just fine with Azime. The old woman teaches her to do everything that she does. And if Fatma is too small or lacks the coordination for a task, Azime explains it carefully to her, so she will know exactly what to do once she is able.

"I'm going to sew a button on Baler's shirt now. See how I thread the needle? Then I make a knot like so. Then you go in and out of the button with the thread like this. Do you see, child?"

"Yes, *Babaanne.*" Fatma calls Azime grandmother, even though she is really Fatma's great grandmother. "May I try to put the needle through?"

"Yes, but be very careful. Here you go." Azime gives Fatma the needle, but she guides Fatma's small hand so that Fatma is successful in pushing the needle through the button's hole and the material. "Well done," she praises Fatma.

Fatma follows Azime around most of the day. The war has made regular schooling impossible, but everyone teaches Fatma what they know. She is a smart child and catches on to everything quickly. The adults are rarely frustrated and enjoy watching her accomplishments. Fatma has learned to read and write simple everyday words. Of course, very soon, by decree of Atatürk, the Latin alphabet will replace the Arabic, and Fatma, as well as everyone else in Turkey, will have a whole new alphabet to absorb.

There are several children of Fatma's age who also live in the cave dwellings. Ada is nine and her sister, Esme, is just a few months younger than Fatma. Sometimes Ada can be bossy and when that occurs, Fatma doesn't like to be around her. But Esme follows Fatma the same way that

Fatma follows Azime and for the most part, the girls get along. Ada and Esme's parents work in the village, and so Azime looks out for the children during the day. Azime finds their parents irresponsible, and they are more than half her age, so they do not socially interact other than around the children. Often, they aren't home until after supper, and Ada is in charge of feeding herself and her sister. Sometimes there isn't any food, and Azime and Baler sacrifice to feed all three children. Baler has become very frail and sleeps off and on. The loss of his sight has aged him.

After Fusun has left and Azime has finished sewing the button on Baler's shirt, Azime begins to prepare food for the day. She has soaked beans and rice the night before, and now she has Fatma rinse them until the water runs clear.

Baler sits outside drinking *çay* with his old friend, Ahmet. Shortly they will begin to play *mancala*. They will do this for several hours until Azime has cooked their lunch. Ahmet is a widower and eats with whoever can feed him. Quietly he sometimes slips some money to Baler, or whichever man of the house he sups with that day.

Mancala gives the men a focus. It is an excuse for them to sit together, to gossip, to pass the time and to drink their *çay*. They talk about the Sultanate, the Caliphate, the Young Turks, the Nationalists and Mustafa Kemal. They never know if their information is up to date, as no newspapers reach them. Ali brings the news when he comes, and Azime and Fusun bring the news they overhear at the pottery shop. Real coffee is almost impossible to find, and there is no cafè until one gets to one of the nearby villages. So the two men sit at a wobbly wooden table with four chairs around it, should anyone pass by and wish to join them. The weather is mild, but both men wear jackets until the sun is fully above them. The morning air still has a chill. A few puffy white clouds idle overhead. This is how the days pass in the caves at Goreme. There is little to do but survive and yet, there is much to do in order to survive. Frequently, most of the work that has to be done is done by the women.

Baler puffs on a hand-rolled cigarette. He coughs, takes a sip of *çay*, and sets the small tea glass onto the rickety table. "If Azime tells me that the potter says the big war has been over for a long time, why are we the only ones still at it? What do you suppose this Kemal fellow is up to?"

Ahmet, who is also smoking a hand-rolled cigarette, pauses to clear his throat and spit out some phlegm. "Nothing good, I suspect," Ahmet tells him. He breaks into a vigorous coughing spell, spits out another glob of phlegm, and takes a sip of tea. "None of them are up to any good except when it comes to themselves." He manages to get the words out before he's overtaken by a fit of choking.

"This tobacco will be the death of all of us," Baler comments. "The young ones will go down in the fighting and us old timers will gag and suffocate from our own smoke; that is if we don't die from the *raki* first. If only we had some!"

"That's the sad truth," Ahmet says. "But if we had the *raki*, we'd both fall asleep."

"Those are true words," Baler says, nodding to his friend. The men are quiet as they puff and drink. They finish their *çay* and set their empty glasses on the tray Azime has left behind.

"*Mancala*?" Baler asks.

"Why not?" Ahmet agrees. He opens a cloth bag and extracts the wooden box of stones from it. This is the same conversation they've been having for several years now. Both men have long since ended their working lives. Ahmet's two sons have not come home from the Great War. He never mentions them anymore, but he has confessed to Baler that he believes they are dead. These two old men take great comfort in each other's company and its predictability. And the fact of the matter is that there is no one else for either of them, so it is in their best interest to get along.

There was a time when the two friends would go into one of the nearby villages together. They would sit in the café and smoke and drink most of the day and on into the evening. Ahmet still goes once in a while, but Baler hasn't been in some time. Baler feels uncomfortable with his sight so impaired. He senses his vulnerability. He is wary of soldiers on any side and doesn't want to encounter any. Baler is content with staying at home. He waits behind for Ahmet to bring him news.

The day slowly progresses outside. When the sun is overhead, the men remove their jackets. They sip and puff and move the stones. It matters little who wins, even though they make a pretext of its importance.

"Ach," Baler cries, "you've beaten me again!"

"After winning all day yesterday, you can say this to my face?" Ahmet shakes his head in disbelief and the two men chuckle. The object is not to win but to play the game.

The day gallops along inside. There are lessons for the girls, more advanced ones for Ada and simpler ones for Fatma and Esme. Azime answers their questions and checks their work, to the best of her meager ability, in between preparing the lunch and housekeeping chores. Sometimes Ada assists the two younger children.

"Fatma, what is this word?" Esme asks.

"I don't know," Fatma says, a bit frustrated. Azime is bent over the cooking stove. "Why don't you ask Ada?" Fatma doesn't like to ask Ada because Ada is contemptuous of their ignorance.

Esme takes the children's storybook over to Ada and points out the word. Ada takes a quick look and tosses the book back to her. Esme misses, and the book lands on the floor. "Stupid!" Ada growls.

"Ada, please. Apologize to your sister," Azime admonishes. She keeps an eye on them, whatever else she is doing.

"I didn't call her stupid. I called the language stupid. It's impossible. The letters don't match what we say. I know the word, but it's written funny. It happens all the time. I don't want to read. I'd rather make up my own stories."

"She makes up scary stories," Esme complains, retrieving the book.

Azime doesn't know how to respond. The language baffles her as well. Baler was able to read, but he has difficulty now making out any of the letters. His sight is too weak. But even when his sight was good, Baler complained about the same problem.

"We have the most stupid written language. Arabic doesn't have the letters that match our ways of saying things. It makes it so difficult to read or to write anything. And there are five ways to write it and five ways to read it! No wonder this country is in such a mess." Baler would shake whatever book or paper he was trying to make sense of in exasperation. But he has read nothing in the past couple of years.

Now Azime shakes her own head in frustration. "I wish I could help you, but you'll have to wait until your *anne* comes back, Fatma."

Ada jumps up from where she is sitting and working on her numbers. "I'll tell you a story," she says.

"No," Esme insists. "I don't want one of those stories you tell about that ugly witch who comes into the caves at night and steals the children. I won't be able to sleep, or I'll have a bad dream."

"After lunch," Azime intervenes, "I'll tell you a nice story, one my mother used to tell me." Without a functioning school, without anyone who can transform the Arabic, Persian and Turk letters into words, Azime cannot do any better. She is more illiterate than the children. It will be six more years before Mustafa Kemal Atatürk is able to institute a plan to change the alphabet to Latin with vowels and symbols that match the Turkish language pronunciations.

CHAPTER 4

Fusun barely recognizes the neighborhood she left eight years ago. Many houses are now demolished rubble and quite a few of the neighbors have disappeared. It doesn't feel at all like the Great War is over. The streets are filled with Allied soldiers who mill about, sit in cafès smoking and drinking, replacing those Turks, Greeks and Armenians who've been killed or are missing in action, marched off to death or refugee camps, or who have simply disappeared and are surmised to be dead. There are many things that obliterate folks during a war, including disease, starvation, and murder of the soul.

The house inside is much the same but seems darker and smells musty. Nur is wrapped up in blankets on her bed like an Egyptian mummy. The windows are covered and Fusun cannot see if her mother is awake or asleep. Will her mother even recognize her?

"*Anne?*" she inquires softly. "Are you awake? It's Fusun. I've come to see you."

"Fusun?" Nur's voice is raspy and distant, as if she has been miles away and just returned from a deep dream sleep. Fusun sees the bundle of blankets move. She leans in closer and is shocked when she can see her mother's face. The color of her skin is a greenish gray wash. Her lips are dry and cracked, and she seems even smaller than the woman Fusun left behind.

"Fusun? Is that you?"

"Yes, *Anne*, I am here. What has happened to you?"

"I have the fever. I don't know what it is. I feel there is nothing left of me." Nur begins to shake with sobs. "I'm dying, I think. Can you help me to sit up?"

Fusun bends over to try to lift Nur. A terrible odor rises from the bedding. She reaches underneath to raise Nur and her hand sinks into something wet and sticky. She immediately withdraws her hand to find it covered in blood and excrement.

"*Anne*, what's happened to you?" Fusun reaches for a cloth to wipe her hands, realizing that won't do it. She'll have to boil some water quickly.

"I'm so sorry, Fusun. Zeynep *hanım* was supposed to come to take care of me while *Baba* went to bring you home. She stopped coming two days ago. I couldn't get up. I soiled myself."

Now it is Fusun's turn to look at Nur with disgust, although Nur doesn't see her face. She's unable to move more than a couple of centimeters on her own.

"I'll be right back," Fusun tells her. Fusun wants to vomit. Besides feeling sick to her stomach, she is outraged. She finds a large bottle of water, pours it into a pot and sets the pot onto the fire. She's careful not to touch anything with her fouled hand. She curses her mother and then her father. How will she ever manage this on her own? Ali left for the restaurant immediately without even checking on his wife. He's so terrified that his boss will hire someone else in his absence.

As soon as Fusun sees the water beginning to boil, she dips a bowl into the pot and retrieves some to wash her hands. She fully expects she'll have to do it many times again. How could her father expect her to do this? Her parents abandoned her with her grandparents, not even knowing if she was pregnant. Azime and Baler went through so much caring for her and Fatma. Where had Nur been all this time? And what if after Ali left, Fusun walked in to find her mother dead? She feels the heat from her mother's body, and the blankets are soaking wet. Her father has to know better. Is he blinder than his father? Baler would never allow something like this to happen.

After scrubbing her hands raw, Fusun looks around for something to cover them. She remembers that her mother sometimes wore gloves. She goes back to the bedroom, takes a deep breath, and begins to search through drawers. She finds a fine pair of cotton gloves and decides she doesn't care if she ruins them. They're a bit small for her, but she stretches them on anyway.

When she turns again to Nur, she tries to assess the best way to handle all of this. Nur is small and phyllo pastry thin, so Fusun thinks she might be able to pick her up on her own. She spreads a clean blanket from the cupboard onto the floor and attempts to hoist the still sobbing Nur from the bed.

Nur cries out, "Please don't hurt me. I'm so weak. I can't stand."

"I'm going to lay you down on a clean blanket. Just relax."

"No," Nur chokes, "there aren't any more blankets. Please, just let me be. I don't care anymore. I don't care if I die."

"*Anne,*" Fusun tries to make her voice sound like Azime, soft and gentle. She emotionally summons the spirit of Azime to assist her in these unpleasant tasks and to ward off her disgust. Fusun knows if Nur fights her, even in her fragile condition, she might not be able to move her. "There is a clean blanket and it's on the floor. I'm going to pull these dirty ones away, wipe you off as best I can, and then I'm going to try to lift you onto the clean blanket. Then we'll figure out what to do next."

Nur's sobs begin to subside as Fusun, gently as she can, raises her mother slightly to pull the soiled bedclothes away from her. The stench is overpowering, and Fusun has to turn her head away and take in gulps of air in order not to wretch. Since she is unable to extricate her mother from all her wrappings, she rolls Nur out of them to the very edge of the bed. She throws them into the corner of the room until she can take them outside to wash them.

Fusun whispers softly to her mother while tending to her. "You're okay, *Anne*, I've got you. Don't worry." Nur's nightgown is now up around her neck. Fusun has never seen her mother naked, even with the close proximity of their living space. Fusun tries to imagine that Nur is not her mother; that she, Fusun, is a nurse in an army hospital and this strange woman is her patient. Fusun reminds herself: gently, gently.

Fusun carries a fresh bowl of water to the bedroom and washes Nur's body with clean rags she has discovered in the cupboard. Nur quickly passes into a faint, or sleep, no longer shaking or resisting Fusun at all.

When Fusun is satisfied that her mother is as clean as she can get her at this point, she removes the gloves and carefully raises her from the bed to the clean blanket on the floor. She rolls her in it until her mother is completely covered.

She's like Fatma was when she was a baby, Fusun thinks. Well, she is even like Fatma now when she's too sleepy to move and I bathe her.

Fusun looks at her mother, squints, and detects a slight sign of Fatma in her features. She finds it difficult to be enraged with this helpless woman. Without any conscious awareness, she transfers her angry emotions onto her father. Ali is an easier target.

Fusun savagely strips the rest of the bed, and exerting herself against Nur's dead weight, she gathers her mother in the blanket and boosts her up onto the mattress that somehow, due to the thickness of the blankets, has miraculously not been soiled. Her rage at her father not yet spent, Fusun spends the next couple of hours heating water and scrubbing the dirty blankets and sheets. By the time she has them hanging outside to dry, the late day sun is at its strongest. Perhaps it will only take them a couple of days to dry. In the meantime, she places a warm coat of Ali's over the clean blanket, keeping Nur covered and warm.

Nur opens her eyes and tries to focus. "Zeynep, did you come back?"

"It's Fusun, *Anne*, remember? *Baba* brought me back to take care of you."

"Fusun," Nur sighs. "Is it really you? Did you have a baby?"

"Yes, I did, *Anne*. Her name is Fatma and she's almost seven years old. Didn't *Baba* tell you?" Is Nur delirious from her sickness or has Ali really told her nothing? No, Fusun decides, this is so typical of what she remembers about Nur's relationship with Ali. Afraid to ask, afraid to say anything to set him off, more than likely she hasn't asked about Fusun in all the time she's been gone. Or perhaps she did ask, and Ali silenced her in a way that prevented her from asking again.

"I've been so ill," Nur mutters. "There is some soup that Zeynep *hanım* left. Would you warm some for me?"

"Do you feel up to eating?"

"Yes, a little bit. Not too much. I feel a bit better now after that nice sleep. Thank you so much, *benim küçük kizim*, my little daughter." Fusun cannot remember her mother ever using such affectionate words with her. Perhaps she had, and Fusun merely couldn't remember. Now Fusun feels a rush of warmth in her belly, a sensation she sometimes experiences as she watches Fatma sleep. Quickly she turns away from Nur. It's too dangerous to have those feelings now. There is so much to do.

Zeynep's soup sits in a clay pot on the table near the stove. Fusun holds the lid up and sniffs to make sure it is still good. She takes a large wooden spoon and stirs it a few times and sniffs again. The soup consists of mostly broth, rice, beans and potatoes. Fusun sets the pot on the fire. Once bubbles begin to form, she takes a small taste with the wooden spoon. Not too bad, she thinks. Azime's is definitely better.

Fusun takes a small bowl and fills it with broth. Solid food might be too much for Nur. She props Nur up on pillows and spoon-feeds the soup to her slowly. Nur gulps it greedily.

"Slow down, *Anne*, there's plenty more. You don't want to be sick."

Nur relaxes at the tone of Fusun's voice. She has a few more spoonfuls before she falls back against the pillows and drops into a deep sleep.

Fusun takes the bowl into the kitchen and dumps the remaining broth. She washes the bowl and the spoon in boiling water and then fills it for herself. She has barely eaten in several days but didn't feel hungry until she smelled the soup. Exhausted herself, she lies down on some pillows in her old sleeping spot on the floor and closes her eyes.

Fusun is running and out of breath. She wants to scream for help, but she cannot get any words to come out. An arm reaches out to grab her and she turns to run in the other direction. There are arms there, too. There are many, many arms that grab at her. She desperately tries to push them away. There is a strange man standing over her.

Fusun opens her eyes to a strange man standing over her. "Fusun?" he asks. He is a stocky fellow, not too tall with strong, wide features and black bushy hair. He's sloppily dressed in slightly soiled trousers and a shirt frayed at the collar.

"Who are you?" Fusun asks, still partially in her dream and frightened, although her question is barked and rude.

"I beg your pardon, excuse me," the man says. "I am the husband of Zeynep, and I come to check on your *anne*."

Fusun springs to her feet, knocking the empty bowl of soup and spoon across the floor. The man bends down to retrieve them and puts them on the table.

"Where is Zeynep *hanım*? *Baba* has gone to the restaurant and left me here on my own. I am afraid to go into the street—the soldiers are everywhere—and my *anne* needs a hospital or a doctor."

The man stares at the floor. "My name is Mehmet. The hospitals are overflowing. They cannot take anymore. And all the doctors who aren't sick or dead are working twenty-hour shifts in the hospital. Some don't rest or sleep at all. I know this because they would not take my Zeynep, and I could find no doctor to come to see her. Nobody. The typhus is everywhere."

"Is Zeynep *hanım* sick?" Fusun asks. She is petrified. If Zeynep is sick, she will have to do everything on her own.

Tears roll down stocky Mehmet's swollen, lumpy face. "Zeynep died last night."

CHAPTER 5

November 1, 1922, Mustafa Kemal proclaims the abolition of the Sultanate. November 17, 1922, Sultan Mehmed VI flees Constantinople. November 23, 1922, Fusun flees Constantinople.

When Mustafa Kemal moves, he moves quickly. The same can be said of Fusun.

Once Fusun realizes who Mehmet is, she takes him immediately to check on her mother. Nur is shaking in her blankets, eyes closed. Fusun looks around for anything to warm her, but there is nothing. She drapes herself over Nur who momentarily opens her eyes, shakes violently in Fusun's arms, and finally collapses there. Nur discharges one long, raspy noise and is quiet and still, as only death can be.

"Just like Zeynep," Mehmet sighs. "She's gone. So many are gone so quickly. I don't know why I'm still here. The typhus is killing everyone. It should have killed me too."

"Don't say such things. I might like it to take me as well, but I am still here and so I have to deal with what is happening now." Fusun is too angry to cry. She wants to screech into the universe. She wants to strike out at someone. If her *anne* were not cradled against her, she would pound the walls with her fists. Finally, when she is able to achieve some positive feelings for Nur, Fusun is abandoned once again.

"You need to go get my father," Fusun tells Mehmet. "Please, go quickly. He'll have to take care of all of this. Go! I'll stay here with her."

"Where is your *baba*?" Mehmet asks.

"At his restaurant. Do you know it?"

"No," Mehmet shakes his head. "We are not really friends, just neighbors. Zeynep was a friend to your mother. They used to shop together and drink *çay*."

"Okay," Fusun says. "I'll draw you a map of how to get there. There is paper and a pen on the table in the other room. Get them for me quickly, please."

Fusun relives the trip to the restaurant in her mind, scratching out mistakes and correcting them. It has been some time since she has been there. Mehmet only hesitates long enough to make sure he understands the crude drawing that Fusun makes for him.

"Tell him *onun için bekliyorum*, I am waiting for him." Fusun knows that if Ali is in the middle of work, he will just expect her to accomplish everything on her own and that he might not come until the end of his workday. What can he do? After all, Nur is gone. This is how he thinks, or so Fusun believes.

Under normal circumstances, Fusun would go to the mosque or her neighbors and ask for help to wash her *anne's* body properly, according to ritual. But these are not normal times. She is too afraid of getting sick herself and bringing this terrible disease back with her. Fusun knows she could very well be in danger right now from Nur's deceased body. She's heard that they've been burning the corpses of the fever victims to stop the spread of this plague. She isn't quite sure about such things, but she does know not to bring in any others who might be carriers or who might contract the illness from Nur. She will have to do the best she can. Nur would have been horrified at cremation. Fusun thinks Nur could not be received in paradise if her body was not whole and intact. If she is irresponsible with her mother's burial preparations, who knows, all of Islam might suffer for her sins. Religious law is explicit. So very cautiously, she prepares warm water on the stove and fetches some clean, white bed sheets in which to wrap Nur afterwards for burial.

Fusun raises Nur by her armpits and drags her over and up onto the wooden dining table. Her feet hang slightly over the edge of the table, but it is the only high enough spot in the house that Fusun can find to place her.

Fusun does not remove the cloth undergarment covering Nur's private parts. Fusun presses on her mother's stomach, wiping the extricated liquids away from her mouth. She rolls the body onto its right side and loosens her mother's braided hair. She takes the bucket of clean, warm water and pours it over the body from top to bottom; then she turns the body to its left side and repeats this. After Fusun has done this, three times, she wipes down the body, folds her mother's hair back into braids, and begins to wrap Nur's remains in the sheets. There are only four sheets. Fusun remembers that a woman should be buried in five. Four is an even number. This cannot be. Even numbers of sheets are taboo in death. She must find another one somewhere.

Fusun remembers the sheets and blankets hanging outside. She knows the laundry won't be dry yet, but somehow getting the number right seems more important to her than using a damp sheet. No one will know. She would rather do that than knock on strange doors or try to buy a new one. There is so little money in any event. Nur would not want her to buy a brand-new sheet only to bury her in it. And there is so little time. The burial must take place before sunset or within the next twenty-four hours, if at all possible.

When Fusun pulls the sheet from the clothesline, it is a bit more than damp. Men are buried in three sheets, women in five. The reason behind this is unclear to her, but no one has ever said anything about the sheets having to be dry, just clean, and the number of sheets necessary. Fusun has never wrapped a dead body for burial or seen it done. She remembers that there can be no stitching, and so she removes all the hems.

Fusun uses two dry sheets first, folds Nur in the damp sheet next, and then carefully rolls her in the last two dry ones to conceal the dampness of the middle sheet. Allah will forgive me, she thinks. After all, what else can I do? She thinks there is a specific method to the wrapping, and she has simply rolled her mother up in the sheets, but if this prevents Nur from being burned in some mass grave to stop the infection from spreading, this is good enough. Everyone around her will be much too preoccupied to ask questions. Her mother's heart simply stopped. Ali himself has not mentioned the fever, just that her mother was ill and dying. Giving Nur a proper burial is the only thing left that Fusun can possibly do for her.

Fusun steps back to assess her work. She realizes that when the body is lifted, the sheets will fall away, exposing Nur's body. She remembers then seeing a photograph of bodies being buried during the war. They were somehow tied with strips of cloth around the sheets to prevent this from happening. She finds a white tablecloth and cuts three long strips from the center of the cloth where there is no stitching. She ties one strip around her mother's feet at the ankles. She secures another strip just below her abdomen. Making sure that her mother's eyes are closed, she wraps the third strip under the jaw to keep the mouth from opening.

Satisfied now with her work, Fusun runs water over her hands and scrubs them. She rinses them and scrubs them again. She does this until her hands are red and raw. Is it possible to wash away the disease? She does not know. Fusun pulls a chair over and waits for the others to come. She is so exhausted that she drifts off into sleep.

Fusun is clutching the edges of a raft in a large, dark sea. The water is choppy, rough, and she has to hang on for dear life. She is terrified. She doesn't know how to swim. Off in the distance, Fusun can hear Nur shouting at her, "I'm over here. Come on, Fusun. Come to me." Fusun tries frantically to locate where the voice is coming from, but she cannot. A large wave comes toward her, rushes over her, water fills her lungs—

"Fusun, wake up, wake up please, what is happening to you?" Ali's hands grasp her shoulders. Fusun pushes his hands away. "I'm fine, *Baba*. It was just a dream."

Fusun's eyes adjust to the darkness of the room. She sees Ali has brought the Imam and the Imam has gathered the required six women to prepare the body. Mehmet the neighbor is there as well. The new widower's arms hang down by his sides, like a mournful scarecrow, a drawing done by a child.

"It's all done," Fusun tells them. "I've properly washed her and wrapped her. She is ready. You can see for yourself."

The Imam doesn't question her, and the women step back. They are used to these situations now. They do not wish to touch the corpse any more than Fusun wants them to. And in these circumstances, even the most religious simply pray to Allah for forgiveness when they are forced to shortcut on ceremony. The times require this.

The men bring in a simple wooden box. They carefully place Nur inside. There are no questions. Fusun is not the only one to cover up a cause of death. She knows how her *baba* would respond to the idea of burning the body, even if its purpose is to save the lives of others.

Fusun walks behind the men carrying the coffin. The women who walk with her are not anyone she knows. In more normal times with possibly a more normal family, there would be a procession of family and friends. The only friend Nur had in Constantinople was Zeynep, and Ali has no friends, not even the Imam. Ali works too many hours in the restaurant to attend to the calls to prayer. And the friends they once had remain in Salonika, if they have even survived the war. No one has kept in touch.

Fusun stands back as they place the wooden box inside the grave. The Imam says the necessary prayers, and then he shovels dirt inside. When the dirt hits the coffin, Fusun jumps at the sound. It is so final. She will never see, hear, or touch her mother again, a mother she has never been so intimate with as she has in the past two days. The Imam hands the shovel to Ali who grasps it tightly. He shovels forcefully, rapidly, shovel after shovel, as if he is eliminating his feelings with each thrust, until the Imam finally wrestles it from him. "Enough," he says. He hands it to the gravediggers to finish the job.

The Imam takes Ali aside and talks to him for several minutes, but Fusun is not privy to the conversation. She assumes he is trying to comfort her father and to get him to come to prayers. She knows her father will not do this but will pray in private, and that the Imam's efforts are fruitless. She expects that Baba will return immediately to the restaurant.

But Ali surprises Fusun by joining her. He doesn't say a word as they walk, and Fusun knows enough to remain silent. She is curious. She thinks he might have said good-bye to her after the burial and that she would return to the house alone to pack her things. And when they arrive there, Ali simply says, "I will take you to Goreme. It is much too dangerous for you to travel alone."

"Thank you, Baba. I will feel better if you travel with me." Fusun is relieved. She is afraid to travel so far on her own. There are so many reports of rapes and beatings, and she continues to relive hers in her frequent night terrors, when she awakens in a cold sweat, not remembering anything.

"We will go early tomorrow," Ali tells her. "I won't go to work at the restaurant again until after I come back. I want to see my granddaughter."

Fusun looks up at Ali. She is sitting by the table where she washed and wrapped her mother's body only a couple of hours ago. As always, it is difficult to read Ali's expression. Has he softened towards her or is it merely the ordinary curiosity that any grandfather would hopefully have about his grandchild? Has Nur's death affected him in ways she cannot fathom? Whatever it might be, she is grateful for these moments.

"Thank you, *Baba*. Should I try to find us something to eat?"

"I brought food from the restaurant. We can warm it on the stove."

Fusun has always loved her father dearly. Nur always seemed distant and critical of Fusun until the very end, when Fusun cared for her. But even in the worst of his moods, up until her rape and possible pregnancy was revealed to him, Fusun has always believed that Ali loves her. His rejection of her only added to her feelings of disgust for her body and recrimination for her actions that day. When she awakens from her worst nightmares, she insists to herself that there must have been something she could have done to fight off those horrible men. Sometimes she is so angry with Ali for blaming her, and at other times she believes that he is right. She is guilty of seducing the soldiers. She brought it all on herself. Well, if this kindness from Ali is a passing fancy, she is willing to bear the disappointment that might come later on. And Fatma is such a delightful child. She knows Ali will love her the moment he sees her.

Fusun rests her head on her arm. "I will be very grateful and happy for you to meet her. Now let me get to the food so that we can have a good supper and get some sleep. I don't know about you, but I am so tired."

While Fusun unwraps the packages of several different kinds of kebab, salad, olives, bread and cheese, Ali lights the stove. "Let's eat in the bedroom," Ali says. "I don't know if I'll manage to sit at this table again."

"I'm sorry, *Baba*. There wasn't anywhere to put her that was high enough. It was the only way I could do it by myself. I didn't want anyone else to see or to touch her body."

Ali looks at this daughter he can barely recognize. She has matured so beautifully. Once again, he has to acknowledge the skill of his mother's parenting, his mother's genuine love and kindness. And his father, not always right, but steady as the rock that forms the caves they live in. He sighs. He has always struggled, no, "warred," with the strict laws of his religion. Sometimes life itself seems to require a bending of these rules, and it makes him furious to be put in such a difficult position: a defiled daughter. How can this be? How could this ever happen to him?

Ali's faith is being tested. He still prays five times a day, even at the restaurant. Actually, he is not the only one who prays there. The owner prays as well. But how can he love a God who seems to have assaulted him and then abandoned him? He feels Fusun's humiliation and self-abasement as if he himself has been violated. This, too, is a source of his anger.

And how can it be that Allah could allow such destruction of his beloved country? Now even the ground under his feet is no longer solid. Nur is no longer here to care for him, and the lives of his child and grandchild hang in the balance. His own life is one big question mark. The world is most certainly upside down. He turns to watch Fusun carefully warming the food.

"I am so sorry, Fusun," he says. "My daughter, I am so sorry for what has happened to you." Ali bursts into sobs that shake his large body.

Fusun still does not know what to make of these sudden changes in her father. The sobs overwhelm her. She has never seen her father cry. She doesn't know who the tears are for, for her, for Nur, for Fatma, or for the despair Ali might feel in this outrageous disruption of his ordinary life. She holds back any emotion, which she is well accustomed to doing by now. She has been doing this for years, not wishing to cause any pain to her grandparents or to her child.

Fusun simply says, "Thank you, *Baba*. I am so sorry, too." Fusun notes that he has apologized for what has happened to her but not for his behavior towards her afterwards.

Fusun fills two plates with food and hands one to her father. They go to the small bedroom that once was Nur and Ali's, but when Ali lifts the curtain that separates the two rooms, he stops and looks at the bed. "I can't eat here either," he says. "I'm going to sleep." He hands Fusun his plate and closes the curtain behind him.

Fusun carries the plates to the table and sets them down. She listens to the sound of Ali getting onto the bed and his muffled sobs. Fusun wishes she could cry. She has not wept since Fatma's birth.

Fusun feels she knows Ali better than anyone, as she is so like him. Tomorrow he will look past her and walk past her as if his tears had never been. To even mention them would be an attack on his manhood. She is curious as to how all of this will play out, but only as a bystander, watching with interest, not as a daughter invested with emotion. She turns to the plate of food and eats with a heartiness that she finds appalling. But she continues, mechanically, finishing her plate and even some of her father's.

Depleted from the day and the effects of the food, Fusun pulls out her old sleeping mattress and to her surprise, discovers a clean white sheet. For a moment, she is struck by this irony, a clean white sheet in the last place she would have thought to look, and she laughs. But then she is overcome with sadness. There was another sheet all along, but Nur was buried with the damp one.

CHAPTER 6

Fusun awakens to Ali's morning prayers. It is dark in the kitchen where she is sleeping, dark and chilly. She tries to roll over and return to sleep but the discomfort of the bare floor reminds her of where she is, why she is there and who is praying. Ali is not so gruff in prayer as he is in speech, Fusun notices. She sits up and gathers her bedroll around her for warmth. Some *çay* would be nice right now. She reaches for her clothes before realizing that she has slept in them. She sighs. This is hardly the first time.

Fusun gives up the warmth of her bedroll, struggles to her feet and wipes the sleep from her eyes. She sees that Ali has already prepared the water for the *çay*. She is surprised to have slept through that or that Ali allowed her to sleep. She knows he is determined to leave as early as possible. She has her first cup of *çay* and heads for the tiny bathroom to clean her teeth, wash her face and use the squat toilet. She has just dumped water from the small bucket in order to clean the toilet when she hears Ali moving about in the kitchen. When she has washed her hands and come out into the room, she sees he is laying out a small breakfast of bread, cheese, and olives.

"Many thanks to you, *Baba*," Fusun says.

"You are welcome, *kızım*, my daughter. Let's eat and be on our way." They take chairs and sit away from the table. Fusun sets two chairs between them to create a makeshift table for the food and the *çay*. Nothing is said, but Fusun knows that neither of them wants to eat at that table, the very table where Fusun washed her *anne's* body and Ali saw her lying dead only yesterday.

They straighten up the apartment as best they can without spending too much time, and just as the first rays of light press through the dark windows, they step out of the door and Ali bends down to lock it. A woman's shrieks bring him instantly upright.

"Murderers! Let thieves and devils find you on the road! Go, get out of here, and curses on the both of you!" Fusun feels a shower of stones falling over her head. "Go on, get out, you filthy murderers!" The woman's harangue is halted by a burst of choking sobs.

"Whatever is wrong with you?" Ali shouts up to a tiny, wasted figure of a woman on the balcony above. Fusun looks up to see their assailant.

"You are nasty, filthy murderers," she sobs. "My little Ayşe is gone, only three years in this world! And why? Why is she gone? She is dead because you left that dead woman here, that dead woman with that evil disease. You stupid asshole villagers. I saw the Imam. I know you washed her and left her. Allah doesn't want the dead to kill innocent children! Why didn't you get her out of there and burn her?" Her voice trails off into more sobs.

"Hush, woman," Ali calls back to her in a much lower voice than she has used. "You'll wake up the neighborhood. I am so sorry for your loss, but we have our own to bear. We want to go in peace."

The woman aims a wad of spit at Ali but misses. "I hope you never see another day or night of peace again in your stupid life, you and your ugly daughter." She spits again and Fusun has to lean out of the way to avoid her more accurate aim.

"We are so sorry for you," Fusun tries.

"And I am so sorry for you," the woman shouts back. "I am sorry for you because I will curse you both every day of my life!"

Fusun and Ali don't wait to hear anymore. They head off in the direction of the buses. The hollering of hungry morning seabirds drowns out the bereaved woman's remaining cries. For the first time, Fusun feels gratitude for these noisy scavengers. When they are well out of the distance of the apartment building, Fusun shakes her head and bursts into tears.

"Did I kill her child, *Baba*? I knew I shouldn't do it, but I was afraid you would be so angry and hurt if *Anne* didn't have a proper burial. I am so sorry for that woman and her little girl."

"It isn't anyone's fault. It is the times. It's all the wars, the fighting and dirt and the disease. Let's not think about it again."

Fusun knows that Ali's words mean please, never bring this up again. She is left with so many thoughts racing around in her head, things she can confide to no one. It is true that Azime will listen and comfort her in the best way she can, but Azime is old world, filled with superstitions without even realizing it herself. And Fusun knows that some of these same superstitions torment her. How can she help it? She has been raised with them. She trips over a large crack in the road.

"Careful," Ali warns. "I won't be able to carry you back to Goreme." His voice has gained some of its normal gruffness.

Fusun tries to focus on walking, but her mind will not rest. Suppose what the woman has accused her of is true? What if her mother did infect the child? It could have happened before her mother died, couldn't it have? And surely there were others close by with the awful disease. Why didn't I get sick? Why isn't *Baba* sick? Maybe we will still get sick. We could be carrying the disease and infect Fatma. Oh, my god, think of it! And Azime and Baler. They are old and weak. Her pace automatically slows down at this thought.

"Come on," Ali urges. "If we miss the first bus, we will be waiting for hours to get another."

"Sorry, *Baba*," Fusun tries to follow Ali's footsteps in order to keep up. This helps her to concentrate. But her mind will not rest and after a few more steps forward, the pesky voice in her head starts up again.

Yes, it's true; I could die, Fusun thinks. That would be good. Fatma is probably better off without me. And if I die right now, I won't infect anyone but *Baba*. But I don't want to infect him; I don't want him to die before he meets Fatma. And Fatma: what if I did infect Fatma and then I would lose my daughter and my mother? These thoughts torture her, but Fusun forces her feet to move, one step after the other. And every now and then she checks herself for symptoms, a sore throat, fever, and she feels relief that she doesn't seem to have any.

The line of people waiting for the bus surprises Fusun. Who would want to be on the road these days? The buses are hardly safe, and their experience traveling here in the first place is proof. The bus they took from Goreme to Constantinople was robbed and they'd been lucky nothing worse had transpired. Fusun and Ali join the line behind an old woman and a middle-aged woman who appears to be her daughter. They are sitting on a large duffle bag stuffed and bulging on the sides. Ali greets them.

"*Merhaba, gunayden*. Hello, good morning."

"*Gunayden,*" the younger of the two women says.

"Do you know when the bus is scheduled to leave?" Ali asks.

The woman lets out a dismissive sounding chuckle. "The driver came and said we would board the bus soon. It is difficult to know what *soon* means. We've been waiting here for one hour already."

"Ah," Ali murmurs, "Thank you very much." Ali motions to Fusun to have a seat. He places his bag next to her. "Wait here and I will try to locate the driver."

The older of the two women turns to Fusun. "Are you running from the sickness?"

"No," Fusun only partially lies. "We are going home to my daughter."

"How old is she?" the woman asks.

"She will be seven soon," Fusun tells her.

"Seven," the old woman reflects. "That is a good age, no?"

"Yes, it is," Fusun smiles, relieved that the conversation has taken a turn away from the typhus, the plague that they have hopefully left behind them. But Fusun is exhausted and fresh from the nightmare of their departure. She prefers not to be engaged in conversation, and she is skilled at making conversation go away. Fusun stands up and pretends to be looking for Ali. He is nowhere to be seen, but the interruption does silence the two women. When she sits down again, they are looking away.

It is a while before Ali returns. When he sits down beside her, he gives no explanation for his absence. When he finally does speak, Fusun can smell the *rakı* on his breath. She stares at him and he suddenly breaks into laughter. Then he lowers his voice to a whisper.

"You look just like your mother with that face. The bus driver was in the restaurant. He asked me to sit and have a drink with him. He had a small bottle with him."

"And now he's going to drive us?"

"Ah, you are like your mother. It was only one drink, and after his breakfast." Ali looks away. As far as Fusun knows, it is the first alcohol he has had in a very long time. Nur's death is harder on him than even he knows, she thinks. And it appears to Fusun that he was also jarred by the neighbor woman's ravings.

Fusun doesn't understand that his looking away from her is his shame. She thinks he only wishes to silence her. Fusun worries that silence will be the case for the entire trip. Whatever has made Ali so closed, so quick to shut down? She has only known peace in his parents' home.

Fusun thinks she must have inherited this detached quality from Ali. No, maybe not. She was not always this way. Since the rape, she does not talk with men at all outside of the family. Mostly she talks to Fatma and Azime. And her conversation is limited with each of them. Fatma is still just a child, although a very smart one. And Azime's world is narrow. Fusun wonders if Nur had lived, would they have become better friends? She wants to believe so.

A large man with a ruddy face and unkempt black, curly hair drooping over sleepy thick eyelids strolls up to the line of passengers. His smile is contagious, but his eyes are serious.

"I am your driver," he announces. "We will be boarding in a few minutes. Please have your tickets ready." Fusun decides in an instant that she need not be concerned with this man's sobriety. She is sorry that she responded as quickly as she did to Ali. Is she like her mother? Does she always seem distant and angry? Yes, she decides. Yes, she does.

Fusun watches Ali stand up and reach into his pocket for their tickets. He seems older. She wonders if he will marry again, and she thinks it unlikely. Fusun gets up slowly, brushes herself off from the sand and dirt and lifts her bag. The front of the line begins to board and Fusun's thoughts return to more immediate concerns. Will they reach Cappadocia safely? Will the bus break down? Will there be robbers or soldiers to stop the bus? And the last question that she cannot help asking herself, although she wishes that it would go away: will she be attacked and raped again? Will she ever stop asking? Will she ever feel safe again?

CHAPTER 7

Fusun is jolted awake by the screech of the bus brakes and the banging of her head against the steel bar bracing the window. Ali is leaning forward in his seat. His body is tense. He doesn't look at Fusun. As the bus doors screech open, Ali pushes Fusun down onto the floor beneath the seats. "Stay there. Don't move," he warns her. He places his bag on top of her seat and throws his jacket over it. She catches a whiff of cold air mixed with gasoline.

Fusun's left ankle is twisted under the bar of the seat in front. She tries to straighten it or move it as stabbing pain pierces her foot. The heavy thuds of men's footsteps enter the bus. Their guttural shouts push her farther under the seat. She knows these men. She has smelled their bodies before, the stench of them. She is afraid to breathe.

"All peoples off bus!" a voice demands in poor Turkish. "Leave your stuffs here."

"Don't move," Ali whispers before he stands up.

Fusun knows she must not move or cry out, but the thorn jabbing thrusts are accelerating from her foot up through her ankle. Allah, she prays silently, please let these men go quickly. Her breaths are short and uneven. Allah, let them take what they want and leave me alone. Please, let them leave me alone.

Zippers tear open and rip apart as the men hurry to examine the contents of the passengers' bags and then toss them from the bus onto the ground outside. Something that sounds like metal is thrust from its container and clanks against either the ground or hard rock; Fusun cannot know from her hiding place. The men laugh and shout as they ransack the meager possessions.

Fusun can hear and feel footsteps approaching. She can smell the male sweat and stink drifting into her nostrils. Bile rises in her throat, and she chokes it back so as not to vomit. The images flooding her mind are impossible to block or erase.

Filthy boots caked with mud stomp into her view. Rough and swollen hands grab her father's bag and jacket from the seat. Fusun tries to scoot back farther. Please, God, make me invisible. Please, please, don't let him see me. But one of the hands reaches down and brushes against Fusun's knees. He shouts out a coarse word in his guttural language and grabs onto Fusun's hand, yanking her from under the seat. Fusun can see the swollen fist, the rough calluses strangling her wrist. Before she can cry out, a large hand with cracked and bloody knuckles pulls on her other arm, and two men wearing soldier uniforms, filthy and torn, from what country she is not sure, pull her upright.

"What, you think you hide from us?" The spit of the first soldier sprays her face. The two men drag her to the door of the bus and fling her down the steps onto the ground. Fusun lands on her side and feels a jagged stone scrape against her face. When she touches the spot with her finger, there is fresh blood.

The bus balances precariously on the side of the highway, dust and dirt in front, dust and dirt behind. Fusun realizes, in her shock and fear, that the soldiers must have waved the driver over at gunpoint. There are no road signs, no phone wires, no villages or towns in sight. The soldiers have herded the reluctant passengers into the barren field away from the road where they huddle together in fear. Fusun can feel the early morning chill on her face, the clench of the men's hands on her wrists and the pain of her twisted foot and ankle. She sees the mother and daughter who spoke to her in the line for the bus as she was waiting for Ali. From what she can observe, the remainder of the passengers are all male, about a dozen of them, including Ali.

"Make like this, circle," the man who appears to be in charge of the soldiers shouts to the bus passengers and the driver. When the driver sees that they have pulled Fusun from the bus and recognizes that she is Ali's daughter, he tries to free her from the soldiers' grips. One of them lets go, grabs his gun and shoots the driver in the foot. The driver lets go and falls, screaming, to the ground, crumpling into a ball and grabbing the bloodied foot in pain. The soldier shoots another round above the driver's head and the driver falls back, silenced, and subdued.

"Okay now," the leader says. "Circle now." The passengers mill about in confusion but slowly obey. Ali tries to move in closer to Fusun.

"Good, Good." The leader flings Fusun into the middle of the circle. She loses her balance but does not fall. "Clothes off," he commands. "We will sing now. All of you sing! Sing!" He begins to sing in a droll voice an old Turkish children's song. The melody only encompasses a few notes and is easily followed, but the passengers mumble, some making no sounds at all but merely mouthing the words.

Şeftali ağaçlan
Türlü çiçek başlan
Yaktı yandırdı beni
Yarin hilal kaşlan
Tin tin tini mini hanım
Seni seviyor canım

"Sing," he shouts to everyone. "You know the song!"

"And you," he motions to Fusun, "dance and take clothes off. Come on, all of you, let's go!" He claps his hands and motions to the other soldiers to follow suit.

Peach trees
Bouquets of many flowers on top!
She set me aflame with
Her beautiful crescent eyebrows
Tin, tin, tin, mini lady
I love you with all my soul

Fusun knows the dance that accompanies this music well. She and Fatma have danced to this in the village with the other children and their mothers during special festivals. They form a long line and dance through the center of the village. She has always loved to participate, but now what she has once loved is turning into a demonic torture. She stands there, frozen. The man raises his rifle and points the barrel at her.

"I shoot, believe me. Dance. Clothes off."

Fusun begins to move in what could hardly be considered a dance. She shuffles forward, limping on her injured ankle. She removes one sleeve of her jacket.

"That's it! Keep going. Sing with me or I shoot," he threatens the passengers.

As Fusun removes her jacket and lays it on the ground, the singing takes on the tempo and feel of a dirge. Her eye catches the daughter of the mother and daughter pair. She can read the fear in her eyes. Will she be called upon to perform next? Will they all die? Fusun has to look away. Even through the fear, Fusun can also read her sympathy. Sympathy will do her no good right now.

Fusun removes her shoes and her socks, and when she slowly removes her pants, the passengers look away. Now she is down to her blouse. She unbuttons it slowly and finally slips it off to reveal her bra. The passengers continue to sing, as the soldier first waves his rifle at them and then at Fusun. The other soldiers, there are three of them, stand and watch and sing and laugh. They only know the chorus, but they clap enthusiastically. The passengers are mumbling and staring at the ground.

Fusun removes her bra. Her breasts are large since Fatma's birth. They flop against her chest. No man has ever seen her breasts. Even the soldiers who raped her entered her from behind. Fusun has never been exposed in this way. She is no longer aware of anyone. She is floating somewhere above the crowd. Someone else is performing these macabre movements. As she pretends to do the jumping steps of the dance, her breasts bounce up and down against her chest. All that is left of her clothing now are her panties.

Ali has had enough. Rage and humiliation are boiling within him. Silent tears are streaming down his cheeks. He moves before he really understands what he is doing. He no longer cares if he is shot. He runs into the circle and hands Fusun her bra and blouse. "Put them on!" he commands. "Now, it is enough!" He turns to face the soldier in command, "Shoot me if you want! Shoot all of us! This is my daughter! Leave her alone or kill us now!"

The passengers and soldiers freeze. The singing comes to a halt. Fusun begins to dress. No one stops her. The soldier in command lowers his rifle. "Brave father. Very brave but foolish father." He raises the rifle again, points it at Ali before he moves in and cracks Ali over the shoulder with it. Ali is doubled over and sinks to his knees. The soldiers laugh. The leader points to the bus driver still lying on the ground. "Very brave men. I like to shoot you, but no time." He motions to the other soldiers and in his language orders them to pick up the belongings of the passengers and to load them into their vehicle.

"Go on, get out of here before I kill you!" he orders the stunned passengers. They begin to walk like mechanized zombies towards the bus. Fusun, now fully dressed again, sees that Ali and another passenger are assisting the bus driver. "I'm okay," he insists, "I can drive. It's my left foot. I only need it for the clutch. I can do it."

"I can drive the bus," the other fellow supporting him says. "You can direct me. And you," he says to Ali, "go take care of your daughter." Fusun recognizes that this "fellow" is not a man after all but only dressed as one to disguise herself. Fusun only wishes that she had thought of this.

Ali reluctantly leaves the two "men" to the task of driving. They must go quickly as all the supplies are gone, including the food. But now he must tend to Fusun, sitting stone-faced and staring straight ahead. He anticipates tears. He sits next to her. She does not move. Her hands are folded in her lap.

"I am so sorry, *kızım*."

Fusun can hear Ali's words, but they sound so far away. It is as if he is speaking from a tunnel. She thinks: If I sit very still, if I don't move, if no one can see me, I can disappear. I can be invisible. "Please, *Baba*, please don't touch me. I do not want to know I am alive."

Ali does not touch her. He sits back in his seat and remains as silent and immobile as Fusun.

CHAPTER 8

When Fusun and Ali finally make their way back to Azime and Baler, they are hungry and silent, but Ali is not able to remain so, once he lays his eyes on Fatma. He hugs her to him, strokes her messy curls and says, "*Kızım, torunum!* My daughter, my grandchild."

Fatma backs away from Ali's embrace and runs to her mother. "*Anne, Anne,* I missed you so much!" Fatma wraps her arms around her mother, who has lost so much weight during her absence as to almost be unrecognizable. Fusun's arms hang at her sides. She allows the little girl to embrace her for a moment and then, without a word, she pries the child's fingers loose and goes back to their bedroom. Fatma bursts into tears and Azime and Baler look at Ali in shock.

"Why don't we let her rest? She has had a difficult time. Nur is gone. Fusun took care of her at the very end. We buried her the next day. Fusun did everything. I thought it was too dangerous to allow her to travel back here alone. And I wanted to see Fatma."

Baler shakes his head. "I am sorry, *oğlum,* so sorry, my son."

"Thank you, *Baba.* She and Fusun—well, I think they made it up at the end."

"That is good," Azime says. "That will make things both harder and easier for Fusun, I think. Are you hungry, my son?" Azime quickly slips into the role she knows best, feeding the men and the children in her life.

"I am starving to death, *Anne.*"

"Good, good." Azime takes refuge in the kitchen.

Ali has not spent much time around Baler recently, but even for him, a man of so few words, he is silent. He has not even greeted them.

"*Baba,* you are so quiet there. Are you not happy to see us?"

Baler has seated himself at the large table he made so many years ago. His movements are slow and determined. For the first time in his life, Ali sees his father as aging, frail. He feels the passage of time.

Baler doesn't answer but motions Fatma to the kitchen. "Please go see your grandmother, dear one. I think maybe she might need your help." Fatma is still upset by her mother's lack of response to her, but she is not rebellious. She knows that those around her have their hands full with life and that she must do the best she can. Fatma is a fighter, but she also understands that Baler is sending her away so that he can speak privately to Ali. And although she would much prefer to stay and listen, she makes her way towards the kitchen.

After a few moments pass, Baler asks, "Has she done as I asked?"

"Yes, *Baba*. She's gone. But can't you see for yourself?"

"If I could see for myself," Baler replies softly, "I would have no need to ask you, would I?"

Ali sighs. He has known for some time that this day would come. Baler has been steadily losing vision over the years. He traveled to Ankara some years ago to see if anything could be done, but the doctors told him no. He is suffering from a rare retinal disease that he inherited from his mother, or so they believe. Baler's mother was completely blind when she died.

"Yes, *Baba*," Ali leans forward to lower his voice. "Does *Annem* know?" In all these years, Ali has not figured out the communication between his parents, what passes between them and what does not.

"What is there to discuss?" Baler shifts on the bench, clutching his cane in one fist. "She can see what is in front of her. There is nothing to be done. I can manage well here. I know where everything is. I don't really enjoy playing *Mancala* anymore. Ahmet feels sorry for me and lets me win, and when I accuse him, he lets me lose. It comes down to him playing both hands, and so we sit and talk. It's okay. I am old. Everything is as it should be with us."

Ali is unable to think of a response until he realizes that there is none. "I will stay here for a week or two, and then I will travel back. I thought perhaps I could take Fatma with me."

"What?" Baler chokes on his question and begins to cough. The spasm overtakes him, and Ali is afraid he will lose his balance and fall from the bench. But Baler leans over the table, takes a sip from his *çay*, now cold, and manages to curb the coughing. "And why would you take Fatma with you? What do you think Fusun would say about this? And Azime? She lives for the child."

"I know, I know," Ali tries to keep his tone soft. "But there is no education for her here. The schools are closed, and there is only so much she can learn from the three of you. I have no education. I have a skill, but where does it get me? Long hours and nothing to show for it."

"But she is a girl. She will marry and have children. Of what use will an education be to her?" Baler takes another sip of the *çay*, more to reign in his emotions than for the now tasteless tea.

"Things are changing, *Baba*. Atatürk is devoted to change. It will be a new republic. If you were in Constantinople—no, Istanbul now—you would see it clearly."

Baler laughs. "I see nothing clearly, only that these women are living for each other. To separate them is a disaster. I am set against it."

These are not words Baler has often uttered and certainly, never lightly. He is more apt to say something like, I will consider this, or I will think it over and let you know. Ali knows that the subject is closed. And perhaps it is a foolish idea anyway. Would he only be bringing Fatma into his home to serve his selfish purposes, just as he worries now that he did with Fusun? If he had not gone to fetch her to take care of Nur, she might not have gone through that horrific humiliation. He was not a particularly good husband or father, and now he is asking to take charge of his grandchild? His father surprises him. He understands him better than he understands himself.

"I am in agreement, *Baba*. You are right. I will not suggest it."

Baler nods his head but says no more. He does not express to his son that he is also concerned about Fatma's schooling. But he knows his son. He is not gentle with women. He suspects that this is some of the reason why Fusun is who she is. He knows that Nur could also be harsh with Fusun. He has listened to her talking with Azime about her parents. He knows that Ali has the best of intentions, but he will go off to his restaurant and assume that everything is fine with Fatma, that he is sending her to school and that is all she needs.

Baler is a practical but kind man. If not for Azime, he does not believe his kindness would have come to light. She has brought out everything good in him. And there is some of her in Ali as well. He can be kind, but he is caught up with making money. Perhaps there is some sort of schooling in Avanos, or even someone with an education who can take Fatma further along. He will ask Azime to speak to the potters.

Azime enters the room with a large tray of food. Fatma follows her with a basket of bread. Once the trays are safely on the table, Fatma announces, "I'm going to get my *anne*." Before anyone can try to stop her, Fatma rushes from the room towards the bedroom they share. A few minutes later, Fatma reluctantly joins the others at the table. She sits next to Azime before she whispers, "My *anne* is not hungry now."

"That's okay, dear. She will eat later. We can let her rest. She's had a long journey." Azime puts one arm around Fatma's shoulder.

Ali lets out a sigh of relief. Even if Fusun is not speaking with anyone else, she is responding to her child. He chooses to take this as a sign of hope, especially since there is little else he can hold onto at the moment.

CHAPTER 9

Later that same evening, once they are alone, lying in their bed, Baler describes some of his conversation with Ali to Azime, eliminating any suggestion of Fatma going off with Ali to Istanbul.

"I thought maybe you could speak to someone at the pottery shop. There are several children there. Is there a school where they send them that is still open?"

"No," Azime slowly shakes her head. "There are three children there, and they have hired a tutor. He is living with them now. They brought him from Ankara. Lucky for them, the school where he taught is closed and they can afford to pay him a bit, plus room and board. There is one boy, around the same age as Fatma, and there are two girls, one a couple of years older and one several years younger, I think. The tutor works with all of them."

"Do you think they would let Fatma sit in on these classes? We could offer them some money. Ali is worrying about her education and would be willing to help out as much as he can."

Azime hesitates. She has also been thinking about Fatma's education. She knows how limiting it is not to have one. Her life has been a simple but happy one. Nonetheless, since Fatma has come to live with them, Azime always wishes that she could teach her more. It has made her so much more aware of her own ignorance. But she is wary to ask more of the potter's family. Perhaps she will injure the relationship that she has established with them. If she did not have that bit of work, it would be hard to feed everyone. Perhaps they might find it too bold of her to ask to put her great grandchild with their children. Or it could be that the tutor might not wish to take on another child and asking might be experienced as intrusive or demanding too much from them. Baler used to be able to read her expressions, but now he cannot see them. And in any event, the lamp has been extinguished.

"I will have to think on this," she says. "I would not want to place a burden on them. The shop is suffering from the wars as well. Who can think about buying pots and plates when there is no food to put on them?"

Baler sighs. "Maybe it is too much and maybe it is not. There is only one way to know. You are good in your ways with people, and the potter and his family are fond of you. Fatma is quick to learn, and she is an easy child. Once the tutor sees this, what is one more child to him? And if the boy is about the same age, they could learn together. I think you can find a way to ask that will not hurt your position with them."

"I hope you are right." It is Azime's turn now to sigh. The potter and his wife are so generous. She hates to have to ask for anything else. But she says, "You are right, my husband. I will think about how to do this."

"Good. Now let us get some rest. Fusun can go with you and help out with the cleaning. She needs to get out of that bedroom. She is so strange since her *anne* passed."

"Yes, I have thought about this, too. And some days she can go alone after I show her what to do. I do not complain, but I get more tired and achy."

Azime's resolve grows overnight. Fusun can take Fatma to the potter's household alone once she has the job down. Azime does not think that Fusun will have any objections as she has accompanied her in the past to help.

Azime is even more convinced in the morning that the time has come for her to work less. She does not like to be away from Baler too long in any event.

While Fatma is occupied playing and attempting to read with Ada and Esme, Azime goes to Fusun. She is listless in her bed, her face to the wall, but she rolls around to face Azime when she enters the room. Azime says, "*Selam*, Fusun."

"*Günaydın, Babaanne.*"

"This is what I have come to say. It is no longer morning. It is now afternoon. You do not eat and lie in here all day. This is bad for you, bad for your daughter, and bad for us."

"I'm sorry, *Babaanne*. I know that this is true, but I am so tired. I have no wish to move or to talk to anyone."

"I know you have had a hard time, but this cannot continue. I am thinking to ask the potter's wife if Fatma could study with their children. The situation with Ada and Esme is not so good. Ada is frustrated because too many times she does not know the answers and it makes her mean. Esme is too far behind Fatma to help her. I thought I would ask if she can sit with the children and their tutor if she doesn't interrupt. You can start coming with me to clean regularly and eventually take this job over for me. I worry too much about Baler."

Fusun raises herself up on her elbows. "What a wonderful idea, *Babaanne*! It will be so good for both of us to have something to do. And you do work too much." A bit of color seems to push through the gray pallor of Fusun's face. Azime thinks how hard these years have been on all of them, how awful they have been on Fusun, how glad she is to have followed Baler's advice as well as her own instincts. But she did not dream that Fusun would be so enthusiastic. What if the potter's wife says no?

"I will speak with them this week. Nothing has been decided yet." She tries to keep any anxiety from her voice. The last thing she wants to do is to disappoint Fusun now. Azime is suspicious that something else took place during the time Ali and Fusun were away, but it is something they are not sharing with her or Baler. Baler is right. Azime does have a way with people, and she is quite sensitive to their moods. She does not push though. Fusun has been through so much.

The brief conversation with Fusun brings results. Her granddaughter gets out of bed and eats for the first time since she has arrived. She washes and ventures outdoors where the children are playing, and Ali is watching Fatma interact with her companions. He has a wistful expression on his face. Fusun sees his sadness.

"It's not you, *Baba*. She is shy," Fusun tells him. "And I have not been any help. I will explain to her that you are my *baba*. She is not sure who you are and so she is afraid."

"Thank you," Ali says quietly. He does not understand what has roused Fusun from her stupor, but he is grateful for this change in her.

Fusun approaches the children. They are sitting together with a book on Ada's lap, Esme on one side of her and Fatma on the other. Ada is too tall and skinny, awkward, and ugly in her need to be correct. She becomes even louder and more insistent in her claim that the word in question means "goat," but Fatma argues that it is "cow." Esme has no idea. She is a tiny creature with stringy yellow mop-like hair, and almost seems to disappear when Fatma and Ada quarrel. Fusun knows better than to enter this squabbling, even though the children plead with her to resolve their dilemma.

"*Anne*, it is a cow, isn't it?" Fatma presses her.

"No, no, it is a goat." Ada pushes the book in Fusun's face. Still Fusun ignores them.

"Come Fatma," she says, negotiating the book back into Ada's lap. "I want you to spend some time with my *baba*. He has come just to meet you, and he is sad that he has not spent time with you before now. He thinks you are a very nice and smart little girl, and he would like to get to know you a bit. Please come."

Fatma looks at Ali and back at her mother. "This is your *baba*?" she asks.

"Yes," Fusun tells her. "He has come to bring me home and to visit you. He will leave one day soon, so you must give him your attention while he is here."

Fatma slowly rises and says to Ada and Esme, "I do believe it is a cow that has made the milk, but it could also be a goat. The letters mean cow." Ada screws up the lines of her mouth and argues, "It is a goat."

Fatma shakes her head and takes Fusun's hand. Ali makes her nervous. How can she speak to such a man, the father of her mother? She has picked up whispers about Ali and Nur.

Fatma is unsure of Ali. There is something about him that makes her uncomfortable. She feels cautious. Fatma is not ready to trust.

But Ali is a man who can shift on a dime. He uses his gentle prayer voice and calls her to him. "Come, little one. Come closer so I can talk with you."

Fatma is not easily won. She turns her face into Fusun's body. This time Fusun cups Fatma's face with her hands and turns her back towards Ali. "*Lütfen, küçüğüm*. Please, my little one." Fatma allows Fusun to direct her face towards Ali, but she remains where she is.

Ali laughs. "If the mountain will not come to Mohammed, Mohammed must go to the mountain." He takes a few steps towards Fatma.

"I am not a mountain," Fatma tells him.

"I can see that very well," Ali says seriously this time. Fatma will not be addressed as a simple child. She will not be talked down to. "But you are a strong one. I can see that, too," he adds. "So, when you are ready, you can give me a big, strong hug. I am your grandfather, you know."

"I am not ready today," Fatma tells him.

Fusun stifles a laugh and chides Fatma, "Don't be rude to your grandfather."

"I'm not rude," Fatma retorts. "He said I can hug him when I am ready. I am not ready."

Now Ali has to laugh. "She's right," he says. "No question about it."

Ali sits down, cross-legged, under a barren tree. Several evil eyes hang from the branches. Fusun pulls Fatma along and settles down next to Ali. Fatma allows Fusun to pull her onto her lap.

Ali asks Fatma, smiling into her amber eyes, "Do you know how to use a donkey?"

Fatma turns to Fusun, looks back at Ali and mutters, "I don't have a donkey."

"But do you know how to use one?"

"Sometimes I see the donkeys crossing in a line, several of them, on their way to market. They carry bundles on their backs."

"Aha, you are observant. Yes. But do you know the story of Nasrettin Hoca and his donkey?"

Fatma shakes her head, "No, I don't know that story, but I know Nasrettin Hoca. Grandpa Baler has told me about Nasrettin Hoca. Did he tell you as well?"

"Yes, he did. When I was just about your age, maybe even younger, my *baba* told me many stories of Nasrettin Hoca. Sometimes I think he even made them up himself if he wanted to teach me something special."

"*Anne,* you know Nasrettin Hoca?"

"Of course, I have heard a few stories, but not this one about the donkey. *Baba* was always working and didn't have time to tell me any stories. This is very special that he is taking the time to tell you."

"Tell us now, *büyükbaba.*" It is the first time Fatma has addressed him as her grandfather. She even inches forward a bit.

"Okay. Do you want to ask your friends to join us?" Ali asks.

"No, just tell it to us." Fatma shakes her head vigorously. "Just us."

Fusun does not chide her daughter for being selfish. This is a rare moment with Ali, and she does not wish to share him with anyone other than her daughter.

"*Tamam,* okay, here we go. Once a long, long time ago, Nasrettin Hoca and his young son, maybe just your age, Fatma, were going to the market with their donkey. Hoca was riding on the donkey and his son was walking along beside him. When some of the villagers saw them, they began to talk amongst themselves: Look at Hoca. He rides on the donkey and lets his little son walk in the dust. What kind of a father does something like this? Hoca thought about this and decided that perhaps the villagers had a point. So, he got off the donkey and set his son to ride on the donkey's back. Soon more villagers saw them. One said to another, just look at the times we are in. The little boy rides on the donkey while his elderly father walks along in the dust. This is a terrible state of affairs. Hoca thought about this, too. He decided that both he and his son should ride on the donkey. So, he joined his son on the donkey's back. They rode along for a little while like this when some more villagers passed by. One of them said to the group: Look at this poor donkey. He is such a skinny fellow, and it is unfair to use him this way. It is too much of a burden for the little fellow. Hoca considered this. He dismounted the donkey and lifted his son off. He took the donkey's forelegs in his hands and told his son to lift the back legs. And so they both carried the donkey to the market."

Fatma laughed with delight. "And what did the villagers have to say about that?"

"I don't have the slightest idea. That is where the tale ends. It is not possible to please the villagers no matter what one does." Ali nods to Fusun. "Isn't that the truth?"

"It is, *Baba.*" Fusun broke into a very rare smile.

"And what do you think the villagers would say, Fatma, if they saw Hoca and his son carrying the donkey to the market?" Ali winked at Fusun.

Fatma thought for a few minutes before she replied, "I think they would say: Look at that silly Hoca and his son! Don't they know how to use a donkey?"

CHAPTER 10

Fusun has confided to Ali that he should not press Fatma for physical affection. Fatma has been raised fairly sheltered from the world of men. She continues to withhold her hugs from Ali. But the two of them are now thick as thieves, sharing stories in hushed whispers when others approach. Ali has stayed on longer than he initially planned, and this is due to his infatuation with Fatma. First thing in the morning, Ali and Fatma look for one another. Before she goes to bed at night, Fatma always wishes Ali "happy dreams," and hopes he will follow her to tuck her in and tell her a story.

Fusun is in awe of Fatma's sudden attachment to Ali and now privy to a side of him she has not known. Sometimes Fusun is already in bed when Fatma comes to join her. Although Fusun often pretends to be asleep, she listens intently. Fusun does not wish to lose this new and better version of her father. He is smitten with Fatma. And Fusun does not want Fatma to be scared away by the gruff Ali with whom Fusun is familiar, and who is still quite present with her much of the time.

It is now two and a half weeks since Fusun has returned. Azime has cleaned for the potter's wife, Cemal, twice now without mentioning a word to her with regard to her plan. She watches the children with the tutor from the doorway, leaning on her floor mop.

The children are lovely, she thinks. And there is laughter emanating from their schoolroom, a converted nursery. Cengiz is a stocky little dark-haired fellow, all muscle, like his name which means "strong." He teases his two sisters, like any normal boy will, but he is also kind and solicitous of them. Cengiz will become eight years of age in the spring, making him approximately one year older than Fatma.

Badia's looks, unfortunately for her, do not mimic her name. She is most definitely not elegant. Although it is possible that she might grow into it. The stockiness that Cengiz wears so well is ill suited to her ten-year old frame.

Little Elif, just five years old, is a wisp of a thing, the slender branch of a weed blown about in a summer breeze, wheat-colored strands of translucent hair tousled and strewn in many directions.

The tutor is a tall, skeletal young man whose face is pockmarked from pimples, some of which remain. His name is Ilhan, and the children refer to him as "Ilhan *bey*." He is strict but patient, allowing for some of the excited interruption that is inevitable for children of these young ages. They are enthusiastic and jump up from their pillows on the tile floor to wave their hands at him, calling, like children do everywhere, *Biliyorum*, I know.

Azime feels a hand on her shoulder. Cemal has come up behind her. "They are good children, aren't they? Smart children?" She says quietly so as to not disturb the lesson.

Azime nods, not daring to utter a word. How long can she go on without asking? Fusun looks to her every day, but she does not ask anything either. Azime knows she must speak now.

"Dear Cemal *hanım,* there is something I have on my mind."

"I do as well. Let me go first. I have been thinking a lot about Fatma."

"What have you been thinking, Cemal *hanım?*"

"I have been thinking," she gives Azime's shoulder a slight squeeze, "I have been thinking that Fatma is a smart little girl and that if you all agree, we should let her study here. I know it is presumptuous on my part—"

"Not at all, Cemal *hanım.* We would be honored. *Teşekkür ederğim.* Thank you very much."

"And what was on your mind?" Cemal asks.

"I am getting old, and so is my Baler. He needs more attention from me. I am thinking to train Fusun to take over my cleaning here. She might come more days, if you like, and bring Fatma with her."

"Oh, that is perfect, Azime. I could use her just about every day. Besides the cleaning, she can help me with the cooking and shopping." The two women embrace. Suddenly Azime bursts into tears.

"Whatever is wrong, dear friend?"

"You are so good to me, to us. I do not know what we would do without you." Azime pulls out a handkerchief from her apron pocket and wipes away her tears.

"Please, it is a good thing. We help each other this way." Cemal squeezes Azime's shoulder again before she walks away, leaving Azime to watch the children alone. She already sees Fatma there, waving her hand and joining in the chorus of "I know, I know." The tutor looks up, and Azime looks away, shy and embarrassed. She takes her mop and picks up where she left off.

Azime thinks, the world out there is still fighting and killing. But here in our village people are good and kind to each other. The potters are good people and Fatma is fortunate to have this opportunity. Ah, if only her mother could have it also, but maybe she will learn some things from helping Fatma and just being in the lively atmosphere of the potter's household.

Azime is overwhelmed with sadness for Fusun. Life is not fair, this she knows well. When she was a child, the family all stayed together, living next door or down the road. But Ali chose to move away. And he took her only grandchild with him. And now that she finally has her grandchild with her, that child is depressed and withdrawn.

Maybe working, having a schedule, will be just the medicine Fusun needs to bring her back to life. Maybe, Azime thinks. If only Fusun would confide in her, the way she once did. Since she is back, she is more withdrawn than she has been since Fatma's birth.

When Azime returns that afternoon, she sees that Ali has packed up his things. His bag is sitting by the front entranceway. Ali is outside with Fatma, and Fatma is hugging him. He has picked her up, and her little arms are around his neck. Ali sees Azime approaching.

"Now that I am leaving to go home, the little mischief will finally give me a hug! How I had to wait for this. She will break hearts, won't she, *Anne*?"

Fatma sees that it is Azime coming and struggles to have Ali put her down. He does so immediately, Azime notes, following Fusun's instructions to be gentle and cautious with her. Azime is glad to see this. Her son has been good for the child, and she has been good for him.

"You are going," she says to Ali, a little out of breath from her walk from the bus.

"I must go back to work, or my boss will hire someone else. He may have already. But I will leave very early in the morning to catch the first bus."

"Ah, good. You will have supper with us then."

"Yes, and maybe if I'm lucky," Ali winks at Azime, "I can get one more hug before I go."

"If you tell me a good story tonight before I go to bed, maybe," Fatma says with a precocious nod of her head.

Ali laughs. "Since she has not lived much in the world of men, where does she get her flirtatious flattery from?"

"Oh, she can get what she wants from all of us, man or woman," Fusun, overhearing them, has come outside. "And I have no idea where she gets it from."

"Ah, Fusun," Azime says, glad she is not asleep, "good news. Cemal has agreed to have you work for her and she suggested that Fatma come to study with her children. I did not have to ask."

"*Baba* is leaving in the morning." Fusun makes no indication that she has heard Azime's news. She looks away from all of them and stares down at her feet, something she often did when she first came to live with Azime and Baler.

Azime is disappointed. She hopes that something has not occurred to make Fusun change her mind. But to her surprise, Ali offers the idea to Fatma.

"So, you are going to have some real lessons, little one. Will you become smarter than your grandpa?"

"Will I go to a real school?" Fatma asks Azime, as she is unfortunately used to her mother becoming vacant and silent. She doesn't wait for an answer but grabs hold of Ali's wrist. "If you stay away too long, Grandpa, when you do come back, I might be lots smarter than you."

CHAPTER 11

It is the spring of 1924. Fatma is eight years old. Atatürk is busy abolishing, first the Caliphate, then the Ministry of Religious Affairs, religious schools, and religious courts.

Turkey is in a state of division and revision, not that the people who reside here are not used to conflict, upheaval and change by this time.

And Fatma? This is the best time she has had in her young life. Ilhan *bey* is patient and kind. Quickly Fatma catches up to Cengiz and surpasses both of his sisters. Badia does not seem to mind, and both Badia and Elif have often heard their *baba* say, "The cock that crows too early gets his head cut off." And because Elif is small and cute and bright for her age, there is no reason for her to be in competition with Badia.

Poor Badia is the ugly duckling in the group. Fatma is a pretty little girl with an unmanageable head of thick black curls. Her small bones and fine lines, her large eyes and tiny figure could make one believe that she will one day be beautiful. In any event, Badia and Fatma take an instant liking to each other and Fatma finally has a real friend.

And what of Cengiz? He is immediately taken with Fatma. After a few weeks he asks that Fatma marry him when they are old enough. She agrees. Neither of them can imagine finding a better partner. Naturally, the parents on both sides are ignorant as to this proposal and its acceptance.

Fatma has all the luck going for her that her mother never had. Fusun is both proud and envious. She is cleaning floors and toilets so that her daughter can have a better life. Fusun is glad that her little girl is pretty and smart. But there are days when she finds tears silently and slowly slipping down her face. She is still so young, and her life is over before it has had the opportunity to begin. She sees this more clearly than ever in this normally functioning household.

When Fusun first stays at home with only Azime and Baler, Fusun believes that her life might turn out much like Azime's. Azime and Baler have a content and quiet life. She can see the love and respect they share. Their feelings for one another are nothing like the coldness and antagonism she has observed between her own mother and father.

If not for her pregnancy, if not for the reality of Fatma, perhaps she could still find a husband, a friend, a partner in life. But it is hopeless. No man will ever want her now, and she is unsure if she could ever feel physical desire, if she could ever want a man, after the suffering she has experienced.

When Fusun mops the floor outside of the room that once was a nursery and is now a classroom, she often pauses, leans on her mop and listens. On certain days, when Ilhan *bey* is teaching geography and history, Fusun finds herself unable to leave and go back to work. She is mesmerized by the possibilities of so many exotic places in the world and by events of which she is only somewhat cognizant but curious to know more about.

Fusun is in awe of her daughter. Fatma is able to answer questions that Fusun would not even know how to ask. From her limited experience of travel from Salonika to Istanbul and from Istanbul to Avanos and then back to Istanbul to care for her mother and back to Avanos again, Fusun knows that the big war, the Great War, is officially ended. Now she hears the names of towns and cities, even countries, she cannot imagine, cannot draw any picture of in her mind. Fatma speaks of these places almost as if she has been there.

"And where is the River Arno?" Ilhan *bey* asks. "Tell me, Badia. Do you know?"

A chorus of "Biliyorum, biliyorum," "I know, I know" comes from Cengiz and Fatma.

"Wait," Ilhan *bey* cautions, "Give Badia a chance to think."

Badia does not wish to have this chance. If she gets the right answer, it will only be a lucky guess.

"Paris? Is that the river in Paris?"

Outside, Fusun shakes her head no. The River Seine is Paris. This she knows.

"No, the River Seine is in Paris. Elif, do you know the River Arno? Do you know what city it is in?"

"I don't." Actually, Fatma guesses that Elif might know the correct answer, but she often pretends she does not to bolster Badia's confidence. She is protective of her big sister.

"Cengiz, can you tell us where the River Arno flows?"

"The River Arno flows in Rome." Cengiz folds his hands together triumphantly.

"No, it does not! You have the right country and the wrong city." Fatma sits back on her pillow, folding her legs underneath her. "The River Arno flows in Florence."

Cengiz makes a funny face at Fatma, and she makes one back. It is the flirtation that can only occur between an eight-year-old girl and a nine-year-old boy.

"The young lady is correct," Ilhan *bey* informs them. "And both Rome and Florence are where, Badia?"

"They are both in Italy."

"Very good. It is important to know where we are in the world."

And where am I in this world? Fusun asks herself. I am alone, truly alone. Fatma has already gone off to begin to live her own life and Azime and Baler are old. They will die soon. And my *baba* sees me as spoiled fruit, a rotten pear, an overripe banana. He loves my Fatma more than he ever loved me, even before I was pregnant. My *anne* is dead.

Yes, it is important to know where I am in this world. Fusun traces her thoughts. I no longer live in Salonika in the Ottoman Empire. I am now living in Goreme in the Republic of Turkey. What is different for me? Here I am with the same dirty toilets and the same filthy floors.

Fusun walks out of hearing distance. She only hurts herself when she lingers there. If only she had, if only she hadn't. There are too many of these to count. Fusun sees that Cemal is approaching.

"*Selam*, Cemal *hanım*. Is there anything you need?"

"*Selam*, Fusun. Will it be okay if Fatma stays with us next weekend? Next Saturday is Badia's birthday, and you know how those two are. They are like sisters. I forgot all about it until just now."

Fusun cannot imagine forgetting Fatma's birthday. And then, just as suddenly as she feels a rush of love, she is struck by a brutal stab of what feels like hate. No, she instantly corrects her thought; this is envy that I am feeling.

"Of course," she says, "I will pack a bag for her when I bring her next Friday."

"Good, good. This will make Badia so happy."

And what about me, Fusun thinks, will this make me happy? Is there anything that makes me feel true happiness? Is there love that does not get mixed up with hate? I have never known this kind of love, if it exists. Well, maybe that isn't true. Maybe I do have this love with Azime. Yes, this love does exist, I have seen it, but this is not a love I have experienced. How can I be so jealous of my own daughter? How can I love her and hate her at the same time? What is wrong with me?

Fusun becomes obsessed with these questions, but she talks to no one about them. She does not wish to worry Azime, and she sees that Cemal is busy with village life. This is why Cemal needed Azime and now needs Fusun.

Fusun knows how much Cemal loves to be in the pottery shop. The shop is both located in the center of town and is the center of town. Cemal and Salman know everyone. Cemal has never enjoyed being a homemaker and when she met Salman, she saw her escape from a life of household drudgery and boredom.

Everything from village gossip to local politics to the changes Atatürk is making and the world at large—this is all discussed amidst the dishes and bowls and plates and cups and saucers. And Cemal is at the very front of all of this. She possesses the knowledge to talk to anyone about anything. She is educated. Salman is not. He makes the pottery and oversees the small factory. Cemal rules the sales shop. Cemal is thrilled to have a tutor and a housemaid so that she is able to leave these mundane tasks to others who are better equipped to handle them. Or they are poor, Fusun thinks, and so they do them anyway, mundane or not, like me.

Yes, Fusun has envy and hatred for Cemal as well. The children adore Cemal, including Fatma. They run straight into her arms, except for Cengiz, who has suddenly, since his ninth birthday, taken to kissing his mother on her cheeks, first one and then the other. Since his circumcision, when he was just eight years old, he has become quite the young man. Fusun does not like to think about circumcision. As far as she is concerned, they ought to remove the whole thing. But she knows it was painful for Cengiz, and she cannot help but be fond of him. Sometimes she hates him, too. Sometimes she hates everyone, most of all, herself.

What is so precious about this life anyway? Now that she has gotten out of her bed, out of the house even, what is there for her? The days are all the same. Fatma can already read beyond her and beyond Azime. She brings books home from the potter's library and books that Ilhan *bey* loans to her. Sometimes she reads them aloud to Fusun, but Fusun cannot seem to stay focused. Her mind wanders. She loses track of the characters and the story line. Fatma realizes that her *anne* is not following and begins to read more and more to herself. This is a relief to Fusun.

Fusun begins to withdraw more and more. Azime and Fatma try to bring her back, but she does not respond to either of them consistently. Fatma can get her attention now and then, but Azime does not push her in the same way that Fatma does. She is getting old and does not have the energy that it takes. Some days Azime joins Baler and Ahmet, sitting outside with them when she brings their *çay*. And even though Fusun now works most days for the potter's family, when Fusun sees the three of them out there, talking and laughing together, she feels even more alone. She belongs nowhere and to no one. There is no place for her, no conversation that she might join, no soft place to land.

"Did you have a good day today?" Azime will ask Fusun when she returns from the potter's home.

"Yes," Fusun replies, "it was fine." Her affect is flat. She does not look at Azime when she answers.

If she was working for anyone other than Cemal and Salman, Azime thinks, she might be concerned that Fusun's employers were abusing her. Azime knows Cemal and Salman too long and too well to even consider the possibility. Her suspicion that something else could have happened to Fusun persists, some trauma other than her rape and the death of her mother.

Although Azime is uneducated and inexperienced, this does not mean she is unintelligent. Quite the contrary, for she has listened in on many discussions at the home and shop of Cemal and Salman about the war, about the men and boys who returned but were never the same. She has also heard them talking about the forming of the Republic and longstanding neighbors turning on one another, families being driven out or running from fear, and the rampant slaughter of Turks by Greeks and Greeks by Turks. Armenians who had lived for generations in the Ottoman Empire were marched away from their homes with their babies and their children, with only the clothes on their backs, grateful to be escaping with their lives; those who are able to survive this deadly march.

Cemal and Salman continue to feel devastated by all of this. Salman goes on about "nationalism at its worst," and that the new Republic of Turkey "is losing out by sending so many talented people away."

"Just because they are Christians. We have always lived together," Salman complains.

"But unfortunately, we are not always good neighbors. Just look at our history," Cemal replies.

Cemal and Salman are good people, but they are not able to work miracles. They do so much for her family already, that Azime chastises herself when she thinks there ought to be something done about Fusun. They see her almost every day. Do they ignore her behavior or just not notice how sad she is? They must have observed her silent tears—or perhaps not.

Azime remembers days when she could have been part of their furniture, not because they were actively ignoring her but because they were living their own lives. It is not in our natures to be selfless, she admits. They have every right to live their lives, and I am coming into theirs. They are not coming into mine. Fatma goes there to spend the night, but the children do not come to spend the night with Fatma. How can she even have these thoughts? After all they have done and are doing for her?

"Ach," Azime murmurs. I am human. I am not without my faults. And it is not as if I ever voice these thoughts aloud to anyone. I will never do that. I do not like this part of me who complains when I should be grateful. Perhaps I ought to be complaining to Allah. My son does this all the time, and I'm not sure why. He is blessed in so many ways. We need to be able to see what we have, not always looking for more, she reflects. Azime cannot understand this nature in her son. Neither she nor Baler has ever been like this.

These questions plague Azime from time to time. If not for her worries concerning Fusun, she does not believe these ideas would ever come to mind. But she does not know the answers. How can she expect Cemal to have them?

Finding no solution, Azime loses herself in Baler and Ahmet's now less frequent games of Mancala and the rhythm of their mostly predictable dialogue. Only when Fusun goes to bed right after dinner, or when Azime watches her ignoring or turning away from Fatma, does a sharp pain stick directly under her rib cage and she wonders, what can anyone do?

CHAPTER 12

Spring, 1930, almost three years since Mustafa Kemal was re-elected as President of The Republic of Turkey.

Fatma is floating on her back in a soft, warm pool of water. The sun is strong and embraces her naked body. Fatma has no idea where she is but thinks she would like to remain in this state of bliss forever. Something hot and sticky oozes from between her legs and covers her thighs. Sharp, swift darts of stabbing cramps in her belly, her groin—

Fatma's eyes startle open. She is in bed, but this dream is not only a dream. Has she wet the bed? It can't be possible. She is just a few months shy of fourteen, and she can't remember the last time that happened. Yet, there is something there, wet, and sticky but thicker than pee. She lifts her nightgown and touches herself with her forefinger. When she raises her finger from under the bedding to look, it is red. This is blood. She throws off the bedding. She is bleeding down there. Fatma lies frozen in her bed, terrified. She doesn't want to wake Fusun, sleeping so soundly next to her, but it seems that she must.

"*Anne,*" she whispers. Fusun doesn't stir.

"*Anne,*" she says a bit more urgently, but Fusun still makes no movement.

Fatma now feels a warm rush between her legs. "*Anne, Anne, Anne,*" she cries, loud enough to wake Azime who comes as quickly as she can from her bed. Her arthritis has been bothering her and she cannot move so easily. She pulls aside the carpet door and sees Fatma lying in her own blood. Fusun is lying on her side, facing away from Fatma. One of Fusun's hands is lying on top of a tray filled with cigarette butts, a habit she acquired shortly after Fatma was born.

Azime looks down at the bedding underneath Fatma and takes in a deep breath, covering her mouth with her hand. "Fusun," she walks over to Fusun's side of the bed and nudges her arm with one finger. "Fusun, wake up, please. Fatma needs your help." Fusun still doesn't budge.

Azime lets out a harsh cry that wakes Baler. She is now shaking Fusun violently. Fatma hears Baler's footsteps approaching and his mumbling, "Whatever can be going on in there?" Fatma reaches down and covers herself with the blankets. Azime is too distraught to notice. She seems to have completely forgotten Fatma.

Baler is an old man. He has trouble lifting the carpet to enter the room. The turmoil that Turkey has suffered shows on him. All he has been able to eat for some time is cereal and çay. The cereal is stale and the çay is weak.

"What is the trouble about? Whatever is the matter?" Baler asks.

Azime points to her granddaughter, Fusun. "She doesn't move."

Baler leans over and listens for his granddaughter's breathing. He lifts the upper half of her body, shaking her, "Fusun, wake up. Please, praises be to Allah, please, please wake up. What is wrong with you?" Baler tries to raise Fusun up again, but her arms flop uselessly by her side.

Fatma knows she must move and clean herself up before she bleeds all over the bed. For what feels to her like an hour but is only a moment, she freezes. She waits for her mother to rescue her, but her mother will not move. What if she never moves again? What if she has lost her forever? Fatma breathes deeply and forces her rebellious body into action. She wraps the blanket around herself, prying it away from Fusun's floppy ragdoll body and runs to the bathroom. Baler continues to shake Fusun until Azime grabs his arms and tries to pull him away. "Let her go, please, you'll hurt her," Azime gasps. Baler lets go and Fusun falls back onto the bed.

"She's dead," Baler cries, his body doubling over with grief. "How can it be that she's dead? She wasn't even sick."

Azime leans over Fusun and puts her ear against Fusun's heart. She then lifts up her wrist and tries to listen for a pulse. Azime pulls the remaining bedding away from Fusun. "Oh, my God," she cries out. She points to a puddle of fresh blood before she remembers Fatma. Azime throws the bedding back over the blood and looks around for Fatma. She has run off somewhere, the poor girl has finally become a woman, and her mother is lying dead next to her menstrual blood.

"I must go to Fatma," Azime cries. "Get the Imam, please, Baler. Praise Allah, He has taken my little angel to be with her mother. And I should have gone before them both."

Baler hesitates a moment, afraid to leave Azime but afraid to comfort her as well. He has never had a facility of speech when confronted with strong emotions. He does not possess the ability to think the right words, never mind voicing them aloud. Baler only feels the bursting pressure in his gut.

Azime runs to the bathroom. She pauses at the carpet door and calls out, "Fatma, are you in there? Can you hear me?"

"Go away," *Babaanne*. "Please don't come in."

"Okay, but I will get you something to use for the blood. Did your *anne* talk to you about this?"

"Maybe. I don't know. I don't remember." Of course, Fatma does remember, how could she not, but she is so frightened now that she wants Azime to tell her everything again, to comfort her, maybe to tell her that none of it is true, that Fusun lied to her. Fusun, my *anne*, is dead. My mother is gone forever, Fatma thinks, how is that even possible?

But Azime is not focusing on Fusun's death right now. She wants to expel it from her mind by attending to something she can do. "You're not ill, my dear," she says. "It means that now you're a grown woman. You have your menstruation. You can have babies. I'll be right back with some menstrual rags for you."

"But I don't want babies, *Babaanne*. Please, how do I make it stop?"

"You can't make it stop, and some day later you may want to have babies. Why don't you want them?"

Fatma feels more liquid running down her leg and settling on the side of her left foot. But she ignores it. "Tell me the truth, please, *Babaanne*, did I kill my *anne*?"

"No, little one, of course not. Let me get some clean rags for you and I'll explain what I can."

Azime makes her way to a cabinet in the room where Fusun is lying. Baler must have gone for the Imam, as he is no longer there. She reaches into the back of the cabinet where Fusun keeps her supplies. Her hand brushes against a thick woolen sweater, a striped pattern of autumn colors, reddish browns, golden browns and burnt oranges. When Azime knit the sweater for

Fusun, she hadn't known that it would turn out to be so beautiful. The wool was a soft blend and the colors suited Fusun so well.

Now Azime strokes the wool and sobs quietly. She remembers the Fusun before her pregnancy, the sweet and devoted Fusun, the angel Azime adored as if she had gone through the agony of childbirth herself to bring her into this world. She takes the sweater and holds it against her breasts, then presses her face into it to catch any lingering smells of the child she has loved as her own.

What happened to Fusun? Was it the rape? She seemed to recover from that. But then Fatma's birth? Fusun was so strange after that. But then she seemed to recover from the birth as well, though perhaps never completely.

Azime is uneducated in these matters. Life simply gives and takes away. She does what she must do and carries on, as her *anne* carried on before her. These ups and downs of Fusun's are a puzzle to Azime. She caresses the sweater, folds it, and places it back on the shelf. She made it to keep Fusun warm. Fusun will not need it now.

In the corner of the cupboard, she finds a pile of clean menstrual rags. She lifts the pile and knocks over a small plastic bottle lying underneath. It is empty. Azime picks it up and looks for a label. The label appears to have been scratched off, only a blank scrap of paper remains. She puts the bottle into the pocket of her robe. Could it be that Fusun was sick and they didn't know? She is always so secretive with them.

Worse still, could she have used these pills to end her life? This question darts through Azime's already agitated mind as she heads back to the bathroom. She wants to rid herself of the idea. She has only raised a son, and Ali always says exactly what is on his mind, or so it seems. Maybe she is wrong about this, too. She knows she is ignorant of many things.

Perhaps they have missed something and Fusun isn't really dead? By some miracle, the Imam might revive her. Azime prays that he will come soon. Please come to help us. We need you now.

Outside the bathroom door, Azime hesitates. "Please Fatma, let me come in to help you. I have some rags for you."

Fatma pulls back the carpet with one hand. With the other she is holding a towel wrapped around her. Azime hands her the rags. "Do you need..."

"Turn your back or step outside, please."

Azime turns around but doesn't leave.

Fatma secures a rag in her underwear and removes the tissue paper she has placed there temporarily. She rolls up the tissue paper and places it in the trash basket and covers herself with the blanket. The soiled bedding sits in a pile on the floor. "You can turn around now, *Babaanne*." Despite the blanket, she falls into Azime's outstretched arms.

"Is my mother dead?" Fatma asks in between her sobs.

"Your great grandfather has gone to bring the Imam. I don't know yet." And as she says this, Azime realizes that it is true. Fusun is gone. Only a miracle from Allah will bring her back. She hugs Fatma close to her.

"Did your *anne* not explain all of this to you? Did she tell you about the bleeding, that it's normal for a young woman?"

"Yes, she told me. She told me but I didn't believe her completely. I thought if I prayed and prayed to Allah, it wouldn't happen to me. Can't I make it stop?"

Azime breaks her hold of Fatma and looks into her eyes. "It's not something you want to stop. It means that one day when you are older and married, you will be able to have babies."

Fatma backs away. "I don't want to have them. My *anne* always says she was too young to be a mother when she had me. And what if my husband goes off to fight with Mustafa Kemal like my *baba* did?"

This is the first time that Azime has heard this fabrication, but she does not comment. Instead, she says, "I will bring you some clothes to put on and then let's go into the kitchen and have some *çay*. We can sit together and talk while Baler is fetching the Imam."

Azime must keep Fatma away from her mother's body. Fatma is bleeding and unclean according to Islam. She covers her face with her hands. Why, praise be to Allah, is she "unclean?" Azime does not understand this, never has, although the law certainly made her feel unclean. It has been many years now since she has had that experience. In some ways she misses the bleeding. When nothing else made her feel like a woman, the bleeding did.

Why does she even think about these things now? What is wrong with her? She is so frozen inside. Why can't she feel? Her daughter-in-law is dead, and now her son's daughter, Fusun, is lying dead in her bedroom. Azime beats her fists against the heart she cannot feel. For the first time in her life, she rails against injustice. Like her son, she rails against the absence of Allah.

Where is he? How could he allow all of this to happen? But then she drops her fists. She must attend to her great granddaughter.

Allah be praised, she thinks. The irony of saying this so soon after her tirade against him escapes her. I am an old woman, and I must be a mother again. These events are beyond her. She has lost the ability to think, never mind putting anything into words or to feel. And Baler has become so fragile. Azime knows she should not have asked him to fetch the Imam, but she could not go and leave Fatma there with Fusun.

Azime walks back to the room where Fusun is lying. She peeks out of the corner of her eye and sees that Fusun is still prostrate across the bed. Without looking at Fusun, she goes to the chest in the corner and opens it. She takes out a pair of pants, a sweater, a bra and some shoes and socks, and walks back out of the room, avoiding the body lying there silent and motionless. Azime takes the clothing to Fatma and goes to the kitchen to boil the water for *çay*.

By the time Fatma dresses and finds Azime in the kitchen, the tea is poured in small glasses and the hot kettle is sitting on the wooden table that Baler crafted long ago. It is made from a poplar tree he felled and from which he produced a table and two long benches. They are rough on the backs and edges with the natural ebb and flow of the bark, but they are smoothed to a finish on the tabletop and the seats of the benches. They lend a sense of primitive artistry to this unusual setting. In a modern world, they might become museum pieces. Baler is a talented carpenter. He is an artisan.

Azime takes a sip of hot tea and ponders what to say to Fatma. She feels very close to the child, closer than she even felt to Fusun, whose moods changed like the second hand on a clock.

Fatma holds her cup of *çay* in her hands, warming them, but she does not drink. "*Anne* is dead, isn't she?" Fatma sets the tea on the table and goes to Azime.

"Yes, I'm fairly sure she is, child." Azime rises and takes Fatma in her arms.

"What will happen to me now?"

"What do you mean? You will always be welcome here with us."

"But what about school? *Anne* talked about sending me to Istanbul to my grandfather for school. *Anne* thought I was smart and should have a good education. She didn't want me to have to be dependent on others, like she was."

Azime releases her hold on Fatma and looks at her. "I never knew she felt that way. We've done the best we could."

"No, no, she loves you dearly." Fatma squeezes her grandmother's hands in her own. "But because my *baba* was killed helping Atatürk to win the Republic, she didn't have the choices she wants me to have. She always tells me to go to school, to be independent, become something so I can take care of myself."

It has been months now since Ilhan *bey* went back to Ankara to teach the new alphabet to other teachers. He was offered good money to do so, and the children lost their tutor. Badia and Elif are struggling with the new alphabet at home and Cengiz is in boarding school in Ankara. For the past year, he is only home on the holidays. He has managed to teach Fatma the new alphabet, and she, in turn, tries to help his sisters. Elif will catch on, but Fatma thinks Badia might be hopeless.

"Ach, child," Azime quickly adds, "you have some time to think about all of this. We will talk with Baler. Now we must wait for him to come and bring the Imam." Azime decides she will never correct this fabrication of Fusun's, this fairy tale Fusun has created of a real father for Fatma, a war hero who fell in the fight for the Republic. It is not her right to take this gift from Fatma. She is also in no hurry to send Fatma away and hopes she can wait this one out, as she has been doing since the tutor left. And now Fusun has left them as well.

They sit together quietly for another hour. At last, Fatma hears the soft chattering of women and the sound footsteps of men. She runs to the heavy carpet that separates the inside of the cave from the outdoors and pulls it aside. Coming down the path are Baler, the Imam, a stout heavily bearded man of more than sixty years, dressed in a formal white turban and a long white robe. He walks alongside the Avanos doctor, a short, potbellied man Fatma has seen only once. Four middle-aged women in headscarves follow behind them. The chattering of the women ceases as they approach Fatma. They nod to Fatma and whisper, "*Salaam Aleikum.*" Fatma replies, "*Wa-Aleikum Salaam.*" They remove their shoes and enter quietly, one by one.

The doctor does not examine Fusun. He listens for a pulse and then a heartbeat and declares her dead due to heart failure. No one questions his diagnosis. No one mentions that Fusun never had a heart condition, and Azime is silent with regard to the empty bottle of pills in her pocket. She thinks, why should Fatma have to carry the burden of her mother's suicide her whole life? And now Azime is almost certain that suicide is what it was. Hasn't Fatma's life so far been unfortunate enough? Isn't she the result of the devil's own luck? No, she will not make it harder for her. She will become Fatma's *anne* for as long as she is able.

The four women who have accompanied the Imam proceed with the ritualistic washing of the body. Azime supervises. She explains that Fatma is unclean due to her period and therefore, isn't able under religious law to assist. The Imam returns to the mosque to await the burial service the next day. One of the four women remains behind at the Imam's request to sit with the body throughout the night. Fatma sleeps with Azime. Baler, forlorn and filled with despair about Fatma's future, sits alone outside the cave, contemplating and carefully considering her fate.

CHAPTER 13

Ali does not arrive in time for Fusun's funeral. Fatma sends a wire to Ali's restaurant, hoping that he will receive the news more quickly there. When there is no response, Baler determines that they go ahead with the burial within the twenty-four hours allotted according to Muslim religious law. Fatma tells Baler she thinks they should wait.

Fatma is the only one amongst them who possesses any understanding of what Ali feels for Fusun. Whenever Ali has visited over the past few years, Fatma has observed his love for Fusun, the way Ali checks Fusun's reactions when he tells a story or when he makes Fatma laugh. Fatma is struck by Ali's delight when Fusun smiles. Fatma has tried to help Fusun to see this, but Fusun has no trust in men. Baler is the only man she trusts, and there are times when she questions even that trust. She tells Fatma that Ali behaves as he should to her, as a father is expected to respond to his daughter, but that he does not feel any love for her. Fatma wishes she could prove it to her *anne*, and now it is too late. Fatma does believe that Ali will be terribly upset.

The potter's family are the only ones to come to the funeral, other than Baler's good friend, Ahmet, and several of the villagers. Cengiz is also unable to get there in time. Fatma is glad that he is not there. She cannot stop crying, as she has not cried in years now, and she likes Cengiz to see her as a strong woman, like his mother. "I would not want him to see me like this," she confides to Badia.

Fatma is glad to have Badia and Elif here with her, though. They hold no stigma against tears and are sympathetic. Fusun has always been kind to them, and they are both sad for Fatma. Fusun always hugged the girls and showed them physical affection, even when Fatma sensed that Fusun was not feeling connected to anyone. Perhaps that is how Fatma recognizes Ali's

81

love for Fusun. Fatma, too, has grown up with a detached mother. She can read emotions that are not easily visible to others.

Ali arrives the next day. He has traveled hard to get there.

"You buried her without me? Why did you do this? How could you do this? These are exceptional circumstances, extraordinary times."

"I am sorry, my son. We did not know when you would come. The Imam came and brought the women to bathe her. She was ready."

"I will never lay eyes on my daughter again. How would you feel if I were lying there? What can you say to me?" Ali sits at the table across from Baler and puts his head in his hands.

Fatma is afraid. She has never seen Ali upset with his father or his mother. She knows that he must have been at some time or another, but he is always respectful and deferring. Now Fatma is fearful that he will go to dig Fusun up just to look at her again. Has anyone ever done that? She does not know.

"Please, *büyükbabam*, my grandpa, she is okay. She is at peace. I saw her face."

Fatma goes over to Ali and touches his shoulder. Ali does not move but whispers, "Thank you. It is good for me to know everything you can tell me about what has happened."

Baler looks long and hard at Fatma. "Fusun died from heart failure, the doctor said. And now, Ali, you will take your granddaughter to Istanbul with you so that she can go to school."

Azime is in the kitchen, but she hears him. Baler says it loud enough for her to hear. There is no objection to this, she knows. Well, Fatma's going might be for the best. What will a young girl—no, now actually a young woman—do here anyway? The young people are all leaving these days. Fatma's chances will be greater in Istanbul.

Ali lifts his head from the table. "Seriously? You will let her go with me now?"

"She is your daughter's child. We are old. There is more opportunity for her there. But you will have to make some changes. Fatma can do most things on her own now. Your *anne* and Fusun have taught her well. But you can see for yourself, she is still a young girl. She will need you to be around more. If you can promise me that you will supervise her; that means coming home from that restaurant of yours every day to make sure she is well, that she eats and goes to school, and that she is also feeling well in her heart and mind. If you can guarantee us that you will do all of this, she will go with you. Azime has already spoken with Fatma, and she says this is her wish."

Suddenly, hearing Baler say it aloud, Fatma feels frightened. She has always lived with Ali's parents. She has never even seen Istanbul or Ali's home. Fusun never wanted to talk about what it was like there. Fatma has no idea if Ali can make such a promise, or worse, will he make the promise and not be able to keep it? From Fusun's descriptions, Ali lives in the restaurant and only goes home to bathe and change his clothing.

"Is this what you want, child? Do you want to come back to Istanbul with me and go to a proper school?" Ali's voice shakes slightly, as if he is afraid to ask.

Fatma looks from Baler to Ali, and then her eyes come to rest with Ali. She cannot say what she feels in words. She is fearful, and yet, she knows on some level that this is her time, her chance. Fusun is truly gone forever. Ilhan *bey*, the children's tutor, is probably back in Ankara for good, and Cengiz is only home for vacation breaks from his school. She will come to visit whenever she can.

"Yes, this is what I want." Fatma says this with decisiveness she does not feel. "Why don't we try and see how we get along?" She feels a necessity to give both of them a way out. Fatma has never been without "parents," even though she has never known her father, and her mother was not always able to answer her questions or attend to her needs. Azime and Baler have always been there to fill in the empty spaces. But all in all, she believes that if Ali does anything to hurt her, this will be without any negative intentions. He is more likely to commit sins of omission. She holds out a hand to her grandfather, and Ali pulls her into a hug.

"It's all settled then." Ali actually smiles. Fatma is long over her reluctance to hug him, but he remembers well when she shied away.

Azime enters from the kitchen. "What is settled?" she asks, even though she has heard everything other than Ali's whisper.

Fatma looks at Azime and sees the pain in her eyes. She hesitates, and Baler responds for her.

"We have decided that Fatma will go to Istanbul so she can go to school. That is a good idea, isn't it?"

Fatma watches her great grandmother's eyes. The light is back in them. Azime is a good woman. She wants Fatma to have everything. "Oh, yes, that is good news," she says. "You have missed your lessons with Ilhan *bey*, haven't you?"

Azime notices once again how Fatma is developing into quite a pretty young girl. Her head of wild black curls is loose and hangs down past her shoulders. She is slender with delicate features that seem to have come from neither side of their families. Must have come from the father's side, she thinks. Azime understands that she must let her great granddaughter go.

"I have missed my lessons, *Babaanne*. But I will miss you, too. *Baba* will bring me back to visit, won't you?"

"That is an easy promise to make." Ali smiles again, noticing that she is now calling him *Baba*.

Fatma persists, saying "But not so easy a promise to keep." This surprises all of them. Fatma can be so grownup at times.

Ali looks from one face to the next. He has not promised to follow Baler's conditions. He sees that Fatma is testing him. "*Tamam*," he says. "Okay, I promise to rearrange my schedule at the restaurant and to bring Fatma to visit. You are all witnesses to my promise."

"That's better, *Baba*." Fatma sounds more like the child she still is. She knows she will have to ask him repeatedly for the same things, for he forgets his promises so easily, but Fatma also knows how to catch more flies with honey. She has learned this skill in Cemal's household. Ali needs flattery and so does Badia. To skirt around Badia's potential to be envious, Fatma has observed Ilhan *bey* do this quite often.

Azime has glimpsed this side of Fatma, and she begins to believe that Fatma will handle her son better than anyone has thus far. Fusun did not like her fate, but she attempted to accept her lot in life. Fatma will not accept; she will choose, Azime thinks. She wonders if she will live long enough to assess the finished work. She doubts that she will, but wishes for it anyway.

The next few days are spent preparing for their journey. Fatma still has very few possessions but more than when she first arrived. Cemal has given her some clothing and Ali has purchased some things along the way to replace what she has outgrown. He explains that they will go shopping before she starts her new school. Fatma wishes that her *anne* would be there to help her. She knows nothing about clothing, never having actually selected any for herself. Her clothing has always been too large or too small for her. Badia's hand-me-downs are big, and Ali buys things that are too small, not realizing how she has grown since he last saw her. She hopes she will know how to choose.

Since Fatma now sleeps alone in the room, in the very bed that she shared all these years with Fusun, she dreams of her. Fatma loves these dreams and is afraid that she will lose them in Istanbul. Her *anne's* spirit might not accompany her there.

When Fatma goes to say her good-byes to her friends, she asks Badia what she thinks about her dreams.

"What do you think will happen to my dreams?" Fatma asks Badia.

"Dreams are messages," Badia tells her. "You will always have them. It does not matter where you are."

"But will I still be able to see my *anne* in my dreams?"

"That is hard to know. But if she needs to tell you something, then she will come no matter where you are. And you will come back to see your great grandparents. Maybe when you return, you will dream of her here."

"Does that mean she will, only when I am here?" Fatma is afraid that Ali will not wish to make the journey too often.

"How can I know? No one knows. If your *anne* needs to give you a message, she will come to you. She could come in the form of a bird or a cat or just about anything. You will know from the message that it is your *anne*."

"How do you know so much about dreams?"

"My *anne* lives according to her dreams. Everyone thinks she has no superstitions and that she is so modern. She is no different from the rest of us when it comes to these matters."

"Thank you, Badia. I need to hear this because my dreams are so real to me that when I wake up, I look for her to be next to me in the bed. I am so disappointed when she is not there."

"Why don't you speak to Azime about these dreams? My *anne* sometimes does. Azime is excellent at interpreting dreams."

Fatma looks at Badia with a quizzical smile. "And why is it that I never knew this?"

"Probably because my *anne's* friends always came here to speak with Azime. They did not consult with her in Goreme."

Fatma says her farewells to the pottery family and promises to write to Badia and Elif. On her way home on the bus she thinks, there is too much that I do not know, and possibly, all of my chances of knowing anything have died with my *anne*. Baler and Azime always change the subject when I ask; they say something I have heard before like your father was brave and he died for the Republic, but they tell me nothing about *him* really. They say they never knew him, only what they heard from my *anne* and grandfather. But I might get more information from him, she supposes. He must have known my father. He brought my *anne* to her grandparents when my *baba* was killed. Maybe he can tell me more. Wouldn't he have known my *baba*? Someone must have.

PART II
LIFE IN THE NEW REPUBLIC

CHAPTER 14

I am fourteen years old, and I have been living in what is now called Istanbul for six months. When the sultan was in charge, it was known as Constantinople. Many things are changing under Mustafa Kemal or Atatürk, as he is now known.

I do not think that learning at the big school is as much fun as it was with Ilhan *bey*. The boys are separated from the girls. And I do miss Cengiz. I always worked so hard to keep up with him. These girls do not motivate me so much. I will have to learn to encourage myself.

The teacher, Selma *hanım*, does not like me when I ask her too many questions. "You always have to know why a thing is just a thing. Sometimes there is no answer to why things are the way they are." I am suspicious that she does not know the answers herself, or she would be happy to tell me.

The house in Istanbul is not as bad as I thought it would be. Grandpa cleaned the bedroom when we first got here, and he gave it to me, so now he is the one sleeping in the kitchen where my *anne* used to sleep. He takes me to school in the mornings, and he picks me up in the afternoons. We ride the tram which is lots of fun due to the many varieties of people I see. We get off just a few blocks from my school. We have to walk a bit farther to catch the tram from home though, and sometimes *Baba* is a bit grouchy in the mornings. He says he's not used to the new schedule. I am, though. I make our *çay* and set up our breakfast now, and so he is not as grouchy as he used to be. And I can usually make him laugh at something funny that happens on the tram, like when the little boy handed the beggar with only one tooth a piece of his Turkish Delight. The beggar stared at it for a long time, as if he did not want to hurt the little boy's feelings by handing it back to him. He muttered "thank you" as he walked away, shoving it into his torn and filthy pocket.

Now that I am fourteen, I can do many things by myself. But *Baba* still does not like me to travel anywhere on my own. He once said it was because he'd had bad experiences, but he won't tell me what they were and does not like me to bring this up. Does he think he will always take me everywhere I need to go for the rest of my life, or will I have to marry to end this?

To be completely honest, I like *Baba's* company when he is in a good mood, so I might miss him if he stopped traveling with me. Unlike Selma *hanım*, he tries to always answer my questions. If he does not have the answer, he will tell me. The one exception is anything I might want to know about my *anne* or my real *baba*. He changes the subject, as if I have not spoken at all.

Sometimes I wonder about my *anne*, whatever happened to her? Why did her moods change so? Why is *Baba* so afraid for me all the time? Was it the war that made him so fearful? Was it the fall of the Ottoman Empire? Was it all the killing that went on then? Did something happen to my *anne* that made *Baba* afraid for me? Or is he worried what his *baba* will think of him should anything bad happen to me? I wish I knew these things.

While I am at school, *Baba* goes to the restaurant. He works there until it is time for him to pick me up and take me home. Sometimes he brings food for dinner from the restaurant, and other times we stop at the market to gather the food for our dinner, and then we make it ourselves. *Baba* is trying hard to keep his promise to his father and to me.

Baba always asks me about school and my friends there. But then he is sleepy after eating and goes to take his nap. When I am ready to go to sleep for the night, *Baba* goes back to the restaurant and works until very late at night and often until early morning. Sometimes I hear him come in, but often I do not wake up until it is time to get ready for school. I never feel afraid to be alone because *Baba* always makes sure that the house is securely locked and bolted when he leaves. And Muhsine *hanım* lives right next door.

I love Muhsine *hanım*. She says she comes to visit me, and I believe that is partially true, but mostly I think she comes to visit *Baba*. Muhsine *hanım* is a widow. She married when she was young, but her husband was immediately taken away to fight with Mustafa Kemal Atatürk. He was killed shortly after the war in the fight for the Republic. Muhsine *hanım* never saw him again after he first left, and so she has no children. I like to imagine sometimes that her husband stood alongside my real father and that they were comrades who fought and died together. And since I can never know the truth because they are both dead, I can make the fantasy even more thrilling both in my daytime dreams and in my nighttime ones.

I secretly hope that *Baba* will marry Muhsine *hanım* because she is pretty and kind, but the one time I suggested this, he just smiled. He did not say anything about this to me again. Oh, I would so like to have a mother. I do miss mine.

Muhsine *hanım* is showing me how to cook some of the dishes her mother taught her to make. They are a little bit different from the ones I learned from *Babaanne*, since they grew up in different parts of Turkey. If I am completely honest, her cooking is sometimes even better than *Babaanne*'s. But that may be because she has more of a choice of ingredients. Now that the war is over and Atatürk is running things, there are all kinds of fruits and vegetables in Constantinople—Istanbul, I mean—some I had never seen before I moved here.

Muhsine *hanım* looks very different from all of us. She is tall and slender with blue eyes, but since she wears a headscarf, I do not yet know the color of her hair. Since she is light-skinned, I am guessing that she might be a blonde. When I once asked *Baba* what he thought, he mumbled and stammered something like, "How should I know?"

Muhsine *hanım* is my best friend, next to Badia, of course. I like to think that I am her best friend, too. I tell her everything about me, but she says very little about herself.

I tell her, "Ayşel interrupted me today when I asked Selma *hanım* why she does not wear a headscarf. She said I was being rude."

"Did Selma *hanım* answer you?" Muhsine is busy filling the *börek* pastry with homemade white cheese. She cuts a small piece for me.

"*Teşekküler*, thank you," I tell her before I say, "Sort of. She said Atatürk passed a law about the veil, not wearing a veil. But I told her, the headscarf is not a veil."

Muhsine *hanım* cuts a piece of cheese for herself and hesitates while she is chewing. Then she says, "The headscarf is more of a choice now. I have been married, and so I wear one."

"But Selma *hanım* is married, too."

"Religious customs can be complicated. I believe that Atatürk has banned them from the schools."

"Why?" Fatma asks.

"Atatürk wants women to be more independent, more educated."

"But what does that have to do with wearing a headscarf or not?" I am persistent.

"The headscarf is the symbol of a woman's modesty."

"Is Selma *hanım* not modest?"

"She does not wear the headscarf in the school. Maybe she does wear one when she is not teaching. I do not know."

"If she wears it at all, why would she not wear the headscarf in my school?" This is the very reason why Selma *hanım* gets upset with me, but I know Muhsine *hanım* will not.

Muhsine *hanım* sighs. "I am not sure. Atatürk would like us to appear more Western in our dress. I think some of this is good. The education part is good. That is why your *baba* brought you here, to get a good education."

I am not satisfied. My question has not yet been answered. This seems perplexing to me. "Did Allah change his mind about the headscarf?"

Muhsine *hanım* slices more cheese. "I think Allah has had little to do with it."

"Did Atatürk take over from Allah?"

"No, of course not." Muhsine *hanım*'s tone makes me think I might have gone too far. "Allah always rules over us. Atatürk makes the laws of the government. Allah makes the rules of the universe."

I sit on a stool and help Muhsine *hanım* to prepare the *börek* by layering the spinach on top of the dough and the cheese. I wonder why adults seem to have so much difficulty in answering what seem to me to be simple questions. Why would headscarves be worn in the marketplace or the home and not in the school? The teacher who works with the small children wears one. It may be Atatürk's wishes, but it does not make any sense to me. I would like to ask *Baba* more about it later, if he will even answer me. But maybe he does not know the answer. He is a man, after all.

Many of the girls at school like me, but I never invite them to visit me at home. When I am at home, I want to read, unless I am busy with *Baba* or Muhsine *hanım*. Sometimes one of the girls from my school invites me to visit them, but I would not want to inconvenience *Baba* or Muhsine *hanım*, and I could not possibly ask the parents of my friends to come to get me and to take me home again. *Baba* is adamant that I never travel alone.

The truth is that I am not interested in these girls anyway. They are nice enough, but a bit boring and silly. They are always trying to steal secret looks at the boys outside their classrooms. Sometimes they pass notes back and forth between them. These notes are mostly nonsense, a code they've created just in case they are intercepted. The girls also pass notes back and forth between themselves. I guess I might be interested in what these notes say, but after Selma *hanım* caught a few and read them aloud in front of everyone, I lost interest. The notes run something like this:

Did you see that Ayşa put henna in her hair?
Sera is angry. Her anne would not let her wear her new dress to school today. She has to save it for her sister's wedding.
Do you think we will have a quiz today? I forgot to study.

I cannot imagine "forgetting" to study. Studying and reading are the two most important duties in my life. Cengiz has told me this. And since I have already promised to marry him, I pay a lot of attention to what he has to say. I do believe, anyway, that this is when I am happiest, when I am learning about something new.

Cengiz and I write letters to each other once every couple of weeks or so, and we compare what we are learning in school. He tells me what he is reading, and I tell him what I am reading. Sometimes we read the same book, and we can share our thoughts. We try to write in English because we are both studying the language. Cengiz gets frustrated when he is not able to express his ideas well in English and returns to Turkish. I follow suit because Muhsine *hanım* says I should not be smarter than Cengiz, or let him know it, even if I am. I struggle with this. Cengiz writes:

To my best friend, Fatma,
How are you, Fatma? I hope your cough is all gone now. I am very well.
I am disappointed that my school does not have the English novels yet. I am finding that the Turkish translations, when we have them, are not so good. Sometimes I do not think the words make sense. They must mean something else. But I am not yet able to read a novel in English. I have to look up every other word,

and I am not so patient. Have you tried to read Jane Austen? I have the English copy of Pride and Prejudice, *and if you do not yet have it, I will bring it next time I see you. It might be a long time before I am able to read it.*

I am looking forward to the next Ramadan holiday. I will get to see my sisters and maybe you as well. Do you think your grandfather would bring you to Goreme so we can fast and celebrate together?

How is your grandfather? Is he continuing to keep his promises to you and to his father? I do worry about how much time he spends in the restaurant. Is he taking good care of you?

I think of you every day.

Your best friend, Cengiz

To my dearest friend, Cengiz,

I am happy to tell you that I have stopped coughing. Baba took me to the doctor who gave me some awful tasting medicine that helped me to sleep. I didn't mind because I was able to sleep without the cough waking me up, and in a couple of days, the cough was gone.

Thank you for thinking of me, but I do already have a copy of Pride and Prejudice. *My English language teacher thought I would like to read it, so I mentioned it to Baba, and he bought me a copy. I agree that the English is difficult, and I have had to look up many words. Maybe you will try again? Selma hanım says it will help us to understand the culture of the West. And that is necessary now because Atatürk is our leader.*

I have to pause here for a few minutes. I'm wondering if I should tell Cengiz that I have just finished reading the novel in English. Jane Austen has not yet been translated into Turkish. In any event, I doubt there is anyone capable of doing so at this point in time. Everything about the novel is so different from Turkish writing and culture. I think it might only frustrate Cengiz to tell him that I was able to read the novel in English, not that I got all of it, I am sure. I continue:

Instead of bringing the novel to me, why don't you read as much of it as you are able so that we can talk a little bit about it when I see you? Maybe we can help each other to understand more.

I have asked Baba if we can spend Ramadan with you in Goreme, and he said he would like that very much. He wants to see his parents. His anne makes all of his favorite dishes for iftar. I hope she is able to do all of that cooking. Muhsine hanım has been teaching me to cook, though, so I can help her with her recipes the same way I help Muhsine hanım.

Baba does not seem to notice how his parents have grown older. He thinks we will all just stay as we are. Now the clothing he tries to buy for me here is too big! When he visited me in Goreme, it was always too small. Do you remember?

I think Baba is more embarrassed to take me shopping these days, so he brings my clothing home. I think he will ask me to go with Muhsine hanım soon. At least I hope he does. His choices are not always good, and I am afraid to offend him if I tell him so.

I pause again here. Will Cengiz wonder if I am always telling him the truth if I am sometimes dishonest with *Baba*? I am unsure, and then I decide that they are different. I am only deceiving *Baba* so as not to hurt his feelings. Well, then, perhaps with Cengiz it is the same. I am deceiving Cengiz about the novel because I do not wish to hurt his feelings. Oh, I do wish Badia were here to help me. But I will not rewrite the paragraph.

I am so happy to think of Ramadan now, although you will be fifteen then, and I will still only be 14. I wish I could also be fifteen.

Your best and dearest friend,

Is that too much? Do I care? Yes, but I am going to leave it like this.

Fatma

CHAPTER 15

Ramadan, summer - 1930

It is so lovely to be with Badia and Elif again. We were together all day today. And tomorrow Cengiz will be arriving from Ankara. We will begin our fast the day after tomorrow. I am so excited. Muhsine *hanım* took me shopping to buy two new dresses for Ramadan this year. They really do fit me well, finally something that fits, and they are nicer than the ones *Baba* brings home. They cost a bit more, too, *Baba* says, even though we did buy them in the open market.

One of the dresses is quite long. The bottom of the skirt reaches my ankles. The top of this dress has pretty black swirls on a white background and a bit of white lace at the end of the sleeves. From the waistline down, the pattern is different. The skirt is also on a white background, but there are black dashes in a constant print. This one is my favorite and meant for special occasions. I wish my *anne* could see me in this dress. I think she might have smiled. She never had anything like it that I've seen. It makes me feel like a grown woman.

The second dress is simple and meant to wear to school. The color is a light brown with a slightly darker flower pattern. The skirt comes to the middle of my calf, and so I will wear long socks with it. This one looks well on me, too, and is comfortable for everyday wear. I bring both of them with me. On the bus, I travel with an old, and somewhat faded plaid skirt and a green sweater that once matched the green in the skirt. This is what I wear to cook and help around the house.

The bus from Istanbul is packed! There are a number of families with little children and babies—and so many bags. *Baba* and I are lucky to find seats. The bus carries the aroma of cinnamon and nutmeg, cheese and olives.

Everyone seems to be traveling with more food than clothing. Some even carry heavy covered dishes. I want to look inside to see what they have prepared. Oh, the smells make my mouth water, and I get so hungry.

Baba gives up his seat for a pregnant lady who boards the bus a few stops after us. She is carrying a large platter that she somehow manages to balance on her bloated lap. She sees me watching her and smiles. I am embarrassed because I've been caught staring, but she lifts the cover, so I am able to see inside. The *börek* are so perfectly formed. The pregnant woman lifts the platter and gestures to me to take one. I bite into the pastry eagerly, savoring the meat and spinach. I smile at her and tell her, "Thank you. This is delicious." And *Baba's* kindness is blessed, as the pregnant woman gets off the bus in just a couple of stops, and so he is able to sit again.

When we arrive at Goreme, *Babaanne* is cooking and baking. I am helping her. Even Cemal is cooking and baking. No one complains. A primitive kitchen is no excuse. We make do with what we have and create substitutes for what we don't. Everything here is centered on preparing for Ramadan. The more love that is poured into the food, the easier is our fast. We do more cooking to prepare for fasting than any other time of the year. I love to smell all the spices, the *biber*, the red pepper and the black, the cumin and cardamom, the garlic and the onions, the cinnamon and nutmeg, the heavenly *simit,* and other breads. Only a couple more days and we will begin the fast and, of course, the drummer will awaken us for *suhur*, and we will not eat or drink anything again until the *iftar* feast, when the sun has sunk from the sky.

Some of our *iftar* meals will be with our friends in Avanos and others will be here in Goreme. When the weather is warm in the evenings in Goreme, our neighbors all join us to eat outdoors. When we break the fast in Avanos, we join the family and friends of Cemal and Salman. If it is warm enough, we set up outside of the shop and then we can fit more people around the tables.

Sometimes we also gather for *suhur* breakfast. This is not always planned. When the drummers come to wake us, we wander outside together. We do not like to miss the drummers and always give them some food or coins. They come to announce that we had best crawl out of bed so as to not miss morning prayers or the last meal we can have until *iftar*.

Suhur is not considered optional by my family or their neighbors, even if we are still filled with sleep from our heavy meal the night before. Cemal is too tired sometimes, as she spends hours in the shop, and she is not so strict with our religious customs. So, we tend to spend *suhur* either with our neighbors or just by ourselves. Cemal is funny. She says that the Muslims should learn from the Jews and only fast one day at a time. I know *Baba* and his parents would not like to hear this. They love to celebrate our fast. And Cemal knows this because she never expresses these things in front of them. I wish she would not express herself so freely with me, as I also love the fasting days. I even started to fast with my *anne* before my puberty, and somehow, all the preparations for the fasting days, the early rising and late to bed, the clothes, the smells of the cooking and baking foods and the beautifully arranged platters bring me closer to her. One of the few things that gave my *anne* pleasure was to set the dishes on the table and to arrange them with all of the colors of the rainbow.

Well, Cemal is something of a female Atatürk, that is certain. She would fight to protect her beloved Turkey, but she is not so keen on certain aspects of religious faith or domestic chores. She would much rather be talking about life with the customers in the pottery shop. I am something like her, but I am also like my *anne* and my *Babaanne*.

This is my first Ramadan with my *Baba* and his parents together. They worship together, father and son, as if they were puppets on a single string, and their consideration of all the rules and their adherence to them is something to see. They make me proud to be a Muslim, to be able to take part in such a magnificent tradition. My *anne* always fasted and prayed, but she was missing the joy in this holiday. There was nothing that gave her much joy; not even I could bring many smiles to her face.

I am sorry for my *anne* and the sad life she lived. She could not catch my happy feelings when I tried to lift her moods. I guess I stopped trying. It was easier to be quiet around her. I pray for her every day. She was a sad mother, but not a bad one. *Babaanne* always says that my mother did not have much luck. I have more luck, and so I am happier. I thank Allah for this in my evening prayers.

Here I sleep in my old room, the bed I once shared with my *anne*. Her presence is still here. I can feel it. "Come, *Anne*, please come into my dreams," I call her to me. "I want to see you, even if you are in the form of a bird, or any other form, please come to me. I have not seen you since I left this place. I so wish to see you now."

I try to form her image in my mind, but her face is blurred. Maybe she will not come because I cannot summon her features. I climb into the bed and pull the heavy blanket over me. Shutting my eyes, I can almost recall them. Please, Allah, bring her to me in my dreams.

****

I am in a vehicle—a bus, it seems. I am sitting beside my anne. What seems strange to me is that the columns of seats are empty. We are the only two on this vehicle that is not going anywhere. There is not even a driver. My anne is looking straight ahead. I try to tap her on her shoulder, but my hand goes through her. I pull my hand back in fear. But when she still does not turn to me, I try to touch her hand. It is solid but wet and cold, and prickly, like the thorns on a rose. I immediately drop this scary hand back into her lap. Still, she does not turn her head. Is this what it means to be dead? Is she frozen? I shrink back into my seat. The seat has a big tear in the back and stuffing is spilling out onto the floor.

Then I see that my anne is wearing a veil, a black veil that covers her below her eyes and hangs down a bit past her chin. When I lean forward again to see better, her head whips around and her eyes are filled with tears. The tears melt her face, like the drippings of wax from a lit candle. I am terrified but cannot look away. Now there is nothing left of her at all, but the veil is still there, an empty veil, as though there were a person behind it. I try to run from my seat, but I am frozen. I cannot move.

"That's where I wake up," I tell *Babaanne*.

"Hmmm," *Babaanne* mutters over the sweet honey and nut pastry she is shaping on wax paper laid on top of the long, wooden table. She hands one to me, knowing I love the raw dough. "This is an easy dream."

"Easy? How is it easy?" I am shocked at her response. I have no idea what this dream that is more like a nightmare could possibly mean. I pop the pastry into my mouth. "Oh, this is delicious!" I drool with the sweetness of the honey and the salty flavor of the pistachio.

I sit down across from where my *Babaanne* is rolling and forming the sweets. I think how clever the cave homes are, even though chilly in cold weather; this kitchen and my bed here are always warm. Windows and doors have been carved out and covered so that there is light and air when it is wanted. I am so comfortable here, more so than in Istanbul.

"You are afraid of your mother, so she cannot come to you now. Maybe you were always a bit afraid of her. I know I was."

"No, I cannot imagine you being afraid of anyone. But maybe I was anxious around her. I never felt I ever really knew her. I know I was a burden to her. Sometimes she would simply send me away, tell me to come and talk with you or to play with my friends. Yet, I also know she loved me." I lean over the pastries. *Babaanne* smiles at me and hands me another.

"I think I was afraid of her and for her." *Babaanne* hesitates, as if she cannot find the right words to let me know what she is thinking. "Life was something of a mystery to her. I do not know her exact experience of things. She did not tell me much. I think her *baba* knows more than I do, but he does not confide in me. Life was too harsh for her. It has been hard for everyone, though. She was not able to figure out how she could make it better for herself and even though we tried, there was nothing we could do about that. It is something each and every one of us must do ourselves. Some of us can bear more than others." Her voice drops, and I can see that she is thinking deeply, but she says no more.

Babaanne starts to hand me a third pastry, but I hold up my hand to stop her. "There won't be any left for the others and more important, I will not be able to fit into my new dresses if you keep feeding me this way."

"That's what all great grandmothers should do, and nothing less," she says, but she takes the pastry back and sets it with the others on the baking tray.

"I think of you and Baler as my grandparents and my grandfather as my *baba*." I tell her this for the hundredth time.

"I know," she laughs, "but I need to make sure that you never forget who we really are."

"This does not matter to me in the least. I love you all the same."

"But will you say it correctly for your future husband?"

I wrinkle my nose and say nothing. I know I will marry Cengiz, and he already knows who everyone is in this strange family. But, of course, I cannot tell her that. She thinks of Cengiz as my cousin, even though the family is no relation to us, yet another misnomer of family. And neither family would ever let me alone with him for one second if they knew our plans. They hardly leave us alone as it is.

Instead, I tell her, "I am fourteen years old."

She raises her eyebrows. "In my time, you were old enough to marry when you were old enough to have a baby. And even sometimes before."

I wince at this, but she does not seem to notice. *Babaanne* can be very good at not noticing. I want to get back to the dream.

"Are you saying that my *anne* will not come because I'm afraid of her? I'm not sure that this is true. She would not look at me, and then the empty veil. That was scary."

Babaanne sets down the knife she has been using to spread the honey-nut mixture and looks me in the eye. "You must stay completely calm," she says, "or you will frighten her spirit. Contacting the spirits is not an easy task. We are on different levels and must figure out how to meet in between their world and ours. You must not shy away. You have to be ready to receive her. That is about all I can tell you."

I wonder at how I am to "receive her" more openly. I ask, "Has my *anne's* spirit come to you? Has she visited your dreams?"

"No, and I do not expect that she will." *Babaanne* carefully places the pastries on a large baking sheet.

"Why not? How can you know that?"

"I do not know this for certain, but your *anne* and I had finished our business together in this world. The spirits come when they have a message. I doubt she has any message for me, but there might be more than one for you."

I want to know so much more, but it is clear to me that I will not get more from my *Babaanne* on the spirit world. But there is a possibility I can get more information on the real world. I worry that my *Babaanne* might leave this world before I get the chance to ask about my father.

Babaanne heaves open the ancient oven door and places the pastries inside. So few Turks have ovens, but *Baba* found this one especially for her. *Babaanne* rubs her hands against her apron, shaking a few dots of flour onto the floor. "Cengiz's bus will be here soon. Do you want to go into town to meet him?"

"No," I tell her. "Let him have some time with his family. I will see him tomorrow for *suhur*. You remember, he wrote that he and his sisters would come here with the drummers in the morning to eat and to pray and begin the holiday with us. Today is just for us." I want to stay. I want her to keep talking.

Babaanne folds her arms in front of her in a determined manner. She has something to tell me, but I can see that she is not prepared to come out with it just yet. Instead, she withdraws her arms and the pose, and she tucks her hands into her apron pockets.

"Then let us have *çay* now, and when the *pasta* is finished baking, we will each try one. You can tell me if it is better raw or baked."

"Both!" I clap my hands, delighted at the notion of a day in *Babaanne's* kitchen, with only Baler to wander in and out from time to time, not an unpleasant momentary interruption. *Baba* is off to Avanos to get more coal.

Baler is so old now. I treasure the soft sounds of his voice, knowing as soon as I laid eyes on him that he will soon be with my *anne*. He is only a few years apart from *Babaanne,* but he seems so much older. She still moves with such grace, and he is a bent-over blind man with a cane, like some I have seen in the marketplace in Istanbul. It is only by the few words he utters, the breathy sound of his fading voice, that I am certain this is my great grandfather. And yesterday, just as I was coming into the kitchen, I saw him place his hand on *Babaanne's* face, tracing his fingers across the indentations and lines, memorizing her. I held back a few moments before I came in so as not to disturb them.

I cannot imagine a life without them here, always waiting for us to return, *Baba* and me. What *Babaanne* says is true. *Baba* is not really my father. He's my mother's father and my grandfather. And *Babaanne* is not really my grandmother. She is my great grandmother, the grandmother of my *anne*. And the youngest of them all, besides me, was my *anne*, and she was the first to leave us. Besides my real *baba*, that is. What a mystery.

Why are there no photographs of him? Not even a military snapshot, and one would think there would be one, at the very least. No one took their photo on their wedding day? And where and when did they marry? These are unanswered questions that I'd best ask now. I could never get any answers from *Anne*.

The water for the *çay* begins to whistle. I jump up to pour our tea. The boiling liquid makes a pretty pattern of hot air whirling about above the tiny glasses. *Çay*, the liquid of life. Anything can be discussed over *çay*.

"What can you tell me about my father?" I ask this as casually as if I were asking would it rain later today. At the same time, I set *Babaanne's* tea glass in front of her.

Babaanne stares into her tea. I almost wonder if she is about to read the leaves.

"I never met your father, you know." She stops here. This has always been where everyone stops speaking. Even *Baba*, who surely had to have known him, if anyone ever did, other than *Anne*.

A sharp and furious pain shoots up from my belly and across my heart, scorching my insides. I double over, gripped by the sudden agony. "She was shouting in my head!" I shake my head up and down and back and forth, as if to somehow eject the sounds through my ears. What is this? My hands begin to tremble, and I cannot make the pain or the trembling stop.

Babaanne jumps up from her spot on the long, wooden bench and runs around the table to where I have been perched on the other long bench. She grabs onto me, rather unsuccessfully, because I am afraid if I let go of my gut, everything will open up and spill out onto the dirt floor. She lets go of my arms wrapped tightly around my belly, and then grabs my head in her hands, rubbing my forehead and asking me, "What is happening to you? Ssshhh. It's okay. What can I get you? Some water?"

It takes a few long moments before I can suck in the smallest and shortest breaths of air again. I gasp when I try to speak, and so I touch my *Babaanne's* shoulder to reassure her that I am not dying, that I will soon be okay again, and she lets go of my head and sits back on the bench, not taking her eyes from me.

"Who? Who was shouting in your head?" *Babaanne* looks more frightened than I have seen her. I cannot help myself. I begin to giggle, try to restrain myself, and burst into loud laughter. Now *Babaanne* begins to look at me with something I can only interpret as suspicion.

"She was shouting in my head." I gasp in more air. "I thought it was my *anne's* voice, but maybe it was only mine."

"What did the voice shout?" *Babaanne* watches me closely, still unsure that this is not some foolish thing I've learned from someone at school in Istanbul, some kind of trick.

"Daughter of the Prophet—you! Daughter of the Prophet."

Babaanne slowly rises and moves back to the other side of the table where her hot tea has now grown lukewarm. She takes a sip anyway. "Yes, that's you," she offers. Your name means "daughter of the prophet."

I sigh. "I know that, *Babaanne*. I've known that for a very long time. I know that Fusun was my real mother, and that she was as old as Cengiz is now when she gave birth to me. But my real *baba*; who was he? He is a big shadow at the far corner of my mind. Once he was a blond Arab in my dreams, and then he became more like me, with locks and locks of unmanageably thick and curly hair. I have never seen his face, even a faded photograph of him. You will leave me one day and so will Baler. *Baba* is just like my *anne*, and he will tell me nothing. What is so terrible about my real *baba* that no one will tell me? In some months I will be fifteen years old, the very age my *anne* was when she gave birth to me. I am old enough, whatever it might be. Please tell me now; tell me this very day!" I take in a deep breath and let it out slowly. This has been a great deal to say. My hands continue to tremble, but the sharp pain is gone and what remains is nausea.

Babaanne slowly shakes her head back and forth. "I knew the time would come. I just hoped it would be farther into the future and that your grandfather would talk to you. Now I understand that he will always only see you as his little girl." She gets up and retrieves the *çaydanlık* from the tiny two-burner stove. It is amazing to me, now that I have seen other kitchens, how she manages to create feasts in her humble surroundings.

"Would you like more?" she asks, lifting the *çaydanlık* from the fire.

"Yes, please," I tell her. We are both quiet as she pours hot tea and water into both of our glasses, sets the kettle back onto the stove and sits back down again. Suddenly I am afraid of what I might hear.

"You were always a good and sweet child," *Babaanne* begins. "And now it is time for me to see you as the woman you are becoming, not the small child you have been. I must burden you with what I know of the truth, as I have come to know it. My son has not shared everything with me, and so there are missing pieces, missing blocks of time, but you will have to get him to talk to you if you wish to know more. Please do not let me forget the time. In a few minutes we will take the *pasta* from the oven. While they are cooling, I will tell you what I know."

CHAPTER 16

Clearly, my *babaanne* has not prepared for this confrontation. She hesitates over the *pasta*, fussing with them, arranging them carefully on a large round glass plate on which she creates a circular design. If one is slightly too large in comparison to the rest, she cuts off an end to equal the others. I sit by, quietly watching her, until I finally lose all patience.

I hear the irritation in my voice, "*Babaanne*, please, the *pasta* cannot be more even or more beautiful if you were to go at them like this all day. If you continue, you might just ruin them."

"You are right, Fatma," she sets the knife down on the table and glances at me. "I don't know where to begin."

"Why not begin with my father? Who was he? Where was he killed in battle? Which battle? Did he fight alongside Atatürk? Did he know Atatürk?"

Babaanne gets up from the table and comes over to me. She sits down on the bench close to me and wraps her weary arms around me. "Let me tell you in this way. I do not know a way of doing this gently. You know you are named Fatma for the daughter of the prophet?"

"Of course, I know this. But I am not Jesus. Are you about to tell me that Mohammed is my father? How can that even be? I have been over this a million times. The only reason I can come to is that my *anne* fell in love with a soldier and they never had a chance to marry before he was killed. That is all I can imagine that would create so much secrecy. She had me anyway, and my grandparents had a difficult time accepting this—and me. Tell me, please, *Babaanne*." I can feel her body slightly shaking. Even though I am ashamed for pushing her, I must go ahead with this. She draws me closer.

"Yes, I can see how you might think that. But Fusun did not fall in love. If only she had. All of our lives might have been different. I wish she had had the experience of falling in love. Your *anne* was not fortunate in love. Her *anne* and *baba* did love her, I am sure. But they were so busy just staying alive and safe in a war that was everywhere. I do not think there was much time for love. I do not think dear Fusun even had a friend. She never talked about friends she had left behind, and she did not have them here."

"If that is true, *Babaanne*, then I am even sadder for her. I cannot even imagine a life without my friends." I try to think of a life without Cengiz, without Badia or Elif. Even though Elif is younger, I still think of her as my friend. She is so funny and makes me laugh.

"The war was very hard on us all," *Babaanne* goes on to say. "The schools were all shut down. It was not safe for a young girl to be out on her own. Anything could happen. And when she came here, she was already pregnant with you, even though, at that time, we were not sure. Ali left her with us to find out. And then when it was clear that she was pregnant, she stayed on with us."

Anything can happen. I think of *Babaanne's* words. I wonder about all of this. I have never known an unmarried woman who became pregnant under any circumstances. But if all that *Babaanne* is saying is true, and I have no reason to doubt her, what could possibly have happened? Could my *anne* have been attacked? I have heard of these things, but I never knew anyone who was attacked. If my *anne* was raped—and the word itself frightens me to death—what must I think? I feel shivers at the back of my neck.

"Please, *Babaanne*, if my *anne* did not fall in love with a soldier, who is my father? What happened to him?" I am furious now and not sure why, and I feel more like screaming and shouting at the top of my lungs, punching and kicking the walls, anything other than being the grownup *Babaanne* thinks I am becoming. Was my *anne* attacked? Did she find me on her doorstep? Did she even want me? Did any of them want me? How will I ever know the truth?

Why doesn't anyone tell me what I want to know? I push away from *Babaanne* and run from the kitchen to the back bedroom where I once slept with my *anne*. I hurtle myself across the bed, curl up in a ball and begin to sob. *Babaanne* tiptoes in softly and sits next to me. She lightly strokes my hair. But instead of calming me, I only become angrier. I choke back tears and mucous, sit up in order to breathe, and break into a coughing fit. When the coughing spasms finally stop, I get up from the bed. I look *Babaanne* in the eyes, something I try not to do, as my *anne* taught me that it is rude to look at one's elders so directly. Somehow, I cannot stop myself. *Babaanne* takes a clean handkerchief from her apron pocket and hands it to me, but then she does not avoid my gaze.

"She was attacked, wasn't she? My *anne* was raped? I don't have a real father? I never had a real father. She made the whole thing up."

Babaanne takes one of my hands, caressing it with her own. She sighs deeply. I feel her quieting now, and so I relax a bit.

"Thanks be to Allah, we can talk about this. My heart has been hurting to keep this inside. Don't be angry, child. She only wanted to protect you. She must have thought she would tell you the truth when you were older. Now you know."

I sit back down on the bed and now I take *Babaanne's* hands in mine. "After all the questions, all the make-believe answers—this is the truth. I have no father. I think it is worse to believe something, and then discover that it's all been a lie. I always suspected there was something more," I choke on a sob, "but I never thought of this."

"It will never change who you are or how much we all love you."

"But how can it not change how I see myself, how I see my poor *anne*?" My fingers begin to tremble violently. I let go of *Babaanne's* hand and clasp mine together. I roll over and place them under my belly to stop the shaking. After some quiet moments, the twitching stops. I turn over on the bed and look up at my *Babaanne*. Her eyes are filled with tears.

"And this is why you did not want me to know, isn't it?" I can see the sorrow on her face. My poor, ruined mother, and my poor, sweet great grandmother; how they have suffered over me.

As if she can read my mind, my *Babaanne* says, "Yes, but I did not suffer over you. I was filled with happiness when your grandfather brought your *anne* here. And I do not think your *anne's* suffering had anything to do with you. You must believe me. She suffered things I know nothing about. She never told me about the rape. Your grandfather told us only when he brought your *anne* to live with us. He knew nothing of the details, or if he did, he spared us those. You were the main concern for all of us. And then when your *anneanne* became sick and your *anne* traveled back to care for her until she died—something happened there. I am sure of it. She was never the same when she came back."

"Yes," I tell her, "I also noticed that, but I thought it was the death of her *anne*."

"Yes, I thought that also at first, but she had not been close to her mother. I began to wonder when her sadness, her depression, went on so long." *Babaanne* moves over on the bed so that she can put my head in her lap. She strokes my forehead and asks me, "How is your stomach now?"

"The pain is gone, but I do feel a bit nauseous."

"Let's stay here a bit," *Babaanne* suggests to me. I do not disagree. She begins to massage my head with her fingertips. Her touch has always seemed like it came from an angel, a special gift. I wonder if Baler, my great grandfather, has felt the same way.

My *anne* was raped. Do I even wish to know the details? I am fairly certain that no one but my *anne* knew them anyway. Maybe her *anne* could have talked about some of it with my grandfather. But my grandfather, her father? No, I do not believe she would have told him. I think I may never know. I sigh, and *Babaanne* runs her fingers gently over my closed eyelids. I want to surrender both to her and to sleep, but I know my time here is short. I reach up and take both of her hands and squeeze them in mine.

"The men will invade the kitchen shortly, and we will have no time. Let's go back and drink our cold *çay* before they come." I sit up.

"No," *Babaanne* insists. "There is no place for cold *çay*. I will heat the water, and we will start again." She pushes herself off the bed and heads back to the kitchen.

I get up from the bed and follow her slightly bent form. How long will she be with me? At the thought of losing her, my hands begin to shake again. I hesitate just outside the entryway to the kitchen until the trembling stops. After taking in a deep breath, I let it out slowly before I enter the room. *Babaanne* is heating the water. She looks up when she hears me.

"Please do not mention this to anyone yet. Let us get through the holiday. I will tell your *büyükbaba* (grandfather) and your *büyük büyükbaba* (great grandfather) when Ramadan is finished. Let them fast in peace."

Let *them* fast in peace, I repeat to myself. And how will *Babaanne* and I fast in peace? Suddenly it occurs to me that I have, by the names I am calling them, turned these people into father and grandmother and grandfather, when that is not who they really are.

My real father does not exist. *Anne* is gone now, too. My grandmother has died. I am doing what I have learned from them. Turning them into people they are not. Turning my mother's father into my father and making my great grandparents into my grandmother and grandfather. We are all guilty of this innocent deceit. We make everyone younger than they really are.

In my mind, have I made everyone a generation earlier to keep them with me longer? And can I change what I call them now just to make everything more real for me? They have not asked me to do so, and if I do, the change might hurt their feelings. To make them closer to me is comforting, I will admit. I know that I will pray about this.

Babaanne is looking at me. I realize that I have not answered her. "Yes, *Babaanne*, I can wait until after Ramadan. But you must bring it up before we leave. I have many questions for *Baba*, and I can do some of that on our trip home. Once we are back in Istanbul, he will go to the restaurant, and I will return to school. Even though he does spend more time with me than he ever did with my *anne* and *anneanne*, he is so tired when he gets home." Fatma thinks, if I back away from telling them I know the truth, I may never be able to challenge *Baba*. Even in my thoughts, it is so difficult now to call him my grandfather.

Babaanne pours the fresh tea into two small cups. "I will try. I will do my best."

Something snaps inside me at this response. "What am I supposed to do if you do not tell them? Wait for you all to die, and then there will be no opportunity for me to ask anyone anything?" As soon as these words fly from my mouth, I am ashamed. "I am so sorry, *Babaanne*," I tell her. "I don't mean to say such bad things."

Babaanne places the *çaydanlık* back onto the stove. She comes to the table and sits after placing the two cups across from one another. "Sit down, please," she says softly. "You are a strong and smart girl, maybe smarter than any of us. But you have a quick tongue, and that can sometimes get you into trouble. Men are not like women. They think they are stronger than us, and that is true in some ways, but when it comes to things like this, we are stronger than them. You must wait for the right moment."

I know I should stop here, and tell her she is right and what do I know about men? But again, I cannot keep quiet. "And when will the right moment come?" I ask her. "We have been waiting since the day I was born. That will soon be fifteen years." I pull the bench out on the side of the table where she has placed my cup, and I sit. We sip our *çay* in silence.

CHAPTER 17

The knock on my door comes just after the sound of the drums. I call out to answer, "I am getting up now."

Ramadan is here, and I am filled with joy. Breakfast will have special treats, always served before the sun rises. And everyone comes together to eat which is truly the best part of it all. I rise quickly, throw on my warmest clothing, and prepare to dash outside so as not to miss the drummers, the old man and his adult son who beat the drums here every year to awaken us. And I will see Cengiz. I run a brush through my hair but do not waste more time now. I will bathe and dress up before *iftar*.

The mornings are cool now, and Goreme has taken on its brown cloak, giving us the hint that winter will be arriving soon. Our cave dwelling is dark, and I lift the heavy blanketed doorway to the outside. A small group has gathered around the drummers, who are dressed in heavy but festive dress. Father and son are in blousy long pants with brightly colored cloth waist belts, light-colored sweaters under thick brocaded jackets, purple, pink, green and gold. They are so deep and rich in the light of the oil lamps *Babaanne* has carried outside. I do not see my great grandfather. He sleeps many hours these days, but he will fast, regardless.

The children I played with as a child, Ada, and Esme, no longer live here. *Babaanne* has told me that they were Armenian and that their lives became increasingly difficult here. I never knew they were Armenian. We did all of the same things together, and the girls came to eat with us and fasted with us, even though I realize now that they must be Christians. But when I started to go to school with Cengiz and his sisters, I did not see them so much anymore. I do hope they are okay.

Oh, my, there is a tall and very handsome young man approaching. Can this really be Cengiz? I hardly recognize him. Has he really grown so tall, so strong? From here he looks more like a man than the boy I remember. I suddenly feel shy and awkward. Can all of these changes have taken place in just one year? And who is that ghostly creature walking behind him?

There are Badia and Elif. Badia has grown so tall, but Elif is as tiny as ever. Once Badia and Elif see me, they come running to kiss my cheeks. If this is truly Cengiz, he is lagging behind.

The young man comes into the light, and I see that it is indeed Cengiz. He smiles warmly and nods to me. We are older now, and he is not family, and so we do not touch. And oh, I so do wish to touch him and hug him. My heart has not changed. I can only hope his has not either.

Moving very slowly behind Cengiz is a figure carrying a lamp. I wonder who this is. As the figure steps closer, I see it is a woman wearing a burqa.

"Please don't laugh," Badia warns me. "My *anne* is protesting."

"This is your *anne*? But why?"

Elif laughs. "She is now a prostitute, if you accept Atatürk's thinking."

"What? If this is Cemal, it must be Halloween, not Ramadan."

"Don't worry," Cengiz sighs. "She will tell you all about it herself. Just a few years ago, she embraced Atatürk. Then when he said that women who wear veils are prostitutes, she was furious. No doubt, some of them might be, but *Anne* says it ought to be a woman's right to choose. She is trying to bring a women's revolution to Avanos. Whatever you do, don't encourage her."

The figure emerges from the shadows and into the light. Yes, I can see her eyes now. It is Cemal behind the veil. She sets down the lamp and embraces me.

"You are wearing a burqa now," I gasp.

"Only when I go out." If she is smiling behind her veil, I cannot see.

"Isn't the *tesettür* (headscarf) enough?"

"No, it is the veil that Atatürk has ruled against."

"But you never wore a veil!" I am shocked. Cemal has always been so modern. She has worn the headscarf when she has gone outside the house, but even that is no longer necessary in Avanos.

"These men have been telling us what to do for far too long. So, when Atatürk announced that any woman wearing a veil had to be a prostitute, I complied."

"But *Anne*, please, you are no prostitute. This is all so silly." Cengiz turns to the muffled voice coming from behind the garment. "Atatürk will not see you or care what you wear." I think Cengiz is somewhat embarrassed. I am also thinking that surely, if anyone could lead a women's revolution in Avanos, it would be Cemal. And what would be wrong in that? I wonder.

"Well, someone ought to take my feelings into consideration." The hooded figure that is Cemal stands completely still. She reminds me of a statue in a museum. I am bursting with an urge to laugh.

"Well, *Baba* refused to come with us because of how you are dressed." Cengiz gestures, tracing his hand in the air down the length of her garment.

Now I am thinking that Cengiz is disappointed and angry that his mother might be spoiling Ramadan for them all. I find it funny and have to stifle a giggle. Of all the women in the universe, Cemal is the least likely to be found dressed this way. I look over at Cengiz and find him staring at me. He looks away immediately. He must have seen my amusement and my effort to hide a smile in the light of his mother's lamp. Now I know without a doubt that he feels shamed at her "protest."

I cannot seem to stop myself. "How will you eat with that thing on?" I ask.

There is a long moment of silence before Cemal tries to pull the garment over her head. Somehow it becomes tangled, and she is stranded between the material and exposure. Badia begins to laugh as she moves to help her mother untangle herself. I break out in laughter and not so surprisingly, so does everyone else but Cengiz. When Badia eventually frees her mother, we all stare at the tight black cap she has over her hair, fitting snugly like a bathing cap, only made from cloth, with a tunnel in the back to hold her hair in place. Now even Cengiz loses control and joins us in a circle of howls of laughter.

"I cannot look that bad. Don't I just look like a religious woman?" When we cannot stop laughing, Cemal pulls off her cap and shakes her thick black curls loose. For the first time, I realize that Cengiz has the same hair. Cemal has always worn hers in a tight bun.

Cemal hands the cap to Badia. "Okay," she gasps, unable to control her own laughter, "let's pray and eat. I will bow to Atatürk."

There are some sighs of relief, including my own. Once Cengiz is laughing with us, I can breathe again. Leave it to Cemal to come up with a stunt like this. Now I know she gets these ideas from reading so much, but when I was younger, I thought maybe she came from somewhere else, that maybe she was not really Turkish.

I walk over and kiss Cemal's now exposed cheeks. "Good to see you," I chortle, still in giggles.

Cemal grabs me and embraces me. "Don't think so much of yourself, now that you live in the big city," she whispers in my ear, before she shows me the big grin on her face. "We are still family, *benim küçük kızım,* my little daughter."

I smile back at her, but a lump travels from my gut all the way up to my throat, scraping the edges with painful doubt. There is that word again. Does she consider Cengiz to be like a brother to me? I turn my head to look at him, but he is already outside washing for prayers. I must wash, too, and join the women to pray before we can eat.

The water is lukewarm. I am the last to wash. The men are praying outside on their mats. The women have crowded inside the tiny room in the cave where my great grandfather prays five times a day. I join them, but I mutter words while I think to Allah: Please forgive me, Allah, but I must pray that I am not like a sister to Cengiz. We once made our vows to marry, and I hope and pray to you to make him always remember this. I hope I am not an evil girl for asking you.

I open my eyes and see that Elif is staring at me, and then she smiles. She has caught me. The movement of my mouth does not match the Arabic words. She winks and closes her eyes. Does she do the same thing? Creating her own prayers? Is this selfish, a sin? This cannot be a sin, since I have no idea what the Arabic words mean anyway, but I am not sure. This is a confusing way to begin Ramadan, but there is no one I can ask these questions of other than Cengiz or Allah. For now, I will have to ask Allah because I am too embarrassed to ask Cengiz.

As everyone finishes washing and praying, the guests gather around my great grandparents' wooden table. Badia, Elif, and I help to carry the heavy dishes of food and set them down there. *Babaanne* removes the *menemen* she has been preparing from the stove. I love these eggs and peppers. I try to make them in Istanbul, but for some reason, they never taste as good as *Babaanne's*. She must add something special to them. I will have to remember to ask her.

There is not so much conversation at this meal. We pass the food around quickly, as we must finish eating and drinking before dawn. *Babaanne* has brought us three large pitchers of *ayran*. Cemal helps her to carry platters of the hot and steaming *menemen*. As we help ourselves to the *menemen,* to fill us up and keep us strong during the day of fasting, Cemal carries a stack of hot *bazlama* that was made outside by the women in the communal ovens while we were still sleeping. *Babaanne* loves this aspect of *suhur*. She has baked *bazlama* with these women over the many years she has lived here. Some of these women are now the children of the women with whom she baked years ago. Others have died or moved into the easier homes of their children, homes with faucets that running water escapes from, and lights are turned on with the mere flick of a switch. Their lives are more comfortable for these graces, but my great grandparents will not leave. This is their home.

The *menemen* is lovely and quickly disappears from the platters, along with the *bazlama*. I am careful not to eat too much, just enough to get me through the day. If I overeat, I will become hungry long before the *iftar* meal. I can almost taste the dates we eat to break our fast. I wish I did not love the sweets so much. It is far too easy to get fat, especially when I am here with *Babaanne*.

When the after-dinner prayers are finished, we help *Babaanne* to clear the table and the guests prepare to leave until we meet again at Cemal's for *iftar*. Badia calls out to me from the doorway, "Fatma, come walk with us to the bus. We have seen so little of you."

I look to *Babaanne,* and she smiles. "Please go, Fatma. I will help your *büyükbaba* to wash and dress after I sleep some more. There is no need for you to stay. There will be much time for us to visit later today."

"I am coming," I call to Badia. "Thank you, *Babaanne*." I kiss her cheeks and run to join Badia and her family.

I walk between Badia and Cengiz, one on either side of me, but soon Badia is walking ahead of us. I wonder if Cengiz has arranged for us to have this brief time alone, even though the rest of the family is close enough to be in clear view. The wave of shyness that overcame me earlier washes over me again. I feel a flash of heat under my armpits. My tongue feels too large for my mouth and my lips are locked. I cannot manage any words.

"Are you okay?" Cengiz asks.

I nod, but I still cannot speak. All I can think of is that it is only a short walk to the bus stop, and this is no time for me to feel so awkward. But I walk and wait.

"We are good friends, aren't we, Fatma?"

"We will always be good friends, I hope."

"I know we made promises to each other, but we were just children then. We could not know what we would want in the future. To be honest, I have no idea what I want in my future. Do you?"

I want to tell him, yes, of course I know, I want to live with you always. Instead this new stranger I do not recognize speaks for me. "Of course, I don't know," I hear myself say. "We were just children. You are right." I am still a child inside, and I want to smack him. I want to tell him, I have believed you all this time, and your promise to me meant nothing to you but a childish game. You will now disappear, just like the father who never was.

"Good," Cengiz says. "We do not hold to the promise we made back then, do we?"

"Of course not," I chime back, managing a bit of a laugh. "I am not a child." I wonder now, for the second time, if this will turn out to be a dismal visit. His letters, all those letters, assured me and reassured me that Cengiz would always be mine. Well, if I must think clearly, he did not say as much, but I believed it to be true. I can feel the burst of tears building behind my eyes and throat. I cough instead.

I run ahead to Badia and kiss her cheeks. Cemal and Elif are up ahead. "Please say good-bye to your *anne* and Elif," I tell her. "I will see you all tonight at *iftar*." I make myself wave in farewell.

Cengiz has caught up with us, but I cut off any further discussion with, "Have an easy fast. See you all soon." I run the rest of the way back to the cave, leaving them staring after me.

CHAPTER 18

I am not sure I want to wear my new dress for *iftar*. Part of me hopes Cengiz will be sorry for saying what he did, and that part of me wants to wear the dress, to look so beautiful that Cengiz will have much to regret. For several minutes, I fantasize coldly ignoring his pleas. No, it is too late, I tell the phantom Cengiz. This sets to boil the part of me that is too angry to care about dressing up. Then the mischievousness in me suddenly wishes I had a burqa to wear. That might give Cengiz something to think about.

No, I am going to wear the dress. I will show him. I refuse to behave as if his words have affected me in the least. I must not let him know that he has upset me. I will never tell anybody. No one at all. Not even *Babaanne*. I have learned well to be silent with my thoughts.

Now I wonder if Cengiz has told anyone. Does Badia know? Did she walk ahead of us because she knew that Cengiz was going to hurt me, to disappoint me, and she did not want to see this? Does Cemal know? I do trust that they love me, so I do hope none of them are aware. I always thought I made my *anne* sad, so I try hard not to alert others if I am out of sorts or disappointed. If anyone knows, I will not give them an opportunity to ask me anything.

I brush my hair so hard that I prick my scalp with the bristles. I quietly scream inside my head, turn the hair upside down, and then mess it all up again. When I throw it back and look in the mirror, it actually looks better than it did to begin with. There is something wild, untamed, and exciting about me. I have to laugh. Something tells me my appearance will make little difference. Cengiz is a man, and I have certainly been warned enough about them.

Muhsine *hanım* has given me some rouge for my cheeks and my lips, just to add a bit of color. I did not think I would use it, but I didn't wish to hurt her feelings, so I took it anyway. I look in my bag for it, take a tiny bit and press it into my cheeks. I feel I look silly, so I take most of it off with a cloth. The color looks better on my mouth, but I do wipe most of it off as well, just leaving my lips with a slight hint of color and my cheeks slightly flushed. This makes me look so much older, and the wild hair is a nice effect.

I pull the long dress over my head, shake out my hair again, and I have a look. I am pretty. Muhsine *hanım* teases me, but I think she is sincere. She tells me to enjoy beauty while I am young because soon, I will be as old as she is now. I cannot imagine this, and I do think Muhsine *hanım* is beautiful, even though I have never seen her hair.

I stand in the mirror for some time. I will not be sad because of Cengiz. He will be sad because of me. I will turn this thing around. How could I expect the future to be so simple for me when my *anne's* was destroyed? She often used to warn me when she was especially sad. She would tell me not to be innocent, that life is hard for everyone, that I should be prepared. But I am only fourteen and my life is already much easier than my *anne's*. Somehow this does not seem fair.

But I do trust Cengiz, as I would not trust any other boy. I have seen other boys notice me, but I never pay them any mind. Their attention is flattering, but I know that I am pretty. I have just always believed that I would marry Cengiz, and oddly enough, I still believe this.

Babaanne always tells me that when I know what it is that I want, I must be patient. She used to tell my *anne* this as well, but that one word could make my *anne* angry and frustrated. But my *anne* was so unhappy. I never wish to be unhappy like that. Perhaps if I pretend to be happy, I will be. And I am so glad to be at home with everyone here. I can be patient. I don't mind it so much.

When I finally decide that I am ready, I step out into the kitchen and see that my family is gathered. "*Çok güzel,*" they cry out. Beautiful. *Baba* looks at me with such pride. Since this is a rare enough occurrence, I give him a slight smile, not too big but just enough to let him know that I appreciate his reaction.

Babaanne is wearing a long blue skirt, a blue and gold printed tunic and a dark blue silk headscarf. *Baba* is wearing the special gray suit with a vest that he says he wore to my *anneanne's* funeral services. *Büyükbaba* is wearing loose trousers, a striped shirt and a vest much like *Baba's. Büyükbaba* does not look well. I look from his vest to the color of his face. His face is also gray. He has barely spoken since *Baba* and I arrived. I worry about *Babaanne*. I know she has to help him to wash and dress, and his vision has become so much worse. How will they manage?

I think we are leaving a bit early, but when I watch *Büyükbaba* struggle up the steps and into the bus, I understand that he is even more frail than I had thought. I want to help him, but even *Baba* will not attempt to do so. The Turkish male has so much pride. He only tolerates *Babaanne*, and that depends on his mood. The fact that it is the first night of Ramadan has made him more amenable to her attentions.

Fortunately, the bus leaves us off in front of the pottery store, and the family home is behind the factory. The weather is a little cool but warm enough for Cemal to have decided to set up a big table outside just behind their house, covered by a tent in case of rain.

I gasp at the stunning table settings. "Oh, but these plates and bowls are so beautiful."

Salman smiles. "They are all handmade right here, and Cemal has painted all of these." He holds up one of the plates designed in red tulips with green stems and leaves and a blue design throughout. "She has been helping us with decorating the pottery since you've been gone."

"I did not know you are so talented, Cemal."

Cemal smiles. Thankfully, she has abandoned the burqa and is wearing wide-legged pants that are almost a skirt in a soft wine color and a matching jacket. Her hair is covered by a soft pink silk scarf. She is so pretty. Cemal takes the plate from Salman's hands and places it back onto the table.

"This is not too difficult, Fatma," she tells me. "If you would like to learn, I will teach you one day."

"I would like that very much," I tell her.

Quickly Salman settles my great grandfather into a chair with pillows. This chair has been carefully selected so that he can sit and rise fairly easily. Even so, *Büyükbaba* pushes Salman away when he attempts to assist him. I silently wonder if Cengiz will behave like this when he is old. I know *Baba* will. These men are so stubborn.

But where is Cengiz? And where are Badia and Elif? I enter the house and find Badia and Elif busy in the kitchen with last-minute preparations. They are both wearing aprons over their tunics. Badia is stirring a large pot of something. She looks up at me.

"Whoa, *çok güzel*! You look wonderful! What did you do to your hair? It looks so full and thick."

Since we are alone in the kitchen, I give them a quick demonstration. Badia and Elif giggle.

"Well, that looks easy enough," Badia says. "I will have to try it, but not while I am stirring the soup."

"Can I do anything?" I ask.

"No," Badia says as she taps the big wooden spoon against the side of the pot. "We are finished. We have been working since we got back from *suhur*. There is enough food here for the entire village. For someone who barely cooks, *Anne* outdoes herself for this holiday. And now that we are old enough, we help her."

"It is difficult to fast and prepare all of this food," Elif complains. "I don't understand why we fast all day and do nothing but prepare food. I don't even get to lick the bowls or taste anything."

Badia frowns at her little sister. "*Anne* and *Baba* never insist that we fast. You know that. You are still a child, and it is not required."

Elif sticks her tongue out at Badia. "I am not a child, and that is why I fast."

"Then don't complain." Badia wrinkles her brow to give Elif a dark look.

I think if I were not there, she might be tempted to stick out her tongue as well, but she wants to show me her maturity. And I think she wants to prove this to Elif as well. Badia has turned eighteen, and she is considered to be a grown woman now. I wonder if she will marry soon or continue her studies. Badia never liked school that much. I wonder if she is thinking about someone special, which reminds me that I have not yet seen Cengiz.

"And where is your brother?" I ask her.

"You must have just missed him. A friend from his school is joining us for *iftar*, and Cengiz went to meet him at the bus. They should be arriving very soon."

As if she has read my mind, she adds, "He is an older boy who Cengiz wants to introduce to me. He graduated from Cengiz's school, but they met last year. He is a serious boy who is studying to become a doctor."

I smile. "A suitable boy."

"Yes." Badia smiles back at me. "But I will only consider him if I like him."

"I hope he's not ugly," Elif quips. "I hope he isn't cross-eyed or stupid. Suppose he's short and fat?"

"Now why would Cengiz bring someone to meet me who is any of those things?" Badia fires back.

"Because he will look good with you!" Elif curves her back to extend her stomach in order to emphasize "fat," and stretches her mouth on both sides to emphasize "ugly." We all have to laugh.

"Little sisters. They either adore you or are jealous as can be. This one loves me one day and insults me the next."

"I wish I had a sister," I say.

"That's only because you don't have one." Badia laughs.

"You are our sister, Fatma," Elif tells me.

"Ah," Badia counters. "You are the good sister today. Watch out for tomorrow."

Elif scrunches her face up at Badia, runs behind her and undoes her apron strings. When Badia tries to catch her, Elif races from the room.

"She is at an awkward stage," Badia announces. "She just got her period and she goes from being mature one day to being two years old the next. She is driving us all mad."

I think they are an incredible family. I still wish I had real siblings. My family is all so old. But now I am grateful for Muhsine *hanım*. But even so, I wish I had a brother or sister. I know that Badia and Elif adore each other, but it is a ritual for them to tease each other. I try to imagine what it would be like to love someone so much and to tease and fight with them at the same time. Is this a deeper form of love?

The soup that Badia is stirring begins to give off a tantalizing aroma.

"What kind of soup is that you are heating?" I ask her. "It smells so good."

"Have you never had *ezogelin* soup?"

I lean over the pot and take in the aroma. "I'm not sure. What's in it?"

"Red lentils, rice, bulgur, onion, red pepper, mint, lots of salt, a bit of flour to thicken it, butter—let me think. Oh, yes, of course, beef broth."

"Hmm, no, I don't think I have ever tasted it."

"This soup is not so common here. My *anne* learned how to make it from her *anne*. The recipe is from the south. The soup has a story behind it."

I hear male voices and the door opening and closing. Cengiz enters the kitchen with a tall, thin fellow whose face is angular, as if it had been carved from stone. His thick, black straight hair is pushed back from his face. His eyes are large and dark with bushy eyebrows, and he has a long narrow nose that makes him look like a character in an Egyptian painting. Badia tosses aside her now untied apron and turns the fire off from under the soup, putting the lid on the pot to keep it warm.

Cengiz puts a hand on his companion's shoulder. "This is my friend, Mustafa. He is going to join us for *iftar*. Mustafa, this is my sister, Badia, and this is our friend for a long time now, Fatma."

Badia and Mustafa smile at one another and say, *"memnum oldum,"* nice to meet you.

I turn back to Badia. "So, what's the story behind the soup?"

"Ah." Badia looks slightly embarrassed, but she continues anyway. "Some years ago, maybe twenty or twenty-five years, I don't know, there was a new bride named Ezo. Her mother-in-law did not like her. She tried everything, but she got nowhere with this woman. Then she made this *çorbası* for her, this wonderful soup. She invented it herself. The recipe spread because everyone who ate it, loved it."

"And what about her mother-in-law?" Mustafa asked.

"Of course, she was no exception. She loved the soup. Ezo had to keep making it so that her mother-in-law would love her."

I laugh. "Let's hope we will have simple mothers-in-law like that, and we can find the right recipes to make them love us."

"Who says you will ever find a husband?" Elif has come back to the kitchen, hearing her brother's voice and wanting to meet his friend.

"You see," Badia says, rolling her eyes. "Now that she has declared you her sister, she believes she has the right to insult you."

I laugh again, but Badia looks serious.

Cengiz grabs Elif and hugs her. "You are a rascal." He turns her around so that she is facing Mustafa. "Mustafa, this is my little sister, Elif."

Elif is suddenly shy. She mumbles softly, turning slightly sideways into Cengiz's arm, "*Memnun oldum.*"

Mustafa charms her by bowing slightly. "*Memnum oldum.*"

Elif runs from the kitchen once again, announcing the arrival of Mustafa to her parents and the rest of the gathered guests. She calls out, "Cengiz and Mustafa are here!"

CHAPTER 19

I am not sure why this is true, but only during Ramadan does it take so long for the sun to set. I never mind this, as I am usually helping with the cooking or the serving and cleanup afterwards, no matter where we eat. Somehow, this particular year, I am urged to stay at the table, directly across from Mustafa and Cengiz and in between Badia and Elif. I believe it is not too much to assume that we've all been seated this way while Cemal serves in order to keep the conversation going between Badia and Mustafa.

The sun has just dipped down behind a bed of clouds, leaving a few red streaks in its wake. We begin to pass around the dates to break our fast, when Mustafa says to our little group, "That was an interesting story that Badia told us about the soup. I wonder why we Turks always seem to have a myth or fable about everything. I would like to know them all."

"You will not have much time to learn them if you are going to be studying medicine," Badia remarks.

Cengiz laughs. "Badia believes that studying so much makes one stupid about real life. She would prefer to cook than to read. And her cooking is so tasty that perhaps she is correct in her thinking."

"I like to cook, but I also like to read," I say. Quickly I remember that Cengiz has brought Mustafa to meet Badia, and that I might not be presenting my friend in the best light. I hastily add, "But my food is not so tasty as Badia's. She has a special sense of flavor that does not come naturally to everyone."

"I must have inherited this 'special sense of flavor' from my *anneanne*. My *anne* treats cooking like she is doing math. Everything with her is measurement."

"My *anne* would rather be talking to people in the pottery shop," Cengiz admits to Mustafa. "However, her cooking is still tasty, even if she doesn't do it so often that she can remember how much of anything needs to be added. Badia cooks for pure pleasure."

"Not so much *my* pleasure. Meals must be made," Badia retorts. "However, it is pleasant to cook."

"Admit it, Badia, you'd rather be in the kitchen than in the shop." Elif inserts another date into her mouth as a prelude to the coming soup.

"Oh, that's not something I have to admit to." Badia smiles. "It's the truth and we all know that."

"Mustafa didn't know it." Elif reports this with a sing-song quality that indicates to me some mischievous intent on her part.

As if to defend everyone, Mustafa comments, "But now I do know it," and he winks at Elif. I can see by Elif's look of absolute devotion that Mustafa has won her over with his wink and bow. They are conspirators.

Perhaps Elif will fall for Mustafa as her first crush. I remember her being a bit jealous of my friendship with Cengiz when we were all in school together. I hope not, as that might cause troubles between Elif and Badia.

Mustafa looks to me, "What do you like best about Ramadan, Fatma?"

"Hmm." I stop for a moment to consider; then I look around the table. "I have two answers, one being that I am able to spend time with all of you, when *Baba* and I are able to get away. The second thing is that I am so happy to fast. I feel so cleansed from my ongoing, everyday foolishness."

"And how are you foolish?" Cengiz asks.

"I'm foolish whenever I think about family." I lower my voice and lean forward, so that only the young people can hear. "You will all have your family for many years of your life. Cengiz and Badia and Elif, you have each other and both of your parents. I have no parents. And the most wonderful people who have taken over my parenting are all old. *Baba* is not my father. He is my grandfather. And now my mother is gone." I have told no one the details of my *anne*'s unfortunate life, or her untimely death, and certainly not the origins of my birth.

"But why do you think that is foolish?" Mustafa asks.

"Because these feelings are as selfish as they are foolish. I must be more grateful for all that I do have and not feel so deprived. First, I do not like to be selfish and secondly, when I show that I am unhappy about anything, *Baba* worries about me. Everyone does."

"There is an old tale that my mother used to tell me," Mustafa offers. "My mother was quite ill at the time, and my father was fighting in the Great War. My mother was afraid that I would lose them both and end up an orphan. She didn't know the author of the story or where it came from. It was one of those tales that have been passed down through the years by her mother and grandmother. I don't know if it was ever written down, but I can recall some of it, well, really just the main plot."

"Tell it to us, please," Elif encourages him, "whatever you can remember."

"There is a little girl, I forget her name, who is orphaned. Her father is killed in a war, and she is sent to live with her grandfather on the top of a mountain. I think it was in the Alps, I'm not sure where. Her grandfather is old and kind of a hermit. He is gruff and mean at first, but then they, along with the grandfather's goats, completely win each other over.'"

"How did that happen? Badia asks.

Mustafa seems to acknowledge her for the first time since the topic arose. I think he might be annoyed with her for asking. Badia must think the same, as she looks up at him and says, "Oh, I'm sorry. You already said that you don't completely remember the story."

At the moment that she says this, Cemal enters the room with a tray filled with small soup bowls cautiously balanced, as they are filled to the brim. She starts to carefully distribute them. Badia starts to get up to help Cemal, but Cemal motions to her to stay seated.

Mustafa continues. "I remember that the little girl softens the old man's heart through her love of his goats. They all become a very happy family. Love can come to us in many different ways. My father did die in the war, but my mother's health improved. And my uncle, my mother's brother, helped her to raise me. He is a good man, strict in his ways, but I know that he loves me as if I were his own son."

"This is true, Mustafa," I tell him. "We are both fortunate. Of course, I feel so much love from the family I do have, and that's why I feel selfish when I wish for more. That's why I love to fast. I feel kinder and more accepting."

I rise to help Cemal put the remaining soups on plates around the table. This time Cemal does not stop me. Cemal has a way of knowing things. I'm a bit surprised that they all seem to be so eager to find Badia a husband. Cemal has always been modern. Perhaps there are some areas in which "modern" does not hold so much weight. These types of sudden differences make me wonder and make me think of the women and girls I know. There is both wisdom and superstition in every one of them, past and present, always fluctuating, competing with the present and the future to make sense of our lives.

I place the soup bowls from Cemal's tray onto each plate. Cemal pulls me into the kitchen with her.

"How is it going?" she asks.

"I can't say," I tell her. "My thought is that we are all trying too hard. Why is everyone in such a rush to marry her off?" Cemal is always puzzled and then pleased with my direct manner. She washes the tray free of soup spills and sets if off to the sideboard to dry.

Cemal begins to unwrap the dishes served at room temperature. She gives me a quizzical look. "Whatever do you mean?" She wipes down the serving tray and begins to set the dishes to be served on its clean surface.

"Since we all know why Mustafa is here, we're all stuck on this one point, and the conversation isn't natural."

Cemal sighs. She takes my hand and motions me back to the table to have our soup. She whispers to me, "When is conversation between men and women ever natural?" She smiles.

I think about this question as I spoon the broth into my mouth, letting it roll on my tongue to taste the perfect blend of spices. Badia really is a spectacular cook. She looks at me and I nod my approval of the soup. The entire gathering gives nods and sounds of approval and congratulations to Badia. She shrugs her shoulders, but I can tell that she is pleased.

"Ah, my Badia, you have all the household skills that I lack." Cemal glances over at Badia, and then shifts her gaze to Mustafa. "Well, I don't lack the skills but don't love the tasks so much as Badia."

I cringe, feeling my stomach muscles tighten and then release. How can she be any more obvious? Perhaps I should be glad that there is no one who seems to be dwelling on my future wedding. My *anne* didn't like men, only my *büyükbaba*. She loved *Baba*, but she would say he was "typical," a "typical Turkish man." I think I know what she meant now, but Cengiz and Mustafa are not "typical Turkish men." Well, I don't know for certain about Mustafa, but Cengiz is not. He is sensitive and kind. At least he was until yesterday.

Baba smiles at Badia. "This might be the tastiest soup I have ever had."

"I will make it for you when I visit you and Fatma in Istanbul." Badia smiles at Mustafa, who will shortly be attending medical school in Istanbul.

"Yes, you will make it for all of us," *Baba* informs Badia.

My *anne* was right in thinking that *Baba* knows absolutely nothing about women that has been very useful either to him or to the women he has known. Now I have to wonder who *Baba* means when he says, "all of us." He cannot mean *Büyükbaba,*who is drifting off to sleep, allowing his spoon to slide down into his soup.

Babaanne lifts the spoon out of *Büyükbaba's* soup, wiping the handle on her napkin. She is careful not to wake him. "He barely eats anything anymore," she says to Cemal. "He drinks a few sips of *çay*, and then he falls back to sleep. I think his final journey will come soon."

Cemal stands to collect the now empty soup bowls, but first places her hand on *Babaanne's* shoulder. "Praises be to Allah," she says softly. "Now that Cengiz is out of the house, perhaps you will both come to live with us. It would be easier for you."

"You are too kind," *Babaanne* says. "But Baler needs to be in his own home. It is too late for him to make a change now. He can barely see, and he could easily have quite a bad fall if he doesn't know exactly where everything is."

Cemal nods at this expected answer. She has asked them to move in with her many times, and the answer is always the same. The cave is the home of *Büyükbaba's* family. He was born there and will die there, as his father before him.

I do wonder what *Babaanne* will do once he is gone, but it feels to me pretty much like he is gone now. I never like to think of this future. I have wished that *Babaanne* would come to live with us in Istanbul, but I always feel so guilty because that would mean *Büyükbaba* would no longer be with us. Even though he no longer says much to anyone, he is still important to all of us.

As if someone has just poked *Büyükbaba*, he jerks awake. "Ah," he mumbles, "I almost missed the soup." Slowly he draws the bowl towards him and lifts his spoon. He inhales the soup slowly, as if he were the sultan's taster. After allowing it to sit momentarily on his tongue, he finally swallows. He looks over at *Baba*. "You are right, my son. This soup is perfect."

I cannot help but smile. *Büyükbaba* has possibly heard every word of our conversation. He is still very much with us. Perhaps he has not missed a thing.

CHAPTER 20

The evening is not going well for Badia. This is only obvious to those who are now directly involved. This includes me, Badia, and Cengiz. Although Mustafa is a part of this, it has become apparent that Mustafa has not been told that he has been invited to *iftar* purely to meet Badia. What is also painfully clear to me now is that Cengiz has told Mustafa nothing about our relationship. Though that relationship and our promises appear to be nothing but history as of yesterday. This lack of information has quickly driven Mustafa to become infatuated with me. I cannot get him to stop flirting with me.

I try to include Badia in the conversation, but Mustafa has a skilled way of directing questions specifically to me. Since Badia does not read or study and has not traveled much beyond Avanos, and Mustafa is going to be going to school in Istanbul, there is little I can do to direct the conversation back to Badia.

The adults are now all engaged in a political discussion. Cemal looks over at us now and then to make sure that we are equally engaged with one another, but she is not paying any attention to content, as she is unable to hear us from where she is sitting. Cengiz, on the other hand, is watching with some intensity. Badia is less socially attuned. She doesn't know how to capture Mustafa's curiosity, and so she has shifted her attention to the adults. I decide to try again.

"You may not know this," I tell Mustafa, "but Badia, Elif, Cengiz and I all studied together during the war. Cemal and Salman hired a tutor for them once the schools were closed. I would take the bus with *Babaanne* and then with my *anne* so that I could join them. My *anne* didn't go to school because of The Great War. She and *Babaanne* wanted me to have an education. Badia, didn't we have so much fun with the tutor?"

Badia hears her name and looks over to me. "What did you ask?"

"I was telling Mustafa how we all had our own school at your house during the war and how fortunate I was to study with you."

Badia flicks her wrist in indifference. "You were lucky enough to study with Cengiz. Ilhan *bey* practically ignored me. You two always had the answers, and Elif was too young to participate much."

"I have decided to study to be a doctor, too," Elif offers, taking the attention once again from Badia. Elif looks up admiringly at Mustafa. I decide that she definitely has a crush.

I barely take a breath before I try again. "Ilhan *bey* did not ignore you. He treated every one of us the same."

"Poor guy. He had a handful with us." Badia finally looks at Mustafa.

"Why were you a handful?" Mustafa asks. "Did you behave badly?"

"I was often bored," Badia confesses. "And I would get so sleepy. I did fall asleep a couple of times, but Ilhan *bey* was no disciplinarian. Elif was the one to wake me. Once Ilhan *bey* tapped me lightly on the shoulder with his ruler, but he never got upset. I think he didn't want to lose his job."

"This is very true," Cengiz adds. "With all the schools closed, he was lucky to have a job. I don't think of us as difficult students, though. We had fun, and we worked hard."

"And then Atatürk had to go and change the alphabet," Badia says, screwing up her face and shaking her head. "That is exactly when I gave up."

"You aren't the only one," I add, still trying to protect Badia. "Some of my school friends in Istanbul are still having so many problems with it. All of a sudden an Arabic letter or word appears."

"Well," Cengiz comments after he swallows a large bite of lamb and eggplant. "If we are going to be part of the western world, we have to have a common alphabet. Ilhan *bey* is off somewhere teaching the conversion to adults. It's probably more difficult than it was to teach us."

Mustafa rests his fork in his plate and leans back in his chair. "I cannot eat another bite, even though this food is so delicious."

Cemal passes the food around the table again, but only a few of us put anything else on our plates. We know that there will be a delicious custard for dessert, along with watermelon, and no one wants to miss out on these delicacies.

Cemal carries a couple of the dishes back into the kitchen, and I follow her. Once again, she doesn't protest. When we are out of hearing, she asks me, "What do you think of Mustafa?"

I set the platter I am carrying down on the table. "What do you mean?" I ask.

"Do you find him attractive?"

"He seems nice enough. He's a good friend to Cengiz."

"Do you know if Badia finds him attractive?" Now I am confident that she has noticed the flirting and attention Mustafa has been giving me. Cemal is wondering if I am attracted to him.

"I don't know," I tell her. "They seem to be getting along nicely."

"Good," she says. "Then why don't you stay here and begin to clear the food off the dishes. I will bring them in for you."

"*Tamam*, okay," I agree, only too happy to be taken out of the picture for a time.

I linger in the kitchen longer than necessary, until Cemal asks me to set the custard dishes on the table. I see that Cengiz and Mustafa are talking excitedly about soccer, but Badia and Elif look weary, listless. *Büyükbaba* seems to be asleep again, and *Babaanne* announces that she will have to get him home soon after the custard and coffee. Mustafa will spend the night and stay for another half day before he leaves to be with his *anne* for the rest of Ramadan.

Before I can sit again, Cengiz rises to pour the coffee, but first he tells me, "I would like very much to walk you to the bus again. I have a little gift for you."

I smile and nod, but now I wish that I had brought a gift for him.

After the custard and watermelon, and after the prayers we recite at the end of our meal, it is time to return to Goreme. There is only one late bus, and we must not miss it. The buses run late during Ramadan, but there will not be another one until the morning. We help *Büyükbaba* first, and then *Babaanne*, up onto the donkey that Salman keeps to transport clay and supplies for the pottery factory. Since they are clearly too tired to walk the mile to the bus, Salman has insisted that he walk them on his donkey, Tembel.

Tembel isn't lazy, but that was the name he had when Salman purchased him. Salman saved Tembel's life. Tembel was only four or five, we could only guess, when Salman bought him from an awful man who had abused him and did not feed him properly. Salman already had a donkey at that time, but that donkey was already 25 years old. Salman didn't like to work him so hard. That donkey died several years ago. We all love Tembel, and his life is so much better than it ever would have been with that horrid man.

Cengiz comes out of the house with a tiny parcel that is wrapped in decorative paper and is tied with a ribbon. We walk behind the donkey, far enough from *Baba* and Salman that they cannot hear our conversation.

"I thought this might be a good gift for you." Cengiz hands me the package. I stand still, holding it in my hand.

"Open it, please. I would prefer it."

"But I have nothing for you," I tell him.

"That is perfectly okay. I just saw this in a shop and wanted to buy it for you."

I hesitate for a moment, untie the ribbon, and open the paper. I gasp as I lift the slender chord and pull out the hamsa that is attached. There is a small clasp so that it can be worn as a necklace, as well as hung on a hook

It's not possible for me to say what I feel. I stand there like a speechless idiot. Finally, I manage to say, "Cengiz, this is so beautiful."

"I hope it will bring you luck." Cengiz smiles at me, and I know he is pleased with my reaction.

"Fatma," Cengiz takes my hand in his, "I have been frivolous."

"How?" I ask him, wondering if the necklace has cost him too much.

"The promises we made to each other; I think we need to keep them. I was just afraid that I was being selfish. Perhaps you would meet someone better in Istanbul."

"You might find a better girl than me," I say quickly, hardly believing myself.

"There is no girl better than you for me, my lovely Fatma."

"Now you won't write to me next week, or even next month or year and tell me something different, will you?" I don't resist saying this, even though my heart is beating so loudly that I can barely hear myself speak.

"Ah, I can see that you no longer trust me. I promise to work hard to earn your trust again."

I let go of Cengiz's hand to fasten the pendant around my neck and tuck in under my blouse. "I will wear this always close to my heart where no one can see it but me."

"Come on, you two," *Baba* shouts. "We will miss the bus."

"I will expect you to work very hard at this," I tell Cengiz before shouting back to *Baba*, "We're coming."

Cengiz squeezes my hand before letting it go. "I will. I will," he whispers, "I promise I will." I hand him back the wrapping paper but take the tiny ribbon and stick it under my blouse as well. This is Cengiz's first gift to me, and so this ribbon is precious.

CHAPTER 21

So far, today has to have been one of the worst days of my life. Even after Cengiz renewed his commitment to me, I will never forget this day as horrible. Just before sunset, we buried *Büyükbaba*.

Büyükbaba collapsed in the bus last night. The bus was packed and very warm, so many people were visiting for Ramadan. A young man rose to give *Büyükbaba* his seat. As he went to sit down, he missed the seat and crashed to the floor, his head banging against the bottom of the chair. We all thought he had simply slipped and fallen, but when the ambulance finally arrived, they pronounced him dead of a heart attack.

Even so, *Babaanne* fell on his body and insisted that we go to the nearest hospital to make sure that he was really dead. I still find this aspect of things disturbing, as she was just talking about him taking his last journey very soon. Even so, the shock of it threatened to take her with him. *Babaanne* was insistent. The bus driver had to stop the whole bus, call for the ambulance, and when we could not all go in the ambulance, *Baba* took me back home and let *Babaanne* go with *Büyükbaba*. *Baba* knew his father was gone, and there was nothing more he could do. I was so shaken that I gripped my new hamsa all the way back. *Baba* was too absorbed to notice. This morning, *Baba* went to the hospital and brought *Babaanne* back in a rented vehicle with the body.

It is interesting, but now that the burial is over, *Babaanne* has stopped weeping, at least she has in front of me. I have not seen her cry since the death of my *anne,* even when I left to go to Istanbul with *Baba*. I always think of *Babaanne* as a strong woman, a woman who accepts things as they are. I hope that I am like her in this way. My *anne* suffered her fate so much. Because of this, I am pleased to see that *Babaanne's* eyes are dry, even if they are swollen.

Baba has asked *Babaanne* to come to live in Istanbul with us, but she continues to refuse. She has agreed, though, to finally move from the cave in Goreme to Avanos with Cemal and Salman. We will help her to pack her things and move them into what used to be Cengiz's bedroom, so we will delay our stay. There is a spare room for Cengiz when he visits. *Baba* and I can always stay at an inn or go back to the cave.

Baba will rent a vehicle and a driver to take us back to Istanbul with some of the furniture that *Büyükbaba* made. What we leave behind will either be taken to Avanos or left in the cave in Goreme. I hoped that *Babaanne* would come with us, but she says she is too old now to change her way of life. She knows Avanos, but she does not know Istanbul. And if she finds that Avanos is not good for her, she can return more easily to Goreme. Now that I have school, I cannot stay behind with her. If I am to keep up with Cengiz, I must return to Istanbul.

My heart is so mixed up. In a way, I liked it that Mustafa was interested in me. I will not ask Cengiz if that was the reason he changed his mind, but I am convinced that this made him think twice.

At the same time that I was flattered by Mustafa's attentions, I feel bad that he seemed unattracted to Badia. I also worry that Cemal, since she knows nothing about my real relationship with Cengiz, will stop inviting me if she thinks I am competition for Badia. Since Badia appears to have no ambition, they want to see her married as soon as possible. And they would never want to see her marry down, even if it would make her happy. This would not worry Salman, but Cemal would always remain worried about her. She would not want to see her daughter married to a man who could not comfortably support a family. She might be satisfied if Badia were to marry someone of equal status to her own father but marrying up would be the best. I know Badia will make a wonderful wife and mother, but she is not what some folks might consider a pretty girl. I find Badia to be beautiful, but Muhsine *hanım* would say that she is plain, meaning that she is not ugly. But she is as loyal and loving a person as anyone could be. So I used to believe that anything could be possible for her.

Now that I am older and have gone to a regular school, I know better. I understand from my reading that men who are more upper class either want women who are very pretty and kind or at the least, very smart and shrewd. So, attracting a suitable boy, especially in a small village like Avanos, will not be easy. Ahhh, I think, what if Badia were to live with us in Istanbul? She might agree to come to my school. I will discuss this with Cengiz first and see what he thinks. If *Babaanne* could live with us, why not Badia? This new idea distracts me from my grief for *Büyükbaba*.

I sit down on a bench at the table that was made so many years ago by *Büyükbaba*. The table and benches will come back to Istanbul with us. We will get rid of the table *Baba* brought with them when they came from Salonika to live in Constantinople, the city that I know as Istanbul.

Strange, isn't it, how names and alphabets are changed after a war? Mustafa Kemal is now Atatürk and Constantinople is now Istanbul. The Turkish alphabet is now taken from the Roman alphabet. I understand why the alphabet has been changed, but I do not grasp the name changes. These things make no sense to me. They are still the same people and the same places. I see that some folks never adjust to the changes. Some still refer to Mustafa Kemal and to Constantinople. The older folks, like *Babaanne*, make fun of the changes by always referring to them by both the old name and the new one with a bit of sarcasm in their tones. Now it is all Turkish for the Turks, as if there is no Persian or Arabic remaining. Personally, I think Constantinople sounds better than Istanbul.

"Can you help me load this box of clothing into the truck?" *Babaanne* asks me.

"Certainly," I tell her, rising from the bench and leaving my wandering thoughts behind. "I shouldn't just be sitting here anyway. I should be helping you."

"Thank you, dear, but there is so little that I am taking with me. The box is too large for my clothing, and so it is awkward and bulky to carry."

The box is on loan from the pottery factory, one used for carrying finished pots from the factory to the shop. I grab one end and *Babaanne* grabs the other. *Baba* is outside placing *Babaanne's* few belongings onto the truck. He takes the box from us and easily lifts it onto the truck.

"Not a lot of clothing, *Anne*," he says.

"It's all I've ever needed," *Babaanne* assures him. "After all, I have lived in this cave for most of my life. I've only ever traveled as far as Avanos. Why would I need to waste money on unnecessary clothing?"

"Oh, if only Fatma would feel the same!" *Baba* looks at me and smiles.

"Fatma does not live in a cave," *Babaanne* quips back.

I give *Babaanne* a hug. "That's right."

Baba shrugs his shoulders but smiles. "Always take her side. If she doesn't stop growing, I'll be broke giving all my money to the clothing shops."

I don't pay any mind to this. *Baba* is always complaining half-heartedly about how much money is spent on clothing for me, but I know he prides himself on how well I look. My *anne* was not so pretty, or so he says. After my birth, she lost lots of weight, and I thought she was pretty when I was old enough to notice.

Babaanne has one photo of *Büyükbaba*. They had no wedding photo. *Baba* had the photo taken on his 70th birthday. *Babaanne* is standing next to him. They both look younger. That is the last item she hands to *Baba* to add to the box of clothing.

"I will go in for a few moments," *Babaanne* announces, "and then I'll be ready."

"No rush, *Anne*," *Baba* tells her. I wonder why *Baba* doesn't join her for a last look around the cave, but I suppose he thinks we'll be back and does not regard it as the last time we will be there.

Babaanne doesn't linger in the cave, as I think I might have if I were in her situation. Perhaps she feels that she will be well enough for a time to return here once in a while. She has left a chair and two small beddings there just in case, or for our use should we wish to stay there. For me, it is the end. The cave cannot ever feel the same to me now. Nor do I believe it will ever feel the same to *Baba* or to *Babaanne*, but perhaps I am more sentimental.

I ride to Avanos in the back of the truck with *Babaanne's* belongings. If the two of them are having a conversation, I'm unable to hear it. This suits me, as I am at a loss for words. This does not happen to me very often. *Babaanne* is in deep mourning, and so I feel that acutely. She is a different *Babaanne* from the great grandmother I have known all my life. Now I do more hugging and kissing than speaking.

Since it is Ramadan, we have not eaten since our breakfast before sunrise, and we have all fasted since burying *Büyükbaba*. We did not have a reception for *Büyükbaba* because there was no real community to join with us but Cengiz and his family, and it being Ramadan, we will join them for *iftar* later on. After the burial, we didn't feel any hunger. The movement of the truck lulls me to sleep. I try to stay awake, but the breeze presses against my eyelids, and I am unable to keep them open.

Fusun, my anne, is sitting beside me. She looks alive and well. She is wearing a head scarf, something I never saw her do. I ask her why she is dressing hajib now. She writes on a piece of paper. I am surprised when she hands it to me that it is written in the new alphabet. It says: **Turkey is changing. Be flexible**. *I hand the paper back to her. What do you mean, I ask her? She writes again on the paper and hands it back to me. I read:* **Change can be dangerous**. *I look up at her. She pulls off the scarf and throws it at me, and she begins to howl, to shriek. I cover my ears.*

"Wake up, Fatma." *Baba* is touching my shoulder. "We are here. Help us to carry in *Babaanne's* things. Why are your hands over your ears?"

I realize I am still covering my ears to protect them from my *anne's* cries. "She came into my dreams again."

"Who?" *Baba* asks.

"My *anne*. She came to me only once before this. I think she is trying to warn me." I struggle to my feet and pick up a box to take inside. "She was screaming into my ears."

"Warn you about what?" *Baba* looks at me strangely. "I hope you aren't becoming foolish and superstitious like my *anne*."

"Of course not," I protest. "It was just a dream."

"Well, I'm glad to hear it. My *anne* is a wonderful woman, but she was raised in folk tales and superstition. You are getting an education. I don't expect this from you. When you were a child, it was one thing. I even told you silly tales. But now you are an educated young woman. Your *anne* is no more. She cannot warn you about anything."

"Of course, *Baba*. I know that." But, in truth, I do not know that. I go over the dream in my head, every detail I can remember, so I can tell it to *Babaanne* before we return to Istanbul. I know I should not have said anything to *Baba*. *Babaanne* has warned me not to repeat my dreams or their meanings to men. "They are too weak to believe in these things. They are scared of them and prefer to chastise us women so that we will give them up as well." Once again, I think that my *Babaanne* is a truly gifted woman.

PART III
TRIALS OF TRAVEL
AND SEPARATION

CHAPTER 22

So much has happened in the last two years, Fatma thinks. She curls her legs up under her body and leans back into the pillows stacked behind her on the double mattress that *Baba* and Nur used to share and is now shared by Fatma and Badia.

If only there was someone I could talk to, really talk to, Fatma wonders. If Badia could read her thoughts, she would be so hurt. What do you mean you have no one to talk to, Badia would scold her. Why can't she talk to Badia? And why is it that Fatma cannot talk to Badia?

And what a surprise Badia has been to everyone. Fatma smiles just thinking about this. Badia came to live with them almost two years ago in order to begin her studies at university. Who would have ever thought that this shy young woman would even consider continuing her education? The family might have believed more in her studying to become a chef. But no, Badia is studying to become a journalist.

And Badia is so busy these days with her new organization, The New Turkish Woman. They are only five women now, but they have started their own little newspaper, and so Badia is gone many evenings, either working on the newspaper or studying with friends. Fatma feels her own problems are petty in comparison. They are low in importance when one puts them on the continuum with matters of State and women's issues. And Fatma never wants to put Badia in the middle between herself and Badia's own brother, Cengiz.

Fatma is still hurt by the brief break with Cengiz, even though it lasted just a day. She reaches inside her nightgown and runs her fingers over the hamsa. It's been almost two years since this occurred, she admonishes herself, and she ought to be over it by now, but she's not, and she cannot say why. There is still the fear that he will do this again.

Fatma takes a deep breath and sighs. Men are complicated. How can she ever be sure what Cengiz is really thinking? How can she trust him? Women tell each other I love you so freely. Men tell you one thing one day and change it all the next.

After that same *iftar* when *Büyükbaba* passed away, Fatma had gone home with *Baba* in order to go to school. She had asked Muhsine *hanım* to help her to make *Babaanne's* recipe for *menemen*. *Babaanne* had confided that her secret was in the spices, and she gave Fatma several to take home with her. Fatma waited for a morning when *Baba* could be around to eat with them, and that was how it all began.

When Fatma finished washing up after the meal, she said good-bye to Muhsine *hanım,* and went directly to her room to study. She could hear their chatter and laughter through the curtain separating her bedroom from the eating area. This felt pleasant to her.

Fatma pauses to remember. Yes, after so much death, how welcome that conversation and laughter was! This is how she imagines that others live, normal people in real families. Yes, that is exactly how it felt. She smiles and lingers in the memory of those moments.

After a few weeks, Muhsine *hanım* began to bring over a meal here and there, and a pattern was in place. When Fatma would clean up after each meal, Muhsine *hanım* and *Baba* would move over to the sitting area, relax on the pillows, and talk while Fatma went to her room to study. Their muffled words and laughter made Fatma happy and helped her to concentrate.

The house being as tiny as it is, Badia continues to visit with friends in order to study. She works on the newspaper with her The New Turkish Women's group both at school during the day and at the school library in the evenings. When Badia is at home, the four of them have supper together, and Fatma and Badia whisper in their room like loving sisters. Fatma sighs now, thinking of these precious moments. Yes, though she cannot confide to Badia her feelings for Cengiz, she believes that Badia is her true sister, even though they are not related by any blood.

One day *Baba* meets Fatma after school and suggests that they go to drink some *çay*. This is what *Baba* will do when he has something of significance to discuss. Everything important and everything unimportant happens with *çay*. Fatma cannot remember any important decision in her life being made without *çay*.

Baba and Fatma are seated at a small table in the corner of a pastry shop. They have each ordered a baklava and *çay*.

"How is everything at school?" *Baba* asks.

"Everything is good, *Baba*." Fatma replies. "I enjoy the reading, and I am learning how our new government works."

"And what is interesting to you about our government?"

Fatma thinks that *Baba* is not as self-absorbed as he used to be. He seems genuinely interested in what she thinks. She tells him, "Well, honestly, I think a large part of what goes on with our government is confusing. I never knew that we were living next to Armenians in Goreme. They were my friends. They were poor, but so were we, and I was frightened when I learned that they had been run out of the cave dwellings. I never got to tell them good-bye. They just disappeared. And what in the world is wrong with Kurdish people? I have a Kurdish friend at school. She is so much like me. It seems to me that Atatürk is good for us in some ways and not so good in others."

"Ah," *Baba* laughs. "Just like the sultans, good in some ways and not so good in others. You are a wise one, young lady. I hope it will not lead you into trouble."

"How can my thinking about ideas get me into trouble?" Fatma asks him, already knowing what he will say but wanting to hear him say it anyway. *Baba* is so old-fashioned.

"You see what happened to Atatürk's wife. She was a woman with ideas. She went off to battle with him, and then he said: I divorce you; I divorce you; I divorce you. And that was that."

"I'm not afraid, Baba," Fatma says.

"You are too young to be afraid." He takes a sip of tea, swallows it slowly, deep in thought. "Speaking of divorce, I want to tell you that Muhsine *hanım* and I are getting married."

"Oh, *Baba*, this is wonderful! Now I will have two sisters." Fatma's heart fills with joy. This is the happiest she's been since Cengiz gave her the hamsa and told her he loved her. The family she has wanted for so long is literally climbing over her doorstep!

Fatma thinks back to the guilt she felt at Ramadan a couple of years ago when Mustafa came to visit. This is one of the most incredible things about life, she thinks. Just when a person is feeling hopeless or sad, all of it changes in maybe a day, a week, a month, a year, even years. If only her *anne* could have known that. She might have found Fatma enough to live for.

I ask *Baba*, "But where will we sleep? Both our house and Muhsine *hanım's* are too small for all of us."

Baba grins. "I will take you now to see our new house."

They take the tram to Taksim Square. As they walk along, Fatma's curiosity is too intense to even ask *Baba* where they are going. Taksim is filled with food carts, noisy with people and smells so divine to Fatma. On any other day, she might have been tempted to ask to stop for a lamb kebab, but on this day, she strides right past their tantalizing fragrance.

Finally, *Baba* hesitates at the top of the steepest street Fatma has seen in all of Istanbul, with all of its sloping hills and treacherous inclines. When she looks down, she sees signs for soup and at a small café, a tiny grocer and even a laundry. She looks for a bakery, but she does not see one just yet. Shops, people out and about, so different from their old neighborhood. A million cats running everywhere. This must be their neighborhood as well.

Fatma and *Baba* trip along the crooked cobblestones, straight downhill. Fatma is wearing socks with sandals, so she has to be careful not to catch her shoes on the jagged edges. But it seems to Fatma that the people around them must be used to this because they barely look where they are walking. They talk as they walk and do not seem to notice Fatma and *Baba* at all.

Baba stops in front of a three-story building that stands somewhat lopsided with a crooked threshold and a lock that he is forced to bend over to undo.

Baba hesitates before opening the door. He points down the rest of the hill. "If you continue down there, you will arrive at the Bosphorus. And we will have built-in exercise climbing this hill every day."

Fatma laughs. The hill does not discourage her. She is too excited to see their new home.

Baba opens the door to a tiny lobby. We step inside, immediately confronted with a narrow staircase. "This will give us some exercise, too." *Baba* turns to me and smiles.

Fatma watches *Baba* climbing the stairs. She wonders how much longer he will be able to manage them. Is he sixty yet? she wonders. But then she remembers seeing some pretty old people going up and down that hill. Maybe there is not so much to worry about.

Baba looks back and grins at Fatma. "We now own the second floor."

"Oh, but how? How can we afford it?"

"Ah, I will tell you everything once we are inside."

When *Baba* opens the door, Fatma almost knocks him down to get inside, kicking her shoes off quickly. She waits impatiently for *Baba* to untie his shoes.

"*Baba*," she complains, "you are taking so long with the shoes. I think you are doing this on purpose just to tease me."

"Go in, go!" *Baba* steps to the side. "We will live here for a long time, I hope. You could have waited another half a minute," he tells Fatma, giving her a wink to let her know that he is only kidding.

Fatma can see that Muhsine *hanım* has already had some of her furniture moved, her lovely wooden cabinets with the glass and wood doors, so that you can see what's inside. Now they stand empty, waiting for the pretty pieces they normally hold to arrive. Fatma turns around and around, swinging her arms wide, in the large living room and dining area. She runs to hug *Baba*. "It's wonderful! Perfect," she tells him.

"But you have hardly seen any of it yet."

On the other side of the dining area wall is a large, modern kitchen. Fatma is still trying to believe that all of this can possibly be hers. She has never lived anywhere but the cave in Goreme, and then in the tiny makeshift house with *Baba* in a much poorer section of Istanbul. For Fatma, this is the sultan's palace.

Fatma runs from the kitchen to the large bedroom on the opposite side of the hallway where she stops short. "*Baba*," she calls out to him, "where will Badia and I sleep?"

"In here," he calls to her.

Fatma follows the sound of his voice to a smaller room on the opposite side of the living room. "Oh, my!" She covers her mouth with her hands. "Oh, *Baba*, there is a balcony! And two beds! I cannot wait to tell Badia!"

Fatma opens the door to the balcony overlooking the street and steps outside. It is October, and there is a light drizzle and a brisk wind that sends sealed bags of garbage barreling down the hill. She wishes that Badia could be there to share this with her for the first time. She knows why *Baba* wanted to bring her here alone first. Fatma does not feel that *Baba* completely understands her friendship with Badia. There are times when she believes he is a bit jealous of their secrets, their whisperings at night, their sidelong glances at one another, almost always knowing what the other is thinking. Of course, Fatma thinks, *Baba* will now have Muhsine by his side. But Muhsine is often included in our most private matters. She has become more of a sister than a step-grandmother. Fatma does not expect that to change.

Sometimes *Baba* now jokes about what it is like for him to live with three women, even though Muhsine never moved into their tiny house. (Now that Muhsine is family, she will no longer be known by the name *hanım*.) Badia's presence has so altered the balance of their lives, and it is not uncommon for *Baba* to come home from the restaurant and find the three of them giggling in the cramped kitchen, stirring pots and rolling out dough. It is as if both Badia and *Baba* have been reborn, he through Muhsine, and Badia through Istanbul. Who would have ever thought she was at heart a city girl who had once been stuck in a backward village? Fatma still wonders at this change of events.

Baba steps out onto the balcony and takes Fatma's hand. "This is not all. You never met him or knew him, but the old man who owned the restaurant where I have been working for so many years has passed away. He drove me like a slave, and then, such a surprise, he left the restaurant to me."

"Oh, my, *Baba*! You own the restaurant now?" Fatma is truly astonished at this news.

"Yes!" *Baba* releases Fatma's hand and raises his fist in the air. "Allah has rewarded me for my patience all these years. And so, I was able to sell our place and Muhsine's and make a large deposit here."

"We will own this?" Fatma examines his face closely for any signs of a game he might be playing with her. Although, this would be out of character for *Baba*.

Baba hands a paper to Fatma. It is a signed contract for the apartment. As she is still gasping with excitement and pleasure, he hands her another paper that shows the date and the ownership of the restaurant.

"Are you going to keep the same name for the restaurant?" Fatma asks him. Actually, it has never had a real name. There is a flimsy sign hanging from a chain outside that says "*balık*" with a crudely carved fish below.

"No," *Baba* grins. "It will be called *Balık Baba*. Do you like it?"

"Fish father? That's a strange name."

"Well, I am *Baba*, and it is a fish restaurant. It will be easy to remember. I can hear it in my head now. Let's go to *Balık Baba* for dinner tonight." He gazes at Fatma with a questioning look on his face. Fatma realizes that *Baba* is asking for a sign of her approval. "I will carve a better fish on a new piece of wood," he adds.

Fatma searches his face. Am I so grown up that he now wants my opinion, she wonders? She thinks it will not be a bad thing to encourage him, although she is unsure of the name. "You know best, *Baba*," she assures him. "*Balık Baba*. The more I say it, the more I like it."

A beautiful smile spreads wide across *Baba's* face. Fatma has never known him to be so happy.

Mashallah, Fatma whispers to herself. She clasps her hands together as if she is praying. Who will care what he names the restaurant? It is truly a blessing to see him so pleased.

CHAPTER 23

Packing up to move is much harder than Fatma thought it would be. Since Badia has been living with Fatma and Ali, they have gathered so many cooking utensils specifically designed to prepare Badia's numerous dishes. But now she must be persuaded to cook for them. Badia is much more interested in reading newspapers, and now there are two stacks to move of the ones she wishes to save. Fatma and Ali never thought they would see the day when paper was more attractive to Badia than food.

After Nur died, Ali put some of her things in a large box which he has kept near his sleeping mat. Today he brings this box out and sets it in front of Fatma.

"Please go through these things and keep whatever you would like. All this time I saved it for Fusun, but she is no longer with us, and so this now belongs to you."

"Do you want to keep something for yourself, *Baba*?" Fatma asks.

"I have my wedding ring and my memories. I wish I had been a better husband to Nur and a better father to Fusun. Life sometimes leads us to behave in ways that we wish we hadn't. I am trying harder this time." He walks away, obviously not wanting a reply. Fatma feels so grateful that Muhsine is now in their lives. *Baba* has suffered enough.

Badia is busy in the kitchen wrapping plates and glasses in the newspaper she no longer wants, and so Fatma decides to go through the box alone. Fatma reflects that she never knew this grandmother, her actual grandmother and *Baba's* wife, her *anne's* mother. What was she like? She may never know much about her other than what she has left behind, Fatma decides.

The box is securely taped. *Baba* must have thought he would bring it to Goreme for Fusun on his next visit. There is a dark pit in the bottom of Fatma's stomach. *Baba's* next visit was to bury her, but he did not arrive there in time.

Fatma takes a sharp knife from a kitchen drawer and slowly and carefully cuts through the tape. She watches closely not to cut through anything that might be near the top. Once the flaps of the box are opened, she sees that *Baba* has put a layer of paper over the contents to protect them. Again, he surprises her. She wonders what her *anne* might have thought about this.

Fatma pulls out a large plastic bag filled with Urfa scarves handwoven on the edges in intricately crocheted patterns. The colors are brightly varied, and yet, she thinks that she cannot imagine the Nur she had heard about from her *anne* wearing anything but black.

Fatma sees that there is another bag underneath containing several head scarves of soft pastel colors in silk. They are so soft to the touch. She has not felt silk like this ever. Fatma is puzzled. How did Nur come to have these beautiful things?

Baba passes by and sees Fatma's puzzled look. "They were her mother's. Nur was from a wealthy family. They did not approve of our marriage. And they were right to question what life would be like for Nur if she married me. She was always disapproving of me, and I did not make matters better. After Fusun was born, I was working in the restaurant night and day. I rationalized this as making more money for the family. The truth is that I often could not bear to be at home. Nur's family disowned her when she married me, and so she had no money of her own."

Fatma is genuinely surprised. "I never knew any of this. My *anne* did not say much about Nur. I asked her, but she would give me a quick answer and then change the subject."

Baba sighs. "I do not like to speak ill of the dead, and especially of your grandmother, but Nur could be a selfish woman. She disapproved of Fusun as much as she disapproved of me. When she was young, Fusun was plump and took on my features. When Nur saw your *anne,* she saw me. Nur no longer took much care of her own appearance, as we could not afford the clothing and jewels that her family possessed. She had no engagement ring from me, just the wedding band. Her mother had given her a beautiful ring from her own mother, but then I never saw it again. Truthfully, I forgot about it, and when I did remember, I thought she must have sold the ring during the war for food."

"The war made things even harder for you, *Baba*," Fatma says, trying to soften his harsh self-judgement. "If not for the war, maybe Nur would not have been so afraid and disappointed."

Baba shakes his head. "That I will never know, but her character was weak. I don't blame her for this. Her parents protected her and gave her everything. I don't know if I can ever forgive her for sending Fusun to the market alone."

"But why then did she marry you?" This makes no sense to Fatma. "Surely she could have married someone in her own class. Wouldn't her parents have arranged her marriage back then?"

"They tried. She was engaged at birth, but once we met, Nur threatened to run away. This caused a lot of difficulty between her family and that of the intended groom. They never spoke to each other again, and they were cousins and in business together. Ah, my Fatma, I was so different from what Nur had known that she fell hopelessly in love with me. They say that opposites attract, and this was true for us. Before your mother was born, Nur was a beautiful woman. You favor her. I had never had a beautiful woman fall in love with me."

"How did you meet?"

"I used to work in a restaurant in Salonika. Salonika was a good place to live back then. Nur and her family came to eat there. We were very young. For me, she was unattainable, but I did none of the chasing. To this day, I do not understand what she possibly saw in me. Love is one of the great mysteries of life. At least that is true for me. To be completely honest, I do not understand what Muhsine sees in me either. But I am older now, and so I am more of a companion than I was back then."

"Thank you, *Baba*."

"Whatever for?"

"You didn't have to bring me to Istanbul to go to school. I will always be grateful to you for that. A single grandfather taking care of a young girl."

"And so, what do you think of the job I have done?"

"Not too bad, *Baba*." Fatma and Ali look into each other's eyes and smile.

If only—if only my *anne* could have known this *Baba*, Fatma thinks. If only she could have felt his love. Ah, well, and they do say that being a grandparent is always easier than being a parent. And those were such different times.

Baba breaks the moment by calling out to Badia, "Do you need my help in there with the breakables?"

"It would not hurt," Badia tells him.

Once more, Fatma is alone with the grandmother she has never met. She pulls out several large balls of newspaper wrappings. They are carefully taped closed, but the first she chooses to open is already slightly loosening from the tape. She removes a large piece of linked silver filigree with tiny green stones placed inside each link.

"*Baba*," Fatma shouts, "what is this?" The links are long and connected.

Baba walks back to Fatma, takes the piece from her hands and examines the links closely in the light. "Ah," he says finally, connecting two of the inks with a hook. "It's a belt. I don't remember ever seeing this. Nur may have never worn it." He shows Fatma how to close it, and then opens it again and hands it to her. "See if this fits you," he says. "I think the stones are tiny emeralds. Emeralds were Nur's mother's favorite stones."

Fatma stands up and wraps it around her waist. The belt slides down to her hips where it fits perfectly.

"You won't always be so slender," *Baba* announces, as if it were already fact. "For now, you can wear it around your hips and later, after you gain some weight, it will fit around your waist."

Fatma has no wish to gain any weight, and does not appreciate the inevitability he implies, but she says nothing of this to *Baba*. He is always trying to make her eat more. She unclasps the belt and lays it back down on the paper. Then she has a second thought and picks it up again. "Hmmm, I wonder if this will work." Fatma fastens the belt to another link. "Look, *Baba*," she cries, "I can adjust it. It's beautiful. I wonder why she never wore it."

"It belonged to her mother. Nur stopped dressing up when she became pregnant with your *anne*. After Fusun was born, she never wore any jewelry other than her wedding ring. To be honest, Nur was often depressed. I never felt that I could make her happy, so finally, I stopped trying. Now it is almost nine years since she passed, and my heart still hurts when I am reminded of her unhappiness."

"My *anne* was often sad, too," Fatma acknowledges. "And when she was like that, she would send me out to play or to spend time with *Babaanne*. Well, I will wear the belt for both of them, and I will not be depressed. Not ever, I hope."

"I hope so, too, *benim küçük kızım*, my little girl."

Fatma understands that *Baba* no longer sees her as a child, but that he says this to show his affection.

Badia calls out to *Baba*, "Can I get some help in here?"

"Coming," *Baba* calls back. "Guess I had best get back to work," he tells Fatma. He looks at the belt one more time and then turns back to the kitchen.

In this moment, Fatma cannot imagine ever being depressed like either Nur or her dear *anne*. But now she worries that both her mother and her grandmother were unhappy souls. She didn't realize this before. Does depression run in my family? I must be careful, she thinks. I must be careful of the signs. She runs her fingers over a silk scarf. Oh, she wishes, if only my *anne* were here with me. These things would belong to her, and then one day, she could pass them along to me. That is how this should have happened.

Fatma is learning that life often does not go as expected. When she would feel sad because her *anne* was in one of her strange moods and would not speak, *Babaanne* used to tell her to always be grateful for what she had. Not to moan about what was not meant for her. "Life is not always kind," she would say, "but it is how you feel about disappointments that makes all the difference. Some people have too many, like your *anne*. Later today, or maybe tomorrow, she will be herself again." Then she would turn to Fatma and smile, "Should we bake something nice for her?"

Now Fatma looks back and wonders, who was my *anne* and was she ever herself? What did that even mean to her? She feels tears welling up in her eyes, brushes them away, and tells herself to wear and enjoy all of these precious gifts that might have been her *anne's*. I will enjoy them for her, she determines.

Fatma reaches into the box once again and pulls out the remaining package, a large ball of newspaper wrapping. She peels away the tape, layer upon layer. She begins to question that this might just be paper, when she presses down on the package and feels something hard inside. She rips the remaining newsprint away and calls out in wonder and surprise, "*Baba, Badia,* come here and see what I have found!"

CHAPTER 24

At dinner that evening, *Baba* explains that he will close the restaurant for a few weeks with a sign that will say the place is under new ownership and that *Balık Baba* is coming soon with the opening date. "I want to give the place a thorough cleaning," he announces, "and make it more attractive for the customers."

Fatma sets her fork down on her plate. "I can come after school to help you," she tells him. "It will be fun."

Badia says, without looking up from her food, "*Ben de*, me, too. We can all work together."

"Yes," Muhsine chimes in. "We will turn a dump into a high-class restaurant."

"Not too high-class." *Baba* fakes a frown. "I don't want to scare away the old customers."

Baba takes the bread and breaks off another chunk. He sets it down on his plate. "There is something else I must tell you." He looks at Fatma and then at Badia, so it is clear that whatever he is about to say, Muhsine is in on the secret. Slowly he picks up the chunk of bread, breaks off a smaller piece, tosses it into his mouth and begins to chew.

Fatma loses patience. "Please, *Baba,* tell us now."

"There will not be a wedding."

"Whatever do you mean? You are not getting married?" Fatma is instantly outraged. Whatever is happening here? she wonders. What can they be thinking?

Muhsine breaks in, "We are not young." She winks at Fatma, knowing that she is well aware of the difference in their ages. *Baba* is twenty plus a few years older than Muhsine, who is almost forty now. "So, we went to get married yesterday while you were in school. The war has taken so much from us. We wanted the marriage to be as simple as possible. We are building new lives."

Obviously, Fatma's expression is giving something away because Muhsine looks at her in distress. "Oh, dear Fatma, are you disappointed? Are you very upset? We decided it made better sense to put the money into a new home and to fix up the restaurant. The wedding would have cost so much money. Do you mind terribly?"

Does she mind? Fatma asks herself. Well, yes, she quickly determines, she does mind. Yes, she is terribly disappointed. She has been imagining her dress and Cengiz telling her how beautiful she looks, as he would have certainly come to Istanbul for the wedding. Now she may not see him until the end of the school year. Suddenly Fatma realizes that she has not had one single thought of Muhsine and *Baba*. How can she be so selfish, she wonders? They have only married yesterday, and they are both sitting there staring at her. And so is Badia. She must pull herself together.

Fatma jumps up from her chair and runs to hug them. "*Çok tebrikler!*" she shouts. "Many congratulations!"

"Yes, yes," Badia follows behind her with more hugs. "Many congratulations. Does my family know?"

"Not quite yet," Muhsine answers her. "I will send them a letter."

"And I will write to Cengiz. I know he will be so happy for you." Fatma cannot know that, as Cengiz has never met Muhsine, but she knows he will be overjoyed to learn that *Baba* is finally happy.

That night Fatma and Badia agree that they will stay in the old apartment a few days after *Baba* and Muhsine move to give them some time alone. Of course, when they inform them of their plan in the morning at breakfast, *Baba* protests.

"It is not appropriate to leave you two alone here," he says, returning momentarily to his sober demeanor. "*Babaanne* would never approve."

"*Babaanne* is not even here," Fatma groans. "Just a couple of nights, *Baba*, please? It can be our wedding gift to you." Fatma turns to Muhsine for support.

"Just a couple of nights would be alright, wouldn't it, Ali? The girls are being very kind."

Baba is silent. Suddenly it occurs to Fatma why he is so afraid.

"These are not the same times, *Baba*," she assures him. "We will just go to school and come home. We can move everything except what we will need to stay for two nights. Please?"

Baba laughs, which surprises all three of them. "This is my fate," he chuckles, "to be ruled by women. I suppose I have brought this on myself. Truly, though, do you promise to not go out at night?"

Now Badia speaks up. "We never go out at night. We are too busy with our studies. Why are you so worried?"

Fatma shoots a warning glance at Badia.

Muhsine cuts in. "It is a good thing that *Baba* worries about you. We will talk about it and let you know what we decide."

Fatma is happy and sad at the same time. She knows just how much guilt *Baba* carries for her *anne's* fate. Clearly, he has been sharing his feelings with Muhsine, and she is helping him to settle his mind. Fatma knows the agony he suffers. Muhsine is a wonderful partner for him, she thinks. She reminds herself to write to Cengiz about all of this tomorrow. If only Cengiz and I will always be as happy as *Baba* and Muhsine are today.

Fatma fingers her grandmother's ring. The setting holds a large emerald surrounded by tiny diamonds. The color of the emerald is an unusually bright green, filled with light. As it turned out, Nur never sold the ring. All these years this ring has rested in a felt box, wrapped in newspapers. Inside there was a piece of stationary with tulips printed along the edges. *Baba* has confirmed that the handwriting is Nur's, and the note is written in Arabic script.

Please whomever might find this ring, it is for my daughter, Fusun. May she hand it on to her daughter, should she have one. I hid this away because I wanted to give something beautiful to my daughter, and I wanted to have her give her daughter something from me. My love to them both. Nur

Fatma hopes that wearing this ring will not make her too sad since her *anne* was never able to wear it.

Dear Cengiz,

I do hope that this letter finds you well and happy.

You are not going to believe what I am about to tell you! Baba has gone and gotten married! I have told you so much about Muhsine. She is the best step-grandmother I could ever have wanted. Now with Badia here, we are a real family.

Baba and Muhsine decided not to have a wedding. Baba inherited the restaurant from his boss. A miracle that he didn't work Baba to death first. Anyway, we are packing to move into the new home with Baba and Muhsine. You will hear more news from your family, as Badia is writing to them. I know Babaanne will be beside herself that Baba has found a new wife. She worries about him so. And he is so happy, Cengiz. I am so afraid that I will wake up and find this is all a dream.

I miss you. I hope we will have some time together over the holiday break.

Love,

Fatma

CHAPTER 25

Fatma is lying on her new twin bed watching Badia go through a box of her books. She is putting them on shelves that *Baba* has constructed for the girls, two shelves for each, on the one available wall next to Badia's bed. An armoire for their clothing will take up another wall, once it is delivered, and then there are the windows to the balcony and the door leading into the rest of the apartment. But after the tiny space they've been living in, this room feels palatial in spite of its limitations.

"Too many books," Badia comments, staring at the shelf she has already filled. "I'll leave some of them in the box and shove it under my bed."

"Let's see how much room I need when I get to it," Fatma tells her. "If I have leftover space, you are welcome to use it."

"Thank you, *küçük kızkardeş*, little sister. I can't believe I now have more books than you do. Do you remember when I refused to read?"

"How could I forget? You have changed so much, *abla*, older sister." Fatma props herself up on her pillows so that she is able to look at Badia.

Badia shoves a large collection of articles onto the shelf. The shelf sags a bit under the weight. "I hope *Baba* attached this shelf well enough. I'd hate to have it collapse on me in the middle of the night." She hesitates a moment, takes down the large volume and places it back in the box. She roots around in the box until she finds a lighter volume to put in its place.

Badia has been referring to Ali as *Baba* for some time now. Everyone does. The only people who call him Ali from the family now are *Babaanne* and Muhsine. And when Muhsine is speaking to the girls, she also uses *Baba* instead of Ali.

"Don't worry," Fatma responds. "*Baba* learned carpentry from his father, and there was no better carpenter in the universe. The shelf will not collapse."

"*Inshallah*," Badia mutters. She puts her hand underneath the shelf, steps back and surveys the row of books to make sure there is no sag in the wood.

"Do you want to change beds?" Fatma asks, conveying her confidence in *Baba's* handiwork.

Badia laughs. "If it is going to kill one of us, it should be me. *Baba* could never survive if he killed you."

Fatma silently watches Badia line the second shelf for some moments before she speaks again.

"*Abla*," she asks, "how did you become so confident so quickly? I never thought you would come here to study. You hated books and studying so much. We were all so sure you would marry young and have a house full of children..."

"With pots on the stove all gurgling with soups," Badia interrupts. "I was bored in Avanos. And I was lazy. To be honest, the topics we studied didn't interest me that much, and so I thought school was dull. But I never thought about marrying and having a house full of children. Everyone was mistaken about that." Badia sits down on the edge of her bed facing Fatma. She is cradling a book of poems by Nazım Hikmet. "That was never my plan, although I didn't really have a plan. When you moved to Istanbul, I thought at first that it was my chance to escape from the village. I didn't even expect that the university would accept me."

"You weren't the only one who was surprised." Fatma gazes down at the book in Badia's lap. "You are reading him now?"

"Shocking, isn't it? I love his poems. I never gave poetry a chance. But we are young, my little sister, and we have the whole world in front of us. We can read and do all we like now."

Fatma sits up and throws her legs over the side of her bed, facing Badia. "You make it sound so easy."

"Isn't it? Why, you are the one who convinced me to study. What is difficult? We are living in the center of our culture in the best of times for Turkish women ever. No one is going to try to marry us off to some old man. Can you imagine what that was like?"

"No," Fatma reflects. "In my family, such as it has been, the girls all chose their husbands."

"Oh, in my family, too. But many girls have not been so fortunate. And still today, they aren't so lucky, and that is one of the things I want to fight against, arranged marriages." Badia gets up to place the book of poetry on the shelf in the last open spot. She bends down to shove the box of remaining books under her bed.

Fatma is afraid the moment has gone. There is so much she wants to ask Badia, but Badia's recent self-confidence, her seeming fearlessness, the changes in the Badia Fatma has always known, leave her without words. Fortunately, Badia sits back down on her bed and picks up the conversation.

"What is worrying you, Fatma? Please tell me."

But Fatma cannot tell her. She is unable to put her fears into words. Instead, she rolls back onto her bed and says, "You are right, Badia. There is nothing to worry about. This move has exhausted me. I'm going to close my eyes and try to get some rest."

Badia gives her a doubtful look, but she has learned that it is difficult to push Fatma farther than Fatma is ready to go. Badia lets it drop.

Fatma realizes that she is more different from Badia than she had once imagined. Fatma does want to marry and to have children. Specifically, it is Badia's own brother with whom she wishes to spend the rest of her life. And somehow, it feels to Fatma that her studies will lead her somewhere else, exactly where she is not sure. This is more of a sick feeling inside of her gut than words she is able to express. How could she ever have both? Even Badia's mother did not manage that, as liberal as Cemal has always been. Cemal is the only woman Fatma has known who is modern.

Perhaps, Fatma thinks, if Cemal had been her *anne* instead of Fusun, she might be more like Badia. But this is a fleeting thought and not one that Fatma can hold onto for very long. Her childhood is deeply rooted in the caves of Goreme and part of her nature, however it is to develop, springs from the melancholia of her *anne*, Fusun.

CHAPTER 26

Fatma, Ali, Muhsine, and Badia find themselves occupied with so many changes. By now, everyone is quite used to having Muhsine around, but they have never all lived in the same place at once. Fatma and Badia have been accustomed to fending for themselves in the mornings, and now suddenly they are waking up to the enticing smells of the onions, peppers, and tomatoes sauteed into eggs to make *menemen,* the savory aroma of *pastas* and *börek*. Once they make their way to the kitchen, they are confronted with a pot of *çay* already made and waiting.

They are not ungrateful for this, but anything new requires adjustment. Muhsine has taken over the kitchen quickly. *"Günaydın,"* she greets them. They return her good morning greeting. *"Çay?"* She does not wait for them to answer but fetches the pots and pours hot tea into two small glasses. The brown sugar cubes they like so much are already sitting on the table. *Baba* is still in the shower.

Muhsine fills their plates. This is the most difficult of adjustments for Fatma. *Babaanne* always encouraged her to fill her own plate, and so she was able to measure how much she chose to eat. Fatma is struggling with if or how to address this. If I don't finish the food on my plate, she reflects, Muhsine might feel I'm being impolite. Or even worse, she may think I don't like her cooking. Even if I say to her, please, not so much, she will probably come to the same conclusion.

This is not a problem for Badia. She has always been a bit plump from all the cooking she used to do, and she has a big appetite. Badia has a large frame and can carry more weight than Fatma. Badia teases Fatma that she has a tiny frame with chicken bones. Fatma is afraid to even raise this with Badia for fear that she will talk to Muhsine, thinking, of course, that she is being helpful. Fatma truthfully does not know how to handle this, as she does not wish to offend *Baba* either.

It is interesting for Fatma to note how concerned *Baba* is with their responses to Muhsine. If they leave the house in the morning at the same time, Ali will say something in order to get feedback from them, or rather, Fatma, specifically.

"It's so nice to be so well cared for, isn't it?" He looks in Fatma's direction, but Badia is the one to answer.

"Ah, yes, it is. My *anne* didn't make breakfast. She was always running to the shop or off running errands. We had to fend for ourselves. That's why I learned to cook." She smiles at Ali. He smiles back.

"And what do you think about it, Fatma?" He begs her approval.

"It is very nice, *Baba*," she tells him. But Fatma cannot smile because she has once again eaten too much. But Ali doesn't notice. He is pleased with her words. He doesn't second guess them. Little else is said on the rest of the walk to the tram.

Badia, on the other hand, senses that something is up. Once Ali has left the tram, she asks Fatma, "Whatever is wrong?"

"Nothing," Fatma tells her.

"I know something is wrong, even if your grandfather is too thick to notice. Come on, what is it?" Badia is persistent.

Fatma is cautious not to reveal too much. "Nothing, really, I'm still sleepy."

Badia gives Fatma a hard look before she exits the tram. "Okay, but I don't believe you."

Badia doesn't look back, and Fatma gets off at the next stop, wondering if she will have to buy new clothes when the old ones no longer fit.

Fatma's friend at school, Claudia, also begins to drill her. "You seem down in the dumps," Claudia tells Fatma. It is a question, even though it is not put as such.

"Just tired," Fatma sighs. "The move took more energy than I thought it would."

"And are you all settled in now?" Claudia sets her books down on her desk.

"More or less. The armoire will be delivered this week, so we will be able to sort out our clothing."

"That will make things more comfortable."

"Yes, but they are not uncomfortable now." Fatma does not wish to say more.

Just before class is to begin, Claudia opens her English book and pulls out the homework assignment. "English is worse than Turkish, especially when you have spoken Italian first and then Turkish. My mother still doesn't speak too much Turkish, but she gets by. My father is used to picking up languages for his business."

"I wish I could speak Italian," Fatma replies. "It sounds so pretty. Turkish sounds harsh, but not as harsh as German."

"Hey, why don't you come with us to Italy for Christmas?" The idea comes to Claudia in a flash, or so it feels to Fatma. "You can hear the language, maybe learn a little bit, and see how a real Italian Christmas is celebrated. We'll have so much fun! You don't have to go to Church with us or anything, but the shops and the homes are all lit up like Christmas trees. Oh, Fatma, do come with us." Claudia looks pleadingly over at Fatma where she is seated at her desk.

"Oh, I don't know if *Baba* would allow me to travel so far. Anyway, I'm hoping Cengiz will have a break then and we can all meet in Avanos."

"And if Cengiz has no break then?" Claudia persists.

"Then I will think about this. I'm sure that *Baba* will need to meet your family first. He is old-fashioned and not really my father. He is my grandfather."

Claudia stares at Fatma.

"It's a long story," Fatma does not explain further. Fortunately for Fatma, the English teacher enters the classroom. "Later," she whispers to Claudia. "We can think about it and talk about it more."

Claudia smiles. "I will hope," she whispers back.

Fatma thinks to herself that Claudia is right about the English. In the beginning she found it easy, but now that there seem to be exceptions to just about every rule, she finds it quite impossible to remember them all. Fatma's teacher, feeling this to be supportive for her students, reminds them of the numerous exceptions in Turkish, but they already know all of these and find the teacher's attempts to mollify them of no comfort at all. Fatma's mind wanders.

Will Cengiz come to Avanos over the winter break? He has not said anything, and she has heard nothing for over a week. Every day she and Badia go quickly to retrieve the mail. Badia waits to hear from her family, and Fatma waits to hear from Cengiz. She reads every word of his letters several times. He gives her news of his life, but she yearns for some words of love. This he doesn't do. So, neither does she. They both sign "with love," but Fatma searches for poetry or passion. Cengiz's letters to Badia are not much different from his letters to her. Fatma's expression shifts to one of disappointment, as she mulls this over. She believes romance ought to be more like the novels she reads, at least the ones that don't end in tragedy.

Claudia pokes Fatma. The teacher is asking her a question.

"And why do I put the English word 'will' in front of this verb?" the teacher asks.

Fortunately, Fatma knows the answer. "To show future tense. Sometimes the English tense goes in front. Our future tense is always added as an ending to the word."

"Good, Fatma." She gives Fatma a look which says that she has been lucky this one time, but she had best pay attention. Fatma pries her thoughts from Cengiz back to English.

When the class comes to an end, Claudia reminds Fatma, "Please ask your *baba* if you can spend the holidays with me. Don't forget, Fatma. Honestly, you seem in another world half the time. Cengiz, Cengiz, Cengiz. Maybe it's a good idea for you to have some time away."

"But that's the problem," Fatma replies, an unpleasant edge to her tone that she recognizes and is not sure she likes. She adjusts the negative sound in her voice. "It is just that I don't see him very often."

"Perhaps one day, if you marry him, you'll see him every day and wish you had more time for poor Claudia." She grins at Fatma and Fatma grins back at her. They are okay again.

But Fatma considers that in some ways, Claudia is right. She needs to just enjoy her days while she is living them. Her *anne* lived in her past, and she is afraid that she is living too much in her future. Is that true for everyone, she wonders, or are there people who are able to stay in the present? If one did that all the time, she reasons, how could one ever plan for the life one wishes to live? Tonight, she will attempt to discuss this with Badia.

But that evening in their room, before she is able to raise this question, Badia throws an envelope at her. "I forgot that this came in the mail today." She has gone to the mailbox without Fatma, as she was waiting for a letter from Cemal.

Fatma recognizes Cengiz's handwriting.

Dear Badia,

I am only writing to let you know that I will come to Avanos in December. I have been writing to Anne to let her know that I am bringing a friend home with me. Her name is Azra. I received permission from both Anne and Baba to bring a guest. She can share the guest room with Fatma. I don't know if you know this, but Anne gave up her reading room so that we could have a room for Babaanne and a guest room as well. You, of course, can be in your own room.

I look forward to being with all of you in December.

Your brother,

Cengiz

Fatma looks up from the letter to Badia. "And who is Azra?" Again, she is aware of an unpleasantly accusatory tone. She attempts to annihilate this. "He hasn't mentioned her," she says in a softer, more neutral voice.

"He doesn't say. This is the first I've heard of her." Badia stares at Fatma, unsure what is causing her discomfort. "You can share my room with me, if you'll feel more at ease. We are so used to sharing a room anyway."

"I just have no idea what this means," Fatma blurts, swallowing so deeply that she chokes on the words and coughs. She knows she is revealing too much. Why should any of this matter to her?

"Why does everything always have to mean something with you?" Badia is frowning.

Fatma tries not to sound angry, but the burn in her chest is getting the best of her. "Well, he sounds so formal, like he's bringing home a fiancée!"

Badia screws up her face, and then makes a rattling wail with her tongue, a Muslim death cry. "Are you out of your mind? If you were bringing a friend home for the holidays, wouldn't you ask us first?"

Fatma sees her point, but still she finds herself replying, "Well, Claudia has asked me to travel to Italy on the holiday, and I think it just occurred to her. I doubt she has asked her parents yet."

"But Claudia's parents are not the same as mine." Badia takes the letter back from Fatma's hand. "You know my *anne*. She'll have to prepare. And she might have said no, as it means some cooking on her part, unless she will expect me to do it all, and I would doubt that these days. If I'd known you would find the letter so upsetting, I would never have shared it with you."

Fatma sits down on her bed and thrusts her feet up onto the quilt. "I suppose you're right," she answers. But the seed is planted, and her mind sows it obsessively. Perhaps Claudia is right. I do spend too much time thinking about when Cengiz and I will be together again and when we will finally be together always. I'm not sure if this is normal or that there's something wrong with me. I wish I could talk with Badia about this, but even if she has guessed my feelings for Cengiz, that doesn't seem fair. Cengiz is her brother.

Is she afraid? Is she so like her mother? Does she fear that her children will have no father? Or that she will have no children? In the light of day, these often seem to be foolish questions. At the moment, however, it is dark and chilly outside. Fatma's eyelids are heavy, and she will soon climb under the covers to attempt to sleep. Will she be able to settle her mind, or will her thoughts run away with her? Fatma worries about this, as she is fearful of her dreams. When she is anxious before sleep, her dreams can haunt and chase her.

CHAPTER 27

Fatma is floating on some kind of a raft. It feels like plastic and is cold next to her naked skin. The water is still, almost as quiet as bath water. Someone or something is moving the raft along rapidly. It is her anne! Fatma cannot see her, but she knows her instantly. Fatma is clinging to this raft, which is racing so swiftly on top of the water that it barely makes a ripple. "Anne, Fatma calls out to her, where are you taking me?"

"Home," she replies, "I'm taking you home."

"Where is home?" Fatma tries to ask her, but suddenly the water is rough, waves hurtling against the raft like the ocean in a storm. The raft and Fusun are swept away. Fatma is tossing and turning in a gigantic wave. She is alone and cannot breathe. She tries to call out—

"For Allah's sake, wake up! You'll arouse everyone in the building!" Badia is shaking Fatma's upper body, but Fatma is not yet fully awakened. Water is still surging all around her.

"Are you okay?" Badia 's look of annoyance has turned to one of concern.

"Just give me a minute. I was so deeply in my dream that I don't feel quite here yet. So sorry to disturb you."

Badia sits on the edge of Fatma's bed. "Tell me," she says, "can you remember what the dream was about?"

Fatma rubs her eyes, still shaking off sleep and the dream. "There is almost always water. When I dream of my *anne*, there is water. When there is no water, there is either a train or a bus. We are moving, or she is taking me somewhere. I think she might be trying to save me from something. But I lose her, or I can't find her, or she somehow disappears in every dream."

"You'll have to write it down so that you can remember to tell *Babaanne*. She's the one to help you."

"Yes, and I will miss seeing her at the holiday."

"What are you saying?" Badia looks at Fatma strangely, and Fatma recalls that not only has she said nothing to Badia of her plans, but she has not yet spoken to *Baba*.

"Claudia's invitation is a great opportunity for me to travel. But *Baba* might not let me go anywhere without him. I will have to introduce him to Claudia's family." Fatma cannot believe she's thinking about the actual steps she will have to take to make this plan real.

"What about us? *Baba*? Muhsine? And Cengiz? What about Cengiz and Azra who he is bringing home just to meet us? What about Avanos?"

"I know. I know. Cengiz will have the family and Azra, and you will have Azra, whoever she is. I can see something of Italy. Then soon it will be spring, and we'll have another break."

"Are you actually jealous of someone you haven't even met?"

Fatma throws off her covers and jumps up, wide awake and ready to defend herself. "I'm not jealous of anyone. I just think you will all be busy with a house guest, and I am curious to visit Italy."

Badia shrugs her shoulders, makes a silly face at her, and climbs back into bed. She turns to wink at Fatma. "If you go back to sleep, try not to have any more of those noisy dreams."

"Fine," Fatma mutters. She rolls back the window curtain and sees that it is not even dawn. She is fearful of more dreams, but in spite of this, she turns over on her side, pulls up the blankets and closes her eyes.

Fusun and Fatma are hanging onto a small, overturned boat. No, it is more like one of those lifeboats that are attached to ocean liners in case of emergency. But there is no ocean liner in sight, nor are there any other lifeboats around them. There is only blackness. Now they are suddenly sitting inside the boat. Fusun is using her arms and her hands in the water to push the boat forward. She calls out, "Fatma!" Fusun motions to Fatma to help her, waving her arms to illustrate. Fatma lifts her arms to obey and sees that they are covered in blood. She shows her arms to Fusun, but Fusun does not appear to see the blood. Fusun only shouts at Fatma to help her. In an instant, Fusun has vanished, and Fatma is alone in the boat, blood dripping down from her upright arms. Fatma screams and screams—.

"What? What is it now? Please wake up!" Badia has hold of Fatma's wrists and is pulling her up into a sitting position.

"My arms," Fatma tries to explain, "they're bleeding."

"Your arms are fine." Badia lets go of her wrists. "Look for yourself. You're having one of those dreams again."

Fatma stands up from her bed to inspect them. Badia is correct. Her arms are fine. Fatma walks over to the balcony. When she pulls back the drapes, it is light outside, but gray. There is no sign of the sun trying to break through the overcast layer of clouds. There is a basket of bread making its way up to the window of one of her neighbors by means of a hand-constructed rope hoist and pulley. Two feral cats are curled up asleep together on the seat of the grocer's bicycle. She calls down to the bread delivery boy. She lowers their own basket, filled with coins, and left on the balcony for this specific purpose. The boy takes the coins from the basket and inserts a fresh loaf of warm bread. He motions to Fatma to lift the basket. Badia has come onto the balcony behind her.

"Ah, your arms are okay?"

"Yes, it was another dream." Fatma raises the basket over the edge. The bread is still warm to her touch.

"Another dream with water?" Badia asks.

"Yes."

"You do need to speak with *Babaanne*. Write down the dreams. If you don't come with us to Avanos, I'll describe them to her for you, and maybe she will be able to tell you something. If she has anything to say about them, I'll write down what she says for you. You cannot possibly go so many months without any explanation. Suppose you continue to have the dreams?"

"I will write them down, but I must begin to guess on my own what they are about. We'll see if what *Babaanne* says about them is similar or not to what I come up with. I think I must try to understand them myself."

"What do you think?" Badia pulls off an end of bread, tears it in half, and hands one piece to Fatma.

"At this moment, I have no idea," Fatma lies to her with a sincere face. She isn't ready to speak of this yet. Fortunately for Fatma, Badia believes her.

"You will think about it?" Badia stuffs a large piece of crust into her mouth.

"Of course, I will. And if I come up with anything, I promise to let you know." Fatma slides a much smaller piece of crust into her mouth and begins to chew. And for the moment, that is the end of that. She wants desperately to ask Badia not to mention the dreams to *Baba* and Muhsine, but she is afraid it will only lead to an opening for more discussion.

Badia picks up her bag of toiletries and makes her way towards the bathroom. Fatma perches on the edge of her bed, chewing on the bread and thinking. This is the first time *Anne* has appeared in her dreams since Avanos. She's not sure what to make of it. Perhaps *Baba* won't allow her to go to Italy with Claudia, and then she will ask *Babaanne* about the dreams herself.

Fatma decides to postpone speaking with *Baba* about the trip to Italy until tomorrow, even if he has not left for the restaurant yet. He is always in a rush in the morning and may say no quickly to get it over with. Does she even want him to say yes? Is she hoping for him to say no so that she will see Cengiz anyway, in spite of Azra coming? Her true wishes are unknown to her. There is a part of Fatma that is questioning why she should even sit around and wait for Cengiz. His letters to her might as well be letters to Badia. They are never the love letters that she hopes for. Ah, she will leave it to fate to decide.

Fatma removes the bread from the basket and brings it into the kitchen. Water is boiling inside the *çaydanlık*. Fatma turns down the flame under the teapot as she hears Muhsine's footsteps approaching.

CHAPTER 28

Fatma knows nothing about Claudia's family until Claudia and her parents arrive in the downstairs entryway for dinner. If *Baba* approves, Fatma will travel to Italy with them over the Christmas holiday. She remains of a mixed mind over all of this, but it feels like an opportunity she does not want to dismiss. She has seen photos of the Ferrari family home outside of *Firenze*, and it looks to her like a castle or a mansion at the very least.

At 7:30 p.m. sharp, the buzzer rings. Fatma is quick to make sure that she is the one to answer. She rushes to the intercom phone to tell them that she is coming, pushes the buzzer button to let them in the front door, and then bolts down the stairs to greet them. She is curious to see what she has gotten herself into before anyone else is able to make a judgment. She wants the advantage of just those very few moments to think how she might best defend against any oddities that her *Baba* might perceive in them, these aliens who are stealing his granddaughter for a Christian holiday in their foreign country.

Claudia's parents strike Fatma as pretty ordinary at first glance. However, Fatma thinks they are a bit more elegantly clothed than is required for the occasion. Claudia's father is wearing a dark navy-blue suit, a white shirt, and a blue striped tie. He is a handsome man with a full head of black hair, younger than she had expected, until she remembers that her *baba* is really her grandfather, and so, of course, *Baba* is older. Claudia's mother is slender and quite attractive. She is also wearing a suit, a fashionable tweed, with a skirt that comes just below her knees. Her legs and their shapeliness are accentuated by her very high-heeled and shiny black leather shoes. I am not sure how *Baba* will respond to her sheer stockinged legs, she thinks. The shoes match her black and gray suit perfectly. Underneath the open jacket of her suit, Fatma can see a loose-fitting white silk blouse. Fatma assumes it is silk by the look and drapery of the material. Badia sometimes brings home fashion magazines which she shares with Fatma.

Claudia introduces her parents to Fatma as *Signor* and *Signora* Ferrari. She is once again reminded that her own family does not yet have a last name. Atatürk, it is said, will put this into law to make the Turkish more Western, but this has not happened yet. How should she introduce *Baba* and Muhsine to them? Does Fatma explain that they do not have last names, or are they familiar with this already? They must be. He does business here. But Fatma has no idea. They are dressed so formally. What should she do? Why didn't this occur to her earlier?

Before she can resolve this question, Fatma wonders how *Signora* Ferrari will manage the stairs. And how did they ever manage to climb the hill? Did they arrive by car or taxi? Once again, she has no idea. But in the blink of an eye, *Signora* Ferrari is climbing the stairs as if she has done this a thousand times. Fatma arrives at a solution to her first question, not wanting to emphasize their differences. She will introduce *Baba* as Ali *bey* and Muhsine as Muhsine *hanım*. And by the time they reach the top of the stairs, and Claudia squeezes Fatma's hand, Fatma's confidence returns.

The apartment is warm and smells of Muhsine's cooking. Muhsine has prepared special dishes for the Ferraris. Fatma removes her shoes at the threshold, just outside the door. Claudia and her parents follow suit. Once they have entered and are no longer looking, Fatma pulls the adult's shoes inside the door. These shoes look expensive to her. There is never any theft of shoes in the building, this being part of the culture, but *Signora's* heels might prove to be too tempting to resist. Fatma shudders to think of being responsible for their loss.

Fatma looks down at *Signora* Ferrari's exposed feet. "*Signora*," she asks, "would you like to wear some slippers?" Fatma retrieves a pair that are by the door for just such a purpose. *Signora* Ferrari looks at the worn insides of the slippers and shakes her head. "No, dear, thank you. I'm fine." Claudia and her father walk past the slippers, *Signor* Ferrari mumbling, after his wife, "Thank you, no thank you."

Fatma has never worn shoes in any of the homes she's lived in. She wonders why Westerners have such a distasteful habit. The streets are filthy. Why would they ever want to expose their floors and carpets to the dust, if not the dirt, that is dragged in on one's heels? Fatma shakes her head, looks down at her own feet encased in soft ballet slippers.

Muhsine takes off her apron and comes into the hallway to greet their guests. *Baba* steps to the side of her and reaches out both of his hands in a wide gesture. "Welcome," *Baba* says warmly. "Welcome to our home. Please, come in, come in."

Fatma introduces everyone and Muhsine invites them to sit in the living room. She has arranged olives, cheese, hummus, chickpeas in a spicy sauce in small *mezze* dishes with a basket of bread on a low table.

"Would you like some drinks?" Muhsine asks. "We have Coca Cola for the girls. We are not strictly religious, so we do have some wine to serve with dinner. We also have rakı for the men, if you like. It's too strong for me, and so I will wait to have a little wine with dinner."

Signora Ferrari smiles. "In Europe, we are all drinkers. Even Claudia drinks wine with dinner. This is common in France and Italy. But please, don't worry. We don't have to give it to Fatma, if you disapprove. I will try a sip of my husband's rakı. It's also too strong for me. I'll just have water for now and wine with dinner."

The alcohol is news to Fatma. Other than toasting to their new lives together, she has never seen liquor in the house. Perhaps *Baba* only bought it especially for the Italians and doesn't want to make them uncomfortable. He, too, might not wish to emphasize the differences. Although Fatma knows that abstaining from alcohol isn't an absolute for *Baba*, his family never drank. In Istanbul, the rules are less rigid than in the villages.

The drinks are served. Claudia sits by her mother, and Fatma sits by Muhsine. The two men are opposite one another with their glasses of rakı and water.

"So," *Baba* leans in to speak to *Signor* Ferrari, "Fatma tells me you are living in Istanbul temporarily for your business."

Signor Ferrari mimics *Baba's* movement. He leans forward, takes a sip of the rakı and exclaims, "Oh, this is delicious. Yes, I design and sell women's shoes. I designed my wife's shoes. Oh, of course," he smiles looking down at her stockinged feet. "They are over there by the door."

"And do you have shops in other locations?" *Baba* inquires, perhaps a bit uncomfortable with the attention being drawn to *Signora* Ferrari's exposed and shapely calves.

"Yes, I do, as a matter of fact. I have one in London, one in Germany, and now I have one in Istanbul. I have three in Italy, one in Milan and one in Firenze, near the family home, and one in Rome. My brother, Alfredo, manages the Italian stores while I travel. Istanbul will be the final location for a while. We're trying to set up shipping to Paris and to the United States."

Fatma, Muhsine, and Claudia sit and watch the two men. Fatma thinks, well, at least *Baba* is the owner of the restaurant now. Muhsine is wearing hajib, and Fatma feels a bit like the country mouse with the wealthy city mouse cousin. Claudia is more dressed up than she is at school with a plaid pleated skirt and a soft red sweater that must, Fatma thinks, be cashmere, as it looks so soft to the touch. Fatma cannot bring Claudia's shoes to mind, as Claudia left hers outside the door. What can she possibly have gotten them all into? Fatma wonders. She checks these thoughts instantly. She is proud of *Baba* and Muhsine. I live in Istanbul, too, she reminds herself, so I am not the country cousin.

Finally, *Signora* Ferrari turns to Muhsine. "Muhsine *hanım,* your home is filled with such lovely smells. You must be quite the cook."

Muhsine rises from her chair and motions to *Signora* Ferrari to follow her into the kitchen. Claudia looks at Fatma finally and smiles. "Well," Claudia says, "that takes care of that. Show me your room. And where is Badia? I want to meet her."

"Come," Fatma tells her, pushing herself up from the couch, "Badia is at a friend's house studying for an exam. You probably won't meet her this time. But I can show you our room." Fatma excuses them, and they leave the two men discussing business. The two women remain in the kitchen engrossed in recipes and food. Not off to a terrible start, Fatma thinks.

Fatma imagines that the bedroom she is about to show Claudia is nothing compared to that of her friend's, but Claudia exclaims with absolute delight when she sees the small balcony and the French doors that lead out to it. "Oh, this is too wonderful! Can we go out there?"

"Sure," Fatma says. She is pleased. She opens the doors, and they step outside. There is a chill in the air and the clouds cover most of a tiny sliver of moon. The streetlights sparkle in the distance.

"Oh, my," Claudia says, smiling widely, "you can see everything from here. This is so romantic, like Romeo and Juliet. I wish I had a balcony like this. Why, you and Badia can tell secrets out here and no one will hear you."

Fatma is amazed at the thought of her friend envying her for the balcony, and even more for the secrets. "Yes," she replies, "I loved this room the moment *Baba* first showed it to me. Although, to be honest, it's a bit chilly for secrets out here now. We whisper to each other at night. Badia is just like a sister to me."

"She might actually become your sister if you marry Cengiz," Claudia says a bit too loudly.

"Ssshhh," Fatma warns her. "*Baba* and Muhsine have no idea. I would never have a moment alone with him if they did."

"Does Badia know?"

Fatma hesitates. "I think she must guess something. She knows how jealous I can be. Come, it's chilly out here. Let's go back inside." She wants to change the subject. She thinks she might have already said too much.

As Fatma closes the doors, the light seems to disappear before she can completely pull the curtains. She pushes one aside to check, and yes, the sky is cloudy, but it seems so dark all of a sudden, even though the shops are still lit. This darkness has been descending on her recently. She thinks that she must speak to *Baba* about this. Maybe she should mention it to Badia. No, she decides, she won't mention it to anyone. What if she needs glasses? She won't wear them. People always tell her how beautiful her eyes are. She doesn't want to cover them up. Fatma pulls the curtains together and banishes the thoughts from her mind.

"Let's see what our families are doing," Fatma suggests to Claudia. "I'm not sure it's wise to leave them alone for too long."

Claudia laughs. "I know what you mean. I had no idea we would have to do this before they would consider letting you go with us."

"You have no idea." Fatma makes a disgusted face.

"Oh, but I do," Claudia grimaces. "I'm Italian and Catholic."

"Are your parents strict? They don't seem to be."

"Maybe not strict in the same way as yours. Sometimes I'm surprised by how permissive they can be, but it's usually because they have little imagination. They accept what I say without questioning. If you come, you'll see."

Fatma is not quite sure what Claudia means, but this admission makes her nervous. Does Claudia lie to her parents? Or does she eliminate just what she thinks they might not like to hear, which amounts to the same thing?

Does she want to be in a foreign country with someone her own age who's in charge because her parents are ignorant of what she might do? How well does she even know Claudia? Avanos feels much safer.

Well, Fatma thinks, *Baba* and Muhsine are ignorant of my feelings for Cengiz. But now there is this Azra. What does she mean to Cengiz? No one but Cengiz knows anything of Fatma's true feelings for him with, perhaps, the exception of Badia. Even Badia doesn't know they plan to marry one day. Fatma guesses that Claudia was merely teasing when she spoke of Badia becoming a real sister to her.

It has also crossed Fatma's mind to wonder what she would do if another war starts while she is in Italy. *Baba* says that Mussolini is a bad man, a fascist, like Hitler in Germany. He doesn't think that Atatürk will tolerate another war, especially a war that is not his own. Still, Fatma has questions. What if she got stuck in Italy and could not travel home again? She has read stories about such things happening in the past.

All of these thoughts chase themselves around in her mind as she and Claudia walk back to the living room. *Signora* Ferrari has somehow convinced Muhsine to allow her to help with carrying the food to the table. Since this is unheard of with guests, Fatma realizes that they have established some sense of intimacy.

"Ah, just in time," *Signora* Ferrari tells the girls. "We are about to eat."

Signora Ferrari calls everyone to the table. Fatma wonders as to the appropriateness of this behavior, but when she returns to the kitchen to retrieve another plate of food, she observes the two women laughing together. Muhsine is so gracious and accepting. Whatever Muhsine is thinking, she allows *Signora* Ferrari to feel at home and comfortable. This is a quality Fatma feels she might never possess, although she reflects that she might wish to be more like Muhsine.

Baba sets his rakı down at the head of the table where he always sits. *Signor* Ferrari stands holding his glass in his hand, obviously unsure of where he is to be seated. *Baba* sees his hesitation and says, "Ah, *Signor* Ferrari, please sit wherever you like."

Signor Ferrari immediately walks over and sets his glass next to Baba, where Muhsine normally sits. *Baba* gives him a welcoming smile.

"So, *Signor* Ferrari—

"Please call me Alberto."

"Thank you, Alberto. And you must call me Ali."

Baba asks him a question about the leather he uses to make his shoes, and they are off again. Men in business and women with food seem to be at no loss for words. Fatma guesses that Muhsine and *Signora* Ferrari are on a first-name basis already as well. She is correct. She hears Muhsine telling *Signora* Ferrari, "Yes, Sofia, you can take that now." Well, Fatma thinks, I had best stay with calling them *Signor* and *Signora* Ferrari. She is sure this familiarity does not apply to her.

As Muhsine carries the dishes to the table, she motions to Fatma to sit next to Claudia. Fatma realizes, seeing the number of dishes, that Muhsine has outdone herself with this meal. Even though Fatma has helped her to prepare, the quantity of food didn't strike her until seeing it spread out across the table. Muhsine is entertaining strangers and serving guests for the first time in her marriage and in their new home. She carries each dish to the table with a spectacular flourish. She sets down pickled salad and more bread, a heartier country bread than the flat bread that will soak up the juices of her *Hünkar Beğendi*, Sultan's Delight, a perfectly seasoned lamb dish set on an eggplant puree. This dish awaits, still warming in the kitchen.

Muhsine brings the Sultan's Delight to the table only after she has placed several varieties of handrolled dolma, some meticulously rolled with grape leaves and some with cabbage. There is also a platter with a variety of small colored peppers stuffed with ground beef, rice, onion and spices. As if this is not enough, there are string beans in a tomato-based sauce and a large platter of *pilav* with sliced almonds.

Ali pours the wine. The lamb has been cooking slowly over a low flame for some hours. The aroma fills the air with a delicate scent of meat, juices, and spices. This platter is so large that the other dishes must be moved closer together in order to fit it onto the table.

Once everyone is seated and the wine is poured, *Signor* Ferrari lifts his glass and says, "To our host and hostess, *buon appetito*."

After everyone has taken a drink, the girls from their Coca Cola and the adults from their wine, Ali raises his glass and says, "To our fine guests, *afiyet olsun*." Everyone sips again.

And, Fatma adds, raising her glass, "To Muhsine, *elinize sağlık*."

"What does that mean?" *Signora* Ferrari *asks*.

Ali smiles. "Fatma is wishing health to the hands of the cook. This is an old Turkish expression, something more than compliments to the chef. There is no truly accurate translation."

"Ahhh," *Signora* Ferrari smiles at Muhsine, "those hands of yours are special indeed, if this meal is only half as good as the appetizers." *Signora* Ferrari reaches out for the plate of *pilav* Muhsine passes to her. "And my friends," she looks around the table, "this food promises to be even better."

Dinner is a success, of course. Everyone applauds Muhsine as the best cook in all of Istanbul, and *Baba* is beaming at having captured the affections of such an accomplished wife. Fatma and Claudia communicate through raised eyebrows, rolling eyes and little smirks that never exceed the edges of the corners of their mouths. Fatma thinks that she and Badia often communicate this same way during meals, but that they are never this quiet. Since the adults are so busy with one another, they either don't notice, or they simply take the girls' silence as good manners and a sign of respect. If the girls were asked and they were to tell the truth, they would say that they didn't wish to break the apparent harmony of the adults holding both of their futures in their hands.

CHAPTER 29

We'll be on this cursed train forever, Fatma complains to herself, not wishing to seem ungrateful to Claudia and her parents. She looks around and is thankful that they have seats. Their car, every car for that matter, is filled with families, babies crying, soldiers or police or whatever they are, singing a song or two, the notes dying out, and then suddenly picking up again, as if they are trying to keep one another awake. The few sleeper cars were taken, and so they are "reduced," according to *Signor* Ferrari, to sitting with "commoners" if they wish to get anywhere at all.

At one point, Fatma thinks she will vomit. The jerky movement of the train coupled with the smell of rancid food and unwashed bodies causes her stomach to lurch. But the thought of making her way to the toilets at the other end of the car, through the gun-toting black-shirted men in boots, forces her to swallow the bile and to keep it down. She thinks of her *anne* and the Greek soldiers and shudders. Claudia, who is squashed next to her on the narrow seat, feels her body shake.

"Are you okay?" Claudia asks in a whisper. There is no privacy here. "I never remember the trains being so crowded, especially not with all of these men. I hope they aren't all traveling all the way to Firenze with us. There are a few cute ones, though. Look at that one over there with the black, curly hair. He is so handsome."

"Are you out of your mind?" Fatma is not about to take a closer look. "Look at them. They look like Nazis, or the pictures of them that I've seen. They look awfully scary to me."

"They are Italian, not German. They are Mussolini's men."

"These men are soldiers from your country?" Fatma whispers into Claudia's ear.

"Yes, of course. Nothing to worry about."

"They look like Nazis to me." Fatma finds herself staring at several just across the aisle. One tips his cap at her. She looks away quickly.

Claudia laughs and says to the group *"Mussolini ha sempre ragione."*

They laugh and respond, *"Mussolini ha sempre ragione."*

"What did you say to them?" Fatma doesn't like the idea of not knowing what is going on. She hasn't really considered the language barrier until this moment.

"I told them, Mussolini is always right."

"That is impossible," Fatma retorts.

"It's one of their slogans, whether or not it's true. Anyway, I only said it to get their attention." Claudia winks in the general direction of the soldiers, clearly flirting now.

"And why would you want to do that?" Fatma thinks that she has never flirted. Well, perhaps, she remembers, I might have flirted with Mustafa. She glances over at Claudia's parents. *Signor* Ferrari's head is deeply buried in his newspaper and *Signora* Ferrari is fast asleep on his shoulder.

Claudia turns her face towards Fatma, away from the soldiers, and sticks her tongue out at her. "Just for the fun of it," she replies.

"I'm glad to hear that." Fatma sighs with relief. "They are way too old for us."

"Not so much," Claudia says, serious now. "Most of them are just boys, eighteen and nineteen years at most. Why, only a year or two older than Cengiz. He could wind up a soldier, wait and see."

"No, he won't. Turkey will not get into another war. That's what *Baba* says."

"Well, he'll have to do his service, in any event. I'm glad I'm a girl."

Fatma is relieved that she has gotten Claudia's attention away from the young men across the aisle. She sneaks a peek at them and realizes that Claudia is right. How young they are. The uniforms are deceiving. Please Allah, she thinks, half as prayer, half as plea, don't let my Cengiz go to war. Fatma catches one of the soldiers staring at her and Claudia appraising them. She turns abruptly away, gazing over Claudia and her parents out the window at the passing hills and forests. She doesn't look back again to the other side of the aisle.

She is tired of the train and a bit bored with Claudia. She would never have thought so prior to this trip, as she hadn't spent hours with Claudia up until now. Fatma reflects that Badia is her only true girlfriend. She speaks to the girls at school, but she shares little about her life with them. Claudia is the only one to whom Fatma has even mentioned the somewhat odd structure of her family. When *Baba* has met her after school, since she always calls him "*Baba*," the girls just assume that he is her father. She has never thought to explain anything to anyone, as she has not brought anyone to her home until Claudia. Why she has bothered to share this with Claudia, she isn't sure. But now, she hopes she has no reason to regret this. She has tried to raise several topics of conversation, but it seems that Claudia has only the soldiers on her mind. When Fatma asks Claudia questions about Italy, she says, "Wait, you'll see for yourself."

Claudia smiles across the aisle. Fatma ignores her, closing her eyes and pretending to sleep. Suddenly, Claudia pokes Fatma in her side and announces, "I'm going to the W.C. Be back in a few minutes." She climbs over Fatma in order to get to the aisle, and Fatma watches her make her way in the direction of the toilets at the far end of the car. Claudia disappears into the sea of crowded bodies. Fatma turns to say something to the Ferraris, to let them know that Claudia has gone to the toilets, but now they are both asleep, *Signor* Ferrari's newspaper fallen from his lap and hanging over his seat into the narrow space where his legs are tucked. No point in waking them, Fatma thinks. Claudia will be back before they even notice that she's gone.

But the minutes pass, and Claudia does not return to her seat. Not even consciously aware that she is doing so, Fatma glances across the aisle. The soldier with the dark curly hair is not in his seat either. Several of the young men are missing.

Fatma's mind begins to speed to a dark place, where it always sprints at even the mention of foreign soldiers. She tries to rid herself of these thoughts by visualizing Cengiz in a uniform. This she is unable to do. She finds herself picturing Claudia being cornered by a group of Italian soldiers. She begins to shiver and shake, and her movements awaken *Signora* Ferrari. *Signora* Ferrari yawns, looks over at Fatma and quickly assesses her condition.

"Whatever is the matter, dear? You've lost all the color in your face. You're as white as a ghost. Are you ill?"

Fatma is too upset to think of ways to hide her distress. "Claudia went to the toilet some time ago. I'm worried that she hasn't come back."

Signora Ferrari laughs. "Oh, is that all? Claudia is a curious girl. She often disappears for a while, but she always returns. You don't have to be concerned. She is very capable for her age. She is sixteen. At her age, I was never allowed to be out of my parents' sight, and I was as capable as she is, I'm sure. I hated that they seemed not to trust me. I don't want Claudia to feel that way. Her father agrees. How else will she learn? Ah, you see. She's coming now."

And just as *Signora* Ferrari utters these words, Fatma sees Claudia approaching from the direction of the toilets. Fatma feels a stab of anger at the look on Claudia's face. She is smiling as if she has just accomplished something memorable, oblivious of Fatma's worry. Fatma thinks of *Baba*. He never lets her out of his sight unless he is forced to do so, such as school. Would he have let her go on this trip if he'd known how much freedom Claudia's parents allow her?

Claudia bounces into her seat triumphantly. She announces, "He spoke to me. I knew he was flirting with me."

Fatma is shocked that she speaks so freely in front of her mother. How can she say this to her mother? Doesn't *Signora* Ferrari know about soldiers? They are to be avoided at all costs.

Instead, *Signora* Ferrari appears to be as delighted as Claudia. "Of course, he was, darling. What boy wouldn't want to flirt with my beautiful daughter?" They laugh.

Claudia notices Fatma's expression. "Why are you looking at us with such a strange face?" Claudia asks.

Fatma doesn't want to voice her displeasure, so she sticks to fear. "I have learned to be afraid of soldiers."

"But why? They aren't fighting with us. They're just young men, like young men anywhere. Who taught you to fear them?" *Signora* Ferrari appears to be genuinely surprised and curious.

Fatma leans forward to face *Signora* Ferrari. "We've had so much war. *Baba* is very careful and strict in these matters. I'm not free to speak with strangers. So, I was afraid for Claudia when she was gone so long."

"And exactly what were you afraid of?" Claudia asks.

To Fatma it is so obvious that she is frankly surprised at the question. She doesn't think at all before she blurts out "Rape. I was afraid you'd be raped."

Claudia and *Signora* Ferrari both look at Fatma in astonishment.

"And how would anyone accomplish rape in such a crowded train?" Obviously, Claudia finds this thinking inconceivable. "And I can take care of myself. Do you mean to say that if your *baba* were here with us, he would accompany you to the toilet?"

Realizing that both Claudia and her mother are staring at her, awaiting a response, Fatma replies. "Well, yes, he would. He might not come all the way but close enough that he could keep an eye on the door."

"And this doesn't disturb you?" *Signora* Ferrari asks.

"No. I feel safe with him. He's right to be concerned." Suddenly Fatma finds herself feeling defensive for *Baba*.

Signor Ferrari shifts in his seat. His newspaper falls the rest of the way to the floor. When *Signora* Ferrari bends over to rescue the crumpled pages, *Signor* Ferrari stirs. "I wish they had food on this train," he grumbles. "Do we have anything to eat? I'm starving."

Signora Ferrari stands and reaches above for a large sack. "There is bread and cheese and water here. Oh, and some cookies and grapes." She sits back down, opens the sack and begins to break off bread into chunks. She has cut the cheese into pieces prior to packing. She pulls out some napkins and offers them. "Do you want to eat?" she asks Claudia and Fatma.

"I don't want anything now," Fatma replies. "Thank you. The motion upsets my stomach. I think it would be best if I wait until the train stops for a bit."

"We will stop for an hour in Paris," *Signor* Ferrari says, "but I'm too hungry to wait. And as many folks who will get off the train there, just as many will board. We won't want to lose our seats." He takes a bite out of the makeshift sandwich *Signora* Ferrari has handed him. "We can take turns stretching our legs there."

Signora Ferrari offers Claudia bread and cheese, but Claudia shakes her head, "No thanks, *Mamma*. I'm not hungry. I will have some water, though, please."

Fatma drifts off into a chaotic sleep. Whenever the train slows or speeds up, she is thrown into consciousness briefly. As the train resumes a consistent speed, she nods back into a series of short, intense dreams.

Fatma is running. She is not yet sure from what. She senses an essence behind her, an apparition, something, or someone chasing her. She can feel the heat of this thing closing in on her. She tries to call for help, but her voice will not work. Something is smothering her.

Fatma lurches in her seat and awakens to find that someone has covered both her and Claudia with a blanket. The train has become chilly. Claudia and her father are sleeping. It must have been *Signora* Ferrari, who is completely absorbed in reading a book. Fatma tries to shake off the nightmare and go back to sleep. Sleep is her only answer to this long and taxing train trip.

Water. So much water. Loud and angry water crashing against rocks. A waterfall. Fatma looks up. Fusun is at the very top. She hollers to Fatma, "Come up! I'm here! Come up." Fatma tries to ask over the pounding water, "How, Anne? How do I come up there?" But Fusun is unable to hear Fatma. She calls back, "What? Come on!" The water recedes and Fusun fades away with the waterfall.

Fatma sits upright in her seat. Why is the *anne* in her dreams so impossible to reach? Why doesn't her *anne* hear her? Her groggy eyes begin to adjust to the daylight and slowly she comes back from the dream. Will I ever get off this train, she wonders? If only she had thought to bring a book. But within a few moments, her head is nodding again from the motion of the train, and she falls back into sleep.

Fatma is sitting on a bench in the park next to the Bosphorus. The black water is still. Fusun comes and sits down next to her. Fusun takes Fatma's hand, places it in her hand on her lap. "It's your turn now," she says softly, without looking at Fatma. A man appears out of nowhere. He is faceless and dressed in a black shirt with high boots. Fatma yanks her hand from Fusun's to push the man away. Her hand passes through him. Fusun laughs. "He's not real, you know," she says. Fatma feels the weight of the thick, heavy air that contains this ghost-like entity. Her heart is pounding. "Go away," Fatma shouts. "Get away from me!"

Fatma opens her eyes to a genuine and very real man in a black shirt and tall boots. "Go away," she pushes him with her hand, and yes, this man is very real.

"I'm sorry," he says. "You seemed to be having a bad dream and your family is asleep. I thought I should wake you."

"Thank you," Fatma tries to manage a smile. "That's very kind of you." The three sleeping bodies next to Fatma begin to stir. The man returns to his seat before anyone else is aware of him. Waiting for the Ferraris to completely awaken, Fatma peers over them and out the window. They are coming into a city, and the train is slowing down. Paris. It must be Paris, Fatma thinks.

CHAPTER 30

Paris is a disappointment. Fatma has seen pictures of the Gare du Nord in magazines that Badia has brought home. Those photos showed a large and lively space with women flouting fashionable frocks and men meandering about in stylish suits. This Gare du Nord is devoid of color. The train makes this stop early in the morning, just as dawn is breaking, but the gray of everything is not at all what Fatma is expecting. When Fatma leans out an open window, she can feel the cold moisture in the air, like a blanket of dew that seems to have settled on everything. Wet and cold. Badia would be so let down, Fatma thinks. But would she be?

Of course, Fatma notes, Badia would get off the train to be certain. She would not even hesitate. Badia would hail a taxi to the Eiffel Tower, telling the driver that she had to be back at the train station in one hour. Fatma wishes she were with her now, as the thought is tempting. How odd that Badia has turned out to be so much more adventurous than Fatma could ever be. And why is Fatma on this trip anyway, she wonders? Azra, she reminds herself. She bites the inside edge of her mouth. So foolish of me! Fatma takes her prior thoughts to task. She feels gritty and definitely out of sorts.

Fatma notes that no family or group completely abandons their seats. After those whose destination is Paris have disembarked the train, those who wish to get off for a bit of air, a nonmoving restroom or to quickly purchase food to bring back to the train only do so when leaving someone in charge of holding their seats and keeping an eye on their baggage. Fatma looks out at the heavy grayness and decides to volunteer to stay behind.

"You aren't bold enough," Claudia complains. "Where's your spunk? Papa has been here many times. He'll stay behind, won't you, Papa?"

Signor Ferrari is halfway up from his seat but sits back down abruptly. "Of course. Fatma, you should have a look."

"That is very thoughtful of you," Fatma says politely but firmly, "but I do honestly prefer to stay behind." Claudia is clearly not happy with this decision. She makes a grouchy face, scrunching her teeth together and shaking her head to show her disgust, but she pushes Fatma no further. Once the Ferraris have stumbled from their stiffness, and finally, from their seats, Fatma settles back again.

The seats across the aisle are empty now. The soldiers must have departed without her noticing. She is saddened by this, as she realizes that Claudia is correct. Fatma has little sense of adventure. She is only brave when in the loving arms of her family. The soldier who woke her from her dream is just a boy. Fatma understands that it cannot be true that all soldiers are rapists. Now she wishes she had said good-bye and thanked the young man.

Why is she so cautious with boys who are not quite men? Why is she afraid of men she doesn't know? Why does her breath shorten when she sees a uniform? Did this begin before or after she learned of her *anne's* rape? Has this always been the case? Fatma tries to think back. She sighs. I never went beyond Avanos until I moved to Istanbul, and by then I knew about the rape. She is unable to know which came first, as her early years were so sheltered.

Suddenly it occurs to Fatma in a single lightning strike of recognition; she is the child of a most horrific rape. Even though *Babaanne* finally shared this with her, and she has known it for some time now, experiencing this fear and her discovery of it in this moment smacks her hard in her gut. Fatma cannot breathe. Her being born is the result of her *anne's* worst trauma. She is the product of the event that eventually took her *anne's* life. She is the offspring of the most violent act capable of destroying a woman.

Fatma's head falls forward into her hands at the force of this, her elbows digging into her thighs. Nothing about me is normal, Fatma protests. She fights against tears. Enough with the tears, she chides herself. I don't want to be angry, afraid, sad like my *anne*. I want to be like *Baba* and make a happy life in spite of it all. *Baba* was angry and sad. Now he is living a good life with Muhsine. Maybe he isn't rich or famous, but he's no longer angry or sad. With all of his difficulties in the past, he is a happy man now. He turned his past around. I will do the same. I will enjoy this time in Italy. Fatma is proud of her ability to make such a shift in her thoughts. Thinking itself is such a complex conundrum.

Fatma leans across the empty seats to see what *Signora* Ferrari is reading. The cover looks like a mystery. There is a man in a suit, wearing a hat, brandishing a lit flashlight on a dark road. The writing is in French, *Double assassinat dans la rue Morgue.* Hmm, Fatma thinks, *Signora* Ferrari reads French. She isn't as bad with languages as Claudia reports. Actually, her Turkish is not so bad either, even if she stays mainly in the present tense. Fatma is impressed. *Signora* Ferrari reads French. Fatma reads a bit of French herself. She picks up the book and flicks through the pages. She has heard of Edgar Allan Poe, but she has never read him. There are too many words, and she places the book back down in frustration. Close your eyes and pretend to sleep, Fatma tells herself, and then maybe you will. Sleep is the only escape from this interminable trip.

But try as she most certainly does, the thousands of little interruptions that occur on a train stopped in a station prey on her consciousness and keep her from slipping into sleep. A door opens and slams shut. Someone has returned to their seat and is pulling down baggage to get to who knows what. There is a low hum of chatter which slowly begins to pick up as time passes, then dies out and picks up again. Fatma is not always sure of the language being spoken. There is an abundance of French and Italian. Fatma is able to recognize them, although the French is too fast for her, and she understands even less Italian. There is some English; but she has not heard a word of Turkish. How odd to be amongst so many people and not to hear a single word of your own language. She had never imagined what this would be like.

There is an announcement on the loudspeaker. It is in French, but it is rapid and muffled by the static of the speaker system, too distorted for Fatma to make out what is being said. The hum of language begins to pick up, and some folks begin to reach for their baggage and disembark from the train. Fortunately, the Ferraris arrive, in some agitation, looking flustered.

"Hurry," Claudia explains, "we must get our baggage and get to the right end of the train. This one is separating, and we're on the wrong end of it. Hurry, hurry, or we won't have seats."

Signor Ferrari pulls all of their luggage down from the rack, and they each pick up whatever they can carry. Meanwhile, the announcement is repeated over and over on the loudspeaker. "This train--Istanbul." Claudia hurries after her in the sea of passengers.

Claudia nudges her forward. "This way, Fatma. Only this part of the train will go on to Rome. Stay close to me. Mama and Papa will race ahead and try to get seats."

Fatma has no idea which end of what part of the train is going where, but she forces herself to keep up with Claudia and boards another train section right behind her. Claudia shouts, "Roma?" to a man in a railroad uniform, and he nods, yes. Now they must find Claudia's parents. Bodies are swinging bags and pushing through the aisles, tossing parcels and suitcases in the luggage racks above them. There is no "first class" here, even though Fatma understands that the Ferraris have paid for first class seating. In this car, it is every man, woman, and child for himself. Beyond an enormous man trying desperately to squeeze into one seat, Claudia spies her mother and pulls on Fatma's arm. "Just behind this next set of seats. Do you see them?"

Fatma cannot see over this fellow, but she follows behind Claudia and finally discovers the Ferraris. They have spread baggage all over the seats in order to save them. The large man is insisting that they cannot hold seats in this way. He is shaking his fist at *Signor* Ferrari. He doesn't have a seat for his daughter. The fat man's wife is squeezed onto the seat and a half that will eventually become his. The little girl, a child no more than five or six years old, is being crushed by an unrelenting group of passengers still clamoring for seats.

"Ignore him!" Claudia yells. "Get in there before he throws the poor child onto our seats. She can sit on their laps." Fatma feels she is in no position to argue, and in no mood to give up her seat to the child. Ordinarily, Fatma might even offer to hold the child on her own lap and to entertain her with stories, but she is tired, nauseous, and beginning to feel dirty and disheveled. If this man is going to stare across at them with angry eyes all the way to Rome, so be it. Fatma will simply keep her eyes shut. She feels any good will she might have had towards her fellow passengers slipping away after this upsetting incident.

Fatma turns and whispers to Claudia, "Do trains all of a sudden do this? Do they start off going in one direction and then someone decides they are going in another? How do you even know where you are heading if you don't speak the language?" Fatma recognizes that in spite of her discombobulated state, she has not lost all compassion. She is concerned that there are people still on the other part of the train who have no idea what is happening.

Claudia laughs. "This is the way of travel. You have to be alert."

Fatma helps the Ferraris lift the baggage up onto the rack. After being packed together so closely for so long, Fatma is hoping to have her own room in Italy. In the photos she has seen, there certainly seem to be enough rooms to provide one for her.

The giant across the way lifts the little girl onto one massive knee. She looks dismayed and shifts her body, trying to seek a comfortable position. Her mother reaches out for her and settles her onto her own lap. They do not glare across the aisle but settle quietly into their own space. Fatma is relieved. She has seen much worse on Turkish buses. So much for Paris, she thinks. She has seen nothing of it. And if she must stay alert, as Claudia has suggested, she is not so sure she likes the idea of travel at all. What if she had been on her own? She might have stayed on that train and been on her way back to Istanbul. Would that have been so bad? Fatma is unsure. But she can just hear Badia: You didn't get off the train in Paris? How could you not?

Fatma closes her eyes to banish these thoughts but fails. Soon she has opened them again. She tries to take in the passing landscape with Badia, *Baba* and Muhsine in mind. They will want to know all the details, as they have not been to France or Italy. She should be writing something down, she thinks, but then, she has not really experienced anything but inconvenience. They already know about this from precarious bus experiences in Turkey. Fatma is disappointed that train travel seems to be only slightly more glamorous than bus travel, and glamorous would not be a word she would use to describe this trip or any other she has taken.

Claudia has purchased some chocolates at the Gare du Nord. She offers one to Fatma. "You won't get chocolates like these anywhere but in Belgium or, of course, if they are exported. And this was one of the last packages left in the station. Things are becoming scarce again. Papa says that soon he doesn't think they'll be able to export them to France anymore. Papa feels sure that there will be another war. This is one of those rare times that I hope Papa is wrong."

Fatma takes the chocolate and lets it melt slowly in her mouth. "Mmm, this is delicious. I've never tasted anything so good."

"These were expensive," Claudia reveals. She bends over and whispers to Fatma, "I had to beg Papa to get them for us. They were so much more than the last time we were here. The prices are all going up."

Fatma leans across Claudia to thank the Ferraris for the chocolates. They smile and nod. *Signora* Ferrari returns to her book, and *Signor* Ferrari has purchased another newspaper at the Gare du Nord. This one is in French. He is as engrossed in the news as *Signora* Ferrari is in her mystery. Fatma wishes again that she had thought to bring something to read. She never could read on a bus as the movement made her nauseous, but the train motion is not quite as bumpy. She will definitely purchase a book or a magazine for the return journey.

Fatma notices that often Claudia busies herself watching other people. Sometimes she includes Fatma in her appraisals of the people she is observing. "Look, Fatma. Do you see that couple in the next row over there? The young blond girl in the blue dress sitting with the fellow in uniform. The French uniform. The boy in the glasses. Do you think they're married?"

Fatma tries to look interested. "I can't see if she's wearing a ring or not. Men don't always have them."

"I can't see either because his hand is over hers. I wish he'd lift his hand." Claudia raises up her body in her seat a bit, as if this will give her a better view.

"Why do you want to know?" Fatma asks, curious about this friend she realizes now that she doesn't know very well.

"Just curious. They seem isolated in a cloud of intimacy. I was wondering if they are newlyweds. Maybe they went to Paris for their honeymoon. I would like that. I would eat these chocolates all day long!"

"Then you'd never fit into your wedding dress again," Fatma warns, always conscious of her figure.

Claudia looks at Fatma as if seeing her for the first time. "I never gain any weight," Claudia declares. "I'm just like my mother. She never gains any weight, and she eats whatever she wants."

"I wish I could be like your mother, too. She's so slim and pretty. She doesn't look much older than you."

"Did you hear that, Mamma?" Claudia says to her mother, pulling her momentarily from her book. "Claudia says you could be my big sister because you're so slim and pretty."

Signora Ferrari looks up and over at Fatma. She gives her a big smile. "Why thank you, Fatma." She uses the informal Turkish with Fatma, something she hasn't done until now. Fatma has thought that perhaps *Signora* Ferrari didn't know there was a formal and informal way to say thank you, but she knows a bit more than Claudia is willing to acknowledge. Although, Fatma thinks, *Signora* Ferrari's French is more than likely better than her Turkish. Well, it seems that Claudia is quite proud of her mother's appearance and wishes to be like her. Interesting, Fatma reflects, she will do her best not to live her life as her *anne* lived hers. Fatma doesn't think she looks anything like Fusun. But *Baba* has commented that Fatma does resemble her grandmother Nur, even though Fatma doesn't think of herself as being anything like the spoiled and petulant Nur.

"Oh, yes, she is wearing a ring. How sweet. They must have just gotten married. Look." Claudia is smiling across the aisle at the couple. They see her and nod back at her. Fatma finds herself smiling first at the couple and then at Claudia. Claudia does have a nice way of engaging people. Fatma's friend might be a flirt, but she is a friendly and kind person. Fatma decides to try to set aside her fears and worries around this trip. I'm here and so I might as well enjoy what I can. She does think it is too bad that she didn't get off the train in Paris. Even though she doubts there was much to be seen from the train station, she should have tried.

CHAPTER 31

Fatma awakens to the sounds of rustling and crackling in the fireplace. Maria, the housekeeper, is stoking another fire. She has filled a large bucket with the burnt wood and ashes of the one that must have extinguished during the night. A few moments pass before Fatma can fully realize where she is and what Maria is doing. Fatma attempts to slowly emerge from her blankets. But before she can manage this, Maria hears the bedclothes stir and turns to shoo her back under them. Maria is deft with hand signals, obviously having entertained foreigners prior to this. She makes the motions of shivering and points to the growing fire. Fatma nods, understanding that it is best to stay where she is until the room is warmer.

She is about to close her eyes again when the door bursts open. Claudia, still wearing a long flannel nightgown, bounces onto her bed. She climbs quickly under the covers with Fatma.

"Goodness, I had forgotten how cold this house can be. Maybe it was never this cold when there was more money! *Nonna* says she cannot afford to heat it as she used to. It will warm up soon. We will drive into Firenze today. *Nonna* will give us her car and driver. It's time you visited Michelangelo. You will see David!"

Fatma sits up, rubbing her eyes. "The real David?" She attempts to visually assemble the statue in her mind. She has only viewed David in a book about Michelangelo that she happened to pull from the shelf in her school library.

"Yes, the real thing! And the real thing is taller than the tallest person. Maybe three to four times as tall! Come on. Up and about. Ignore Maria. She will coddle you all day. You'll miss breakfast and the trip if you wait for her to tell you it's warm enough."

Maria looks up from the fire that is now blazing and giving off a fair amount of heat. She knows her name has been spoken, but she understands no Turkish. She pushes herself up from the fireplace and in turn ignores the teenage girls, Claudia beginning to drag a sleepy Fatma out from under the sheets and blankets.

"Wash up, throw on some warm clothes and come downstairs for breakfast. We'll need to eat a good meal, as we won't be back until dinner. I'll let everyone know you are awake and getting ready."

"Okay," Fatma mumbles as her friend runs from the room, presumably to ready herself for breakfast and the day ahead. Fatma is already wondering about the art she will see. She knows that David is a naked man. She has not forgotten gazing wide-eyed at the penis and then her guilt at having done so. She knows that Catholics, all Christians, portray their religious figures in art, unlike Muslims who are forbidden to do so. Fatma is curious about how she will react to all of these naked bodies. This aspect of the trip has only just occurred to her. She determines that she will react as she reacts. She will not think too much about this beforehand.

Fatma washes her face and cleans her teeth. She quickly selects a warm sweater and a long skirt. She pulls on some socks and grabs a pair of boots. She is not yet sure what to do about shoes or no shoes in this house. She took hers off when she arrived, as they were so dusty from the journey. For the same reason, she guesses, so did everyone else. But she is not yet sure of the shoe etiquette here. She grabs a hat, coat, and gloves in case there is no time to retrieve them after breakfast. Everything here is new and so difficult to predict.

The family, including *Nonna*, is already seated at the breakfast table which is located in a lovely and sunny breakfast nook outside the kitchen. The formal dining room on the other side of the kitchen is intimidatingly large and formal. Ancestors' portraits with unreadable expressions surround and dignify that room, perhaps falsely. Fatma knows nothing of the Ferrari family history yet to either support or disclaim their royal presentation. Fatma has passed through that room only briefly the prior evening. On the other hand, the breakfast nook is decorated with still life paintings of flowers, fruits and vegetables that appear so real to Fatma that she almost believes she could reach inside the frames and pluck their contents. In any event, this is a much friendlier atmosphere and more conducive to her sense of comfort than that dour and foreboding room on the other side.

The greetings to Fatma are warm. Even *Nonna* is less to be feared in the sunlight, sitting amongst the tantalizing varieties of food. Fatma is quite hungry after hours of consuming almost nothing. She digs into rolls and toast and fruit, covering the breads with cheeses and jams. She is even bold enough to ask for tea, as coffee is clearly the beverage of choice at this table. The serving maid is not formally introduced, but Fatma thanks her profusely in her limited Italian when she places a pot of tea next to her plate.

Fatma is still tired and overwhelmed by the journey. She thinks she might sit in this cheerful place all day long, reveling in eating and drinking tea. No one hurries her, but when her plate is empty and she has drained the last drop of some black tea she has never tasted until this morning, Claudia jumps up from her chair. "At last! Let's go. We have to drive for a couple of hours before we reach the center of the city."

More sitting, Fatma understands unhappily. She has not yet discovered what is so compelling and fulfilling regarding travel. Her body is exhausted from lack of movement. She wonders how large a city Firenze might be. She has only seen a map of Italy. Fatma was hoping that they could either walk or take a tram. She is reluctant to voice this, even to Claudia, for fear of the laughter it might induce. Back to being the country mouse, she thinks, not without a sense of the absurd.

The driver, Matteo, is an elderly man with a full head of white hair and an elegant gray mustache. He gives Fatma a dazzling smile that makes her feel that she is a welcomed guest of the family.

Matteo sits alone in the driver's seat. Claudia's parents sit in the seat behind him, but before her parents can get into the car, Matteo pulls the back of their seats forward so that Fatma and Claudia can climb into their seats in the very back.

"What kind of car is this?" Fatma whispers to Claudia, once everyone is inside and Matteo is pulling the car out of the driveway and onto the road.

"Beautiful, isn't it?" Claudia whispers back. "It's a Bugatti. *Nonna* would probably sell it but then, I have no idea how she would get around. Papa says it is what happens to wealthy people down on their luck. She won't take a penny from Papa. I think it's sad."

Fatma thinks about *Babaanne*. If not for the generosity and love of Cengiz and his family, *Babaanne* would have been forced to move to Istanbul. Fatma knows she would not have been happy in such a big city.

Both Fatma and Claudia sleep on the road. The car is spacious and comfortable. At first, the views are compelling for Fatma, but the movement of the car and the heavy breakfast she is still digesting soothe her into a light doze. Her eyes open now and then to the rolling hills, some softly covered by a light layer of snow, and others brown and empty where the snow has melted. But she is unable to keep her eyelids from closing again, even though her brief glimpses out of the window remind her of the illustrations from a Christmas advertisement in one of Badia's fashion magazines. Fatma wonders whatever became of that issue. Does Badia still have it? She also wonders if she is dreaming. The countryside is far too beautiful to be real.

As they enter the center of the city, Fatma sits up to gain a sense of her surroundings. *Signora* Ferrari rolls down her window on the other side of the car. The sky has taken on a gloomy gray countenance, not so dark as to be menacing, but as if a giant dirty canvas has been laid out, blunting the curves and carvings of the statues and architecture. The streets are quite narrow and dark. Fatma worries that a car as large as the one in which they are comfortably seated will be confronted head on by a horse and carriage or some other obstacle to their progress. Where will they ever find a place to leave this monster, and suppose they are forced to back up? There is much to consider.

As it turns out, there are no impediments, and they have already planned to park in a centrally located garage for some "astronomical fee" (as *Signor* Ferrari calls it). One would never know it was a garage, as it is concealed behind huge doors which will only open to those known to the establishment. Matteo will wait with the car. He has a newspaper, a book, a sandwich, and the entire back seat to take a nap in, if he so wishes.

The air is thick and gray like the sky above, and Fatma questions her ability to breathe in such soupy conditions. She tries to take in a deep breath to test this but begins to choke and cough before she can take in any air.

"Goodness, Fatma, what is wrong with you? Are you okay?" Claudia pats her friend on the back, but this only makes matters worse.

"Come girls. We'll have a cold drink before we look at the sights." *Signor* Ferrari sets off in the direction of a café he knows, and the others fall behind.

On the way to the café, some elaborate mosaic tables sitting out on the street and just inside a shop immediately catch Fatma's eye.

"Oh, look at these!" Fatma's coughing dissipates. "Do we have time to stop?"

"We can do whatever we like," *Signora* Ferrari says, shooing everyone towards the entrance.

The small shop is crammed with tables and lamps. It is dark and dusty. Claudia calls out that she has discovered the perfect gift for *Nonna*. "Mamma, over here, look at this one." The three of them cluster around a tiny round table on the other side of the room. Fatma wanders back outside to look at the table which first caught her attention. Now she can see that the mosaic pattern inside this circular table is that of a large peacock, its feathers spread out in abstract tiny blocks of bright blues, reds, greens, yellows, and oranges. The bird is framed in a circle of squares of softer greens and blues. What a beautiful table to bring home to *Baba* and Muhsine! She looks for a price but cannot find one.

The little man who must be the shopkeeper is discussing the price of the table that Claudia wants to get for her grandmother. Fatma can see that it is a burst of flowers in a large brightly colored pot of red and yellow, the flowers in softer, muted colors. "Oh, that is lovely. I think Claudia is right. That would look perfect in *Nonna's* breakfast room."

"Thank you, Fatma." Claudia beams at Fatma's support.

"And which one do you like?" *Signor* Ferrari asks.

Fatma leads everyone outside to the table she has discovered. "Oh, this is beautiful!" Claudia returns the support enthusiastically. "Can't we get them both, Papa?"

"*Baba* has given me some money to spend if I would see something I loved to bring home. But how would we ever carry this table back to Istanbul?"

The shopkeeper smiles. "We can ship it. No problem."

"And we can carry the one for *Nonna* back to her in the car," *Signor* Ferrari says. "Can you wrap it up for protection? We'll pick it up later today. When do you close?"

And so, the arrangements are made. Fatma tries to give *Signor* Ferrari the money for the table, but she never succeeds in discovering the price. He disappears to the back of the store where the old shopkeeper has a small counter and what appears to be a tiny back room where he and *Signor* Ferrari carry the two tables to be packaged and paid for. Fatma is uncomfortable with the Ferraris paying for her table. She follows the two men to the back.

"I must give you some money," Fatma tells *Signor* Ferrari. "This is my gift to *Baba* and Muhsine."

"But didn't your *baba* give you the money to buy something for yourself? Wouldn't he want you to do that? This can be our gift to you. Once we give it to you, you may do whatever you like with it." He winks at her, determined to have his way. The shopkeeper is busy wrapping and addressing the package. *Signor* Ferrari has written out Fatma's address in Istanbul for him.

Fatma doesn't know how to handle this situation. She never thought the money was to specifically buy something for herself. The table would be shared by all of them, something of beauty from her trip. She has thought to get something for Badia, but she has no idea of the prices of things here or what that gift might be. After all, this is the first shop they have visited. In spite of *Signor* Ferrari's protestations, Fatma pulls some bills out of her purse and holds them out to him.

"Nonsense," he responds, "that is entirely too much."

Fatma does not withdraw the money. "I insist," she tells him firmly. She will one day be embarrassed when she finds out the worth of the table is so much more than she has given him. But the shopkeeper is noticeably removing himself from this discussion and *Signor* Ferrari is not telling her the price. Since none of the tables are marked, Fatma has just taken out random bills. She does not withdraw her hand, and so *Signor* Ferrari finally takes the money, pulls a couple of bills from it and hands the rest back to Fatma. "This is plenty," he says. Fatma will discover one day that she has probably paid for the shipping. But for now, she feels relief at having done what she believes to be the right thing. She hopes that *Baba* and Muhsine will love the table as she does. She will find a scarf for Badia. She remembers that Badia has mentioned that silk scarves are abundant in Italy.

By now, Fatma has stopped coughing and so, they decide to see David first and then get a drink and a snack afterwards. The museum that houses David is not far, Claudia tells her. Fatma is looking forward to the walk, however close or far away it might be. There has been entirely too much sitting. The crowded and crooked narrow streets do not bother Fatma. She is quite used to this in Istanbul. She does note that the street cat population, although ample enough, does not seem to compare with the throngs that roam the streets and alleys of Istanbul. The people Fatma passes are dressed from rags to riches, women negotiating the crooked paths in high heels and fur coats to those wrapped in dull woolen layered clothing just to keep out the cold. From exquisite leather boots to ones ragged and exposing holes, the endless march of the affluent to the dirt-poor pushes on around her. Not so different from her own neighborhood.

But once Fatma enters Galleria dell 'Accademia, as if by a gift from Allah, the sun streams down from above through the skylight, basking the naked man in a golden glow. Fatma's heart begins to beat so rapidly that she wonders if others might be able to hear it banging against her chest. Now Fatma understands. This is not any naked man in the sense she has anticipated. This is not even what she saw in the art book. This is the glory, the beauty of man at his best. Almost a god himself. She walks around him slowly, taking in the muscles in his legs, the strength in his thighs, the powerful buttocks, the sensuous curves of his arms and hands, the perfection of even his feet. At last, she allows herself to take in the curves and slopes of his manhood without shame or fear. When she can finally speak, she says, "I never thought I would find it so beautiful."

There is a silence and profound recognition of the unworldly, the quality of a spiritual shroud enveloping the statue and holding everyone in its spell. Fatma is no exception to this. The aura of the place reminds her of entering Hağia Sophia for the first time and feeling that the universe was embracing her. She knows she will not move or look away until she absolutely must.

Michelangelo must have been close to God, Fatma thinks, although this thought brings her back to the question of whose God. Certainly not Allah. Or maybe there are things that cannot be explained. Maybe the idea of being close to God or coming from God is more complicated than she has imagined. Fatma decides that she will talk to *Baba* about these things when she returns to Istanbul. *Baba* is a good man who does not attend mosque frequently, but, nevertheless, he is most definitely a believer.

Has she ever talked about religion with Cengiz? Not really, she reflects. They have spent religious holidays together since she can remember. She has not seen him pray, as he prays with the men. Fatma realizes that she has taken this for granted. She hardly knows what she believes but has simply accepted that they are both Muslim. She has never been instructed to marry a Muslim, as this has been taken for granted as well. To marry out of her faith would never occur to her, especially since she is planning to marry Cengiz.

Her wandering thoughts are interrupted. Claudia is standing next to her. "Have you ever seen anything so beautiful?" Claudia whispers.

"No, I don't think so. At least, not beautiful in the same way. There is something spiritual about being here with this statue that I can't quite explain."

"You don't have to." Claudia smiles. "I feel the same."

Fatma surprises herself by taking Claudia's hand and squeezing it. She has not thought her friend capable of understanding such emotions, let alone having them herself. Once again, Fatma notes her tendency to judge people too quickly. She thinks of Azra and hopes that she has judged her friendship with Cengiz too quickly. When Claudia returns Fatma's squeeze and smiles at her, Fatma feels truly close to her friend for the first time. Tears fill her eyes.

Fatma questions her own reticence. Claudia and her family have been nothing but kind to her. They are so different from her own family, and yet she can find no fault with their intentions. They are simply different. Is she wary because she is afraid of somehow seeming ungracious or making some cultural and thus offensive mistake? Could she have hurt *Signor* Ferrari's feelings when she insisted on giving him money for the table?

This burden of trying to figure out how other people think makes my head spin around, Fatma reflects with some frustration. Other people! She is never at a loss for confusion. Now she contemplates apologizing to *Signor* Ferrari if she has appeared rude. An irritation at not knowing what to do takes her away from the moment. As hard as she tries to strike these thoughts from her mind and to bring back the sensations of David, of this room, she cannot do so. She holds herself quietly, gazing at David as if she is still transfixed, so as not to reveal her thoughts to anyone. Finally, Claudia taps her arm and asks, "Are you ready to move along?" Fatma nods and follows Claudia and her parents into the rest of the museum.

There is nothing in the day's travels that affects Fatma quite like David. She takes in the paintings, The Last Supper, endless crucifixion images. She sees the beauty in them, but the emotional impact is not there. Fatma has some difficulty understanding why people would want to paint such agonizing death scenes, and so many of them. She is fascinated by the variety of halos.

There is a guide taking a group through, but she is speaking in French far too quickly for Fatma to make out much of it. She would love to know what the guide is saying but is shy to ask the Ferraris. She determines to ask Claudia about it later. She feels quite ignorant about this religion. All she has known about Christianity is their persecution of Muslims. She has no idea if Catholicism is different from Christianity or if Muslims are as guilty of persecution as Christians.

As they go from museum to church, paintings and statues after paintings and statues, Fatma begins to feel very tired. By the time *Signora* Ferrari suggests that they rest and eat something, Fatma is quite ready to do so. They have a lovely café in mind with a number of dishes on the menu, all in Italian. The words swim unintelligibly in front of Fatma.

"Would you like some translation?" Claudia asks.

"Please." Fatma closes the menu with some frustration. She is feeling overwhelmed by so much that is foreign. A sudden craving for kebab hits her so hard that she can smell it roasting. And then, just as suddenly, she is nauseous and feels the pang of the beginning of a headache.

Claudia is reading from the menu and yet nothing sounds familiar. Fatma stops her. "What are you going to have?" she asks.

"Ribollita. It's my favorite."

"What is it?" Fatma asks. She is concerned that there be no meat, especially not pork, in whatever it is that she chooses.

"It's a special Tuscan soup made with bread and vegetables."

"No meat or pork?"

"No, only bread and vegetables. It's really good!"

Fatma nods her head. "It sounds perfect for me."

"Especially in this weather," *Signora* Ferrari adds. "Will you get Ribollita, too, my love?"

"It's a good idea. I'm sure such a hearty soup will last us the rest of the day, and then we can have a light supper when we get home. Does that sound okay with you girls?"

Fatma and Claudia both nod their affirmations. Fatma has not announced that she does not eat pork or even meat that is not halal. She assumes that Claudia and her parents are aware of this, as they do live in Turkey now.

Along with very hearty bowls of soup, they are served additional condiments including breads and crackers and cheeses. *Signor* Ferrari orders a bottle of wine for the table. He winks at Fatma, "You don't have to drink it. You can get something else if you like."

Fatma thinks for only a moment and says, "I would like some water with ice. I'm too sleepy for wine." She says this without ever having had enough wine from which to suffer ill effects. The fact of the matter is that she's only had it once to celebrate the new home and *Baba's* marriage to Muhsine. Claudia holds up her glass, indicating to her parents that she will join them in drinking the wine.

The restaurant is packed with families. Fatma reflects that some are visiting for the Christmas holiday. It is just two days away. As Claudia promised, there are decorations everywhere in the town. The trattoria where they are having lunch is no exception. The entrance is embellished by branches of forest pines intertwined with colorful bulbs flashing red, green and a smoky white, like snowflakes, Fatma thinks. Tiny silver lights surround the mirror behind the bar. Each table has a large red candle sitting in a holder with small pine cones dispersed among slender pine branches, their needles winding around both the candle and the holder.

The soup is served individually in large clay bowls with lids. Claudia leans over to tell Fatma, "I love this. You can take a break when you're full, and the lid keeps the soup hot. So, we can take our time."

"Yes, that is nice. I don't think I've seen soup quite like this in a restaurant in Turkey." Fatma is happy to please the Ferraris with her approval. And she has to agree that the soup is some of the best she has ever tasted.

"Not only is it good," *Signora* Ferrari announces, "but it's so warming after being out in the cold. I can feel it down to my fingertips."

Fatma does eat the soup slowly, stopping now and then to indulge in some bread and cheese. The cheeses are much stronger than the white cheese she is used to. She hesitates to bite into a cheese that appears to be moldy. *Signora* Ferrari notices Fatma's hesitation.

"The cheese is good," she tells her, and places some on a cracker she passes to Fatma. "Try it."

Fatma takes it, not wishing to appear rude. The cheese has a strong smell that she's not sure she likes. But when she bites into it, she is greeted by a salty and somewhat smoky taste as the cheese melts on her tongue. "Thank you," she nods her head at *Signora* Ferrari. "I wouldn't have thought so, but it is delicious."

"What did you think of what you saw today so far?" *Signor* Ferrari asks Fatma, shifting the subject away from the food.

"The city is so beautiful with all of the lights and decorations, but nothing is as beautiful as David. I was surprised."

"Surprised?" Claudia asks.

"I didn't expect it to affect me so deeply. Tears actually came into my eyes." And Fatma feels her eyes tearing up again just thinking about it. She wonders if she has exposed herself as simple or foolish.

As if *Signora* Ferrari has read her mind, she says, "Why, I'm also moved by beauty in the same way." *Signora* Ferrari takes a bite of the cracker on which she has placed some of the same cheese she spread for Fatma.

"You cry at everything, Mamma." Claudia grins.

"There are worse things," *Signora* Ferrari defends herself with a slightly cocky grin. "Anyway, I can hardly help it, can I?"

"No, Mamma. I don't suppose you can." Claudia and her mother exchange knowing glances that convey their mother and daughter years of understanding and affection.

Fatma thinks sadly that she and Fusun had never looked at one another with such certainty, never experienced such a familiar interaction that spoke so simply of their mutual love, if love is even what it was on Fusun's part. She could never hope to unravel her distant and often confusing *anne*.

Fatma also cannot ever remember having been in a restaurant with her *anne*. There weren't any near the caves, and back then, only one small café in Avanos. Well, there may have been more than one, but that was the only one she can recall. Eating out was a new discovery from her life in Istanbul. Fatma supposes that Claudia has no idea how lucky she is. How could she? She has never been without parents. What a different life Claudia has led.

The afternoon is spent at the Uffizi Gallery. Fatma follows Claudia and her parents through corridors and smaller rooms magnificent in their display and framing of Western art, most artists to whom Fatma has never been exposed. Eastern art is so different, Fatma thinks. The blatant exposure of naked bodies and violence is frightening. She is drawn to look and then quickly, to look away. There are so many artists, some having their very own rooms. They pass through so quickly that Fatma finds she cannot retain a single painting or statue. Only David stays with her, and the brilliant reds and blues of the cloths in the paintings, golden halos of different shades, shapes, and sizes.

Fatma has to admit to herself that some of the Madonna and child paintings are exquisite. Did her *anne* ever hold her with such bliss? Fatma thinks not. She wonders why all the figures appear to be so different from one another. She would have expected the Madonna to have the same face, hair, and body in all of them. As far as she knows, there is only one Madonna and only one child. She fears appearing ignorant, and so she decides not to ask. Perhaps, she concludes, it is merely the way the artist has chosen to depict them, and obviously, the variety is allowed and accepted, or they would not be hanging in one of the most renowned museums in the world. Fatma wishes they could slow down and not try to see so much at once, but again, she is reluctant to seem ungrateful. And she realizes that the Ferraris have been here many times; even Claudia has been visiting these galleries since childhood.

There is another part of Fatma that wishes they could just leave immediately. Facing what feels to her like hundreds of walls and rooms at once is so overstimulating that Fatma can hardly remember what they just did that morning. She feels a stabbing pain in her forehead and realizes her headache has returned. Then she remembers the table she purchased to send home and hopes it will arrive safely. It is important to her to bring something beautiful back for *Baba* and Muhsine. Fatma tries to recall the pattern of the one Claudia chose for Nonna, but she cannot.

Fatma sits down on a bench and stares at the painting across from her on the wall. It is a huge depiction of what she thinks must be a biblical or historical event, but she isn't able to read the Italian description. She is so visually exhausted that she doesn't really care.

"Are you enjoying this?" Claudia asks, sitting down beside her.

"I don't really know. I've never done anything like this before. To be honest, there is so much. I don't know exactly what I'm looking at and many of them look alike."

Claudia laughs. "I know exactly what you mean. It's better to really look slowly and not see so much. But Mamma and Papa want you to see how big it is, how impressive, how much art there is in Italy. Maybe we can come back one more time while you're here, and I'll just take you to see my favorites. But I can tell you what this one is." Claudia points to the painting directly across from where they are sitting. "First tell me what it looks like is happening there."

Fatma attempts to look at the painting closely. She doesn't tell Claudia that she can barely make out the details of the painting from the bench where they are seated. Her vision seems to be getting worse.

"Are the soldiers taking the babies away from their mothers?" she asks.

"Come," Claudia stands up and takes Fatma's hand. "Let's get in front of it."

The girls wait until a teacher and a group of school children pass. As they approach, Fatma cries out in shock. "Why, the soldiers are killing them! Are they really killing babies? Why would anyone paint soldiers killing babies? How awful!"

Claudia is surprised that her friend is so ignorant of Western religious art. She says in defense, "Fatma, this isn't the only painting of this scene. So many significant artists have painted their own versions. It's called The Massacre of the Innocents. It's in the bible, our bible, the New Testament. It's not in the Old Testament. That's the bible of the Jews."

"You have different bibles?"

"Yes, of course."

"Why?" This seems odd to Fatma, as the Muslims have only one Quran.

"Jews don't believe in Jesus. They think the Messiah is still coming."

"Oh, so this painting is from a story that is only in the New Testament?

"Yes."

"It's not in the Old Testament?"

"No, because it's about the birth of Jesus."

"Did these people want to kill Jesus?"

"Eventually, they did, according to what I've learned. But the Jews don't believe they killed Jesus. I had a Jewish friend here in Italy, and she never spoke to me again after I asked her if she knew why the Jews killed Jesus. She just said, "they didn't," and walked away.

Fatma sighs deeply. "We have these arguments with the Christians. I don't mean that I do. I grew up with Armenian Christians. They used to celebrate our holidays with us. Their parents had so many problems that *Babaanne* took care of them most of the time. They left during the war, and no one saw them again. So why are the babies being killed?"

"Well, there are many versions of the story. Papa says that many people don't even believe this happened. Could be just myth or fiction. Papa says people will say and do anything to condemn the Jews. He doesn't believe we should hold grudges for what happened many years ago."

Fatma thinks about the Turks and the Greeks, and of course, the Armenians. She wishes they were all more like *Signor* Ferrari. She looks quickly at another painting of a different slaughter and then looks back to Claudia. "And the story?" she asks her friend.

"So, as I remember, and I may be mixing things up a bit from one version to another. What I remember is that Herod, who was the King of the Jews back then, got angry because the three Wise Men lied to him. They said they would take him with them to see the baby Jesus, but they went off on their own. When Herod found out, he got really angry and sent his soldiers to kill all the children under two. Papa has said that Herod probably wanted to kill Jesus anyway. He simply would not have liked the competition; kings rarely do. That explanation makes the most sense to me."

"What a horrible story if that is true, and if not, why would anyone invent something so dreadful? And paint it?" Fatma turns away from the painting and begins to walk away.

"But this painting is celebrated. The artist was friends with Michelangelo."

"Who is he?" Fatma has turned to Claudia but not the painting. Maybe she should not have come here. Then she remembers David. "Why would someone like Michelangelo be friends with this man?"

"Oh, Fatma, don't be silly. Other painters have painted this scene. He isn't the only one. This was painted by Daniele da Volterra."

"Never heard of him," Fatma announces, as if that diminishes his importance.

"I would guess that not so many people have. Papa says he is more well known for his friendship with Michelangelo. He's also known for painting a loin cloth and figs over Jesus in Michelangelo's painting of him in The Last Judgement."

"He didn't put one on David. Why Jesus?"

"Fatma, Fatma. You have so many questions."

"I'm sorry." Fatma thinks maybe she should not be asking any more, but Claudia just chuckles, and so it seems to Fatma that she is being teased.

Claudia continues, "Papa says he couldn't be naked like that in the Sistine Chapel. Nobody could, I guess, because da Volterra actually covered all of them. I don't know if we'll get to the Sistine Chapel. Truthfully, I'm sure we won't. The Sistine Chapel is in Vatican City in Rome, and Papa will not want to leave his mother for so long."

"Please don't worry about this. I think I've had enough of art today," Fatma acknowledges. "To be honest, all these naked bodies and pictures of death are disturbing to me. Not growing up with this kind of art, I don't understand. I feel sick to think about the slaughtering of babies and to see so many paintings of Jesus being tortured. Why do people wish to glorify death and suffering so much?"

"I think you need to ask Papa that question, or someone much more knowledgeable than I. I've thought about this question myself, but Mamma and Papa love the art so much that I'm afraid to hurt their feelings. And Papa has tried to educate me about all the great works, so I know that this is something he thinks is very important."

Fatma nods. "We do try to please our families, don't we? I understand, and I will ask *Baba* if he has any thoughts on the subject. Then maybe we can both find out why it's important to know and appreciate this kind of art. But now I think I've seen enough."

"Of course." Claudia takes Fatma's hand. "Let's go and find them and see if they've had enough. If not, there's a café nearby, and we can get some coffee."

"Oh, I would like that very much. We don't drink coffee the way that you do. We mostly drink tea, as you probably have discovered."

"And you probably like your Turkish coffee as much as we like our Italian coffee."

"No, no!" Fatma laughs. "I like your Italian coffee more. And I especially like the sweetened cappuccino."

The girls walk quickly, still holding hands, through the galleries, looking for *Signora* and *Signor* Ferrari. They find them standing in front of a large panel of paintings.

"Aha!" *Signor* Ferrari explains. "Fatma, have you seen this panel of Botticelli?"

Claudia lets go of Fatma's hand and takes her father's. "Papa, I think Fatma and I have seen enough for now. This can be overwhelming, especially for someone who has never seen this art before."

"Of course." *Signor* Ferrari acknowledges the hint in the extra squeeze Claudia applies to his hand. "Should we leave?"

"No, that isn't necessary," Fatma gives a tug to Claudia's sleeve. "Claudia has promised to take me to a café nearby for another one of those delicious cappuccinos."

Signora Ferrari gives each of them a brief hug. "You go along then. We'll meet you there. Italians rarely turn down a stop at a café for a coffee."

CHAPTER 32

The café is crowded. Fatma notices a few people she recognizes from the museum. An elderly couple vacate their table slowly, and Claudia grabs a chair before anyone else can step in front of her. "If we're too polite, we'll be here all day," she tells Fatma. She pulls two other empty seats over to hold for her parents.

Fatma accepts the menu that the waiter hands to her. The writing is in Italian, but Fatma panics as she realizes that she would not be able to read it even if it was in Turkish. Intermittently, the letters swim in front of her.

"Do you want a cappuccino?" Claudia asks. "You don't need the menu for that. Should we share a pastry?"

"Oh, yes, please," Fatma replies. When she hands the menu to the waiter after they have ordered, her hand is shaking slightly.

"Are you tired?" Claudia asks her. "Being a tourist can be exhausting."

"I'm fine, really. The thing is—" Fatma struggles with the decision to confide in Claudia, but she feels closer to her now.

"Whatever is wrong? You must tell me now." Claudia will not allow Fatma to run from her thoughts.

"My eyes have been weird."

"Weird how? What do you mean? Do you need glasses?"

Fatma takes a deep breath. "I don't know. That's just it. I'm afraid to tell anyone because I don't want to wear glasses. They're ugly."

The waiter brings the two cappuccinos and a plate with a pastry that has been cut in half at Claudia's request. Fatma sees that it is rolled and baked dough with some kind of jam in the center. There are strips of icing across the top.

"Mmm, looks good," Fatma says as she takes a piece and lets the icing melt on her tongue. It's not too sweet, which surprises her.

The girls sip their cappuccinos slowly. "This is good," Fatma comments, taking another bite of the pastry.

"No," Claudia is adamant. "You are not going to avoid this, Fatma. You have to tell somebody and have a doctor examine you. What if it's more serious than just needing glasses?"

"A doctor? Oh, no. I don't want to go to a doctor. Really, most of the time, I don't even notice that anything is wrong. This only happens once in a while." Fatma is regretting that she has said anything.

"My Papa's first cousin is an eye surgeon. He lives not too far from *Nonna*, and he works at the hospital right here in the city. I'm sure Papa could ask him to examine you while you're here. Then if everything turns out to be okay, and you are merely near sighted, we can leave it up to you to decide what to do. But what if it's more serious? Wouldn't you want to know?"

"I'm not sure I would. Please let me think about this. Oh, I never should have said anything." The pastry is suddenly making Fatma nauseous. She sets it back on the plate half eaten.

"Of course, you should have said something. You're my best friend. I would tell you now, wouldn't I?"

Fatma takes another sip of her cappuccino. This is news to her. She has become much closer to Claudia, but best friends? Badia is her best friend, and she has not really confided in Badia about this. Badia has questioned her, but she pretends it's nothing when Badia notices her squinting to make out the small print on a label, even at times the larger print. She has been afraid that Badia will respond as Claudia is now.

"Look," Claudia goes on, "I will swear Papa and Mamma to secrecy. You can decide for yourself whether or not to get glasses. I will make them promise. But you will need to see in order to go to school. You will need to see if you want to become a journalist like Badia, won't you?"

Fatma looks around the café. She is afraid that the Ferraris will turn up in the middle of this conversation and demand to know what they are discussing. But then she takes another deep breath. Maybe this is good. What Claudia is saying makes sense. She has been worried that the blurring of her sight might indicate something worse. And suddenly, the relief of having told someone brings her to tears.

Claudia rushes over to hug and to comfort her. Just then, the Ferraris enter the café. Claudia looks up and sees her parents approaching. She immediately runs back to her seat. They sit down next to the girls, giving Fatma just enough time to compose herself. Claudia's instant reaction to protect Fatma from exposure leads Fatma to believe she can trust her, and perhaps, also trust her parents.

"It's okay, Claudia. I think you're right. But only if I decide to let my family know."

At this moment, the waiter stops to hand menus to *Signor* and *Signora* Ferrari. "Just two espressos," he tells the young server and hands back the menus.

Signora Ferrari presses on. "Let your family know what?"

Claudia looks at Fatma. "Do you want to tell them?"

"Yes," Fatma decides. "But first, let them know my conditions."

Claudia explains to her parents and catches the expression on her mother's face.

"Don't worry, Mamma," Claudia chuckles, guessing her mother's first thoughts. "Fatma is not pregnant."

Everyone laughs with relief.

"I would never think something like that," *Signora* Ferrari defends herself.

"Right, Mamma. You say you would never think something like that. Papa would never think it, he's such an innocent, but you would." They both smile, more from relief, Fatma thinks, than anything else. It has certainly not occurred to her that this would even cross their minds. She is a good Muslim girl, for Allah's sake.

The waiter comes with the espressos. "Anything else?" he inquires.

"Not right now, thank you," *Signor* Ferrari says to the waiter in Italian. "So," he turns to Fatma, resuming in Turkish, "whatever is this deep secret?"

Fatma sighs. She knows she cannot take back what she has revealed. She can only go forward.

"I notice that I am losing some of my sight."

"How long has this been going on?" *Signor* Ferrari inquires.

"I couldn't say exactly. For a while now. It comes and goes. It's worse at night."

Without any prompting from Claudia, *Senior* Ferrari says, "There's a phone booth just around the corner. I'm going to call my cousin. He's an eye surgeon right here in town. Is that okay, Fatma? We're already here. Perhaps he can somehow have a look at you today. Will you let me do that?"

Once again, Fatma bursts into tears. These people are so kind. Now *Signora* Ferrari leans over to hug her.

"Oh, I'm so sorry," Fatma says. "I'm ruining your holiday with this. Perhaps it is time for me to tell *Baba*, and then I can see someone at home."

"Nonsense, my cousin is an acclaimed professor. He may not even be in his office today, but please let me try."

Fatma doesn't know what to do. From an early age, she has been trained by her *anne* not to be a bother to others. Fusun would send her to *Babaanne* when Fusun was tired or depressed with the expressed order not to bother Fusun's grandmother too much. *Babaanne* never gave Fatma the feeling that she was a bother, but she was always careful to try not to be.

On the other hand, Fatma thinks, Claudia and her parents do appear to be sincere. Perhaps a doctor she doesn't even know in Istanbul would not be as good a doctor as *Signor* Ferrari's cousin. After all, she reasons, he is a specialist.

"Okay," Fatma tells them, extricating herself from *Signora* Ferrari's arms and straightening herself back up in her chair, "Thank you. Go ahead." She wipes her face with her napkin.

"Why don't you all wait for me here?" *Signor* Ferrari suggests. "It might take a few minutes to get a hold of him."

The rest of that day is lost to Fatma. *Signor* Ferrari is gone from the café for some time. He returns to say that his cousin will see Fatma at the end of his day, as he is fully booked until 6:00 that evening. *Signor* Ferrari is further delayed, as he must call his mother to let her know that it is likely that they will not be back in time for dinner. She tells him that food will be saved and waiting for them should they return hungry.

Since it's already past 4:00, he suggests that they go back to the garage. They will make a quick stop to pick up the table for *Nonna*. The hospital is located on the other side of town, about a twenty-minute drive from the city center. This will allow them to get there close to the time of the appointment.

Fatma mumbles softly, "I've ruined everyone's day."

"Now that's silly," *Signora* Ferrari intercedes. "Please don't think like that. This is about your life, not just one day."

"Mamma is correct, Fatma. And I think I've seen enough for one day anyway."

"Yes, I'm tired, too. But I have to admit, I do feel better now that I've told you. I've been holding this in for too long. I think it will be a relief to finally know what is happening."

Signora Ferrari nods her head, and her eyes linger over Fatma tenderly. "Good," she says. When Fatma feels *Signora* Ferrari's gaze for too long, she looks away and quickly gathers her coat and purse. This kind of sympathy makes her uncomfortable, and yet, there is something so gratifying about being the recipient of such genuine concern from an older and wiser stranger she has already begun to admire. She is confused as to what she's feeling. She senses that she is being hurled into these circumstances, this quest for an answer, that she has been avoiding for so long, because they truly care about her. And yet, Fatma knows all of this action is occurring due to her own confession. No, she's not being hurled into anything. She's being encouraged, not forced.

Signora Ferrari and the girls wait just outside the café while *Signor* Ferrari pays the bill. The air is crisp and welcoming to Fatma after the stuffiness of the overfilled café. Fatma tries to control the warring voices her mind evokes. Run, girl, you still have time. Don't be a fool, now is your chance to find out what's going on. It could be nothing. Then again, it could be something. In the time they have left the table and stepped outside, Fatma has turned inward to the churning sea of conflict in her mind.

The walk from the café to the garage, picking up the table, the drive to the hospital, all of these little events Fatma feels she will not remember. She is residing in an alternate space. Her mind is too preoccupied with what the doctor might say for anything else to register.

The office of Dr. Lorenzo Alesso is not situated in the hospital itself but in a separate wing of the hospital where all of the doctors' offices are located. Obviously, *Signor* Ferrari has been here before, as he does not stop to ask for directions. Fatma thinks that if she had to find her own way out of this place, she might be terribly lost in the labyrinth of these busy corridors. Fatma is concentrating as hard as she can to numb any feeling in her body and to stay removed from her emotions. She treads behind them, determined not to give in to the urge to suddenly charge off in the opposite direction. As if they are all awed by her apprehensions, Claudia and her parents are silent.

They sit quietly in the waiting area of Dr. Lorenzo Alesso's office. Three rows of chairs are lined up as if in a classroom. There is a woman with a seeing eye dog. The dog is large, and the breed is not familiar to Fatma. Male or female, Fatma does not know which, the dog sleeps at the blind woman's feet, oblivious to the humans around. There aren't many waiting, as it is almost after hours for Dr. Alesso. There is an elderly man with his wife or sister, or maybe only a friend, Fatma cannot guess, who is accompanying him. They do not touch or even speak. It is as quiet as a funeral procession, Fatma thinks, maybe quieter. For her, she imagines, it might be a funeral procession on the way out, if her news is as bad as she thinks it will be. She is glad that the office makes no attempt to soothe waiting patients. The furnishings are simple, colorless. Only photos of eye procedures, charts with signs and symptoms of diseases of the eye, doctor degrees and qualifications line the walls. Well, Fatma decides, this man will be honest, as he does not try to sweeten what takes place here.

The door from the inner sanctum finally opens, and a nurse dressed in full white uniform steps inside and hands what appears to be a prescription to the woman with the dog. The nurse says something to her in Italian that Fatma doesn't understand. The woman with the dog thanks the nurse. She places the prescription in her pocket, and after slowly maneuvering her large and infirm body from her chair, she gently rousts the slumbering dog. Like his master—it is a male, as she calls him Fredo—his movements are slow and labored. As they make their way out of the office, Fatma wonders which of them will die first. Will this woman have to get another dog, or will the dog need a new blind owner?

The nurse comes back a few minutes later and addresses *Signor* Ferrari. "*Signor* Ferrari, we are sorry to keep you waiting. There is only the one patient before you. The doctor will be with you very soon. And who is the patient here?" she asks.

"This is Fatma." He reaches across to put his hand on Fatma's shoulder. "She is my daughter's friend and is traveling with us."

"Hello, Fatma. I am Nurse Ricci. So nice to meet you. It might be as long as a half an hour if you would like to go to have something to drink." She says this in Italian and Claudia translates.

"I'm fine, thank you," Fatma responds in Turkish, and Claudia translates back to the nurse.

"Okay then," Nurse Ricci says. She motions the man and woman to come inside with her.

Fatma wonders if it is the man or the woman who is the patient now. She has assumed for some reason that it is the man.

Claudia turns to her. "Do you want to talk, or would you rather just be quiet?"

"Thank you. I think I'd rather be quiet." Claudia takes her hand, squeezes it, and then lets it go.

It occurs to Fatma once again that she has not given her friend enough credit. Claudia has proven herself to be an unselfish and kind person. She is like her parents. They surely would have liked to have spent more time with *Nonna*, or at least gotten back in time to join her for dinner, but not a word has been said. Matteo is sleeping in the car, preparing to drive them back in the evening after the appointment. Fatma reflects that she would not like to have Matteo's job. Sitting around and waiting for people all day would be totally unsuitable for her. Then she remembers that *Nonna* rarely leaves the house, so this is unusual for Matteo as well. But no one complains or gives her the least indication of impatience or irritation. Still, she feels that she is a huge inconvenience.

Time passes slowly. Claudia's parents have brought their reading with them. Claudia rests her head on *Signora* Ferrari's shoulder and closes her eyes. Fatma begins to read the charts on the wall. She is impressed. Lorenzo Alesso has a number of credentials. He has graduated from Baylor University Medical School in the United States, somewhere in Dallas, Texas, a place Fatma has never heard of until now. But a university in America must be very good, she thinks. There is some other writing on plaques she cannot read but what she has seen is enough. She did not expect to see a doctor who had studied in the United States. She doesn't think they would find someone like this in Istanbul. She hopes it will not be hard to communicate with him. Her English is not strong, although she has studied English in school. Anything complicated, she fears, will go completely over her head. And she has less Italian than English. Oh, the complication of language. She has never felt this so acutely as she does now.

The man and the woman finally emerge from the inner office. Now the woman puts her arm through the man's. Still, Fatma thinks, there is no way to tell their relationship. Suddenly she has to acknowledge that a curiosity about people she doesn't know has suddenly developed within her. This comes from being with Claudia. Fatma is amused.

Several long minutes pass before the door to the doctor's inner office bursts open. A tall, slender man, with shaggy but fashionable blond hair and a carefully trimmed mustache and beard, emerges with arms open wide for *Signor* Ferrari. Dressed in slacks with a long white jacket over his shirt and tie, Fatma gets her first glimpse of Dr. Alesso. The two men are embracing one another. They hug and plant a kiss on each cheek. Fatma wonders if this greeting is for family only, or do all Italian men greet each other this way. Clearly there is much affection between the two men.

To Fatma's unexpected surprise and pleasure, Dr. Alesso greets her in Turkish when she is introduced to him by *Signor* Ferrari. "Do you really speak Turkish?" she asks him in astonishment, fearing that this greeting is all he will be able to say.

Dr. Alesso laughs. He is warm and friendly, not at all stuffy, as Fatma would expect from an esteemed surgeon. "My stepfather is Turkish, and so my mother became fairly fluent. I had to learn if I wanted to understand what they were talking about when they didn't want me to know. I learned purely as a defense."

Fatma takes the hand he holds out to her in greeting. She is not used to shaking hands with men she doesn't know, but she is not shy with this one. "Your Turkish is so good," she says in earnest. "I thought I would have to have someone translate for me. My Italian is very poor, and my English is not good either. Oh, I am so glad you can speak with me in my own language. I want to make sure I understand everything you have to say."

"Well, let me have a good look at you first," Dr. Alesso says. "Come back inside with me. I understand you may wish to be private about all of this, so what you wish to share with the Ferraris is up to you."

"Thank you, Doctor." Fatma is relieved. She is unsure how she wants to handle the news, whatever it might be. Will she even share it with anyone other than the doctor? She is grateful that everyone is listening to her and guarding her right to privacy.

"We're going to be awhile, so if you folks would like to come back in an hour, there's a coffee shop and a cafeteria one floor down. If you aren't back yet, we can come to get you. Fatma is, of course, my last patient of the day."

The Ferrari's are still seated in the waiting room when Dr. Alesso takes Fatma to his examining rooms. She had wondered if the exam would hurt, but there is nothing like that in this consultation. Dr. Alesso asks her to cover one eye and read from the uncovered eye. He introduces lights, lines of lights, flashes of lights. He puts drops in each eye that he says will help him to see better what is going on inside. All of these procedures are exhausting for Fatma. In any event, she complies with all of the doctor's directions, as she wants the best exam she can possibly obtain from him. She knows that she will not be able to explain to anyone later on exactly what all of this maneuvering has entailed. She is too busy focusing all of her attention on the doctor's directions.

At one point, Fatma says to Dr. Alesso, "I saw outside in the waiting area that you went to school in America. That is impressive."

"Ha," he laughs, exposing all of his very white teeth. "That was all my mother's doing. She prodded me to apply, and then she prodded my stepfather to pay. It wasn't easy for me. It was easier for my stepfather, as I did manage a scholarship. But I was the one who had to make the grades and to work in the lab to be eligible for the scholarship. Truly, I saw very little of America. I'm glad that I did it, though. My English improved and patients love to see the diploma among my credentials. Just like you did."

"Was it hard for you to live in another country?" Fatma asks.

"Very hard," Dr. Alesso says quickly. "I missed speaking my own language. So, I was always looking for other Italian speakers. They weren't so easy to find in Texas. I never had a single dream in English. Okay, now, I'm going to darken the room. You'll see different flashes of white light. Please tell me when and where you see them."

Fatma's eyes are heavy. Just when she feels she will have to stop the testing, Dr. Alesso switches the overhead lights back on. "That's all, Fatma. You've done very well. I'll need a few minutes to look at all of these results. Why don't you just relax here while I do that. Would you like a glass of water?"

"Yes, Doctor, thank you."

Dr. Alesso brings her a large glass of cold water from another room; then he shuts off the lights so that Fatma can rest her eyes. Fatma takes long drinks of the soothing water until the glass is empty. She sets the glass down on a nearby table. She closes her eyes and tries to take in deep breaths. What will the doctor say when he returns?

When Fatma opens her eyes, Dr. Alesso has quietly entered the room and is standing over her. "Are you okay?" he asks.

"Oh, yes, I'm fine. I was just resting my eyes."

"Good," Dr. Alesso tells her. "These exams can be pretty tiring. He pulls a stool across from Fatma. He sits and looks directly into her eyes. "I do not have good news," he warns her, "but it could be worse."

"Tell me," Fatma says, awake now and ready to hear whatever Dr. Alesso has to say.

"It's simple and not so common. We're still learning. There are a series of rods and cones in your retina, as there are in all of our eyes. Some of yours have died and still others are in various stages of dying. The good news about this is that this process could take many years, and you may never become completely blind. And we can fit you with glasses that will help somewhat for a while. The bad news is that we don't have a cure for this. We also can't predict how much sight you will lose or at what rate. Medical science, unfortunately, doesn't have all the answers."

Fatma feels the tears silently gliding down her cheeks. "Does this disease have a name?"

"It's called retinitis pigmentosa, but it merely means that the rods and cones in the retina of both eyes are dying. We don't yet have a procedure to stop this."

"And you won't have one in time for me?"

"That I don't know." Dr. Alesso sighs, leaning forward with one of his large hands spread across each of his knees. "We are studying and trying to see if something can be done, but we don't have anything yet. We learn more and more all the time, so it's possible but uncertain. Did anyone in your family have a loss of sight?"

Fatma thinks for a few minutes. "My mother died when she was still very young, so I can't say if she would have lost sight when she was older. I don't remember her ever complaining about her vision. I never knew my father."

Fatma finds her voice slightly cracking at the first utterance of these words. "My great grandfather, my grandfather's father, lost much of his sight before he died. He never went to see a doctor, as far as I know. I think they just came to the conclusion that it was old age. It wasn't really noticeable until he was old. He used a cane and didn't really go anywhere. He died a few years back."

"It's possible that he left you an unhappy inheritance, but hard to know." The doctor gets up from his stool to hand Fatma a couple of tissues from a box on his desk. Then he sits back down in the swivel chair behind his desk. Fatma thinks that Dr. Alesso must be quite tired, too. The clock on the wall indicates that it is close to 8:00 in the evening.

"I thank you, doctor." Fatma manages to get the words out without bursting into sobs. "What do I owe you?" Fatma reaches for her bag.

"No, no. That isn't necessary. You are like family to Claudia and her parents. They are my family. We never charge family members."

"Are you quite sure?" Fatma asks. "I have money to pay you, and I'm not really family."

"Is this a strange Turkish custom that I know nothing about? My stepfather would say thank you and walk away happy."

"I'm sure that your stepfather is a good man, but we Turkish have a lot of pride."

"Well, today you will have to let go of some of that pride. I refuse to take money from you." A little smile turns up the very corners of Dr. Alesso's mouth.

This smile lets Fatma know that he will continue to refuse payment. "Then I will be grateful and say thank you. I will always remember your kindness."

Dr. Alesso starts to give Fatma a hand to help her from her seat and then just as suddenly pulls it back. Fatma thinks he must be aware of Muslim restrictions around non-married men and women touching. She silently appreciates his consideration. He doesn't ask if she will share her diagnosis with the Ferraris. He walks her out to the waiting area where the Ferraris are still sitting. Dr. Alesso hugs all of his cousins affectionately and tells them that they are always welcome. They should visit him at home more often when they are back in Italy. There are other farewells in Italian, but there is no need for Fatma to know what they are saying. She knows it has nothing to do with her.

Matteo is waiting for them where they left him with the car. He greets them politely and asks no questions. He surely must be curious how a day planned full of sightseeing has brought them to the hospital. He knows not to ask. Fatma admires his instincts. Of course, Fatma thinks, this is crucial to his job and thus, to his life.

The ride back to *Nonna's* is enveloped in silence. Fatma has said nothing about the results of her tests, and the Ferraris, like Matteo, have enough sense not to ask. Fatma is so impressed with this that she determines that she will tell them, but not just now. She needs time to digest the information herself. Since there is no cure, there is also no rush. At this point, she has no intention of getting glasses. She closes her eyes and pretends to be asleep. Fatma is not up to any conversation. She doesn't stir until they have reached *Nonna's* home and Claudia taps her shoulder.

"We're here," Claudia tells her when she is conscious again.

Fatma asks if it will be okay if she skips dinner and goes straight to bed. No one objects. It appears to Fatma that *Nonna* also has some good judgment regarding when not to ask questions.

And so, without further ado, Fatma goes to her bedroom. The fatigue in her eyes from the lengthy examination will not allow her to sort out her muddled feelings. The fire has been lit, Fatma assumes by Maria, and as soon as her head hits the pillows, she is sound asleep.

CHAPTER 33

Fatma wakes to the sound of knocking. She rolls over once to face the door and then asks, "Who is it?"

"It's me." Claudia asks if it is alright to enter. Fatma thinks this is strange. Yesterday Claudia came in and bounced into bed with her. Today she is asking if she can come in. Are they all afraid of her now? Does she seem too vulnerable? But she hasn't told them her diagnosis yet. Perhaps they have guessed that it could not be good.

"Come in!" Fatma says this in what she thinks might be an excited, enthusiastic voice. She doesn't want to ruin another day of their vacation. If they are all so wary of hurting her, nothing is going to feel natural.

And it does appear that Claudia is approaching Fatma's bed self-consciously, tiptoeing cautiously and sitting with unusual delicacy on the edge of her bed.

"Is something wrong, Claudia? Well, come over here and tell me what it is." Fatma pats her hand on the quilt next to her.

Claudia jumps off the bed and comes running around to Fatma, taking her in her arms. "Oh, I'm so sorry, dear Fatma. You don't need this bad news on top of everything. *Babaanne* has taken a bad fall and broken her hip. She's in hospital in Kayseri. Your *baba* is on his way there. You can see the wire he sent. It arrived this morning. How awful for her and how awful for us. Why, you've just begun your vacation." Claudia hands Fatma the telegram.

Babaanne fell. Broke her hip. Going to Kayseri today to hospital. Cemal and Salman there now. Sorry to give you bad news. No need to come home. Love, Baba.

Fatma fingers the telegram, reads it several times, as if she might have misread it the first time. Tomorrow is Christmas. Today they are supposed to hang decorations on the large pine tree that Matteo will erect in *Nonna's* living room. Fatma has planned to wrap the little gifts she has brought from Turkey to place under the tree. She had determined to go with the family to church, the midnight mass, purely out of curiosity. She thought the opportunity to see a Catholic Christmas ceremony might never come again. Claudia has told her the music is beautiful. On the other hand, if *Babaanne* should die before she can say good-bye to her, she doesn't know if she will ever be able to forgive herself. Suppose she never gets to see or to speak with *Babaanne* again? Is this what life is like? As soon as she recovers from one assault, must she keep up her guard for yet another? Whatever is she going to do now? Even though the answer is fairly clear, she can't embrace it.

In some ways, it's typical of *Baba* to tell her that there is no need to come home. He knows that will be her first thought, and though he wants to make sure that she doesn't consider this event lightly, he is giving her the facts without pressure or judgment. Muhsine is such a good influence on him. His marriage to her has made him a softer, more considerate person.

And there is, of course, the train ride home. It will take so long. No, there is no way she can wait until after Christmas. She must quickly dismiss all her anxiety of traveling alone. Her fears could stop her. She doesn't want to make such a difficult decision out of fear. What shall I do, she asks herself? Whatever shall I do?

Fatma realizes that Claudia is still standing at her bedside, waiting for some reaction from Fatma, any reaction at all. But Fatma cannot seem to tear her eyes from the telegram.

Claudia says, "Please come down when you're ready. We can talk about what to do then."

"Thank you," Fatma says again, recognizing Claudia's kindness. "I'll freshen up and then come down. I need to think a bit on my own."

"I understand," Claudia says, and Fatma believes finally that she does.

Fatma takes a long, hot bath. Since she has already decided what it is that she must do, she allows her mind to be empty during the bath, but once she is dressed and her bag is packed, her determination waivers. Her memory of the long trip here is too fresh in her mind to have faded at all. The thought of the trains and how they might suddenly change route merely by an announcement only in French or Italian, the number of soldiers packed onto the train, and worst of all, the number of hours of sitting—this is all too much for her.

And now Fatma feels even more vulnerable knowing that even though it will be a slow process, she will eventually lose either most or all of her vision. She leaves her suitcase in the room and slowly makes her way downstairs and into the breakfast nook. When she passes the large window there, she sees that it is snowing lightly. The long line of cypress trees are only lightly dusted at this point, looking like someone has spread powdered sugar over them from above. She pauses there, taking in their magnificence, trying to imagine what her future darkened world will be like. She cannot.

Claudia looks up and sees Fatma at the window, just outside the breakfast nook. She gets up from the table and walks over to her. "Those trees are stunning in the snow. We're lucky to see them like this. Snow doesn't happen too often here at any time, never mind Christmas."

"Yes, they are straight out of a fairy tale," Fatma tells her, while thinking to herself, I have to put everything into my memory so carefully now. There are many sights that I may never see again, and not only because I may never come to Italy again. Should I tell them?

The two girls join the family at the table. Everyone greets Fatma, but they don't begin to quiz her as her own family would have done. Once again, the breakfast choices are numerous. This morning there are also chocolate croissants, along with cheese and plain ones. There is a variety of fruit, homemade yogurt, and muesli. No eggs, Fatma notes. They don't appear to eat them for breakfast here. And of course, a cappuccino is brought out for Fatma by Maria, who smiles at her and whispers, "Now you are Italian, coffee instead of tea." Fatma understands the meaning and smiles back at her.

When Fatma finishes the food on her plate and is sipping her coffee, she looks around the room. She almost wants to giggle at the family's restraint. But the urge passes quickly, and she announces, "I must go home. I am so sorry to do this. You're all so lovely and kind."

Nonna looks puzzled and turns to *Signora* Ferrari who translates for her. She shakes her head and mutters something in Italian. *Signora* Ferrari says to Fatma, "She's not happy that you have to leave, but she understands. She says you are a good girl to love your grandmother so."

"She is actually my great grandmother," Fatma corrects her. "We don't really know her exact age, but she must be close to ninety, if not beyond."

"Does that make *Baba* your grandfather?" *Signor* Ferrari asks.

"Long story, Papa," Claudia cautions him. "Let's talk about all of that another time."

"Of course," he responds quickly. "Okay then. I will pack a small case, get you back home and come back here. The holiday itself is not so important to me," he tries to reassure Fatma. "Please don't try to argue with me, Fatma. The times are not good. I must see you home safely."

"Oh, but I must object, *Signor* Ferrari. I've taken too much time from your family already. You can't possibly take me all the way back to Istanbul and then turn around and come all the way back here!"

"Oh, yes I can," *Signor* Ferrari insists. "You forget that I'm used to traveling for my business. What may seem like a long distance to you is quite manageable for me. And letting you travel alone is out of the question. The trains will not be crowded on Christmas Day. We will each choose a book, and we can read all the way." He looks winningly at Fatma. "Before you know it, you'll be home again."

And then off to Kayseri, Fatma thinks. What she says is simply, "I will never know how to thank you." What a relief it is to Fatma that she will not have to make this trip alone, but she feels guilty for taking *Signor* Ferrari away from his family Christmas celebration and from his elderly mother. Fatma also knows *Signor* Ferrari has already made his decision and that he will never allow her to travel on her own. Maybe there is one way to thank them. And Fatma decides quickly that she owes them a diagnosis.

"I'm sure that you're all curious as to what Dr. Alesso found," she says, looking down at her plate. "The condition I have is called retinitis pigmentosa. The rods and cones of my retina are slowly dying. It might take a long time for me to lose all my vision, and then again, I may not lose it all. The science isn't there yet. They just don't know. Dr. Alesso says there is currently no cure. Those thick glasses that I don't want will help somewhat. I don't know yet what I'll do. Please, *Signor* Ferrari, please don't tell my *baba*. I will tell him, but not just yet."

"I give you my word, although I might push you from time to time to know if you've told him. He does need to know eventually."

"I know," Fatma replies. "Just not yet. We must all give our attention to *Babaanne* now."

PART IV
AVANOS

CHAPTER 34

Fatma rolls from side to side, but she gains no relief from the stabbing and piercing of her labor pains. She curses everyone who comes near her, which is why Cemal has ushered Cengiz out the door and off to make more pots. Salman, Cengiz's father, is working at a much slower pace these days, and he really does need Cengiz to keep up production. Salman and Cengiz are both hoping that Fatma will deliver a son who will be able to eventually come into the pottery business. Fatma, on the other hand, is praying for a daughter. She has no idea what she will do with a son.

Badia is wiping the sweat from Fatma's brow, but Fatma finds it is more annoying than comforting. She pushes the cloth away. Badia lays it down on the table next to the bed and takes Fatma's hand in hers. "It will be over soon," she tells Fatma.

Fatma lashes out at her, "Since when have you become the baby expert? You've never been through this!"

Badia smiles at Fatma, "And it's a good thing, too, since I'm not married and probably never will be. If only you would stop groaning and push my niece out of that big belly of yours, I would at least have the pleasure of being an aunt." Badia is the only one who can make Fatma stop screaming and shouting at the people who are trying to help her. This time she almost gets a smile from Fatma, although many would see it as more of a grimace.

So much time has passed since Fatma returned so hurriedly from her trip to Italy. *Babaanne* is gone now, but she did live for another six months after her fall. Her hip never healed properly. She fell again. Cemal found her outside in the small vegetable garden. There was a large basket lying next to her half-filled with the weeds she had obviously been pulling at the time. No one knew why she'd been out there, probably a lifetime of working so hard and the frustration and boredom that comes from not being able to do very much.

And when Fatma and Cengiz met again, after *Babaanne's* first fall, so much had changed for both of them. Azra, Cengiz's friend, had only stayed one more day after Fatma arrived. As it turned out, Fatma discovered the letter that Cengiz had written to her explaining why he was bringing Azra home. The letter had not arrived in time for Fatma to see it before she left for Italy. *Baba* had carried the letter to Avanos with him. Fatma had instantly liked Azra and regretted her foolish jealousy. Both girls expressed how sorry they were that the visit had to be cut short, but everyone was so involved with caring for *Babaanne* that Azra ended up leaving early by her own decision. "I will try to visit again," she promised. "This is just not the right time. You all have so many decisions to make. And there is Salman to consider as well."

"Salman?" Fatma had asked, looking directly at Cengiz.

"We will talk about it all later," Cengiz had assured her.

And when they had talked about it later, Fatma learned that *Babaanne* was not the only casualty of the time she'd been gone. Salman had suffered a heart attack. He had been ordered to bed rest and of course, had taken no time off at all. The upshot was that Cengiz had decided not to continue his education but to stay in Avanos in order to help his father with the business. First of all, of course, he would have to learn the business. As a young boy, he had never been interested. Now he was determined to be.

Cengiz encouraged Fatma to go on to university, but she had lost interest. She no longer wished to leave Cengiz or *Babaanne*. She knew that she would miss *Baba* and Badia terribly, but she could always travel to Istanbul to spend time with them, or so she thought. And now that *Babaanne* was so weak, she was sure that *Baba*, at the very least, would come to Avanos more frequently. She felt that they would resolve these issues in the best way that they could.

Salman and Cengiz built an add-on room where Fatma could stay comfortably with *Babaanne* until she and Cengiz married. Fatma had determined that she would marry Cengiz at age eighteen. And so, eventually, Cengiz got his old room back after sleeping for a couple of months on pillows in the family gathering room.

And now, almost one year to the day of their wedding, Fatma is delivering her first child.

"Right at this moment," Fatma groans, "I would wish neither marriage nor childbirth on any woman. One does lead to the other, you know!"

"It's much too late for that now," Badia insists. "Just push as hard as you can."

"It hurts too much," Fatma protests. But then Cemal and the midwife enter the room together. The midwife is skinny, and Fatma is willing to bet her whole future on the assumption that the midwife has never had a baby. Fatma is surer of this than she is of the midwife's name, which escapes her now.

Everyone is telling Fatma to push. And then, Fatma hollers, "shush, all of you. Just be quiet." She takes in a deep, deep breath, pushes with all her might until Badia shouts, "Here's the head! Look!"

The midwife is stronger than she appears. She pushes everyone out of her way and dives in to rescue the infant who finally, after a bit more coaxing, lies limp and naked in her hands. "It's a girl," she sings out, pushing the infant into one arm, turning her over, and smacking her into the first cries of her life.

Fatma holds out her arms. "Oh, it is a girl. Give her to me. I so hoped it would be a girl, but ssshhh, Cengiz wanted a boy. Oh, I'm so happy!" For the first time in many months, Fatma laughs with glee. Her pregnancy has not been easy, but this baby is so perfect, so beautiful; her skin is so soft. She counts every finger and toe and checks both thumbs. She cannot resist taking a good look at the baby's genitals, as a penis is not something she wishes to see. Ah, indeed, this baby is perfect she thinks; she has finally stopped torturing my insides. "Cut this damn cord, will you please? I'm ready for us to be two people."

"Not so fast," Cemal cautions. "You think it's over? The cord is cut and that's it? Heaven help the poor baby who has a mother who can't wait to have her child's umbilical cord cut. This is the beginning, my dear. Now you must learn to be a mother. Believe me, I've had three of them."

The midwife picks up the knife she has prepared for this task, and Badia quickly looks away. "Sorry," she mumbles. "I'm okay with the baby coming out, but I think I will not watch this."

"What will you name her?" the midwife asks as she reaches to take the baby from Fatma in order to wash her, give her a diaper and dress her in her soft baby dress.

"I have a name picked out for her." Fatma gently hands the baby over to the midwife. She does not relinquish her easily.

"What will you name her?" Badia asks. "And don't you have to talk this over with Cengiz?"

"We had already decided that if it was a girl, I would name her. And if it was a boy, Cengiz would name him. We asked Cemal and Salman, and then we asked *Baba* and Muhsine. But they are all so modern." Fatma grins at Cemal. She would have been Ahmet if she'd been a boy."

"So?" Badia asks, impatient.

"She is Pinar, a spring, flowing in the mountains. Pinar, a spring of mountain water."

"Pinar Celik," Cemal tries it on her tongue. "I'm still not used to having a surname," she says.

"Ah," Fatma sighs, reaching up to take back her freshly cleaned baby. "So, I'm calling her a fresh mountain spring of water against her last name meaning 'steel.' I don't know how I feel about getting a surname. Somehow it doesn't feel right to me yet either."

"But the surname is good," Badia says. "She will flow like a mountain spring that is protected and surrounded by a guardian of steel."

Fatma looks up at Badia and smiles. "And saying those kind words will get you to be the first to hold her after me." She hands the now sleeping baby to Badia.

"You see that," the midwife cries. "I never get any credit. I was the first to hold her."

"I'm sorry," Fatma tells her. "I don't even know your name."

"It is Nehir," she says. "I am the river who has delivered the mountain spring."

"Deliver, ha!" Fatma watches Pinar nestling against Badia's breast. "This baby delivered herself, and she took her time in doing it, I might add."

"But there is that element of flowing water," Cemal exclaims, "and that's a good omen. We are in the desert, after all."

Fatma's eyelids begin to flutter, and she knows she will soon be asleep. "I'm so happy," she sighs. "Her life won't be easy. A woman's life never is. But we will do all we can for her, won't we?"

"Of course, we will," Badia declares. "Let's all hold hands and make it a contract."

Badia hands the baby, now fast asleep, to the midwife, Nehir, and the women join hands and close their eyes. Badia says, as if she has been doing this her whole life, "Praises be to Allah, we will love this little one and cherish her. We will teach her everything she needs to know. And...," Badia opens her eyes and lifts her voice to a sharp wail. "I will be the best auntie who has ever lived, *mashallah!*"

The women open their eyes, grinning ear to ear. Badia looks over at her mother. "You know, *Anne*," she says, "we will have to make this pact all over again when Muhsine gets here."

"They are on their way," Cemal says. "Muhsine didn't want to travel without Ali. And you know how your *baba* is about the restaurant, Fatma. He has good help now, that Armenian fellow, but he still doesn't trust anyone else to run *Balık Baba*."

Fatma sees that Cengiz is making his way into the room. She guesses that he's been just outside the door for some time now and listening, and so he must know that he has a baby girl.

The midwife offers the peacefully sleeping Pinar up to her father. "Ah, here is my beautiful daughter. I guess I will have to wait for my sons, eh? But now we have you to help your mother with them when they come." Pinar suddenly squeezes her face into what must be a gas bubble but looks more like protest. This passes quickly, and they all laugh but Fatma.

And Fatma mutters under her breath so that no one hears her but Badia, "And that will be a long wait, Cengiz, if I have anything to say about it." Fatma's eyes stay open long enough for her to catch the look of disapproval on Badia's face. Fatma's thoughts still pierce in her sleepy state of mind. You just wait, Badia, she thinks. You will marry one day, and then you'll find out all about this. It's not a picnic to be pregnant or to give birth. Her eyes do not open again, as she is now fast asleep.

CHAPTER 35

Fatma awakens to the gurgling ripples of baby sounds. She rolls over onto her back and sees Cengiz quietly waltzing around the room with the bundled Pinar in his arms.

"I am sorry that she is Pinar and not Ahmet," Fatma says softly.

"But she's my beautiful Pinar! That's enough for me now. The sons will come."

Fatma sighs. "It's a bit soon for me to think of that. First, I must learn how to be a mother. It's good that I have your *anne* to help me. Oh, Cengiz, I so wish *Babaanne* could have lived to see her and to help me raise her. *Babaanne* had enough love in her heart for all of us."

"You will have plenty of help in raising her. And plenty of love as well. First of all, I'm here, and I'm her *baba*. My *anne* is already swelling with the pride of her first grandchild. She has been holding court in the shop and promising everyone that as soon as Pinar and you have had forty days at home together, she will bring Pinar for everyone's observation, and we will have a naming dinner. What do you think?" Cengiz shifts Pinar's head so that she can see her mother's face. "What do you say to that, Pinar?" He lifts the baby up and turns her face towards him. She begins to cry, and just as suddenly she begins to holler.

Fatma raises herself up in the bed. "Give her to me, please, my dear Cengiz. Our little girl is hungry."

"You see," Gengiz says, grinning as he hands Pinar to Fatma, "you know just what she needs and what to do. You are a natural mother."

"I don't know about that," Fatma takes Pinar and pulls down her nightgown to expose her breast.

"I will be back." Cengiz looks horrified that he might possibly observe breastfeeding and practically runs from the room.

Fatma laughs. It is her second burst of laughter since her water broke. Pinar fits snugly against her breast. Fatma adjusts the baby's mouth slightly, but she and Pinar seem to be doing quite well with the feeding. Fatma knows that this was not true for Fusun. Fusun had refused to breastfeed, and *Babaanne* had to hire a woman from the village who had lost her child at birth. Once Pinar is peacefully sucking, Fatma finds the experience surprisingly pleasant. My goodness, she thinks, I'm feeding my baby from my own breasts. How absolutely lovely this is. I think it is much better than sex.

Although Fatma has adjusted to her sexual life, she cannot, no matter how hard she tries, see the big deal. Although Cengiz is tender, and she knows he loves her, she wonders if her husband is a poor lover, an inexperienced lover, or that this is all there is. In which case, why does everyone make such a huge fuss about it? Or could it just be her own failure? Fatma has no idea. She would have felt comfortable asking *Babaanne*, but she does not feel comfortable asking anyone else. After their wedding night, all Fatma could think about was her mother's rape. How did she ever withstand such a thing? Cengiz is so careful with her. Fatma tries not to think of how her *anne* must have suffered. She has found it a bit painful herself, but she keeps that hidden from Cengiz. Of course, it is now much better than the first night. She cried and cried, and poor Cengiz didn't know what to do. He completely misread her tears. "It's okay that you're no longer a virgin," he consoled her. "You are a married woman now."

Oh, if only *Babaanne* were here. She certainly can't talk to Badia. She is a virgin, as far as Fatma knows. And Muhsine? She's too shy and embarrassed to do so. Cemal is Cengiz's *anne*. She can't possibly talk to her.

As if she has been summoned, Cemal enters the room. "Can I help you with anything, dear? Oh, my, she's feeding so easily. Cengiz tried to bite off my nipple."

"If you can take her as soon as she's willing, I do need to use the bathroom." Fatma is a bit unsettled by the picture now in her mind of an adult Cengiz biting his *anne's* nipple. No, she determines, I won't talk to anyone. Maybe one day. What a crazy thing life is. People are so difficult to understand. I wonder what Cengiz would say if I talked to him. I'm too afraid of hurting his feelings. He asks if I am okay, and I say, yes, of course and smile, and I pretend to have enjoyed it as much as he seems to.

When Pinar's sucking slows and then stops, Fatma hands the sleeping infant to her *babaanne*. "She is drunk on my milk, so I'd better get to the bathroom before she cries for more."

"Shall I change her diaper while you go?"

"Please." Fatma struggles to disengage herself from the bedclothes. "Thank you." Well, Fatma thinks, as she heads as quickly as she can to the indoor western toilet Salman has installed with Cengiz's help, having parents around to help is good, even if there is no one she can ask about how to make the sex better. At least they can cook and change diapers.

How far I have come, Fatma thinks, as she flushes the relatively new toilet. And yet, I have not really gone anywhere at all. But I do have a loving family, a child born out of love with a husband, something my *anne* never had. And something she did not live to see me have. What a shame and a waste of Fusun's life.

Fatma takes her time washing her hands, happy to be on her feet again. She sneaks a brief look at her face in the mirror; then she lifts her gown to stare at her distended belly. She pats herself and smiles. Fat in the name of childbearing is not such a terrible thing, she reflects, but she knows she will want to get rid of this as soon as possible. She runs her fingers through her hair and picks up a brush for the first time in what feels like days. I would love to wash this messy mane before *Baba* and Muhsine arrive, she muses, but I will be doing well to brush my teeth. She does this slowly and deliberately before returning to Cemal and Pinar. Pinar is fast asleep with a clean diaper and a tummy filled with intoxicating breast milk. Fatma takes the infant, sits in a large chair by the bed, and is soon sleeping almost as peacefully as her child.

Fatma is sitting alone on a stone bench dressed in a white lace wedding gown. She looks down at the intricate patterns of henna someone has painted on her hands. She watches for Fusun and Babaanne to appear. How can she possibly marry without them? Fatma notices that she is surrounded by giant stalks of sunflowers in full bloom. When she rises to pluck one, she almost trips. Her floor-length veil has become hooked to a crack in the stone. She turns to detach the caught threads, dismayed to see that she has now created a hole in the delicate material. Fatma stops and stares at the ruined lace. This is not my bridal gown or veil, she realizes. She reaches out to grasp hold of a sunflower stem and tries to pluck it from its thick stalk. There is a struggle before she can finally break it loose. When she looks down at the bench to sit again, a young woman is seated there in the very gown and veil she had been wearing. Fatma's own clothing is transformed to simple dress. Who are you? she asks the young woman. The girl doesn't answer, but gazes straight ahead, as if she has not seen Fatma at all. But Fatma knows. She cannot help but to recognize her daughter, Pinar.

****

Finally finding herself alone in the kitchen with Muhsine that same afternoon, a couple of hours after *Baba* and Muhsine have arrived and fussed over a somewhat cranky Pinar, Fatma decides to tell her stepmother about the dream she's had. The others are in the outside courtyard that separates the pottery shop from the living quarters. The early fall air wafts through the open door and windows, embracing Fatma with cool breezes. Fatma looks outside and sees that Cengiz is struggling to keep Pinar's head from slumping down into the crook of his elbow. She considers that Cengiz is slowly discovering and adjusting to the physical demands of fatherhood, albeit a bit awkwardly. Most fortunate for Pinar, he isn't the one doing the breastfeeding.

Fatma turns to Muhsine who is sipping the last of a cup of *çay*. They are both seated at the long wooden table Fatma's great grandfather made years ago. The family salvaged the long and heavy piece of furniture from the cave dwelling in Goreme where Fatma was born.

"Just before you and *Baba* got here, I fell asleep and had a dream. This dream felt more like a warning than a dream. It wasn't a bad dream, but it did seem strange."

Muhsine looks across the table at Fatma and shakes her head. "I am not your *babaanne*. I cannot make much sense of my own dreams, never mind yours."

"That's okay. I understand. I don't expect you to interpret but just to listen. Between the two of us, we might have a thought."

"Sure, go ahead." Muhsine takes her last sip of *çay* and pushes her now empty glass to the side.

"I'm sitting on a bench somewhere in a field of sunflowers. I'm wearing a beautiful and very elegant wedding dress, much fancier than the one I wore to marry Cengiz."

"Oh, but your dress was gorgeous," Muhsine interrupts.

"I didn't mean that mine wasn't." Fatma responds quickly. Muhsine helped her to pick out that dress, and it was lovely. "But mine was of much simpler lines. The dress in my dream was covered in lace with a very long veil. I almost tripped when I caught it on a crack in the bench when I got up to pluck a sunflower. Now that I think about it, I don't remember any shoes."

"Maybe that's because you pulled yours off so quickly after the ceremony," Muhsine laughs.

"Oh, my poor, poor feet," Fatma recalls. "I had never worn shoes like that. I was so afraid I'd fall and break my neck. Not a good omen for a wedding day."

"Praise be to Allah; all went so well. But what happened next?"

Fatma rubs her left breast, now a touch tender from Pinar's hungry sucking. "Well, this is the weird part. Suddenly, I'm not the woman on the bench. I'm standing and looking at her, but she doesn't see me. She's wearing the wedding clothes, and I'm dressed in my everyday working duds." Fatma stops there, hesitating.

"Is there more?" Muhsine asks, running a forefinger over a natural wood marking in the table.

"It sounds so odd," Fatma tells her, leaning forward as if revealing a secret. "I knew in the dream that the young girl was Pinar."

"Really? How could you know? Pinar has only been in this world a couple of days."

Fatma wonders if Muhsine is joking or serious, but her expression indicates that no humor is intended. Muhsine is often concrete in her thinking. Fatma reflects for a moment. "I honestly could not tell you how I knew. I just did. And I am quite sure of it as I sit here now."

The two women are interrupted by the cries of either a hungry Pinar or a Pinar who needs a diaper change. "Sit," Muhsine says. "I'll go get her and bring her in. You'll only have my help for one more day, so please take full advantage."

"Okay," Fatma nods. "But I think it must be a dirty diaper. She just ate, *mashallah*. They do keep you busy, don't they?"

Muhsine jumps up as the cries intensify. Fatma gets up and watches *Baba* hand over the now screaming Pinar to his wife.

Muhsine runs past Fatma, carrying the red-faced and contorted Pinar, arms and legs flailing, to Fatma and Cengiz's bedroom where there is a table for diaper changing. Fatma starts to join her but then sits back down. There will be plenty more diapers to change once Muhsine returns to Istanbul. She hears an "ugh" and smiles. It must have been a nasty one. Muhsine has never had children, so this is a new experience for her. Fatma senses that Muhsine will not be unhappy to return home. But now all is quiet in the other room.

Muhsine returns with empty arms and sits back down at the table. "She's fallen asleep again, so I put her in her crib. Now, tell me, what is worrying you about this dream? There doesn't seem to be anything bad in the dream. You are simply looking ahead to when Pinar is grown and when she will marry. Why does this concern you? I think it's a good sign."

"Maybe you're right." Fatma sighs and rubs her hands over her stomach. "Perhaps I make too much of dreams. But *Babaanne* always took them so seriously, looking at each symbol for its meaning. So now I'm inclined to do the same. And it is also the feeling."

"What do you mean?' Muhsine asks. She leans forward, her attention now totally drawn to Fatma.

"When I see her sitting there and I recognize that it is she, Pinar, I have a sense of dread, fear. I feel something in my throat, caught there, stuck, like I can't take in a breath. It's only for a brief moment, maybe even a second, but still, it's there."

Fatma pauses, stops rubbing her stomach and takes hold of Muhsine's hand. "No more," she says, looking into Muhsine's eyes. "I'm sure you are right. I will put it to rest for now. I think I am a bit afraid of being a mother. Will I be a good one? I had such a peculiar mother myself."

Muhsine wraps her other hand around the one Fatma has placed over hers. "I am quite sure you will be. Remember, you also had *Babaanne*, and she had love to spare. She will always be with you, even if she's no longer here in the flesh. And Cemal is here with you. And no one can be a perfect mother, I think. Mine certainly wasn't, but she did the best she could. In my opinion, that's all that can be asked of any mother." She strokes Fatma's hand gently and rises from the table.

"And now," Muhsine says, "if you don't mind, I'm going to freshen up and join the others outside. It's such a beautiful day. I love the fall breezes. How fortunate Pinar is to have been born in October. I think it is the best time of year."

Fatma grins. "Unless it means you have to be pregnant all summer. I'm going to check on the baby, and then I'll come outside. I don't know why I look for everything sinister, but you're correct, Muhsine. It is too beautiful a day to wallow in future misfortunes when there are none at present."

Fatma peeks in at Pinar, who is sleeping peacefully. She sits for a few moments in the armchair. How can she possibly be a good mother when she is holding on to so many lies? No one knows about her pending loss of eyesight. She could never bring herself to tell anyone. And although her sight has not changed much in the past ten years, only ever so slightly, she lives in fear that she will pass this disease on to her child. Then Cengiz would have to discover that she has deceived him, and not about something minor.

Fatma regrets not keeping in better touch with Claudia and her family. When she moved to Avanos, there were letters. And Claudia and her parents did attend the wedding. But Fatma's fear of Claudia or her parents revealing her secret kept her from continuing their relationship. When *Signor* Ferrari moved the family back to Italy, Fatma breathed a sigh of relief. Sitting here now, Fatma wishes she hadn't let the friendship slide. *Signora* Ferrari would have been the perfect person for her to consult about sex. As it stands now, they don't even know she's had a child.

Fatma rises from the chair slowly and thinks, perhaps I can confide in Badia. Not about the blindness but about the sex. Badia has friends in Istanbul, and I know they're not all virgins. I'm not even sure about Badia anymore, but she insists she will never marry. I wonder about that. But I do know Badia is trustworthy. I know it would give me great comfort to talk to someone. Fatma checks one last time on Pinar before she shakes off her thoughts and steps outside to join the others in the small garden.

"I never found it easy," Cemal says.

"That is exactly why I will never marry." Badia replies.

"What are you talking about?" Fatma seats herself on a chair she pulls up between the two of them.

"Being a mother," Badia informs her. "I don't believe I could ever do it."

"Don't be silly," Cemal intercedes quickly. "If I did it, anyone can."

"Yes, you did. And you were not always terribly happy about it, as I remember." Badia winks at Fatma.

"Look at what you're doing now," Cemal chides Badia. "She's a new mother, and we must give her all the support we can. Talking about how difficult motherhood is can't be helpful."

"In a way, it is." Fatma reaches over and takes Badia's hand in hers. "This way when I'm feeling that I'm not doing so well, I will know that you have felt the same way, Cemal. I won't feel so alone."

"You will never be alone as long as I'm here." Cengiz defends himself.

"But you're a man," Badia counters. "You are not the mother."

Fatma takes in a deep breath. "No," she says. "I am the mother. There is no changing that now."

CHAPTER 36

Avanos is damp, wet, and cold. It is December, and Pinar is now close to three months old. Elif, Badia's younger sister, is back from Istanbul where she was living with Badia. She is the most attractive as well as the most spoiled of the Celik family, small-boned, slender with high cheek bones and dark features. Her prominent sculptured nose has sometimes caused people to mistake her for Egyptian, as she does look foreign and exotic. She tags after Fatma and Pinar in her current state of disgrace.

Folks outside of the family tell Elif she could be a film star. Alas, Fatma thinks, there is almost no film in Turkey. She would have to go to America, and there is little to no chance of that. Fatma believes that people should stop putting lofty ideas in Elif's head. She is a pretty girl with little motivation or thirst for learning. Fatma does not believe that Elif has the stamina or even the personality for becoming a film star. The industry is small and new and too expensive for Turkey, as the infant republic stumbles along. This is all a pipe dream, anyway.

Turkey is still recovering from the Great War. The economy has gone up and down as leadership pulls forward one way and stumbles back another. Money is scarce, and now there is concern there might be another war. Adolf Hitler is ranting and spewing his hatred, creating quite a storm in Germany, along with raising much anxiety throughout Europe. Just after Pinar emerged from Fatma's womb, all hell broke loose in what is now Nazi Germany. Kristallnacht or Night of Broken Glass, two bloody days and nights of vicious pogroms against German Jews, sent shock and fear into every European's sensibilities. November 9 and 10. As if a madness had overtaken otherwise normal citizens. And even more fearful was that the police participated. And everyone knew, even if they refused to acknowledge the truth, it had not been so long ago that these awful things had happened in Turkey with the Armenians. Fatma still thinks about her childhood friends in the caves and their disappearance.

Word is that Turkey will not enter another war, but who can be sure? And Cengiz's temporary deferment, due to his recent onset of asthma from working with the pottery, would be ripped out from under him with the onset of a war. Elif's delinquent return is yet another worry for the Celik family, as tourism and pottery sales are down, and they scarcely have time to concern themselves with her.

To top all of this off, Atatürk has finally succumbed to years of imbibing too much rakı. Just one month after Pinar's birth, on November 10, 1938, the second day of Kristallnacht, Mustafa Kemal dies of cirrhosis of the liver. The Republic is in mourning. Fatma is grieving deeply. She remembers well what life was like prior to Atatürk. Even though she was just a child in the forming of the Republic, he has been the only leader of Turkey she has really known. He has lifted Turkey up in the eyes of the world. She is not alone in feeling much pride in his accomplishments. Various factions are striving to take power, and no one is sure what will happen or how long any government will survive.

Initially, Elif moved in with Badia to begin university, and "begin" was all that she did. Instead of attending classes, she wandered the streets, gazing longingly into shop windows and sitting for hours to drink çay in cafes. After the first term, she was put on notice. At the end of two terms, she was asked to leave. Although the Celiks might have bartered and bought her another term, they knew nothing of these developments.

Elif did not inform her family that she was no longer in school. Badia finally did when she discovered Elif at home sleeping one day. Badia had returned from work to recover some papers she mistakenly left in the apartment. She confronted Elif, and Elif finally confessed that she had whiled away the next semester's tuition money from her parents after having been dismissed from the university. Badia was furious, and after some fruitless efforts to regain some of the financial loss, put Elif on the first bus to Avanos.

"How could you take the money from them when you know it's a sacrifice. The shop is not doing well, and *Baba* and Cengiz are working so hard just to keep it going." Badia opens the closet where Elif keeps her belongings and begins to pull out purchases with the price tags still attached. "You bought these things with the tuition money? You will take everything back and give the money to *Anne* and *Baba*! How could you do something like this?"

Elif begins to sob, and between sobs she blurts out, "The merchants won't take them back. They'll refuse. I know they will. The times are too hard, and I never paid the price on the tags. I bargained, and they accepted. They know I didn't pay full price. How can I take them back?" She gives Badia a defiant look, her wide eyes contracted, her mouth a determined line.

"I'll go with you," Badia insists. "Get dressed and gather all these things. We're going now. I'm going downstairs to the phone to call my work. Hurry up. I have a deadline and now I will have to work late to meet it. You should be ashamed of yourself. I hope you are." Badia runs out and slams the door. Elif can hear her footsteps barreling down the two flights of stairs and then the slam of the heavy door to the street. Badia cannot afford a phone and must go to the booth on the corner.

Elif was correct. The merchants refused to accept the returns, and after wasting her words and her time in several shops, Badia is forced to admit that her exertions are useless. She later admitted to Cemal that she had gotten so angry that she had slapped Elif when Elif refused to enter one of the shops with her. Cemal is shocked when she repeats this to Fatma. "We have never used any physical punishment in our family," she tells Fatma, once she knows that Elif is on her way home.

"Perhaps you should have," Fatma responds.

Cemal looks in horror at Fatma and then down at the sleeping Pinar. Fatma follows her glance to the child.

"No, I wouldn't choose to slap her. Badia was right to be angry, though."

Cemal sighs. "Elif always wanted pretty things more than books."

"You excuse her too much, I think." Fatma is displeased with Elif and understands Badia's anger and frustration. In these times, who could have patience with this behavior? No wonder Elif acts so irresponsibly when Cemal is so accepting. And so, they leave the subject and don't discuss it further. And Fatma does not broach the topic with Cengiz, who is becoming a slave to the pottery business and speaks of very little else. These days he coughs and chokes and sneezes more than he speaks.

Now Fatma wraps another shawl around herself to keep out the damp. She is tired of Pinar's incessant needs but also not eager to engage with Elif. The girl is looking for sympathy anywhere and Fatma is not only unsympathetic but irritated by Elif's persistence. She has now been back for two weeks.

"I didn't mean to upset everyone so," Elif begs her.

"Well then, you might have thought more of everyone before you acted so poorly," Fatma responds. Pinar has been plagued with colic, and thus Fatma sleeps poorly. It is only when Pinar ceases to scream and cry and collapses into sleep that Fatma is able to shut her eyes. Cengiz is so drained when he finally comes to bed that nothing, even Pinar's shrieks and his own coughing, awakens him. Fatma's lack of sleep and constant fatigue causes her to be short-tempered with Elif.

Fatma is at her wits end. Nothing she does quiets this infant. Cemal has no experience of this. She insists her own babies slept through the night and sometimes half the day. This news, of course, does nothing to reassure Fatma. When they seek the help of a midwife and then finally a doctor, they shake their heads in empathy but without suggestions that have not already been tried. "It happens with some," they say. "It will pass."

When will it pass, Fatma wants to know? No one is able to tell her. In the meantime, she walks and rocks and rocks and walks throughout the night and into the day. Pinar seems to sense when Fatma is finally able to nod off after hours of soothing her to sleep, and then she is at it again, wailing at the top of her tiny lungs. This is astonishing to Fatma. How can such a small creature expel so much noise? If Pinar is disturbing anyone else with her constant protests, no one is coming to her aid but Fatma. After Cemal tried once and was clipped by Pinar's arms lashing out into the air, she quickly handed her back to Fatma saying, "I've never seen such a thing. She despises her own *babaanne*."

"Then she despises her *anne* as well," Fatma had muttered.

So Fatma is in no mood these days to pamper or pacify Elif in her struggles for redemption. Elif is afraid of Pinar and her violence and so is unable to give Fatma any relief by holding her. Instead, she follows Fatma and Pinar everywhere until bedtime when she disappears to the sleeping couch the Celiks have temporarily prepared for her. Everyone is too busy to listen to her pleas for forgiveness. Even Cemal.

Fatma knows that her husband and his family are worried about their finances, but this is not unusual in these times. The whole world is concerned with finances. Fatma has read about the stock market crash in America and heard about the resulting suicides. This collapse has cascaded throughout the world. Badia has written about some of this, Fatma knows, and Badia brings some of her articles home to discuss with her family when she visits. Fatma is always interested. Since America put a hold on credit for Turkey and for Germany, both economies are suffering. Neither country can afford to keep up the banks without American credit or loans. The banks are rapidly faltering. These world problems take Fatma momentarily away from the constant tyranny she is living with Pinar.

Fatma is appalled by her hatred of Pinar. The infant is helpless to her care, and Fatma is constantly aware of this. But does Pinar have no gratitude? No heart? Does she feel nothing at all for the minutes, the hours, the days that Fatma is laboring for her? The sore breasts. The never-ending washing of diapers. The rocking to and fro with no end in sight. Sometimes the urge to throttle Pinar, to choke her, to throw her against the wall is so strong that Fatma is afraid of herself. She completely understands that the gentle Badia had to have been driven mad by Elif's behavior to have hit her. She feels that she is being driven mad every day now. If only there was someone who could be effective with Pinar, but Pinar only shrieks louder when handed to anyone else. There is no way known to Fatma to put a stop to this torture. There are times when no one is watching that she dumps Pinar into her crib and just lets her scream to keep herself from inflicting a violent act on her own child.

But Pinar does not seem at all like a child to her. Pinar feels more like a satanic explosion that has burst from her womb and is punishing her for even thinking she could be a mother, a wife, have a family or experience anything that is taken for granted by most as normal life. Is Pinar Allah's punishment for her lie?

Fatma has tried to make herself believe that keeping her fading vision a secret is not a lie, and so she is hesitant even in her own mind to refer to it as such. Up until the rantings and ravings of Pinar, Fatma has thought of her withholding of information as a confession she needs to make. But now, it seems to her that she should have made this confession to the whole family prior to the wedding. If not the whole family, at the very least, she should have confided in Cengiz. Now her dreams have become nightmares. She sees Pinar as an older child walking with a blind user's stick, poking her way through the uneven stones and dirt of Avanos, screaming as she stumbles along a deserted path. In these nightly torments, Fatma is a mere observer until she awakens and sees her frightening fantasies as a real possibility.

But, Fatma rationalizes, Pinar may never be afflicted. Even if she is, it is not likely to affect her until she is older, an adolescent as Fatma was, or even later in life. So she calms herself momentarily, only to relive the same episode in a precious moment of sleep. There is no rest, there is no sleep, and there is no escape.

As if Elif is pursuing an evil spirit in order to relieve her of her own shame, she traipses behind Fatma as a sore reminder to Fatma of her guilt. And with the never ceasing cries of Pinar and Fatma's resulting shortness of temper, she becomes more convinced of her inherent badness every day.

"Why don't you find something to do?" Fatma entreats Elif. "If you can't help me with this demon child, just go away. You can see that I'm busy. I have no time for you." Fatma places Pinar on the changing table and shakes out an unused diaper.

"Here," Elif offers. "I can take the dirty one."

"By all means, take the dirty one." Fatma unpins the filled diaper and attempts to hand it, half open, to Elif, who cannot resist bringing her fingers to her nose.

"You see," Fatma barks, "you are no help at all. You can't even abide the smell. You are the pretty girl who has no shit of her own."

Elif looks genuinely shocked. "Shit" is not a word used in the Celik household. She has never heard Fatma curse. She stares back at Fatma in disbelief.

Fatma takes hold of herself, realizing that she must appear to have lost her mind. Carefully, she secures the dirty diaper and tosses it into a nearby trash can. "I'm sorry to have cursed," she tells Elif calmly. "There's no reason for it except that..." At this moment, Pinar begins to kick and holler, as if she is explaining her mother's loss of control. Elif is not of sturdy material, and so she almost runs to the nearest door. Fatma laughs. The wind is howling, and the temperature is close to freezing. In her light fancy outfit, with only a jacket to cover her, Elif will be back before anyone can notice she is gone.

However, Fatma is wrong. When the family is gathered for dinner, Cemal asks, "Where is Elif? Has anyone seen her?" When no one responds, Cemal looks around and then calls out, "Elif, it's time for supper. Where are you, dear?"

Fatma flinches at the "dear." Cemal is entirely too indulging of this family anomaly. They are all so hardworking, and this one just goes off and does as she pleases, never caring how what she does or doesn't do impacts her family. When Fatma looks back in time, there was always a streak of this selfishness in Elif.

When there is no reply to Cemal's calls, Cengiz says, "Sit and eat, *Anne*, everyone. I'll go and see to it. Maybe she just fell asleep." Cengiz pushes back his chair and rises, suddenly convulsing in a coughing spell. "No," he motions Salman back, "no *Baba*, I'm fine. You need to eat and rest. I'll be right back with her."

But the minutes pass, and Cengiz does not return either alone or with Elif. Cemal lays her fork down on her plate. "I can't eat another bite until I know what's going on here." Fatma rises with her, as she can hear the beginnings of a new tantrum emanating from Pinar. Fatma has left her in the next room long enough to try to eat.

But just as they move to exit the room, the outer door slams shut. A terrified and windblown Cengiz enters the room with the limp form of Elif in his arms. Her head is cracked open and soaked with blood that has seeped through to her fine clothing and oozed onto Cengiz's work clothes. Cengiz falls to his knees and places Elif on the floor.

"It was a tree," Cengiz cries. "It was my fault. She turned when she heard me calling to her. If she hadn't turned, if I hadn't called to her, it would have missed her. It was all my fault." He breaks into choking sobs. The room is frozen as if a mysterious force has stopped all time.

Suddenly it occurs to Cemal that even though Elif has given no indication of life, she may still be alive. She rushes to the lifeless and blood-spattered body, lifting her and shaking her in her arms. "Wake up, Elif. Please, wake up. Salman, go get the doctor! Now! Why are you all just standing around? Help me! Help her! Help—" Her voice dissolves into sobs. Her sobs incite Pinar, still lying in her crib. Fatma ignores her.

"*Anne*," Cengiz chokes on his words, "she died instantly. She was not breathing when I lifted the tree. It took me so long to lift it. So heavy, that old tree by the well. I knew we should have cut it down."

"Ah." Salman speaks for the first time. His voice is not his own, the whispers of a ghost. "This is my fault, not yours. You told me about that tree, that we should take it down before it fell on something or someone. I was so busy. I was so tired. Why didn't you insist?" Without realizing what he is doing, he shifts the blame back to Cengiz.

"Stop it now, both of you!" Cemal has recovered her senses. "This is no one's fault. This was an accident. A terrible one, an unnecessary one, but still an accident."

Fatma is still. She does not rush to Cengiz. Something roots her feet to the floor. Pinar's cries are slowing down now, probably from the futility of them—no one is coming—and her energy for emitting them is dissipating. Fatma thinks, this is truly my fault. This is my doing. If I'd had one ounce of patience with the girl, she would not have run off like that. This family must be so tired of me and this monster I have produced. I'm sure they believe I could keep her quiet if I only tried. Can I possibly confess to having killed their child, their sister? I'm cursed and my blood is cursed. Fusun, my poor lost *anne,* you and I are not so different after all. We hide and live in our awful secrets and pass them along to the daughters we bear.

No, Fatma thinks, as she goes to see to Pinar and observes the group huddled around Elif, I do not belong here. It has always been impossible. This is the family I have sought to make my own and now I have killed one of them. And I'm very afraid that if someone does not separate me from this infant of mine, I will kill her as well. Poor Cengiz. What a curse you have taken for a wife!

CHAPTER 37

The year is 1951. As *Baba* predicted, Turkey stayed out of the war until it was over. They joined the Allies at the signing of the treaty. Although there had been mass migrations of refugees, including many Jews fleeing Hitler, this had only affected the larger cities, for the most part.

The war had been hard on tourism, but it is picking up again. The Celiks are not wealthy, but they are more comfortable than many. And somehow, *Baba* has kept his prices reasonable, and so the restaurant has survived.

Pinar unravels the ribbon tied on the birthday gift that Fatma hands to her. She is nine years old today and already disappointed. The box is too large for the mirror, comb and brush set that she showed Fatma in the marketplace. It was gold-plated and ornate. Her *anne* does not seem to pay attention to her about such things. Her Auntie Badia is so much better at buying her gifts.

Everyone tells Pinar that she must be kind and forgiving with Fatma. Fatma suffered so much when Pinar was born. Pinar remembers nothing of this, which everyone tells her, is fortunate. Pinar only remembers when Fatma went into the hospital.

Pinar was just five years old then, and it was her first day of school. Fatma had helped her on with her new dress, a plaid with a velvet collar that she had chosen herself with Fatma's help in the department store in Nevşehir. This was a big day for Pinar. Her *anne* and *baba* told her about their early years in school right here at home with the tutor in the Celik house. Pinar felt special that she would go right away to a real school with other children. She was not the least bit nervous but excited at the thought of a new experience. Since she already knew her letters and could read, Cengiz, her *baba*, told her she would be a step ahead of some of the other children. This idea appealed to her. She wanted to be smart.

There was a bus that would come and pick her up to take her to the school and home again, but on the first day, Fatma arranged that she and Cengiz would take her and pick her up. The school advised this, and other parents would be doing the same. Pinar felt important that this new adventure was to include both of her parents and her new dress and shoes. The shoes were black patent leather and came from a catalogue. She had not been allowed to wear them until the first day of school, but she opened the box they came in and felt the shiny leather every day until then.

When they left for the bus that would take them to the school, Pinar felt some tension between her parents and wondered if they had argued that morning. Cengiz picked her up and told her how beautiful she looked in her new clothing and how smart her teacher would find her. She would be the best pupil in her class, as her own mother had once been.

"I studied all the time," Cengiz told her, "but your *anne* was always ahead of me. What I went through to make her believe that wasn't true. She thought she was working to keep up with me. Isn't that right, my love?" Cengiz looked to Fatma for confirmation. Pinar thought it took her mother a long time to even realize Cengiz was speaking to her.

Fatma seemed to suddenly awaken. The three of them were standing at the bus stop. Fatma looked down at Pinar. "Yes, it's true. I always worked hard to keep up with your *baba*. I thought he was the smartest of us all. Your Auntie Badia did not care for school at all back then, but she ended up ahead of all of us."

Pinar had heard this many times before, but today she only cared about how smart she would be. She wished her *anne* would confirm this for her as her *baba* had done. But Pinar knew her *anne* spent much of her time in the past. Sometimes Pinar liked that, as well as Fatma's stories, but today was her day, Pinar's day, and so Pinar only wanted to hear about herself.

When the bus came, Cengiz took Pinar's hand and started to help her onto the bus. Fatma stood where she was. "Come *Anne*," Pinar cried out. "Aren't you coming with us? Please come on the bus, Anne."

Fatma stood where she was. "I'm so sorry, Pinar. I'm not able to come with you today. I am sick again, and your *babaanne* will take me to the hospital. Please don't be upset with me. If I don't go now—I must go now. I will try to make it up to you, I promise. Please be a good girl. *Baba* will take you today."

Pinar stood by the stairs to the bus. She let go of Cengiz's hand and raced to her mother, wrapping her little arms around Fatma, tugging at her as if to pull her onto the bus. "*Anne, Anne*, please come with us. Please, please."

Fatma bent down and held Pinar's face in her hands. "My sweet girl. Please understand. I must go now. But I will do my best, I promise, not to have to do this again. For all of us, I will try." Tears ran silently down Fatma's cheeks. She knew she was losing control again, and she did not want Pinar to see her in such a state. She and Cengiz had planned this after Fatma had broken down in the night, losing her grip on reality and knowing she needed to go back to the hospital. Cengiz had agreed.

When Pinar saw her *anne's* tears, she knew her pleading was useless. She let go of Fatma and returned to her waiting father, still holding out his hand to help her up the steps of the bus.

"Be brilliant, my child," Fatma called to her before she turned and began the walk back to the house. There she would wait for the car coming to take her and Cemal to the inpatient hospital where she had been several times by now. This time she had been able to see it coming before she became irrational and what the doctors called psychotic. Fatma believed it was a good sign. And because of the warning signs she has learned to recognize, Pinar will not see her at her worst. She will get help before then.

But Pinar had been affected by Fatma's absences. When Fatma returned home this time after one month, Pinar was cool at first. About three days after Fatma was back, Pinar approached her when she was alone.

"*Anne*," she said, with more gravity and composure than would seem possible for a five-year old, "I want you to promise me that you won't go away again."

Fatma was sitting outside the kitchen shelling peas into a bowl for their dinner that night. Pinar had just come home from school and had not yet changed out of her school uniform into her everyday trousers and shirt.

Fatma set the large bowl on a table and took Pinar's hands in hers.

"I know it was hard for you *kızım*, my daughter, and I'm so sorry for that. I wish I could promise you that I won't ever have to go to the hospital again. In this moment, I don't feel I will ever have to go back, but I cannot know the future."

Pinar persisted, "But will you try your best, *Anne*? That is what Miss Hürdür says we must do. She tells us if we try our best, that is good enough."

"Your teacher is very wise, and if you follow her advice, I think you will be, too. Yes, *kızım*, I can certainly promise you to try my best, *Inshallah*." Fatma squeezed her daughter's small hands and let them go. "Now let me finish these peas or we won't have any supper."

But now, Pinar is nine years old on this day, and she is opening her first birthday present from Fatma. The box is filled with tissue paper and when Pinar pulls it out, there is the very mirror, brush and comb set that she loved. "You fooled me, *Anne*! The box is so big! I didn't think you remembered. *Teşekküler, Anne*! Thank you so much."

Fatma watches her daughter run her fingers over the elaborate filigree bordering the mirror and brush handle. In this moment, Fatma feels the happiest she has been in some time. The love she feels now for Pinar allows her to believe, in this moment, that she might be able to have more children. The doctors have assured her that not every mother who goes through this type of depression with one child will necessarily go through it with others.

"I'm going to put these on my table, just as you told me your *Babaanne* put hers." Pinar runs to her room to do so. Fatma knows the birthday is over in a sense. This was the one thing Pinar had wanted, and Fatma is so glad she was able to note this and return to purchase the set. She does not want to be a disappointing mother any longer. She had one herself and knows all too well what that is like.

The rest of the day will make Pinar happy, the birthday cake at school, the little presents from her friends, the dinner at home with another birthday cake to follow. She will love all of it. But even Badia's gift will not outshine the fact that her mother remembered how she had fondled the set, her desire clear to not only the merchant but strangers passing by.

Fatma is dressed and ready with the birthday cake when Pinar returns with her school bag in hand. Fatma is going with her today to oversee the birthday celebration with her teacher, Miss Öztürk. Fatma has met with this teacher on several occasions. She is a sympathetic woman and has said to Fatma, "Pinar is a wonderful child. She is very bright. But she has a difficult time trusting herself. She needs a great deal of approval." This worries Fatma.

Fatma has told Miss Öztürk about her condition and her hospitalization when Pinar was five. She also tells her that Pinar has never seen her in a psychotic state. Miss Öztürk had cautioned her. "Children can seem unaware, but their memories start before we think they do. Even if it is only a shadow of a memory, it is possible that she does know something or feel something she can only find in her dreams."

Fatma thinks a lot about these words. She knows about dreams. She lives with her own. Now she has the doctor from the hospital to talk to and that helps so much. Dr. Tabak is kind and listens to Fatma as no one else has listened to her in her life. Maybe *Babaanne* was the closest, but even she cooked and cleaned while Dr. Tabak just sits and listens. It is as if Fatma is the only obligation Dr. Tabak has in the world. Dr. Tabak, Fatma guesses, is in her mid-forties. She has one daughter and one son and a handsome husband who appears to be only slighter older than Dr. Tabak. Fatma sees them all in a family photograph that Dr. Tabak keeps on her desk. Her husband is also Dr. Tabak, and he is a psychiatrist in the same hospital. This seems to cause much more confusion for staff than patients who know exactly which Dr. Tabak they are seeing. Even now after all the years she has been coming, whoever the receptionist is always asks, "Is it Zeynep Tabak or Alp Tabak you wish to see?" And Fatma always replies without expression, "Zeynep."

Now Pinar comes running back. "I love my present so much, *Anne*. I can't wait to show it to Badia *Teyze*, Aunt Badia."

Fatma is pleased that Badia and Pinar have such a close relationship. She marvels at how Badia works to please her daughter. Fatma loves Badia as much as she always has, but she sometimes feels that Badia judges her. Badia knows the strain that Fatma's depression and psychosis has put on her brother, her whole family for that matter. And even though Badia knows, Fatma believes, just how hard she is working to fight against the depression, it does weigh heavily over the Celik household. Her hospitalizations and therapy have been costly as well. Even though Fatma knows that no one complains to Badia, most especially not Cengiz, Fatma wonders if Badia feels that her brother could be happier. Fatma knows that Cengiz still blames himself for the death of Elif, and now he worries over his father's heart condition. Fatma is concerned about Cengiz's health, as the constant work in the pottery factory has created a bronchial condition along with his persistent asthma. None of these kind folks should have to worry about her mental health, Fatma concludes. But she reminds herself that it has been four years since her last hospitalization.

Fatma and Pinar walk to the bus stop. Fatma carries the cake in a box, and Pinar carries the bag of treats she will give to her classmates. This is how the children's birthdays are celebrated in her day school. Once they are settled on the bus, children from Pinar's class wish her a happy birthday, and this continues along the way as the bus stops to pick up other children. Fatma notices that some of the children are shy and that others appear to know Pinar quite well and don't hesitate in the least to convey their good wishes. Fatma wonders at how popular her daughter seems to be. A feeling of happiness rushes through her again. She is lucky to have a daughter like Pinar.

Miss Öztürk greets them at the bus and takes the cake box from Fatma. "Here, let me help you," she says. As they walk to the classroom, a group of girls surround Pinar. There are no boys in Pinar's school, as boys and girls are separated. Fatma cannot help feeling some jealousy along with her pleasure and her admiration of Pinar. Oh, to have had such a school herself. To have known the joys of being with so many girls. And then she remembers that she had this in Istanbul after they moved. That is where she met her Italian friend, Claudia. Poor Claudia, Fatma ponders. She didn't deserve such a bad friend as I have been. I haven't been a friend at all.

The cake is lit with candles, ten in all, one being for good luck. When Pinar blows them out in one long breath, the girls clap and squeal. Fatma cuts the cake and hands each of the children a piece on a paper plate. The cake is chocolate, Pinar's favorite. It is topped with a thick chocolate icing made with mostly butter and sugar. The one waiting at home is the same. Fatma could not convince Pinar to have two different cakes. She had laughed at her daughter's insistence. She is a girl who knows exactly what she wants, and in many cases, manages to get it. The cake is delicious. Fatma's heart is filled with pleasure seeing the joy in Pinar.

The children are pleased with the hair ribbons and barrettes that Fatma and Pinar selected from the market, the same day and the same market where Pinar had spied the brush, comb and mirror set. They have handmade cards for Pinar and little gifts they have also purchased from the market or made at home. They are simple gifts all around, but the children are enthusiastic about each and every one of them. When the party comes to an end and the class resumes their studies, Fatma calls a taxi to take her back home.

In the afternoon, the family from Istanbul arrives together. In his old age and his middle-class status, Ali has purchased a car. It is a used Fiat, nothing fancy, but as Ali loves to say, "It gets me where I need to be." The sole purpose of the car is so that he and Muhsine can travel to visit Fatma and the Celiks more comfortably and frequently. And when Badia is free to join them, she does. None of them would miss Pinar's birthday. Ali has wooed Pinar in the same way Fatma remembers him winning her heart. He tells Pinar old Turkish tales that she loves and reads to her from books of Turkish folklore.

Ali is the first to greet Fatma with his arms wide open. Muhsine and Badia are removing packages and food from the car. "Oh, *benim küçük kızım, my little daughter,* come here, come here!"

Ali has been worried about Fatma's well-being since her first psychotic break shortly after Pinar was born. He is as warm and loving as he has always been, but Fatma notices from time to time that he treats her as if she is a precious flower that might break at the stem and die.

As soon as Pinar returns from school, the family birthday party begins. The food has been planned ahead, and so everyone contributes to making Pinar's favorite dishes. Badia has brought the ingredients for *patlıcan kızartması,* slices of eggplant deep fried with a tomato sauce and usually served with a dollop of garlic yogurt. But since Pinar prefers *cacık,* a traditional yogurt dip that is made with grated cucumber, dill, mint, lemon, and olive oil, Fatma has made that to go with it instead. Badia will fry the eggplant slices now so they will be fresh. Muhsine has made *sigara böreği* that very morning and carries it inside on a large tray. This is an appetizer made with *yufka* dough and filled with parsley, scallion, egg, and feta cheese. This is a favorite of the whole family. Cemal has prepared *kısır,* a dish that Pinar would eat for every meal of the day, if only she could. Cemal makes it so often for Pinar that Cemal could do it in her sleep. It is a spicy bulgur wheat salad made with a special red pepper paste and pomegranate molasses, onion, scallion, parsley, mint, tomato paste, tomato and *biber,* a lovely red pepper that Cengiz and Salman put on almost everything. Salman cannot eat as much of it as he used to, at least not on his doctor's advice.

Fatma is now in the midst of making *mercimek çorbası*, a creamy lentil soup that is light enough to eat with this huge meal. Badia has also brought a massive tray of rice *pilav* with vegetables. Yesterday Fatma put the chicken marinated with sumac, cloves, garlic olive oil, salt and pepper, lemon and chili flakes in the refrigerator to soak overnight. She did the same with the marinated lamb for the kebabs. Cengiz will grill them, as he is the best at the barbeque. And the chocolate birthday cake is waiting. This is not traditional, but Pinar has insisted that she wants this more than anything else on the menu.

Food was less plentiful during the war with the overcrowding of refugees and various difficulties transporting certain staples. Fatma and Cengiz are delighted to be able to procure what they need to make this birthday special for Pinar. Food is bountiful again, even though medical expenses have not allowed them to live extravagantly. At least people are traveling to Turkey once again as tourists, not just to escape from autocrats threatening their lives.

The kitchens in both houses are bursting with lively energy. Badia runs from Fatma's kitchen to her parents' kitchen and back again. Fatma shakes her hand away as Badia attempts to add more salt to the soup which she has tasted while Fatma is not looking.

"No, no more salt. You know it's not good for your *baba*. If you think it needs more, please add it at the table. Salman really has to watch what he eats. And believe me, he will complain that it needs more salt, so keep it at your end of the table."

Badia's bottom lip curls outward. She appears wounded. "Oh, Fatma, I'm sorry. I'm so careless because I don't live here anymore but even so, I should know better." She puts the salt back where she'd gotten it on the counter next to the stove.

Fatma takes Badia in her arms. "Of course, you didn't mean to hurt your *baba*. It truly is difficult to keep up with everyone's dietary changes. I have to think about these things myself. I'm so used to using so much salt. Salt makes everything taste better. But his doctor—"

Badia returns Fatma's hugs, and then releases her. "They're getting old, especially Ali. I always think of him as your *baba*, so I think of him as younger than he is. He doesn't look like your grandfather, even though he does sometimes have trouble with his hip and doesn't walk so well."

"I know." Fatma lets out a deep sigh. "When I noticed that he was leaning forward a bit when he walks, he admitted to having pain in his right hip. I am so grateful that he has good help in the restaurant now. I do worry about him, even though I know no one could take better care of him than Muhsine. And Cemal and Salman have not been the same since Elif's death. For that matter, neither has Cengiz."

"Does he still blame himself?"

"I'm afraid that will never go away. I try to get him to see Dr. Tabak, but he refuses. I tell him that we all contributed to Elif's death, but most of all, Elif contributed to her own death. I've talked with Dr. Tabak about this many times. She believes that it was no one's fault, but it is human for each of us to feel responsible." Fatma stirs the soup one more time, turns off the fire and lays the spoon on the stove.

"I know I feel responsible." Badia runs her fingers through her hair.

Fatma remembers how unattractive Badia was as a child and how much she has blossomed. The family never expected her to amount to anything. As it turned out, Badia was simply not stimulated. Once she left Avanos, she lost weight and began to take an interest in her appearance. Now she has a good and interesting career. Funny how that happened, Fatma thinks. Fatma often wonders what would have happened if she had gone on with her studies. Dr. Tabak tells her she still can, but Fatma no longer sees school as a possibility. How could she leave Cengiz and Pinar?

"I was so hard on her," Badia continues. "Oh, and that day that I humiliated her, forcing her to ask those snooty merchants to take all the clothing and shoes back, and she knew they would never do that. I ignored her because I was so angry. I guess I wanted to shame her. I could not understand how she could take advantage of *Anne* and *Baba* and me. Now see, I'm angry all over again."

"Of course, you are. There is no excuse for what she did."

"No excuse for what who did?" Cemal has entered without either of them hearing her. Neither of the two women answer her. Cemal looks long and hard at both of them.

"I have a feeling that this topic is not healthy for any of us. Going over and over it again will not change a thing." Cemal sets a large platter of *kısır* on the counter. She has placed the beautiful bulgur salad on large lettuce leaves and surrounded the salad with oil-cured black olives.

"*Anne*, you have outdone yourself this time. If it tastes as good as it looks, we'll have to watch that Pinar doesn't eat it all herself." Badia attempts to stick her finger in the salad to taste it, but Cemal slaps her hand away. "I'm getting my share of slaps today," Badia moans as if injured.

Cemal takes a little bow at Badia's compliment. "You have always stuck your fingers in the food. That's why you get so many slaps." The topic of Elif is dropped, exactly as Badia wishes.

"The school bus will be arriving soon," Cemal reminds them. "Let's get the meat out by the grill and tell Cengiz it's time to get started. Pinar is so hungry when she gets home from school. And she is such a skinny thing, in spite of the fact that her appetite is enormous."

The family rushes around to get the table set and the food laid out before Pinar arrives. And just as everything is ready, Badia calls out, "The bus is here!"

Moments later, Pinar rushes into the house, throws her schoolbag on the floor. Fatma tells her immediately, "Take your books to your room, please."

Pinar obediently picks her bag back up, runs to her room, and is back again with flushed cheeks from the cold, planting kisses on everyone. A chorus of happy birthday and I love you fills the room. Cengiz comes over to Fatma and hugs her. "See what a wonderful mother you are."

"With lots of help," Fatma replies, but she is pleased.

"When it comes to being a mother, we can all use lots of help." Cemal discards her apron over the back of a chair.

"I guess that's true," Muhsine says. "Although Fatma and I were bonded before I even met Ali. You were quite the matchmaker, Fatma."

"I know a good thing when I see it," Fatma replies.

The dinner is delicious. And as is the habit of excellent cooks, possibly with the exception of Cemal who has never made a better bulgur salad, each of them humbly expresses some fault with their preparation. Quick mumbled utterances such as *needs more salt, needs less salt, should have used more parsley, the marinade doesn't taste the same as the last time, I don't know what's wrong,* followed by adamant denials, *no, no it's perfect, this is the best you've ever made, what are you talking about—it's perfection.*

Fatma looks around the table and in this moment could not feel more fulfilled and content. Perhaps Dr. Tabak is right, she thinks. Maybe I am too hard on myself. Perhaps I can be a mother again and give Cengiz a son.

CHAPTER 38

Fatma is sitting on the edge of her bed. She is wearing a light blue nightgown with lace around the collar and the bottom of the sleeves. It is a gift from Badia that she has never worn. Badia presented it to her shortly after Pinar's birth. "This might cheer you up," Badia told her. Of course, it hadn't, but tonight Fatma remembers and thinks it's as good a time as any to retrieve it from its box. The material is soft and feels good against Fatma's freshly bathed skin.

Sex has greatly improved over the last few years. At first, after Pinar's birth, and through the following horrific depression, Fatma could not bear to think about sex. Cengiz was kind and understanding. He never pushed. But once Fatma began to return to the land of the living, she talked with Dr. Tabak about how to speak to Cengiz. Fatma had been surprised and pleased with how easily this had gone. It had taken some time for both of them to make adjustments in their thinking as well as in the physical act itself, but over time and playful practice, they are now enjoying their intimacy. However, they have taken steps, such as they are, to keep from becoming pregnant. On this particular evening, Fatma is ready to discard all precautions.

Cengiz enters their bedroom with a towel over his damp body. "That shower felt so good. It was a long but beautiful day. You threw a terrific party for Pinar, my darling." Cengiz takes a closer look at Fatma. "I haven't seen this gown before." He comes closer. "You look beautiful."

Cengiz sits down beside Fatma, takes her in his arms and they kiss. Fatma looks Cengiz in the eye and says, "You don't have to pull out tonight."

"Are you very sure?" Cengiz gazes back at her. "There's no rush."

"Your daughter is already nine years older than any prospective brother. She'll be ten, and that is only if we are successful tonight. It's time, Cengiz. I'm well. I know I can be a good mother. Time and love have healed me. I'm not perfect, but I'm good enough."

"You are perfect for me." Cengiz throws his damp towel on the chair where Fatma used to sit with baby Pinar. He lifts Fatma's gown and begins to caress every part of her body. As Dr. Tabak has advised, they linger now, slowly drinking in the other. Cengiz has been pulling out prior to ejaculation for so long now that the intensity he feels in his orgasm is explosive.

Fatma laughs. "It must be a boy. What shall we name him?"

"Not so fast," he cautions. "We don't know if you're pregnant."

"I know," Fatma insists. "What name do you like?"

"We must consult my parents first."

"Honestly, Cengiz. You are so old-fashioned. It's 1951."

"Okay, my modern lovely. Okay, I have always loved the name Ahmet. I think it's a name my parents would also like. What do you think?"

Fatma rolls back into Cengiz's arms. "I think it is a beautiful name. I also think a man who has waited so long for a son should be able to give him his name."

"You are so certain, my love." Cengiz gives Fatma a playful kiss. "What if you're wrong?"

"Then we'll keep trying. But I'm not wrong, Cengiz. You'll see."

The very next morning, Fatma is sitting on the bus to take her to Kayseri and to Dr. Tabak. When she focuses on what she must talk about today, she can feel her heart rate increase, hearing the rapid pounding in her ears. She was never so certain with Pinar, but she knows that Ahmet, her son, is on his way into the world. She must rid herself of this burden for his sake, for her own sake.

Even though there were many times when Fatma has thought she might be about to speak of the sexual problems she was having, she never did say a word until she worked up the courage to speak with Dr. Tabak. And then, although she had been embarrassed initially, Dr. Tabak managed to make her feel she was talking about something as everyday as making a special *börek* recipe. Fatma grins about this now, how shy she had been and how long it had taken her to bring up the matter in her sessions. Fatma knows that revealing this darker secret to Dr. Tabak will force her to reveal it to others, most essentially Cengiz. She sighs with a certain resolve. Now is the time. Ahmet is on his way, and surely they will want to have Pinar tested. But that is getting way ahead of things, she reminds herself. The first step is to speak to Dr. Tabak. Does she even suspect? Fatma is so used to covering up her lack of vision that she doubts very much that Dr. Tabak has any idea. It was months before she could even look Dr. Tabak in the eye, keeping her eyes lowered so as to avoid giving any hint of her facial expression or being able to read Dr. Tabak's. Fatma once read about Freud and his use of the psychoanalytic couch. She often wished it was a method employed by Dr. Tabak.

The bus is quiet and empty this morning. Fatma is glad that no one is sitting by her, trying to engage her in conversation. The two-hour bus ride has become a haven for her thoughts both prior to her sessions and afterwards. She likes to imagine how things will transpire, but she knows she is often wrong. She can never predict Dr. Tabak's responses, if there are any, to what she has to say. Fatma likes that there are often long moments of silence where they can each reflect on the words they have uttered and the words they have not. Sometimes Fatma finds herself on a completely different path than she has imagined on the bus. She hopes that she will have the courage to do what she must do today. Somehow the party for Pinar has helped Fatma turn a corner, she thinks. She is ready to move on, to stop dwelling on herself and to consider others.

Fatma feels fortunate that this bus stops directly in front of the hospital as one of its regular stops. She does not have a long walk or have to take a taxi. She is able to get some complimentary çay and biscuits in the reception area. This relaxes her from thoughts of that cold, gray and windy day that reminds her of that fateful time years ago when Elif met her death.

Fatma takes a crowded elevator to the third floor where both Tabaks have their offices. After she announces herself at the reception desk, Fatma pours herself a hot çay in a paper cup and takes two biscuits that she sets inside a paper napkin. She seats herself in a corner by a window, away from other waiting patients. She wants to think. But when she looks out the window, the gloomy day brings her back to Elif. And when she tears her gaze away, the constant ringing of the phones, the never-ending chitchat between the three receptionists and the opening and closing of the door to the offices inside will not allow her to focus. She finishes one cup of tea and both biscuits, then procures a second tea before her name is called.

Dr. Tabak's door is ajar. She has a desk, but when she sees patients, she never sits behind it. She has two large comfortable chairs that are more at an angle than facing one another. She always sits in the one closest to her desk and it's known, without ever saying, that the other chair is for her patient.

Zeynep Tabak is a tall and slender woman. She has strong features, a rather large nose, and a long face. Fatma would not call her pretty, or even attractive, but her dress is smart and professional. Dr. Tabak wears her hair short. It is quite thick, with developing gray streaks at her part that almost form a flower. Her eyes are large and hazel, her best feature, Fatma believes. Those eyes can drink you in so deeply. Dr. Tabak has a presence which Fatma finds compelling. She is both intelligent and compassionate. Zeynep Tabak is someone to be trusted.

Dr. Tabak is sitting in her therapy chair. She gets up when Fatma enters, greeting her warmly with a light kiss on each cheek. "*Selam*," they greet each other. They both settle into their respective chairs.

The office is what one would expect in a hospital setting, although Dr. Tabak has decorated it in such a way as to make it relaxing for her patients. There is a beautifully woven carpet with rich reds, blues, and greens in a pattern Fatma guesses is from somewhere in the south of Turkey. On one wall hangs a kilim in similar but darker colors, an antique Fatma knows is from a small village in southern Turkey near the Syrian border. She once asked Dr. Tabak about the kilim's origins, and she guessed by its pattern that it once served as a prayer rug. On another wall is a watercolor painting of the fairy rocks of Cappadocia. Fatma has spent many hours fixated on this painting. She knows that Dr. Tabak painted this herself.

"I have much to talk to you about today," Fatma tells Dr. Tabak. "I must do it quickly or I won't do it at all." Fatma catches Dr. Tabak looking at Fatma's hands. Without realizing it, Fatma has been kneading her fingers nervously.

"Of course," Dr. Tabak says. "Please go on."

"This is something I've never told you. For that matter, my family knows nothing. I've kept it hidden from them, but I'm afraid I can't do it any longer. Cengiz and I had sex last night, and I'm sure we've conceived another child."

Dr. Tabak waits. She does not interrupt the flow of Fatma's thoughts.

"I am happy about this, as I do wish to give Cengiz the son he wants so badly. I do feel it is a boy this time. But I haven't been completely honest with Cengiz. And now that Pinar is nine years old, and it could happen to her, I feel I must reveal my secret to Cengiz and to his family. Even my family knows nothing of this."

Dr. Tabak is silent. Fatma sometimes wonders how she restrains from interrupting, but she admires this quality. If Dr. Tabak were to break in with questions, Fatma knows she would clam up.

"You remember that I told you about the trip I took to Italy with my friend Claudia and her family when I was sixteen?"

"Yes, yes, I do." Dr. Tabak reassures Fatma.

"Well, there is a part I left out. Before the trip, actually for some time before the trip, I was having problems with my vision. I was a silly girl back then, vain, I suppose, but I was afraid I was nearsighted and would be forced to wear thick, ugly glasses. I did mention this to Badia, holding her to secrecy. Over time, I have learned how to cover my problem pretty well. My vision has only changed slightly in the years since I married Cengiz. But I do know it will become worse. When I was in Italy, I did lose more vision, and so I confided in Claudia. Her father's first cousin is a renowned ophthalmologist in Firenze. Claudia convinced me to tell her parents, and they took me to see their cousin. He examined me and gave me the diagnosis of retinitis pigmentosa." Fatma pauses. Saying the words is more difficult than even she has anticipated.

"Ah, a difficult secret to keep," Dr. Tabak finally comments.

"Yes, it is difficult. It haunts me. I have deceived my husband. I knew about this before our marriage. And worse, I knew it could be hereditary. The doctor told me this when I saw him. It might have been passed to me by *Baba's* father."

Fatma pauses to reach over to the small table next to her where Dr. Tabak has thoughtfully placed a box of tissues. She lets loose a sob and blows her nose.

"Such a difficult thing to keep to yourself for so long," Dr. Tabak says.

"Yes." Fatma is silent. She feels some shame but also some instant relief at having told someone. She remembers telling Claudia and the relief she felt back then.

"You know," she finally says to Dr. Tabak. "I do feel relief at telling you. I remember feeling this way when I confessed to Claudia and her parents. I wonder why I'm so afraid to tell Cengiz, to tell anyone for that matter. Why is this so hard?"

Dr. Tabak looks directly into Fatma's eyes. "You were a little girl when your great grandfather lost his sight, just a child. I remember you telling me that he aged significantly from that loss. He changed. These changes had to be frightening and incomprehensible to you. No one talked about it, as I remember you shared with me. How scary that had to have been for you. But Fatma, that was many years ago. He lived in a cave which made it difficult for him to get around. He never saw a doctor, and you don't know that he even had the same disease." Dr. Tabak does not take her eyes off Fatma.

Fatma's eyes well up. She shifts her gaze downward, taking another tissue to wipe her eyes. "I was a little girl, and it was scary. *Babaanne* somehow must have communicated to me not to talk about it, not to question it. You know, the Turkish manhood thing and how it must have frightened both of them for him to be losing his vision, getting older and weaker. I never really thought about these things quite this way before today."

"As a child, you didn't have the words. But now you are an adult and have the capacity to use words to express your feelings." Dr. Tabak sits back in her chair. She has been leaning forward and into Fatma's space.

Fatma sighs. "With your help, I have been able to think about so many things. When you put it this way, I don't feel so ashamed, so guilty."

"Good." Dr. Tabak leans forward again. "So, what do you imagine will happen when you tell this to Cengiz?"

"I don't know." Fatma shakes her head and then looks back at Dr. Tabak. "I've imagined so many things as I've imagined telling him over the years. Then it just somehow became all these years, and I think that is what will make him the angriest, that I have continued to keep this from him. We always tell each other that we should not have secrets from each other."

Dr. Tabak smiles. "Do you think that Cengiz has no secrets from you? That he shares every thought and fear with you? I don't think that is possible for any human being. This is just not in our natures. If we are completely honest, we must keep some things to ourselves in order to be individuals, to hold ourselves intact. Yes, you want to be as honest as it is possible with your husband, and he with you, this is true. But I cannot imagine that someone as kind as Cengiz would not be able to understand what has held you back. You did not have a normal childhood. He knows this. There were so many secrets." This is a lot for Dr. Tabak to say, and it is also a good deal for Fatma to absorb. They sit for some moments in silence.

"You are right about Cengiz," Fatma finally says. "He is a good and kind man."

Dr. Tabak nods.

"I think I might be able to find the right words to tell him. I feel lighter already. I know I must do it before Ahmet comes."

"Ah, you have named him."

"Yes, it is Cengiz's choice, and I like it, too." Fatma is so grateful for Dr. Tabak. She wants to tell her, but instead, she is quiet, still overwhelmed by her powerful feelings. And she has expressed her appreciation many times to Dr. Tabak. Now she is thinking that it is only through Dr. Tabak acknowledging and reminding her that she can truly accept how odd and painful her childhood really was and how much those years influence her even today.

"Hearing from you how difficult, how unusual my childhood really was helps me to accept its influence on me." Fatma finally tells Dr. Tabak.

"Soon you will be there on your own, Fatma. You will no longer need me to remind you."

"I will miss you terribly when that day comes."

"And I will miss you, too," Dr. Tabak replies. "But we will always be together in our hearts.

"I know that is true," Fatma says. And she does genuinely believe that this is an indisputable fact.

CHAPTER 39

Fatma is in the throes of all the positive feelings she has received from Dr. Tabak. She does not wish to wait another minute to speak with Cengiz. She is jittery and impatient during the bus ride home. She repeats her opening lines to Cengiz in her head. Then she changes them and repeats her new lines. An older woman gets on the bus at the first stop and sits next to Fatma. She has an overactive little boy bouncing and twisting on her lap, who is most likely her grandson. The bus is too crowded now for Fatma to move. The child cannot seem to restrain himself from a frenetic state of movement. He kicks the seat in front, his little feet striking out and coming close to striking Fatma in their wild and uncalculated movements.

What the hell am I thinking? Fatma wonders. What am I going to do with a little boy of my own? If he is like this one, I might murder him. Thankfully, I never strangled Pinar. Oh, how awfully close I came to it some days. But there is no predicting these things. Our son could be calm, like Cengiz. I wonder if it is bad luck that we named him. As she has these thoughts, the little boy lets out a shriek, and the helpless grandmother gives Fatma an apologetic and somewhat sheepish glance. There is also some shame in that look, Fatma thinks, much like the looks she herself gave when Pinar would refuse to be consoled and Fatma felt embarrassed and humiliated.

"It's okay," she says to console the grandmother. "I have one of my own who used to be like that."

"Whatever did you do?" the grandmother asks.

Fatma cannot tell the grandmother that she went to a mental hospital. She laughs on the inside at how the old woman might respond to that information. Instead, she says, "She grew out of it. He will, too," although

Fatma knows well that these identical words did little to comfort her. But the grandmother smiles, nods her head, and thankfully, she disembarks with the little devil at the next stop. Peace and quiet at last.

Fatma returns to thinking about what she will say to Cengiz. *There is something I have wanted to tell you for some time now*—no, no, that's all wrong. If she had wanted to tell him, then surely, she would have done so. *Cengiz, I have a confession to make*—do I really want to begin with calling it a confession?

What did Dr. Tabak say? Fatma struggles to recall the exact words. Oh, I can't remember. I should have written it down. Something like, *there is something I have been wanting to talk with you about. Unfortunately, it has felt so difficult that I have put it off far too long.* No, that isn't at all what she said. Didn't she say I should just come out with it and then answer his questions? That might be easiest. Maybe he'll never ask me when I began to lose my vision because he'll be so concerned with what is happening now.

Yes, Fatma decides. I think coming right out with it is the best way. So, I'll start with *Cengiz, I have something to tell you. I am slowly losing my vision. I may not lose it all, but it's possible that I may be blind when I'm older.* Yes, I like putting the blind part into the unknowable future. Fatma hopes that she will be able to wait until Cengiz is finished working for the day. She will have to keep her plan solidly in her mind until they are alone.

When Fatma finally arrives, Pinar is singing in the kitchen as she chops onions and garlic for their dinner. This is a tune Pinar must have picked up from the radio. The song is unfamiliar to Fatma. Pinar loves to cook. She often hums or sings as she works at her tasks. Once she is home from school, she often prepares a part or even all of dinner. She reminds Fatma of Badia when she was young. She is smart but doesn't like to do her schoolwork. This doesn't concern Fatma very much. After all, Badia was a late bloomer. And if Pinar is never a serious student, that doesn't worry either of her parents too much. As long as she finds a proper husband, they tell each other, her life will be good. After all, neither of them went on in school.

Pinar stops what she is doing to hug and kiss Fatma. "What are you cooking?" Fatma asks.

"I thought I would make a lentil soup with potatoes and carrots. It's chilly outside, and I've been thinking about this soup all day. I want to put tomatoes in it also."

Fatma takes off her coat and throws it over a chair. "Have you seen your *baba*?"

"No." Pinar has returned to chopping. "He hasn't been in from the factory since I've come home." She pours some oil into a pan. When it begins to sizzle, she throws in the onion and garlic, and then sprinkles cumin, salt, and pepper into the mix.

Fatma nods approvingly. "Oh, that does smell so good. I'm already getting hungry." Fatma watches as Pinar adds sliced potatoes and then carrots to the pan. She quickly dices tomatoes and peppers, tosses them into the pan, along with lentils and broth she has already prepared. Fatma sits and watches her with pride. She is only nine years old and cooks with the skill of an adult, perhaps even with a bit more joy than the average grownup.

"How was school today?" Fatma asks.

"Okay, I guess." Pinar stirs the soup mixture, pours it all into a large pot and adds more broth, more salt, and some red pepper. Again, she sprinkles more cumin and then some coriander. She lowers the flame and covers the pot. Now she turns her full attention to Fatma. "Maybe school was a little bit boring. Math is boring. I don't see the point, *Anne*. How was your visit with Dr. Tabak?"

Fatma refrains from saying too much about her sessions with Dr. Tabak. She knows that Pinar worries that her mother will have another episode and have to leave them again to stay in the hospital. Fatma knows that Cengiz also worries about her state of mind. She is confident that she will be fine from now on. She has learned a good deal about who she is from those terrible breakdowns and the intensive therapy that followed them. Initially, she was terribly frightened. There were many days when she could hardly believe she would ever be whole again.

Fatma remembers well how Fusun would have moods and would shut her out completely. Now she is quite aware of how all of this affected her. She is determined that Pinar will not suffer the same. Fatma prays every day for the strength to break the cycle of sorrow in three generations of unhappy mothers.

She answers Pinar. "We had a good session today. We even mentioned a future in which I will not go to have sessions anymore."

Pinar leaves the soup and comes to sit by her *anne*. "Does that make you happy or sad?" Pinar asks.

Fatma is once again surprised by Pinar's level of maturity, her capacity for insight. "Both," she tells her daughter. "I am very fond of Dr. Tabak. She has helped me in ways I could never have imagined. But we can now be much more confident that I have truly overcome my illness. Yes, I will be sad not to see her, but I will also be happy and grateful that it is no longer necessary. And she will be available should I need her again, just to consult here and there."

"Thank you for telling me, *Anne*. I will try to be helpful to you in any way that I can."

"You already are, my darling one."

Fatma is amazed at how Pinar has grown. From the colicky infant she once was, the child who refused to be consoled, Pinar is hardly recognizable to her own mother. Fatma believes that this deep depression will not occur again with the birth of another child, even if the infant should be colicky. She hopes and prays that the baby will be much easier to handle than Pinar was, but even so, she thinks she could manage.

"I'm going to go see how your *baba* is doing and when he will want his supper. We have some things to discuss later. I'm hoping to eat a bit early; first, because the smell in this kitchen is tantalizing, and second, because I want some time with your *baba* before he falls asleep."

"You go ahead, *Anne*. I can clean up after dinner. I did my homework on the bus, so I will take care of everything. Tomorrow you can make the dinner and clean up, okay?"

"Who is mother and who is child here?" Fatma asks in a half-scolding voice. Then she winks at Pinar. "You've got a deal," she says.

Salman and Cengiz have just completed a new round of bowls. The women they've hired on a job-to-job basis will come tomorrow to paint them. They are in three different sizes and meant to be sold as sets. Both men look dusty and tired, Salman more so than Cengiz. Before he leaves, Cengiz cautions his father to get more rest. "Now that we've finished these, *Baba*, we can take a little time off. Once these are painted and displayed in the shop, we can get on to the next project. What do you think?"

"That sounds good to me," Salman quickly agrees. Fatma notices that Salman is more bent over than usual. He has been using a cane.

On the brief walk to their home, Fatma comments to Cengiz, "Today is a day when the children are telling the parents what's to be done."

"What do you mean?" Cengiz asks.

"Well, you just told your father that you and he will take off a day or two, and Pinar is cooking our dinner and will clean up after so that we can have some time alone."

"Did you have to bribe her?" Cengiz smiles. "And if you did, what with?"

"Nothing at all, really. Tomorrow I cook dinner and clean up afterwards. I would have anyway, so it was easy."

"That Pinar. What a girl. She got off to a rough start, but look at her now." Cengiz shakes his head as he opens the door to their kitchen. "Someone is making a miracle in here. I will hurry and wash so that we can eat immediately." Cengiz hurries to the bathroom. Mother and daughter scrutinize each other, the feelings too strong for words. Pinar breaks the gaze and returns to stir the soup. Fatma can barely control her happiness.

CHAPTER 40

Dinner is so delicious that between Fatma, Cengiz and Pinar, a whole loaf of bread is consumed with the soup. Pinar rises to collect and wash the dishes while Fatma and Cengiz have a Turkish coffee to complete their meal. They compliment Pinar on her cooking and her kindness to her parents. Pinar is glowing with pride.

As soon as they finish their coffee, Fatma and Cengiz retreat to their bedroom. Fatma sits in the large armchair and Cengiz spreads himself out across the bed. "Ah, I have not felt so content in some time. That soup is magical. Maybe we could sell it and make a fortune. Aha, we sell the bowls with the soup in them! What do you think, my love?"

"I think you are infatuated with our daughter." Fatma grins at him.

"I think you might be right. Now what is it you wanted to talk about?" Cengiz turns on his side to face Fatma.

"I am going blind," Fatma announces, fearing if she makes a preamble of any kind, she will lose her courage.

"What?" Cengiz sits straight up and throws his legs over the side of the bed, facing her.

"You're going blind? I thought you were near-sighted, but it never seemed to bother you enough to get glasses. Blind? Like completely blind?"

"I don't know yet."

"You don't know? How can that be?"

"I have a condition known as retinitis pigmentosa. It is possible that I inherited it from my *büyük büyükbaba*. You remember how blind my great grandfather was at the end. This condition is genetic and rare. But who knows? I never knew my father."

"So what can we do? Is there anything we can do to stop it from getting worse?" Cengiz gets up from the bed and goes over to her. He takes one of her hands in his.

Fatma wonders if he will ask how long she's known. Maybe he won't.

"It is possible that my sight will never get any worse than it is now. But there is also the possibility that I might end up completely blind. There is no way to know."

Cengiz takes Fatma's other hand and lifts her from the chair. He puts his arms around her. "I'm so sorry, my love. But we'll handle whatever comes together. Now tell me, how did you find out about this?" They sit down on the bed together, side by side.

"Oh, Cengiz. I'm so sorry. I've known about this since I took that trip to Italy before we married."

"And you never told me?" Cengiz's face flushes with a burst of red that Fatma has never seen before. He pushes away from her and jumps up from the bed. She feels her chest begin to pound.

"Why?" Cengiz asks. He makes a fist and bangs it on the nearest table. A couple of books crash to the floor. "Why haven't you said anything in all of these years?"

Fatma cannot stop herself from crying. "I don't know. I was afraid. Maybe you wouldn't want me anymore."

"How could you think that?" His shoulders are taut, his fist still clenched. Then with a sigh, and then another that Fatma hopes is a sign of defeat or resignation, he releases his fingers. He bends down and retrieves the fallen books. He stares at Fatma as if he cannot recognize her. He finally says, "Sometimes I feel that you will never completely trust me."

"But I do trust you," Fatma sobs. "I was young. Yes, I was stupid. I didn't know any better. And I never told anyone except for Claudia and her family. They are the ones who had me examined by a doctor, a cousin of Claudia's father. Then time passed and more time passed, and I didn't know what to do."

Cengiz clenches his fist again and smacks it into his open palm. Sweat breaks out on his forehead, and he begins to pace the floor.

"So, why are you telling me now?"

Fatma thinks now that perhaps Cengiz is more hurt than he is angry. This calms her to the point where she can speak again. "Dr. Tabak has thought that keeping secrets and feelings inside contributed to my illness. I don't want to keep things from you ever again. I can see how I've hurt you. Cengiz, my darling, I am so very sorry." Fatma bursts into more sobs and covers her eyes with her hands. She feels Cengiz sit down again beside her. He pulls her close to him.

"You must learn to trust more. You must believe that I will never leave you. No matter what, I love you too much. Yes, I am hurt that you couldn't tell me back then when you discovered this. But in a way that I can't explain, I think I understand."

"Do you think you can ever forgive me?" Fatma looks into Cengiz's eyes, her own still filled with tears.

"I have already forgiven you. What else can I do? Our lives are entwined. They have been so since we were children. I never loved anyone else, and I never will."

Fatma is struck by this. How does Cengiz know he will never love another woman? What if she should die? Would he stay by himself the rest of his life? *Baba* certainly didn't. But now she is finding fault with him when he is just proclaiming his commitment to her, his love. Why does she always do that?

"I can't imagine ever loving anyone but you either," she tells him. "I wish I could be a more secure person. I really do try."

Cengiz reaches over and wipes a tear from her face. "Why don't you talk about more of this with Dr. Tabak? I know you're thinking of ending with her soon, but there's no rush."

"No, there isn't. That is exactly what I will do."

But Fatma remains perplexed. She is skeptical. She does not trust Cengiz's reaction. She knows that she would have been furious with him if he had deceived her in this way. Just suppose, she thinks, as she rides the bus two weeks later to her appointment with Dr. Tabak, just suppose he'd been the one going blind and hadn't told me for all these years? And he knew about it before we married? And it was genetic? Why, it didn't even seem to occur to him that Pinar might end up with this awful disease. And what about Ahmet?

Fatma has missed her last period, but she has not yet made an appointment to see the doctor. She wants to miss a second period before she says anything to Cengiz. He will get so excited, she knows, and if it's a false alarm, he will be terribly disappointed. She gazes out the window at the dreary landscape, high desert, small bushes for trees, rock formations that she has seen a million times. She wonders if she will be disappointed if she isn't pregnant. Or will she feel relieved? She isn't sure. Her initial elation and desire have dissipated. Now Fatma is unsure what she feels. This is a good day to see Dr. Tabak, she decides.

Unlike her last bus ride to her appointment, Fatma wishes for some distraction. The man sitting next to her is deeply engrossed in his newspaper. He gave her a perfunctory nod when he sat down next to her at the last stop, but that is all. Fatma knows that she would not have engaged in conversation with a strange man even if he had attempted to speak with her. She almost wishes for the shamed granny to divert her attention from her obsessions. Just when she thinks she knows herself, knows exactly what she wants, her anxieties resurface. What is it that will make her happy for longer than five minutes, an hour, a day? If she only knew.

Her seat companion folds his newspaper and gets up and off at the next stop. A few more folks board here, but not the older woman with her grandson. The seat next to Fatma remains empty. Fatma tries to redirect her thoughts to why granny might have been on the bus that day. Perhaps she was babysitting and had to return the child to her daughter and son-in-law. Hmm, Fatma reflects, maybe there is no son-in-law. The husband has died or left her for another woman. The little boy is stuck with granny all day while his mother works. He's a nice little boy most of the time, but he is angry with his granny. She's too old to play with him, and when he finally gets home to see his *anne*, she's too tired.

Fatma chuckles to herself. Her imagination is always taking her on journeys, fantasies, Badia would call them. Maybe Badia is right. She always teases Fatma that she should be writing a novel. Okay, so she doesn't have the time for that. How about short stories? Badia insists. Fatma shakes her head at the thought. The days of being able to concentrate like that are behind her. Since her breakdown, she is barely able to read. She loses her ability to focus so easily. Dr. Tabak has told her that this is normal, and that it will more than likely pass with time, but Fatma finds this aspect of her illness very difficult to accept.

After she speaks with Dr. Tabak, Fatma feels empowered, strong, capable. Somehow though, at some point in time after she leaves, certainly within the two weeks until the next visit, some little germ will begin to fester, and her doubts invade her like a flu that will not go away. She wonders then if she will ever be able to thrive without these visits. She has many things to discuss with Dr. Tabak today.

When Fatma arrives, the waiting area is fairly empty, but there are screams coming from one of the offices. "What's going on?" Fatma asks the receptionist.

"Dr. Tabak is admitting a patient. Poor thing is pretty upset." The receptionist casts her head and eyes in the direction of the offices.

"Which Dr. Tabak?" Fatma asks.

"Zeynep," she says, glancing at the clock. "You might have a little bit of a wait, but I'll let her know you're here."

"Tell her I can wait, there's no problem." Fatma remembers her own state of mind when she was admitted. She doesn't remember if she screamed, but she knows she was quite psychotic. Her heart goes out to Dr. Tabak's patient.

Fatma wonders again, even after all the years of self-exploration, how she ended up in such a state. This is still somewhat of a mystery to her. She has the intellectual information, but even when she repeats what Dr. Tabak has told her about women becoming psychotic after delivering a child, she has some difficulty accepting this explanation. Of course, Dr. Tabak has also pointed out the history of depression in Fatma's family, the nature of Pinar's colic and the resulting behavior, and Fatma's self-critical beliefs that she should be able to handle everything on her own. Yes, Dr. Tabak has covered everything. Fusun was unable to be a mother, and *Babaanne* did the best she could, but she was old. Fatma always felt that she had to keep a low profile and stay out of everyone's way. Dr. Tabak has told her many times that Fatma has paid dearly for this. All of this makes sense to her, all of this except for the psychotic break. A crazy woman, a woman who has lost all control. Fatma doesn't see how this possibly could have happened to her.

The screaming subsides. Fatma guesses that Dr. Tabak has succeeded in calming the patient and is now going about the business of the admitting process. Fatma hopes that things will go as well for this patient as they did for her. The care here is excellent, she thinks. How fortunate she was to have this hospital when she needed it most.

Some minutes pass, and the receptionist informs Fatma, "Dr. Tabak will see you now. You can go in. Thank you for your patience."

"Thank you," Fatma tells her and makes her way to the door leading to Dr. Tabak's office.

CHAPTER 41

Dr. Tabak is hanging up the phone on her desk as Fatma approaches. She comes quickly to the door and welcomes her with a hug and a kiss to each cheek. "Thank you for waiting," she says as both women settle into their respective chairs.

"Funny thing," Fatma tells Dr. Tabak, "I really don't remember being admitted here. I don't know if I was screaming or crying or how I behaved. I feel for your patient. Being admitted to a mental hospital is traumatic, I think."

"Yes," Dr. Tabak agrees. "But for many it is also a relief."

"Ah, that's true. I think I felt relief that I wasn't on my own anymore. But my mind was so mixed up that I'm not even sure that was true. It's easy for me to say that I felt relief now. Being locked inside because you have lost control of your mind is a terrible thing to have to accept. I still don't accept it."

"What do you mean?" Dr. Tabak leans forward, turning her head to almost face Fatma.

"I still believe in my heart that I failed everyone, most obviously myself. I've gone over this many times, and just repeating that it was not my fault does me no good. I can't rid myself of the belief that I could have prevented all of this. I could have been a better mother to Pinar and prevented her rages. I do try so hard, Dr. Tabak, but as soon as I soothe myself with your words, within minutes I'm berating myself with my own."

Fatma bursts into tears, partly from frustration. "And this is not at all what I wanted to talk about!"

"What did you want to talk about?" Dr. Tabak's tone of voice is soft and genuinely curious.

"I want to learn to trust the people I love." Fatma chokes out the words through her tears. "I told Cengiz about my eyes, and he was too understanding. Oh, he was hurt. He's not an angel. He's human. But he forgave me so easily. I couldn't trust him. Why isn't he furious with me? Pinar might inherit this. And Ahmet." Fatma's tears cease and her eyes flash with anger. "I know Ahmet is here. I have missed two periods. Will Ahmet end up blind? How do I know?" Fatma shakes her fist and withdraws it as soon as she realizes what she's doing.

"You don't know." Dr. Tabak says. "I'm sad to tell you this, my dear Fatma, but life is a continuous state of not knowing. If we allow it, that state of not knowing can drive us crazy or prevent us from living. Your *anne*, Fusun, never left the house again. Oh, she worked with your in-laws for a while, but the recognition of her loss of opportunity and her lack of will to do anything to change her circumstances, understandable as this was, led her to give up on life. She once went to the market to buy food, and her life was changed forever. A simple act of buying food. Her mother could not have predicted this. Fusun could not have predicted this. And yet, the guilt and shame they both suffered dictated the remainder of their days."

"What are you saying?" Fatma doesn't see the connection or the point Dr. Tabak is making. "Somehow I got lost in what you're trying to tell me."

Dr. Tabak takes a sip of water from the glass on the table by her chair. "There are things we cannot know and cannot prevent, Fatma. We do the best we can to protect those we love, but there are forces beyond our protection. War is one of them. War is particularly cruel to women, and men become cruel because of war. Your family did the best they could with what they knew and what they had."

"But Dr. Tabak, I don't blame my family. I blame myself."

"What if no one is to blame? Suppose there is no such thing as blame here?" Dr. Tabak moves her chair slightly so that she can look Fatma directly in the eyes.

Fatma looks down to avoid her gaze. "Are you trying to tell me that the war was to blame? How can the war be to blame for my lack of mothering to Pinar? That seems totally removed. I was a little girl during the war. The war was many years ago, at least the one that affected my family."

Dr. Tabak is silent. By now Fatma knows that she is giving her time and space to think, but for some reason, today this silence makes Fatma angry. Her body tenses until she is no longer thinking at all.

"Why don't you say something?" Fatma is angry. She glares at Dr. Tabak. "You're confusing me today. I don't understand."

Dr. Tabak leans forward and places her hand on Fatma's. "I'm sure it's infuriating that I'm unable to help you to trust. If I could do that, Fatma, I would never withhold that from you. Trust is something you must build in yourself. This takes time. I raise the war and your family history because in those years there was no trust or hope in the future. Fusun only knew to hide as best she could from violence, shame, humiliation. She learned this during the war."

"But what does all of that have to do with me now?" Fatma knows at this point that she is refusing to accept what is obvious, but she doesn't stop herself.

"You lived with this mother for eleven years. She hid in those caves from everyone, from you, from life. Then, we guess, she ended her life, leaving you behind in an unpredictable world, as unpredictable as her moods and her love for you. Why would you not have difficulty trusting? Love can disappear in the blink of an eye. You feel you have no power to sustain love in yourself or in others. But Cengiz loves you. Pinar loves you. This love doesn't come and go. This love is there for you every day."

Now it is Fatma's turn to be silent. She understands now, but she is stuck with how she can sustain belief, how she can hold onto trust over time.

"There is no magic to this, Fatma," Dr. Tabak continues. "Trust comes with time. Your mother was never really there after her rape. Fusun couldn't help herself. She was too traumatized to be a mother to you. Rape was a part of the war and people didn't understand the long-term consequences for the victims. We know much more today than we did back then. Fusun had no one to help her. I think in some ways you relived this violence with Pinar as a raging infant, feeling victimized and not being able to stop her. But now she is a lovely, bright child. You have helped her to become who she is today."

"And Cengiz? Do I fail to trust him because of my mother?" Fatma grips Dr. Tabak's hand without being aware she is doing this.

"I wouldn't exactly put it like that, but basically, the answer is yes. The circumstances that shaped your early life and your learning of the interactions of love, however unconsciously formed, do impact your relationships today. We rid ourselves of these disruptive influences by knowing and understanding them. Then you can say, oh, I know why I'm feeling this, and it actually has nothing to do with Cengiz."

"Ah, I think I'm beginning to see." Fatma relaxes her grip on Dr. Tabak. "And so that must be why I sometimes don't trust your words. Like my mother, you will disappear, and that will blow up all the work we've done and make it nothing. I feel that about my mother. My time with her was nothing."

"No, Fatma, it wasn't nothing. When you miss her the most and wish for her to have stayed and been a mother to you and a grandmother to Pinar, these feelings are too painful. So, you snap your fingers, like this—" Dr. Tabak snaps her fingers to illustrate. "And you make her disappear."

"That's true. I know that is true. I still summon her in my dreams. Sometimes she comes and sometimes she doesn't."

"Exactly how it was in life, isn't it?"

Fatma smiles. "However did you come to know all of this?"

Dr. Tabak shakes her head as if to deny. "I have studied so hard and seen so many patients, but I will confess to you, Fatma, the mind remains a mystery to me. Why we humans do what we do, and so offensively and violently to one another, that is beyond me. I suppose I will always be in search of answers as to why we do what we do, why we think and behave in inexplicable ways."

"But you seem to have answers for me. Do you believe in the answers you give me?" Fatma confronts Dr. Tabak.

"That's a good question, Fatma. I don't like to think that I'm giving you answers, though I can understand why it might feel like that to you. I like to think I'm giving you some explanations for your feelings and different ways to consider them that might be helpful for you. And yes, I do believe in them, although I'm far from infallible. I'm human. You must examine these possibilities to see if they ring true for you or not."

"*Mashallah*, Dr. Tabak, now that is an answer I can trust. I so appreciate your honesty. Thank you."

Fatma isn't sure why, but she leaves this session feeling more empowered than she has in a long time. *If my words ring true for you.* Fatma goes over what Dr. Tabak has said on the bus ride home. If my words ring true for you, she thinks. I decide if they ring true or not. This is my mind, and no one can know it better than I. What a relief that is. And the truth of the matter, Fatma thinks, is that her words do ring true to me. Especially that part about reliving my *anne's* rage and helplessness through Pinar's tantrums. I never thought of it, but when Dr. Tabak said those words to me, they hit me hard. Her words make perfect sense, but if I had to explain it to someone else, I don't think I could. There is a language, Fatma thinks, that Dr. Tabak and I speak within those walls that are only understandable to us. And what a spectacular language that is.

CHAPTER 42

Fatma decides that she will do her best to trust Cengiz despite her worries from the past, despite her fears of being abandoned. After all, her thoughts about how she might react to learning he had kept a secret do not define him. He is a different person. She cannot expect him to react the same as she would or suspect him because he doesn't. Fatma believes that Cengiz is a kinder person than she could ever hope to be. Perhaps if Cemal had been her mother, things might have been different, but who can know? Having Cemal for a mother did not save Elif.

Life is so contrary and complicated, Fatma reflects. If I could only just enjoy all that I have and stop myself from playing my mind like a yoyo. One minute down, the next minute up. I read about a mental disease like that in Dr. Tabak's waiting room, but when I asked her about this, she said that I didn't have this disease. She reminded me that I woke up in a mixture of my menstrual blood and my mother's death blood. She reminded me of all the reasons that my diagnosis was trauma. I don't think of myself as a victim of trauma at all. I think of soldiers returning from war as traumatized. Even so, I'm still confused as to what any of this means in terms of my own illness.

I am a simple woman, Fatma thinks. I am a wife and a mother. I live in my husband's family compound. We run a pottery business. How complicated is that? My mind is what I must cure. I must tame it, keep it from jumping up and down and taking me with it.

Fatma nods at her seat companion before the young woman leaves the bus. On this trip, she did not seek any conversation with the village woman sitting beside her. If detectives had questioned her afterwards, she could not even have described how she looked or what she wore, so deeply engrossed as she was in her own thoughts.

I'm going to create some words that I will say to myself when my yoyo mind tries to take over, Fatma decides, as she meanders along the path towards home. I know, she smiles, how about *no, no, yoyo*. That is simple enough and it makes me smile. *No, no, yoyo*. Yes, I like it. We'll just see if it works.

Fatma repeats the words aloud and begins to sing them to the tune of a childhood song she once knew. She finds herself almost skipping. She stops, looks up at the clouds forming above her and says aloud, "*Anne*, if you can hear me or see me, take notice. I am skipping and singing of my triumph over melancholy. That is not an inheritance I will accept from you. You can have it back! Take it back now!" Fatma stamps her foot three times to sign the deal. A passing vehicle stops beside her.

"Are you okay, lady?" A very young fellow sticks his tousled head out of his car window.

"Never better," Fatma replies.

"I'm looking for the Celik potters. Can you tell me how to get there?"

"Why I'm heading there right now myself."

The youngster leans over and opens the passenger door. "Hop in and I will drive you, if you like."

Fatma looks up to see a Christian cross draped over the mirror.

"Thank you, that is kind of you. But I am a Muslim woman, and I'm not allowed to get into a car with a strange man. I will just tell you. Follow this road until there is a fork and then turn to the right. The sign is on the road. You can't miss it. Don't worry about me. I walk this road all the time." Fatma thinks it is odd to call this boy a man, but she doesn't know another way to say this. "Strange boy" seems insulting.

"Okay," he says, leaning over to grasp the door handle and to close the door. "Thanks for the directions. Be well."

"And you, *Inshallah*." Fatma rebukes herself as he disappears in the dust. Why did she say *Inshallah*? Her experience of Christians goes back to the children in the cave. They all said it, the Christian children, and their parents. Here I go again, she corrects herself. "*No, no, yoyo, no, no, yoyo*." And she hums to herself the rest of the way home.

Fatma sees the boy's big ratty car sitting in front. Whatever does he want with us? she wonders. When she enters the house, she's alone. The boy must have found his way to the shop. He probably has business with Salman and Cengiz, she thinks. He doesn't even seem old enough to drive.

"Who is that boy?" Fatma asks Cengiz when he comes back from the shop for supper.

Pinar pipes up, "Oh, he buys the ruined pots from *Baba* to sell in the villages on his way home."

"They aren't ruined," Cengiz corrects Pinar, "they just have imperfections."

"And how would you know this?" Fatma ignores Cengiz's interruption.

"Sometimes I visit *Baba* when my homework is done, just for a few minutes. I don't bother you, do I *Baba*?"

"How could my angel bother me?" Cengiz reaches over and lightly pinches her cheek.

"The shop is no place for you." Fatma says sternly. "You need to stay here and do your homework. You can always help me with supper."

"But the shop is so interesting, *Anne*. I only go there when you are visiting Dr. Tabak. And sometimes I go visit *Babaanne* Cemal. But it's so quiet and boring here. I like to see the people who come into the shop. I know you do, too, especially the tourists. They sound so funny. Their Turkish is often so bad that I can't understand what they're saying."

"Yes," Fatma says, "it's true. I do enjoy being in the shop. But you be careful in the factory. You could get hurt in there."

"No, *Anne*. *Büyükbaba* and *Baba* watch out for me. They make sure I don't get hurt."

"And you shouldn't be speaking to strange boys or men." Fatma sets the soup tureen on the table with unusual emphasis.

"He's a harmless kid, Fatma."

"No man is harmless," Fatma returns sharply.

"We shouldn't make her afraid of men or boys. Not everyone is out to harm her."

"How can that silly boy harm me? If he tried, I'd smack him. Anyway, he won't be coming back for a while. He said he's looking for work here, but he lives somewhere in the east. Do you know, *Baba*?"

"They are living in Erzurum, and yes, my smart cookie, it is in the east. The family is poor. His *baba* sells junk, well, not junk exactly, kitchen utensils, cloth for sewing clothing, some things that are difficult for village women to find. He also likes to sell pots, and so he sends the boy to find them. The boy likes to travel, and so he sells enough of his *baba's* junk to get around and have some left over to buy pots, the imperfect ones. He takes the pots he can't sell along the way and some extra cash back home. Actually, he's a pretty smart and hard-working kid. I like him."

"Does this kid have a name?" Fatma pours the soup from the tureen into their bowls. Tonight, it's a lentil soup with carrots and potatoes, a hearty soup they eat quite often.

"Kamar." Pinar says too quickly for Fatma's liking.

"You keep your eyes on this," Fatma says to Cengiz. "She only knows the boys and men in the family. We must keep it that way."

"Of course," Cengiz agrees. "Kamar Terzian is as innocent as she is."

"Don't fool yourself, Cengiz. Boys are never innocent. I am asking you now, were you?"

Cengiz breaks off a chunk of bread and dunks it in his soup. "Delicious, my dear Fatma. And no, I don't suppose I was."

Later that night, after Pinar has gone to bed and they are alone, Fatma and Cengiz are together in their sitting room. Fatma is reading a newspaper a tourist has left behind, struggling to read the English, and Cengiz is studying some pottery designs he wants to show to Salman. Fatma looks up from her newspaper and considers Cengiz.

"I'm going to visit the doctor," she tells him. "I'm pretty sure we were successful the night of Pinar's birthday." Fatma is determined to test herself. She doesn't want to keep secrets from Cengiz any longer.

Cengiz throws the drawings onto a table. "That's great," he says and rises to hug her. He stops himself and asks, "Is that great with you? Are you sure you're ready?"

Fatma sets her newspaper aside and gets up to go to him. "Ready? Who knows? If I think about all that this means, I may think it to death. We need a son or two, and so we'd best start now." She laughs as she kisses him on the neck. "I must stop going up and down with everything, one minute yes, the next no. And I have a strong feeling that Pinar will not be the one to carry on the family business."

"You can't know that." Now it is Cengiz's turn to laugh. "Maybe she'll marry a talented, rich potter."

"Do you have anyone in mind?" Fatma steps back from their embrace.

"Of course not," Cengiz replies. "She's just a child."

"But she won't be for very long." Fatma pulls on Cengiz's arm. "Come before we're too tired and I'm so big that you no longer find me attractive."

"You are gorgeous when you are pregnant," Cengiz counters. "I will always find you attractive. And I think those visits with Dr. Tabak are worth every lira."

PART V
PINAR

CHAPTER 43

Twenty-five years have slipped away when Fatma lunges forward at the sudden, sharp jolt of searing pain in her foot. She grabs a hold of the branch of a tree to steady herself and cries out at the twigs that puncture her hand. She struggles to maintain her grasp and secure enough balance to inspect her foot. Ah, now I've done it, Fatma thinks as she attempts to dislodge a broken pottery shard from the hardened sole of her foot with her free hand. Years of running barefoot in and out of doors have left the soles of Fatma's feet calloused enough to avoid almost any kind of penetration. So, when she pulls on the shard to loosen it, Fatma is surprised to see blood running down her foot from around the edges of the shard. "Shit," she curses, something she finds herself more and more guilty of in these trying days.

The injury to her foot is mild, she determines, after extracting the shard. She removes her headscarf and rips off enough material to tie around the cut skin. This temporary bandage will get her back to the house where she can wash her foot and properly bandage the open area.

Fatma stumbles over rock and sand as she makes her way home. She is only just between the house and the pottery shop, in any event. The pain of her foot has dissipated. All she thinks about now is Pinar, her only daughter, Pinar lying and dying in the small bedroom of her childhood. Fatma doubts that Pinar will survive more than another day.

Pinar is still young. After a series of miscarriages, and years in between, Pinar was finally able to carry a pregnancy through to the end. Now, the very breasts with which Pinar fed her daughter, Meryem, have betrayed her. Those breasts will take her away from Fatma and Meryem for the rest of their lives. Fatma has thought many times of bringing Meryem, Pinar's daughter, here to say good-bye to her mother, but Fatma is overwhelmed as it is. And Meryem is still just a child in the beginning of her teenage years. Fatma believes she is ill prepared for the additional responsibility of Meryem.

Fatma regards the slice that the shard has made in her foot. She thinks back to all of the cuts, minor and major, that the women in her life have sustained. She remembers her first menstrual blood and how it covered the sheets of the bed she slept in with Fusun. Fusun had died sometime during the night. The blood had been Fatma's.

Pinar's death will be an extraction. Part of Fatma, she knows, will follow this bitter-sweet relationship into her daughter's grave. The colicky beginning of Pinar's life had brought Fatma over the edge into insanity. But she had learned to love Pinar with a fierceness, an intensity of which she had not known she was capable. This made Pinar's betrayal all the more intolerable. Her marriage to Kamar was more than a slap in the face. This had been an explosion of the very earth under her feet, an earthquake creating a gulf that had only been repaired by the onset of Pinar's cancer. And whatever is to become of Meryem? She has not been raised as Muslim or Christian. And now that she has been abandoned to the care of Kamar's irreverent and irresponsible sisters, who can know what will become of her? Well, Fatma reconsiders, she may be judging them unfairly. Their husbands seem to be in and out of the picture, their children wild like wolves. Fatma has never met any of them, but from the little she has been able to extract from Pinar, she has built a sizeable case against them. Fatma is not normally bigoted, but after all the hard work she put into developing a strong relationship with her daughter, she believes this Armenian Christian family stole her away.

And the poverty. Kamar is not here with Pinar now because he has continued to travel and sell as his father before him. Neither father nor son ever made enough money to support a family. Even though Cengiz had offered to take Kamar into the pottery business, mostly to keep Pinar close, Kamar was intensely independent. Fatma sensed that Kamar was afraid that he would lose Pinar if he worked and lived with her family. Fatma also sensed that Kamar was not too fond of her and wanted to remove Pinar from her mother's influence. But what does Kamar do once Pinar is sick and dying? He brings her back to Fatma's care, as he is unable to undertake this responsibility. Well, Fatma thinks, there is nothing to complain about. This has given her these last months with her daughter, and she has no regrets in the way she has loved and cared for her.

Fatma reflects that the years have been both kind and unkind to her. If she is being generous to herself, she's not yet an old woman. But she is no longer young. The death of Cengiz this past year, another victim to cancer, took the last vestiges of youth from her soul. The rest had already left her. Fortunately, Fatma thinks, Cengiz's mother did not live to see him agonize his way through lung cancer. If Cemal had not already departed, that surely would have killed her. Fatma is amazed that Cengiz's horrific suffering didn't kill her.

And where is this magnificent Allah everyone talks about? Surely a man as good and kind as Cengiz should not have had to bear such torment for so long. If he hadn't spent so many years in the pottery factory—but this is merely whistling into the wind, Fatma reminds herself.

And Badia. Badia the survivor. Badia is still living in Istanbul and working as the editor for a fairly big newspaper. She's planning to start her own women's magazine. Badia never married, but she leads a busy and contented life. She visits Fatma whenever she can. She will be coming soon to say good-bye to Pinar. Badia and Pinar have remained so close. Badia is devastated by the thought of losing Pinar. Fatma thinks that Badia had better arrive quickly. Pinar has not been eating for two weeks now.

As it turned out, those many years ago, Fatma was pregnant as she suspected, and so Ahmet was born. He was an easy baby, no tantrums, and he slept through the night early on. Fatma's depression did not return. And so, just a couple of years later, Bekir arrived. He wasn't quite the easy baby that Ahmet had been, but he was never as fussy as Pinar, and Pinar was there to help with him. Fatma remembers those years as happy ones. Her children were the joy of the extended family, and at early ages, Ahmet and Bekir followed Cengiz into the shop. Actually, Ahmet followed Cengiz and Bekir went wherever his older brother was. Cengiz was delighted, thrilled even, to have two sons. "This is a blessing from Allah," he used to say. Fatma now considers that Allah is quite the inconsistent entity. He gives generously in one minute and snatches away in the next.

Now Allah's demands feel beyond her. Fatma endeavors to find reason, but it seems to her that the stability in her life has always been challenged by forces beyond her control. Pinar is dying. All that Fatma can do at this point is to watch her slip away. She has scrimped and saved to buy Pinar additional treatments, but none of them has kicked the cancer. False hope after false hope. Now all Fatma can do is to make Pinar as comfortable as possible. Kamar is traveling to sell goods and to make money to send to Fatma for Pinar's care, but it is never enough. All the insignificant liras do is buy food, which after all is better than nothing. Her granddaughter, Meryem, is back home in Erzurum living with her aunts and their unruly children.

Fatma is alone now but for Bekir. Ahmet has been sent to Cyprus to fight the Greeks, a never-ending story so it seems. Turkey and Greece. Turks and Greeks. They've been at each other as long as Fatma can remember. Now they are at it again. Fatma only hopes it will be over quickly and that Ahmet will be stationed closer to home for the remainder of his military obligation. That is if he makes it home, of course. Fatma doesn't often allow her thoughts to take such a terrifying path. Enough, Allah. Enough already.

Fatma throws the shard that has pierced her foot as far away as she can. She hears it pop against something, a tree perhaps, she can't see, and then it hits the ground. This does nothing to alleviate her despair, and she reluctantly enters her forsaken house to tend to her injury before Pinar calls for her again.

In honesty, Fatma thinks, Pinar can no longer actually call for her. Fatma has given her a bell to ring, but she doesn't even have the strength for that. Fatma must go to check on her regularly and forces herself to sleep on a mat on the floor next to Pinar's bed. Bekir, kept from the army by his inherited vision difficulties, is still able to run the factory and the pottery shop. He has several people working for him since Ahmet is away. His girlfriend, Esen, shops and cooks for them. When she has time from her paid job, which is helping to run the pottery store, she also cleans the house. Esen is a nice, kind girl, hardworking, and Fatma accepts her help and her presence. Esen lives with her mother, a widow like Fatma, and in her spare time, Esen must shop and cook for her. Esen's mother is diabetic and blind. Good that I can still get around and see enough, Fatma reminds herself.

The foot has stopped bleeding by the time Fatma enters the house. If not for the ongoing noise of the factory, Fatma might feel she is living with ghosts. She stops in the kitchen to wash and bandage her foot. She puts on an old pair of house slippers before she goes to check on Pinar. Should Bekir or Esen come to look in on her, she doesn't want them to see that she has cut herself. They will make too much of a fuss over her. Pinar is too removed from awareness to notice.

Pinar's bedroom is stuffy. Fatma has tried to air it out by drawing the curtains aside and opening the window, but Pinar has insisted she keep it closed. Even though it is August and quite warm, Pinar no longer can tolerate light or air. She has to be forced to drink liquids and must be terribly dehydrated by now. But Fatma has promised Pinar that she will die at home without feeding tubes or any other assistance. There is only morphine to alleviate the pain. This puts her in a nonresponsive state for hours, until she wakes briefly enough to beg for the next dosage. Fatma knows that soon she will go to her, and she will have departed from this world. Fatma dreads this moment. Even though Pinar rarely speaks anymore, she is still there, still breathing in those raspy, shallow breaths and letting them imperceptibly out again. Throughout the day and sometimes during the night, Fatma sits and watches these efforts closely.

Now she approaches Pinar cautiously. When she sits and takes Pinar's hand in hers, Pinar opens her eyes. She is barely able to move her lips, but she whispers weakly, "Badia?"

"She's on her way, dear daughter. She will be here by early evening."

Pinar shuts her eyes again. She whispers, "This is good. And my *baba*? Will he be coming soon?"

Fatma stares at Pinar. Does she not remember that Cengiz is dead? What good would it do to remind her? But then Fatma remembers that Cengiz had called out for his mother when he was dying. She had even allowed herself to feel hurt when he'd called her Cemal but had quickly dismissed her feelings as ridiculous. Perhaps this is just the nature of dying, she thinks. Sometimes the truth is useless.

Fatma says quietly, "Yes, my love, *Baba* will be here soon."

Fatma lifts the water glass from the table next to Pinar's bed, removes the straw and dips a finger inside. She runs that finger over Pinar's dried lips. In the past, Pinar would say, "*Teşekküler, Anne.*" Thank you, Mother. But in the last couple of weeks, she no longer responds to these small attentions. Fatma knows that this is because most of Pinar has already departed. She remembers this slowing, this languid withdrawal from life in her caretaking days with Cengiz.

There were moments with Cengiz when Fatma wished to find him gone already. At the end, when pain and suffering controlled every second of his waning life, Fatma had visions of placing a pillow over his face and pressing down, relieving him, and giving him the peace he deserved. These were only visions, of course. She knew she was incapable of doing such a thing. The feeling is not the same with Pinar. If Pinar could stay with her forever, taking these tiny gasps of air that continue to give her life, Fatma would be grateful. There is a sense that Pinar is a baby once again. This time, however, she's not colicky and there are no tantrums. Often when she watches Pinar, she thinks, don't go yet my darling. Please give me just one more day.

Fatma wonders why she hangs onto Pinar in this way. She guesses there is the desire to relive Pinar's first two years with her, the years she did wish to put a pillow over her face. Even though Fatma certainly didn't want to lose Cengiz, their difficulties had been resolved. Their married life together had been peaceful and loving. Although it had never been filled with the excitement Fatma had sometimes thought she wanted when she was young, she had learned contentment with her husband and with the Celik family. Once she had finished her work with Dr. Tabak, she never experienced that kind of depression again. In the deaths, in all the losses of her family, even of Cengiz, she mourned and experienced normal sadness.

Of course, looking back on it now, Fatma realizes that she had not fully expected Cengiz to die. For some odd reason, she'd fooled herself into the notion of finding him there, day after day, year after year, not leaving her before she left him. As ill as he'd been and as much as she'd wished to see him out of pain, the actual loss, the final realization that she would never hear his voice again, feel his touch again, had left her in a state that she could only think of as an emotional coma. There were no words, only what seemed at the time to be an interminable emptiness. Gradually, her body moved, she breathed air in and out, and she forced herself to eat again.

Fatma now believes that Dr. Tabak's diagnosis of psychotic depression due to childbirth had been accurate. Her chemistry at the time had been the cause. She no longer feared that she might plunge so deeply again. Does she miss Cengiz in the very depths of her bosom? Does she speak to him? Does she constantly ask him what he might do in her place? Of course she does. She lives with his ghost but can no longer hear his voice aloud, only in her mind.

Now Fatma sits, still holding Pinar's hand in hers, waiting for Badia to arrive. She both wishes for Badia and hopes for her delay. She knows that Pinar is waiting to say good-bye to her aunt, and then she will be able to let go. Strange, Fatma reflects, that it is Badia she longs for. She doesn't ask for Kamar or Meryem. Fatma suspects that this is because Pinar has regressed into her childhood and no longer recognizes that she has a husband and a child. Since she hasn't asked for them, Fatma has not felt an urgency to contact them. Kamar is probably not to be easily reached in any event. And Meryem is too young to travel that kind of distance alone. Her aunts are too busy and too poor to take her to Avanos, Fatma rationalizes. She will deal with all of this later.

Now she hears a car pulling into the gravel driveway. Badia. As she knew it must, the time has come. Fatma gently removes Pinar's hand from her own and goes out to meet her sister-in-law and best friend.

CHAPTER 44

Fatma stands by the door in her worn black felt house slippers to greet Badia. They hug and kiss each other on both cheeks.

"How is she today?" Badia's voice trembles, as if she might be afraid of Fatma's response.

Fatma looks long and hard at Badia. Why is she even asking this question? Does she think Pinar might have passed already? Badia knows she is there to say good-bye. Fatma has told her that she believes Pinar is only waiting for Badia in order to allow herself to let go of her tenuous hold on life. Fatma doesn't answer. She walks back towards Pinar's bedroom, feeling her anger rising.

When Fatma opens the door, she sees Badia almost take a step back as the smells of sickness and impending death hit her nostrils. But to her credit, Fatma thinks, Badia steps forward anyway, hesitating only once she reaches the bed. "Is she really in there? Oh, yes, I can see her head, but her body is close to invisible, flat as the sheets. She's lost so much weight since I last saw her."

Does Badia really not realize this is the end? Fatma wonders. Death seems to bring out the strangest reactions in people. Fatma has observed this before.

"*Hala*, Aunt, you are here." Pinar floats these words on shortened breaths.

"Yes, my love, I am here." Badia's eyes fill with tears.

Fatma can see the effort that Pinar makes to say these few words. Sweat breaks out on her forehead. Fatma takes a washcloth from a basin filled with water, wrings it out, first wiping the sweat from Pinar's brow, and then leaving it there to cool her.

"I'm going to leave you, *Hala*, very soon. Maybe today." Pinar gasps out the words and begins to cough, a wracking cough that leaves her too exhausted to speak. One arm attempts to rise from the covers piled around her. She tries to reach for Badia, but her arm falls back onto the bed. The movement causes the washcloth to fall over her eyes. Fatma grabs it and dips it into the water again while Badia takes Pinar's hand.

"I love you, *Hala*." Pinar coughs again several times before sinking into unconsciousness.

"I love you, too," Badia tells her, not sure if Pinar has even heard. "I love you as if you are my own. My poor dear one." Badia lets go of Pinar's limp hand and begins to weep. Fatma drops the washcloth into the basin and goes to Badia. They cry into each other's arms.

"Pinar knows how much you love her, my sister. You have always been her favorite."

"And she mine," Badia whispers, her voice having left her. "So young, too young, and with a child."

Suddenly and without warning, Fatma feels rage rising up into her throat. Why is she feeling so angry? Only yesterday she yelled so hard at Esen, sweet Esen, that the girl ran directly to the shop to sob in Bekir's astonished arms. Bekir had come immediately to inquire as to whatever had happened to cause this. Fatma had not been able to give an adequate answer.

"You must try to control yourself, *Anne*. Pinar's illness is not Esen's fault."

Fatma apologized to the girl and to Bekir, something she was not so apt to do these days. But Bekir had never spoken to her this way before, and she knew that he had been more than correct to do so. Fatma recognized that she had crossed a line. She'd had no right to take out Pinar's condition on this girl who was doing everything she could to help them. So Fatma took a few deep breaths before she spoke to Badia again. She'd been ready to lash out at Badia. She wanted to scream at her and ask her why she seemed so oblivious to the death lying before them.

"Now that she has seen you," Fatma says, stumbling over her words, "I'm going to give her another shot of morphine. The nurse told me that if I give her morphine at this stage, she will soon drift into a coma, and she is unlikely to wake up again. I didn't want to do that until you could tell her you love her."

"But Fatma, I don't think she even heard me."

"She heard you as well as she can hear anything. If I don't give her the morphine, too much time has passed since the last injection, and she will be in great pain. Do you want that?" Fatma takes another breath, realizing that the anger is surfacing again. Badia doesn't have to give her the final dose. Fatma has known for some time that she will have to do it.

"No, of course I don't want that. Should I go get Bekir?"

"No, not yet. After she's gone. Bekir is so sensitive that he cannot bear to be here. He comes sometimes in the night to sit with her, but to see her breathe her last breath will stay with him forever. I don't want him left with that. He adores her."

"I know," Badia sighs, "but don't you want to let him decide for himself?"

This is the last straw for Fatma. All sense of control deserts her. "For Allah's sake, Badia, I know my own son. If I give him the choice, he will think he is only pleasing me to come now. Let me save him from himself. He may be all I have left! If Ahmet is killed in this stupid war, he will be all I have!"

Badia places a hand over her mouth. Her expression is one of deep regret. "Oh, I am so sorry, Fatma. Of course you know what is best. But please don't forget you also have a granddaughter."

"My granddaughter, for all I know, is a Christian who has been raised with barbarians. I met her once when she was five years old, the only time Pinar visited until she got sick. She didn't even come to her own *baba's* funeral."

"But wasn't she too sick to come?"

Fatma takes the washcloth from the basin and flings it across the room at Badia "So what if she was?"

Badia retrieves the washcloth which has landed at her feet and washes it out in the basin. "Give her the shot," Badia says. "I'll change the water in the basin."

Alone with Pinar, Fatma touches her face gently with her fingers. Pinar is clammy from sweat and water. Fatma remembers each time she has stroked this face from babyhood through childhood, and even during the visit she has just remembered when Pinar brought Meryem to meet her grandparents. Back then, she had also stroked little Meryem's forehead while they had been sleeping together in this very bed. Kamar had not come with them. He had been on the road, of course, as he now is.

What kind of man leaves his wife to die at her mother's house? Why had Kamar not agreed to work with Cengiz, to stay here as a family? Why had he taken his new wife to the other end of Turkey, so far away from them? Six-hundred ninety-eight kilometers by road. A long way for a mother to travel with a young child. Why couldn't Kamar have taken them with him, selling goods along the way and stopping to visit them? Fatma never asked these questions. She contacted Kamar's sisters to let them know that Pinar was dying, but they had no idea then where Kamar was. What kind of man leaves his dying wife, abandons his daughter and runs off where no one can find him? Fatma cannot for the life of her understand this behavior, so alien to her own experience.

Now she goes to the syringe to load it with the morphine the visiting nurse has left with her. She stares at it for what feels like a very long time. Badia returns with the basin and washcloth, sets it down on the table and backs away to lean in the doorway.

"It's okay," Fatma assures her. "I do want you here and will only yell at you more if you leave me alone with this. Bad enough that her husband has. She asked for Cengiz earlier."

Badia sighs. "What did you say?"

Fatma shakes her head in despair. "What could I say to her now? I told her he'd be here soon."

Badia comes closer and puts a hand on Fatma's shoulder. Fatma lets it lie there only for a moment. Then she shakes it off to load the syringe. She watches the liquid entering the syringe closely, slowly, almost drop by drop. She could not suffocate her husband, but now she must kill her daughter. Fatma stares at the filled syringe, not sure yet if she can do this.

"She will suffer if you don't," Badia tells her. "You just told me that. And I know you don't want her to suffer."

Fatma lifts one skeletal arm searching for a vein. There are none to be found. She tries the other arm, taking it gently from under the covers. There is nothing useable there either. All the blood draws, medications, and chemotherapy have collapsed them. Her daughter has the veins of a drug user. There are no veins that Fatma can find in her arm or her hands. Although Fatma has been using Pinar's feet, it feels inhumane to her, and she wanted to give this last shot elsewhere. Fatma sees this will not be possible. "No veins left," she explains to Badia. Badia is silent.

In resignation, Fatma pulls the covers back up over Pinar's arms and hands and goes to her feet. She looks at Badia. "Hold her hand while I do this," she says. "It will bring her peace, I know. She loves you so much."

Badia's eyes fill with tears, and she does as Fatma requests. Fatma lifts the cover from Pinar's left foot. "This one has the best vein," she says. Slowly and deliberately, as she has learned from the nurse, Fatma pumps up the vein and inserts the needle, drawing enough blood into the syringe to begin to inject the dose of morphine. Slowly, very slowly she empties the liquid into Pinar's vein. When it is all gone, Fatma removes the syringe and places it in the tray with the morphine. "I would have thrown that across the room as well, if I could only be certain that this is the last injection." She goes to the other side of Pinar and takes her other hand, squeezing it, the tears falling down her face. Badia and Fatma sit on either side of the bed, waiting, and then waiting some more, as Pinar's breaths slow. And then, at some point which neither one of them notices immediately, the breaths simply cease.

CHAPTER 45

Fatma sits in her old-fashioned, plush chair inside the pottery shop. Her cane rests against a small table just within her reach. Several newspapers are piled there, her thick reading glasses resting on top. It takes so much effort to read, she thinks. The worst has already happened, but it's not as bad as it could be. She can see enough to get around, albeit with caution and slowly, but where does she need to go? Nowhere, actually.

Life is definitely more exciting in the newspapers she reads, but she has not wished for excitement in many years. Now in her later years, she feels fortunate. Ah, she has had her losses, but is that not true for anyone who lives a long life? Her sons and their wives take excellent care of her, even though she is somewhat impatient with how long it seems to take them to do anything. Fatma sighs. She has always been overly critical, both of herself and others. Even with all the work she once did with Dr. Tabak, she remains judgmental and short of temper. Allah forgive me, she thinks, I will go to my grave in this insufferable condition.

It is early in the morning and Ahmet has not yet changed the 'closed' sign to 'open.' Fatma used to revel in the activity of the shop, but now she enjoys these quiet morning hours alone the best. She uses this time to remember. Ah, my Cengiz, if only you were here to sit by me. But would you sit by me? No, as old as you'd be by now, you would still be in the factory, even if only to supervise. Fatma smiles. Cengiz had grown to love the factory, the making of pottery. When he had decided to stay in Avanos to help his father, that had been a good decision for both of them. Had she ever said that to him? Now she cannot remember.

Fatma smiles. One thing she does remember is how Cengiz would stride in at the end of a long day in the factory. "What's for supper?" he would call while removing his shoes. Then, without fail, he would find her wherever she was, often simply stirring pots in the kitchen, and he would put his arms around her, kissing her playfully on her neck. "How is my bride?" he would ask.

Fatma sighs. There is too much she no longer remembers. She taps her cane on the floor in frustration and annoyance. And now I have the brat coming here from Erzurum, she thinks. Only a teenager and already a pain in the ass. The aunts, Fatma has never known one from the other and so she thinks of even one of them as "the aunts," have called and begged her to take Meryem in for a while. 'A while,' Fatma thinks, I guess I'm saddled with her for good now.

Apparently, one of the snoops living nearby spotted Meryem holding a boy's hand. With her virtue in question, Meryem would be arriving in just a few days. Fatma is guessing that the child is not thrilled at being sent to her grandmother for safety. And her grandmother, Fatma reflects, is not thrilled at receiving her. I'm too old for this, Fatma concludes. But, of course, this is after she agrees to take Meryem in. Nothing is indicated about the length of her stay, and Fatma wonders what the aunts have told Meryem. Well, Fatma contemplates, I will find out soon enough.

Meryem: Fatma considers that the name means both bitterness and beloved. Meryem was a wished-for child. Well, Fatma determines, there is bitterness there, but she is not so sure about the beloved aspect. She knows nothing of this child and cannot remember what she was like at age five, the last time she has seen her.

I am done with raising children, Fatma announces to herself. Ahmet survived his military service and the war, and Bekir's vision has remained stable. They both have loyal and hardworking wives, even if I find them both dull as the dishwater their hands are perpetually soaking in. They keep their noisy little boys away from me, for which I am eternally grateful. I know I'm too gruff and impatient for them, and so be it. By the time they are old enough to have sensible conversations, I expect I will have departed from this world. Both boys took so long to marry and then to have children. Perhaps my presence here was a deterrent to their wives. Who knows? I won't know and frankly don't care. I've had my years with family and children. Now all I want to do is to rest, complain about the government, and hear about the problems of others. Hopefully, my problems are over. Well, except for Meryem.

Fatma reaches into the pocket of her skirt and pulls out a chocolate she has placed there for safe keeping. She savors the rush of the caramel released by her first bite into the chocolate. Her weight or even her health are no longer concerns to her. This is one of the advantages of being old. I can be as fat as I like, she thinks, grinning, and no one cares. The best part of this is that I no longer care. Fatma almost swoons as the chocolate and caramel blend in her mouth. The life of this old woman is not so bad, she determines. And I will not allow my peaceful days to be disturbed. If Meryem becomes too much of a problem, I will put her on the first bus, train or plane that departs for Erzurum and let the aunts take her back. This is good. I know exactly what I will do.

Fatma sits back in her chair, one that has almost become melded to the shape of her body. She pulls another chocolate from her pocket just as the door to the shop opens. She slips it quickly into her mouth before whoever is entering can catch her. Pushing it with her tongue to the back of her mouth where she believes she can suck on it undetected, she sees an obviously American couple enter the shop. Their clothes are a dead giveaway, but the man's calls of "Hello, hello, anyone there?" confirm her speedy assessment.

"I'm here," Fatma calls back in her halting English. And so a new day begins.

****

Fatma takes the worn box from the cabinet where she has kept it hidden all these years. No one needs to know her secrets, and she has not written a letter or an entry in her tattered notebook for many years. Actually, there is very little here, but still, these are her private meanderings and no one else's business. She has not read her own words or the words in the letters since Pinar died. She will not read them now.

For a moment, she fingers the hamsa she has never removed from her neck since the day Cengiz gave it to her all those years ago at Ramadan. She thinks to put it with the letters, but she changes her mind. Let it stay where it has always been. Let it go to the grave with her. The ribbon Cengiz wrapped it with lies in the very bottom of the box.

A stranger will be coming very soon to live with her. She is a teenager, and perhaps, a nosy one at that. Or suppose, just suppose, Fatma thinks, she falls down suddenly from a heart attack, just like Badia did, and this notebook and these letters are discovered for just anyone to read. No, she would no longer be around to suffer the consequences, but there is no sense in taking the chance. Fatma takes hold of her cane, placing the few bound letters and the small spiral notebook in the waistband of her skirt, and she makes her way outside. She hobbles along slowly, negotiating the rocky and risky path she knows so well. When she decides she is far enough away from the buildings and unwanted discovery, she removes the articles from her waistband and takes the kitchen matches from her pocket.

First Fatma lifts the letters to her lips and kisses them softly. She flicks the pages of the notebook and is not surprised at the number of empty pages. Hers has been a simple but a good life. Some things lost; some things found. Good-bye words, good-bye thoughts, good-bye Cengiz and Pinar, *Baba* and *Babaanne*. Good-bye Fusun, my dear *anne*. I know I will be seeing you all sometime soon.

But for now, I say good-bye to my secrets. There is no need to reveal them, to pass them along. I prefer to take you with me. After all, you are mine.

And with these thoughts, Fatma places the articles on the ground with great difficulty, bending down with extreme care. Placing one hand on the notebook, she opens it to more flammable pages. Fatma manages to take the matches in one hand, and with the other, resting her body on the cane, she tries to light several matches without success. Finally, and not without gasps of frustration, she strikes a flame. Quickly she lights a page and watches it ignite the others. She adds the letters to the pile.

The small fire pleases her for reasons she cannot understand. Watching the pages burn away is like a release of all the pain she has known in this life. But inexplicably, there is a sense of joy that feels spiritual. This is an exuberance Fatma has never known. Perhaps it is what freedom means.

Although the night air is becoming chilly, and Fatma gets cold so easily now, she cannot bring herself to leave this spot. And so it is a long hour before Fatma finally turns away from the charred remains. She emits a loud sigh, and poking her cane into the uneven earth in front of her, she makes her way slowly back home.

ABOUT THE AUTHOR

Phyllis M Skoy is the author of two novels set in Turkey, *What Survives*, and its prequel, *As They Are*. She is currently writing the third in the series, *A Coup*, to complete *A Turkish Trilogy*. She is also the author of *Myopia, a memoir*.

Skoy's fascination with Turkey took hold the first time she set foot on Turkish soil in 1998. She saw a story that provided a window into turbulent times, and she became captivated with why "we create magnificent cultures and then destroy them."

Skoy is a retired psychoanalyst living in Placitas, New Mexico.

Note from the Author

Word-of-mouth is crucial for any author to succeed. If you enjoyed *As They Are*, please leave a review online—anywhere you are able. Even if it's just a sentence or two. It would make all the difference and would be very much appreciated.

Thanks!
Phyllis M Skoy

We hope you enjoyed reading this title from:

BLACK ROSE
writing™

Subscribe to our mailing list – *The Rosevine* – and receive **FREE** books, daily deals, and stay current with news about upcoming releases and our hottest authors.
Scan the QR code below to sign up.

Already a subscriber? Please accept a sincere thank you for being a fan of Black Rose Writing authors.